THE GREEN TRAIN

Also by Herbert Lieberman

BOOKS

The Adventures of Dolphin Green
Crawlspace
The Eighth Square
Brilliant Kids
City of the Dead
The Climate of Hell
Night Call from a Distant Time Zone
Nightbloom

PLAYS

Matty and the Moron and Madonna
Tigers in Red Weather

HERBERT LIEBERMAN

THE GREEN TRAIN

G. P. Putnam's Sons / New York

G. P. Putnam's Sons
Publishers Since 1838
200 Madison Avenue
New York, NY 10016

Copyright © 1986 by Herbert Lieberman
All rights reserved. This book, or parts thereof,
may not be reproduced in any form without permission.
Published simultaneously in Canada by
General Publishing Co. Limited, Toronto

Library of Congress Cataloging in Publication Data

Lieberman, Herbert H., date.
  The green train.

  I. Title.
PS3562.I4G7   1986   813'.54   86-12405
ISBN 0-399-13127-2

Printed in the United States of America
1   2   3   4   5   6   7   8   9   10

For JUDY and ZOEY
with a special note of appreciation
to the Funny Lady on the Third Floor,
Dolores "Skip" MacCarthy—not only for
her invaluable editorial savvy and unstinting
assistance, but for all the laughs too.

Why do the nations conspire,
and the people plot in vain?

—PSALMS 2

One isn't born human,
One becomes it!

—YEVGENY YEVTUSHENKO, "Be a Man"

PART I

A SUDDEN LURCH. The shriek of metal grinding against metal. Instantly awake, Stern felt himself fall sidewards. He cracked an eye at the blinding sunlight, even as the images of peaks, crags, glacial pools, and polar meadows fled like flocks of startled birds before his squinting gaze.

For a moment he imagined himself still on the little cog train they call the "Troll." He had taken it at the fjordside railway terminus up from Flam to Myrdal, going on to Oslo. It climbed nine thousand feet in a matter of minutes, up to the top of Norway, where high in those pristine peaks the crystal air of late July had dropped suddenly from sixty to forty degrees Fahrenheit. At the little station at the top they got down and had coffee out of paper cups while a cataract of melting snow roared down from the rocks above, silencing their gay holiday chatter with its booming thunder.

Singing voices, high and sweet, drifted into Stern's lagging consciousness. There was a peal of laughter from the compartment next door where the "Italian Quartet" sat laughing over the tarot cards—La Force. La Mort. Le Mat. Le Bateleur. Le Pendu, L'Ermite, Le Diable. L'Amoureux. Roi des Epées. La Maison de Dieu.

Slowly it dawned upon him where he was. It was not the Troll train at all. That had been nearly three weeks ago. This was another train; the one he had boarded that drab, gray morning, departing Leningrad eleven A.M., scheduled to arrive in Helsinki five hours and fifty minutes later.

A mosaic of fresh impressions bombarded his eyes. His blinking gaze descended slowly from the luggage racks where it had been fixed, to the trio of faces poised across from him.

Paul Blanton leaned forward and touched his arm. "You okay?"

"Fine." Stern sat up and shook his head. "Have we stopped?"

Frau Kunkel made a sour face and straightened her son's tie. "They're not known for speed, these people."

Stern turned his head toward the window where the oilcloth curtains drooped in the warm, unventilated air. Through a crack in the curtains he could hear voices, and see the shiny black visor of an officer's cap slide past, followed by the crunch of boots on gravel.

"You slept well." Nell Blanton smiled.

Stern sat up and raked a hand through his pepper-salt hair. "Too much vodka last night."

"You didn't miss much."

"We changed all our rubles at Vyborg," Frau Kunkel informed him.

"I still have mine."

"I know," she said pointedly.

"The coins are all right, but you'd better get rid of the paper," Thomas advised. "Flush them down the toilet or just surrender them to the inspector when he comes aboard."

Stern sat limply, rolling his head against the backrest of the seat. "Where are we?"

"The frontier, I imagine." Nell had begun to apply lipstick as if she were preparing to make a good impression.

"Just between Vyborg on the Soviet side and Vainikkala on the Finnish," Thomas explained, his teeth clenched on the cold stem of an unlit cigarette holder. "Got your papers? They're coming aboard now."

Paul Blanton already had his passport and visa out. Told the Russians could be sticky, he'd had them out three-quarters of an hour before. A lawyer from Lexington, he liked to think of himself as efficient, organized—a knowledgeable and seasoned traveler, at home anywhere in the world.

Nell Blanton, his wife, was a pretty, fortyish lady. A kind of country-club matron with an air of wistful sexuality that lingered in the rustle and heliotrope fragrance of her clothing as she passed.

Stern wobbled to his feet and reached up in the rack above for the small piece of hand luggage in which he carried such items as traveler's checks, medications, and official papers, plus the half-dozen or so Maigrets he'd accumulated at kiosks and air terminals to read along the way. "What do I need?"

"Your customs declaration," said Karl Heinz, Frau Kunkel's stiffly polite seventeen-year-old son. "They give you a bad time if that's not in order."

"I didn't buy anything."

"Splendid," Thomas replied. "Then just state that on the declaration."

Voices drifted up from outside. Stern pushed aside the sticky, unpleasant-smelling curtain, then caught his breath as he looked down at the sight below. It took him a moment or two to take it all in—the barbed wire, the sentry box, the big smoke-gray shepherds sitting watchfully by the tracks, the stickpole observation towers surmounted by the armed guards, the low green barracks in the nearby trees behind which the soldiers moved, barely visible.

Smiling, Thomas observed Stern's shock. "It's always a bit unnerving the first time. They can't resist putting on a bit of a show for the Free World."

Stern mumbled something and rummaged somewhat more purposefully through the small bag for his papers.

Thomas—Anthony Beech Thomas, as he was known to innumerable Englishmen from his byline—was not properly one of the Intourist Group 409. He was a British journalist and highly regarded Sovietologist within the international press and diplomatic corps. Posted by his paper to the Kremlin, he made his base in Leningrad, the most graceful, the least dour of Soviet cities. He spoke fluent Russian and prided himself on his connections at the highest levels of the Politburo. His crooked, yet engaging smile opened on a ruin of yellow teeth.

Thomas lived in the newish, rather glitzy Prebaltiskaya, where Stern, traveling morosely in a guided tour—"The Treasures of Leningrad" as it was billed by the tour packagers—had come, over the past week, to know him.

Evenings, Thomas could always be found holding court at a raucous table in a corner of the Dollar Bar of the hotel (so-called because they would accept no rubles there, only Western currencies—francs, marks, lire, but preferably dollars), drinking punitive quantities of vodka throughout the long white nights.

In figure he was tall and slight with a sort of elegant emaciation. The paisley ascot knotted loosely round his throat and the cigarette dangling at his lips were all part of the carefully cultivated air of dissolution. The Savile Row suits, a decade old and gone to seed, reeked of Latakia. He could work diligently a ten-hour day, but after seven P.M. he sought with a vengeance the solace of vodka. He had a deserved reputation for unbridled licentiousness, particularly among female colleagues within the press corps.

At his special table in the Dollar Bar, beside his right hand there was inevitably the tall beaded tumbler of vodka which he would drain slowly, his eyes moving restlessly round the room above the rim of the glass. As the night wore on, he would grow increasingly garrulous, raising a long trembling tobacco-stained finger, waving it like a baton while holding forth before an audience of diplomats, journalists, and the occasional random stranger who happened along—all enthralled by that dashing air of jolly doom.

"I've known them all," Thomas would growl boozily, nearly dislodging several glasses from the table with his outflung arms. He struck a match, having to guide it carefully with a tremulous hand to the tip of his Balkan Sobranie. "All the big boys. The marshals and the grand pandjarams. The old and the new. Just about every regime since Khrushchev. Driven about with them in their Chaikas and their long black Zils. Been to all their homes too. The apparatchiks. Their big old dachas in the Crimea or Pitsunda. Gone boar hunting in Zavidovo with old Kosygin. Stayed in all those grand old villas behind the tall fences in thick groves of trees, so the poor proles couldn't look in and get upset. Houses full of expensive Western furnishings. Chocked to the gills with caviar and vodka, the kind only available for export. Fresh meat, fruit, and vegetables. All you want. American cigarettes. French wine and cognac. Japanese tape decks. Sky's the sodding limit when you're one of those good old boys. One of my late Soviet colleagues called them 'our wonderful Communist nobility.' "

His eyes would open like a man waking and he'd look slyly round the table at them. "I say 'late' because the poor sodding chap vanished about eight years ago and hasn't been heard from since." He'd laugh and slap the table, shouting to the barboy for more vodka.

A dog barked at the end of the coach corridor. There was a gruff burst of Russian laughter and the sound of boots clattering up the boarding stair.

"Well, here we go." Thomas winked slyly. Paul Blanton's face was chalky white. A compartment door slid back at the front of the coach and suddenly they were all galvanized into postures of forced gaiety like animated dolls powered by a wind-up spring.

Frau Kunkel produced her backgammon board. Thomas plugged one of his infernal Balkan Sobranies into a cigarette holder and lit it, sending up black choking clouds of Yanidje smelling not unlike dry manure.

Nell Blanton started to tell a rather dull story about trying to find the women's loo at the Ptimorska Department Store on the Nevsky Prospect. It occurred to Stern that she was talking too fast and a bit too loud, and that the smile on her face made her look a trifle queasy.

He'd come to Leningrad six days ago on the Green Train from Helsinki. His decision to go was last-minute, like everything else in his life, an afterthought with little attention paid to the possibility of untoward consequences.

At the end of a Scandinavian tour, Stern found himself late one afternoon reading a flier posted in the lobby of his hotel, "Treasures of Leningrad. Six days, six nights. Via the Green Train. ETUMATKAT, Kaisaniemenkatu 4A, 00100 Helsinki 10." He called the touring agents immediately and booked.

There was certainly no rush to go home. Back in New York it was the dead of summer. His marriage of thirty years had quietly unraveled early that spring. His wife had by now remarried and moved in with a lifelong friend, an old classmate of his from college, and recent widower. There had been no rancor in their parting. It had been more or less expected for several years and when at last it came it was uneventful and all rather distressingly civil.

His daughter, now twenty-seven, and his son, twenty-four, were both out of school and safely established in secure if not rather prosaically respectable careers—the former a patent lawyer, the latter an associate professor of chemistry at a large Midwestern university.

There was not much else in the way of personal or material attachments to keep him home. He had not been abroad for a dozen years. At a dinner party several months before, a Swedish diplomat from the UN regaled him with the glories of his native land. Impulsive as was his wont, he planned a trip there that summer. Talking to his travel agent the following day, the trip had quickly mushroomed from a "quickie" holiday in Sweden into that of a tour of the whole of Scandinavia.

Starting in Copenhagen, where he stayed for a week, he flew on to Bergen, taking there a small packet boat seven hours up the Sonnenfjord, bound for a tiny village with the vaguely unpleasant name of Flam. The boat was filled with tour groups comprising mostly Japanese trussed in camera straps and swarming about the deck like a locust infestation.

He stood outside on the stern deck most of the way, sprayed by a cold drizzle, slightly sick from the warm blasts of diesel fumes exhausted rearward out the engines into his face. A red-blue Norwegian flag flapped at the taffrail and just below that hung an ensign with the motto "Soli-Deo-Gloria" emblazoned on its black field.

At Flam he stayed at the little inn overlooking the fjord, just up from where the ferry docked and at the terminus of the railroad. The hotel was simple, austere to the point of deprivation. Such amenities as radios or telephones did not appear in the guest rooms. Meals were rudimentary, but fearfully expensive. At breakfast the orange juice was watery, the coffee weak, the milk powdered, and the toast both stale and cold. Dinner was mostly dry chicken and frozen vegetables, with the cost of a bottle of wine or beer ruinous. Even if one could comfortably afford it, you couldn't in clear conscience buy it without the feeling that you were somehow contributing to a monstrous evil.

Somewhat more troubling, the dining room was infested with flies, a fact that seemed incompatible with high altitudes and a cold climate. Even the maîtresse d'hôtel, an icy, somewhat disapproving lady with blond hair tied back in a tight chignon, appeared flustered and apologetic for their numbers.

Flam was not a place you came seeking activity or a vigorous social life. It seemed more a kind of retreat for people recovering from recent nervous collapse. Except for the scenery of mountains and fjords, which was staggering, there was nothing to do but sit on the hotel porch and watch the ferry from Bergen arrive each afternoon and discharge its small handful of passengers. Then, of course, there was the little red Troll train which departed each morning for a day's excursion nine thousand feet up to Myrdal. Following that, you took baths and long walks just to use up time. After a while one longed for the oblivion of sleep, but the long white nights and a sun that never seemed to set even begrudged you that.

Just beyond the little balcony outside his room a huge peak soared. Weary from a day of tramping alpine trails, he would spend hours sipping a beer or two and watching it, a peculiar urgency about his face.

It had a fierce beauty. The terrifying height, the awesome tonnage, the proximity to the tiny lodge that stood at the peak's bottom, built so close to it that its presence there could barely be explained save possibly as the result of perversity or the most imprudent defiance.

Everywhere you turned, it was on you, bearing down from above, brooding and implacable, full of unspoken threats. The longer you stared, the more it gripped you, dragged you into its dark, seductive field, threatening to annihilate you in its mysteries.

The more he stared, the more it occurred to him that in its long, slanting planes of light and shadow he could discern the lineaments of a face gouged out by the buckling and contraction of some vast geological upheaval occurring eons ago.

It was all there, a beetling brow, a sharply chiseled nose, a stern unforgiving chin. Along either side of the face were the gaunt, sunken cheeks where clumps and stands of evergreen looking like tangled beard shot vertically upward out of the rock for hundreds of feet. At the very top, several hundred meters above, gray rags of cloud swirled angrily through a line of blighted pine, fringing the peak like the lank dirty hair of some ancient crone.

It was clearly a face, but like no human face—the features, one might imagine, of some prehistoric deity carved out of the rock by a people long vanished. It was a face that bore the expression of nonexpression; a face that was old but ungraced by any of the venerability of age. Stamped upon it instead was a chilling impassivity that, for all its many eons, imparted no wisdom, save possibly the wisdom of noncaring.

Something untoward, a small incident—small because it in no way impinged upon him—occurred one day to finally jar him out of his inertia and set him moving again. A man died trying to ascend the sheer rock face of that peak.

The woman at the desk of the inn, a pink scrubbed Norwegian lady who smelled of soap, told him the story, smiling all the while. It seemed the body had been found the day before a quarter of the way up the slope. The authorities had concluded that the man had started out merely for a walk to the base of the mountain, since he was neither dressed nor prepared for anything more ambitious. Clearly an inexperienced climber, he reached a point where he could go up no farther. More disconcerting, he could not back down. He must have tried several times, lost his nerve, and panicked. He tumbled one hundred meters down the rubble-strewn slope, his body bounced and caromed over the boulders and huge jagged shards until, broken and unconscious, it rolled to a halt somewhere near the bottom. He died of exposure during the night.

The lady reported the incident to Stern in a voice uninflected by any notable feeling. There was none of that hushed awe or mystery people generally reserve for recounting the details of sudden, untimely death. It was to her merely a piece of information, of no special import. It filled a conversational gap with a guest of the hotel, and so, for her, it was useful.

The next morning Stern packed his bag and took the Troll train over the top of Norway, down to Oslo, where he poked around awhile, then picked up a car and drove across the Swedish Wärmland to Stockholm.

He had meant to fly home from Stockholm, but just as impulsively as he did everything else, he took the ferry to Helsinki instead, sitting up all night in the *sitzky,* since there was at that late date no cabin reservation to be had. His fellow passengers were mostly rough Swedish and Finnish youths traveling with knapsacks and little more, who used the occasion of a night crossing on the Gulf of Bothnia to consume copious quantities of Scotch whiskey and Finnish vodka at duty-free prices.

His arrival in Finland that morning coincided with a great wind storm. It swept off the Baltic, causing the big picture windows in his hotel room overlooking the sea to rattle in their frames. The tall, feathery aspens swayed and trembled all that night with a strange frying sound that rose and fell with every suspiration of the wind.

Rough and cold as the sea was, he bathed in it the following morning, feeling that his immersion was both salubrious and mystical, a spiritual purge that signaled the end of one thing and the start of yet another. At any rate, it seemed hopeful.

But Stern's sudden decision to push on to Leningrad from Helsinki was just as mercurial as all his others—more like headlong flight than spiritual mending.

Señor Gonzaga's dreamy smile appeared in the compartment doorway. He stood there peering down at them uncertainly as if bewildered to find them there. Attired in a white tropical worsted suit and a pair of carpet slippers, scratching his rumpled white hair, he had the look of some mildly demented Knight of the Woeful Countenance.

"It appears we are under siege," he spoke in his sepulchral Castilian accents.

Nell Blanton leaned toward the tottering figure as if fearing he was about to topple.

"I gather they're on board now. Up ahead in the next car. They've started with Miss Blaylock."

Thomas' eyes, riveted to the backgammon board, gleamed wickedly. "Perhaps she'll defect."

"We can only hope," Señor Gonzaga nodded sagely. "But the Russians are no fools."

They all roared.

Enrique Gonzaga was a tall, thin gentleman with thick white unparted hair combed straight back from the forehead. His eyes were of a pale, hawkish hue with something both acute and childlike about them. He was a Madrileno who had repaired to Buenos Aires after the war, with vague plans of producing superior Riesling in the Andean foothills. But still he clung to his Castilian heritage and numbered among his antecedents a host of Bourbon kings. Unlike a good deal of putative European aristocracy, his claims were authentic.

As of yet he had produced no significant wine, and had no other discernible profession as such, but if you inquired what sort of work he did, he would smile vaguely and say in his soft musical voice, *"un poeta."* Indeed, he considered himself a part of his adopted nation's most influential literary circle, counting among his closest friends Márquez, Cortazar, and Borges. "Ah yes, Borges." His eyes twinkled naughtily. "An old faker, that one. He knows he has fooled them all."

Whatever difficulties he caused, and there were many, you could not really dislike the old count.

"Are you all right, Señor Gonzaga?" Peter Stern inquired.

"Oh yes. Quite fine." He seemed surprised anyone should ask, but his eyes were a trifle unfocused. He turned for a moment as if about to leave, then turned back. "I appear to have mislaid my papers somewhere. You haven't seen them?" He'd asked the question as if he more than half-expected they all had.

Thomas glanced up from the backgammon board. "What papers? Surely not your passport and visa?"

"Yes, those too, and my custom declaration as well. Everything." He laughed aloud, with a note of glee as if he'd accomplished something remarkable.

Nell Blanton rolled her eyes heavenward.

"Did you have them when you left the hotel this morning?" asked Frau Kunkel.

"Yes, of course. I keep them in my little musette bag, which is always by my side."

"And it was by your side," Thomas asked, "when you boarded the train?"

"I saw it in his hand this morning on the bus coming from the hotel." Karl Heinz looked round at the occupants of the cabin.

There was a moment of uneasy silence. But if they were all concerned for Señor Gonzaga, that gentleman remained grandly unconcerned for himself. From outside the window came the growl of a Russian sergeant major barking orders to one of the railway/military transport platoons assigned to border inspections.

"Please don't distress yourselves." Señor Gonzaga smiled slyly. "I'm sure it will turn up. At this very moment, Señora Gonzaga is looking for it."

Not far from where they sat, a compartment door slid back and suddenly they heard Russian being spoken to its occupants.

One of the female coach attendants appeared, and gesturing with her hand, addressed the Spaniard in sharp peremptory Russian.

"What does she say?" asked Gonzaga, an expression of baffled amusement on his face.

"She wants you to return to your cabin," Thomas explained. "You must be there when the inspectors come."

"Very good. But first I must go to the loo."

"You can't," Paul Blanton said. "They've locked them for the duration of the inspection. Didn't you read that in the customs instructions?"

The tall, stooping Spaniard shook his head at Blanton with a sweet indulgence, as if he thought him possibly demented. "But I must pee or I shall have an accident." He giggled like a mischievous child.

Thomas spoke to the attendant in Russian, trying to explain the situation. She listened stiffly, then grew adamant. The toilets were all closed. Everyone had been advised beforehand that they should prepare for that accordingly. She was very sorry but the gentleman would have to return to his seat.

They hovered there in confusion until the lady attendant took hold of

Señor Gonzaga's arm and tried to propel him back toward his compartment. The Spaniard flicked her hand off as if he were removing a fly, and rising to his full imposing six feet, two inches, glowered down at the poor woman, who appeared finally cowed. He stood there denouncing her in a string of throat-clearing Castilian epithets, the last of which sounded to Stern something like *puta,* then turned and moved off grandly.

A moment later, Jatta, the Finnish tour guide, popped her head in and counted the occupants. She was a cool, blond young woman with darting blue eyes, attired in a jogging suit made of shiny translucent material through which one could see her undergarments.

"Everything all right here?" Checking names on a clipboard, she seemed chirpy enough, but there was a small uncharacteristic quaver to her voice.

"How long does this generally take?" Paul Blanton asked.

The guide checked her wristwatch. "It's just noon. With any luck we ought to be out of here by one-fifteen, one-thirty. Everyone have their papers?"

"What exactly do we need?" Stern asked.

"Passport, visa, customs declaration, and your currency statement with an exact accounting of how and where you spent your money."

"I still have some rubles," Stern said.

"You didn't change them at Vyborg?"

"I'm afraid I slept through Vyborg."

The Finnish guide gnawed her lower lip. "Better declare them, then. Turn them over to the inspectors the moment they enter the compartment. Better that than have them think you're concealing something." She took a quick glance over her shoulder at the Russian inspectors standing far down the corridor. "They can be quite prickly."

"Señor Gonzaga has lost all his papers," Nell Blanton remarked.

Jatta made a face of weary forbearance. "Oh—that one. Our"—she searched for the word—"grandee." She pronounced it with zestful distaste. "He keeps losing everything."

"What will they do?" Stern asked.

"Nothing," Jatta sighed. "Señora Gonzaga has his papers in their compartment. I had her take them from him for safekeeping before we left this morning. I must go now and check the others. Keep your seats and please don't move about. They don't like that."

In the next moment she was gone.

The train they call the Green Train was not equipped for warm weather. It had no air conditioning, and on the day coach that made the daily run between Rautatieasma Central Railway Station in Helsinki and the Finland Station at the Leningrad end, there was only one class—and that was second-class accommodations. There was a dining car but no dining service to speak of. Meals were rudimentary and sporadic at best. Cold dishes such as simple salads tended to arrive warm, while hot dishes came either tepid or cold. The best one might hope for was a simple sandwich and a cup of palish tea drawn from the battered, tranished samovars that stood at the head of each carriage, the contents of which tasted unpleasantly of metal. For that reason people tended to carry their own lunch on the day coach, risk a cup of tea from the porter, and hope the water was at least fresh.

The coaches, too, left something to be desired. There were nine cabins in each, each cabin accommodating six passengers. The compartments were dusty, the seats were of a plain hard wood, the luggage racks screwed to the walls sat low with their burden, disconcertingly close to the passengers' heads. The single concession to decoration was a pair of curtains stamped with a vague floral pattern and smelling disagreeably of oilcloth. The windows themselves were grimy, tinted yellow, and a virtual road map of dirt and rust commingled with rain. Most could not be opened. The windows along the corridors, however, were all open and provided what little ventilation there was.

The night run between Helsinki and Moscow with a stop in Leningrad was far better. There, one had the option of first-class wagon-lits, sleeping coaches, each with ten compartments, a lavatory at either end of each, and an attendant's compartment for each carriage.

There, too, the dining service was greatly improved. At dinner, a very satisfactory array of *zakuska* was laid on—everything ranging from caviar sandwiches, sausage, ham, cheese, mayonnaised egg, and sardines, to entrées of fried sturgeon, and steak of an indifferent quality. Excellent hundred-proof Finnish or Russian vodka could be had at two rubles, approximately three dollars the liter, and a liter of warm, sweetish Russian champagne was available for the trivial sum of ninety kopecks.

The train itself comprised six coaches and an electric engine. The coaches were a dull metallic green. Stamped on a window frame at the center of each carriage was the official Soviet seal, a red wreath above a crossed hammer and sickle, all surmounted by the Cyrillic letters CCCP. Beneath the seal itself was the coach number, and below that the letters SZD. Just below that was a white destination plate such as "MOSKOVA-HELSINKI" or "LENINGRADIN-HELSINKI," "FINSOV-EXPRESS WLABm."

The upper window frames of each coach bore in gold letters such colorful nomenclature as MOKBA, SCHLAFWAGEN, WAGON-LIT, VOITURE. The coaches were Russian, as were all the personnel—conductors, waiters, waitresses, coach attendants, and porters. The electric engines, however, running between Helsinki and Vainikkala, the border station, were operated by Finns.

The joint operation of the train, suggested by the designation FINSOV-EXPRESS, was a source of constant irritation to the Finns, who, living cheek by jowl to the moody, unpredictable Bear, had learned to swallow quite a bit.

The first stretch of the line from Helsinki to Hämeenlinna was built in 1862. The next would be one connecting Finland to the capital of all the Russias, St. Petersburg (now Leningrad). Work on this particular stretch began in 1868. Thousands of starving Finns and Russians flocked to the job, many dying of malnutrition and disease. But the 190-mile railroad was completed in record time and ready for operation in 1870.

The St. Petersburg line connects with Helsinki-Hämeenlinna railroad at Riihimaki, a rather curious twist to the northwest, if you consult a map. One of the reasons for the route was undoubtedly that the railroad from Riihimaki to Viipuri runs along the top of a sandy ridge, Salpausselka, formed by the last ice age some twelve thousand years ago. This ridge made the work of the railroad laborers much easier.

From its very start the St. Petersburg line was run by the Finnish State Railways, including the terminal at the St. Petersburg end, the Finland Station. It became one of the main arteries of a flourishing trade between Finland and Russia and took on even greater importance with the onset of World War I in 1914.

During World War II, the eastern end of the line between Viipuri and Leningrad saw some of the fiercest fighting of the war. As a result of the war, Finland was forced to cede the city of Viipuri and the areas east of it to Russia. In addition, she had to pay the Russians some six hundred million dollars in war reparations. Since the payments were made in the form of various industrial products, the railroad was suddenly very busy. Full-time, regularly scheduled passenger traffic between Helsinki and Leningrad started in earnest in 1953 and has been running hard ever since.

At that particular moment the Green Train was standing still, awaiting Soviet customs and passport control on the Russo-Finnish border in a flat meadow within the low, scruffy pine woods between Vainikkala and Vyborg. It was 1:15 P.M. Finnish time and unusually warm for that part of the world—eighty-eight degrees Fahrenheit and heading up. Most of the northern tier of Europe had been in the throes of a sweltering heat wave for the past three weeks.

Stern, seated nearest the window, glanced out through the streaked yellow pane and looked down at the Russian soldiers marshaling in the tall, dry grass beside the track bed. They moved up and down in small, purposeful groups, chatting loudly, waving their arms at some unseen railroad functionary farther up the track.

Stern gazed out on a scene of barbed wire and sentry boxes. Every fifty yards or so, running perpendicular to the track, were the observation towers surmounted by armed guards.

It was mostly, however, the barbed wire that unsettled him. He was unaccustomed to seeing barbed wire put to such use. In the Midwestern prairie country he had known as a youth, barbed wire was used to demark boundaries or contain livestock. This barbed wire, stretching for as far as the eye could see, and presumably far beyond that into the woods, had none of the nice, cozy look of pasture fence. This was wire stretched taut on big concrete pylons anchored to the earth, wire raised fourteen feet in height with an additional two-foot apron at the top, canted inward at an angle of forty-five degrees. The wire was the tough, stranded kind studded with waspish barbs designed to puncture and shred flesh. This was a structure not intended to contain animals or demark boundaries but to contain human beings, to limit their freedom of movement. Stern had never experienced that before.

In the next moment the tramp of footsteps sounded in the corridor outside, followed by the sudden appearance of a Russian officer attended by a retinue of noncommissioned officers and a pasty-faced coach attendant shuffling nervously behind them.

Scarcely acknowledging their presence, the officer's hooded eyes swerved round the compartment, moving from the floor upward to the luggage racks and on to the ceiling, where they dwelled on the air vents. From within the cabin, they watched him with a kind of stunned fascination as if they feared to interrupt his trend of thought.

He was a short, square man with a thick neck who managed to wear his baggy uniform with great panache. He had the high cheeks and almond eyes of a Tartar and you could tell from the bright gloss on his boots that he took his work very seriously.

Within the cabin only Tony Thomas recognized from the three stars on his striped shoulder boards that he was a full colonel. His arm, sleeve, and collar badges, all with winged wheels affixed on a green diamond-shaped patch, identified him as part of the elite unit known as the Military Border Guard, itself under the supervision of the State Security Police, known more familiarly as the KGB. The two wide gold chevrons on his sleeve proclaimed that he had served for over twenty years.

Thomas had taken all of this in at a glance. The others could only assume from his bearing and from the deferential attitude of the men around him that he was a person of considerable rank.

They were checking passport photos now, making certain that individuals seated in the various compartments were the same as those who appeared on the photos. A sergeant major with a brusque, pugnacious manner entered the compartment unannounced and with no formal greeting commenced the passport check.

Standing just behind him stood the colonel, observing the procedure, and it was clear from the stern self-importance of the sergeant major that he intended to make the most of his moment in the sun.

Lingering long over each photo, he scrutinized its flesh-and-blood counterpart from a variety of different angles. The procedure was painstaking and agonizingly slow. The overall effect of it in a number of cases was to make the passengers profoundly anxious, as if their papers were out of order or possibly they'd done something wrong.

In the case of Nell Blanton, the procedure dragged on to the point where the cabin occupants began to exchange uneasy glances between themselves.

At one point the sergeant major, clearly dissatisfied with the results of mere comparison between subject and photo, indicated by a series of hand motions that Nell was to stand. The moment she was on her feet opposite him, he reached up and without warning took her sunglasses from her face. More of a snatching than a lifting motion, so abrupt and unexpected it was, it caught everyone there by surprise. There was a communal gasp. Blanton half-rose in his seat, but Thomas pulled him back down. The colonel leaned over and whispered something into the sergeant major's ear. Still clearly dissatisfied, the man muttered something and with a decidedly begrudging air thrust Nell's passport and glasses back at her. It was a tense, unpleasant moment.

At the conclusion, the colonel nodded, bowed his head in rather courtly fashion, a stiff Old World gesture that almost made you like him. In the next moment he'd turned his back on them and was gone, followed by his entourage. Only the rumpled, somewhat exhausted attendant continued to hover there uneasily in the doorway, wringing his hands. Blanton's face at that moment was the color of parchment.

"Please to keep seats during inspection," the attendant murmured in hushed tones. "Hope to be finish here as quick as possible. With your kind cooperation." He bowed in that rather formal Russian manner, backed out into the corridor, and followed the colonel on to the next cabin, where the same procedure was just then being repeated.

From where Stern sat he could hear Madam Mukherjee across the corridor in her shrill, clipped English, attempting to communicate with the colonel. She appeared to be protesting something. Madam Muk, as they had come to call her, as always was protesting something. From the curt response, not from the colonel but from the sergeant major at his side, she seemed to be getting nowhere.

"Please to keep seat during inspection," they heard the frazzled coach attendant repeat his polite exhortation after the colonel had moved on. "Please not to leave cabin or go into corridor. Hope with cooperation to finish as quick as pozzible."

Then he was gone, up to Cabin 6, where a number of the youths in the Spanish choral group sat nibbling figs and nuts, laughing and chattering volubly to one another.

Stern glanced up to find Nell Blanton's slightly amused gaze upon him. During the past week, he'd had occasion to find her eyes upon him with disconcerting frequency. "What do you suppose that was all about?" she asked.

"Theater. These people love theater." Thomas dismissed it with a wave.

"Is that all?" Stern asked, surprised.

"My dear fellow"—Thomas studied the game board—"I'm afraid they haven't yet started. Just setting the scene, so to speak. Getting us all into the proper frame of mind."

Paul Blanton was still shaken from the episode of the sunglasses. "For what?"

Thomas rattled the dice in the black cup, then tossed them with a smiling flourish onto the backgammon board.

* * *

The small child propped up rather stiffly in Madam Mukherjee's lap had begun to cry. It had started tentatively with a series of small burbling sounds, then escalated in volume to a long, piercing wail. With its shaved scalp, except for a squiggly corkscrew of black hair near the top, and bulging forehead, a hooked little nose, an overbite, and no chin to speak of, the child had the look of a tiny turtle. Yet it was that sort of unqualified ugliness that almost endeared it to you. That is, until he cried, which he did quite often and which he was doing just then.

A bubble of mucus depended from the child's nose. Katrina Van Meegrin stared out the dusty compartment window trying hard not to see it. She was a young woman, barely out of her teens, of rather fragile beauty, and newly married to Kyle Van Meegrin, several years her senior, and by profession a biochemist. They were from Rotterdam. An extremely attractive couple, they were by popular consensus easily the favorites of the tour. Virtually everyone liked them.

A wealthy upper-caste Bombay family, the Mukherjees were, by process of breeding, imperious, disdainful, and generally discourteous to anyone they knew or even suspected to be their social inferiors. When, however, they encountered someone they perceived to be a "person of rank," they gushed sycophancy. They made it clear to the Van Meegrins from the very start that they did not think highly of them. Also assigned to their compartment was a young couple, an American girl and a young French law student, quite obviously rapt in one another.

Madam Muk was at great pains to cut them dead with her glances. She had learned it from her grandparents, who had been taught it by the English during the "grand old days" of the Empire, where cutting people in that fashion was a social obligation.

Madam Muk herself was a formless tawny shape, some five feet in height in a pale sari with a bare midriff out of which a bulge of quivery flesh extruded itself. A red semiprecious stone flashed at the side of her nose. Now, with the baby squealing on her lap, and having just been rebuffed by the Russian colonel, Madam Muk was manifestly cross.

She blamed her husband for her present discomfort. Mr. Mukherjee had insisted from the beginning that he would take charge of all travel arrangements. In fairness, he had done quite well, transporting his family all over the Continent for six weeks in glorious, unstinting full first class. Responsibility for now finding herself suffering the indignity of a second-class day coach, she placed squarely on Mr. Mukherjee's shoulders. The fact that the Russians provided no first-class accommodations for the day run seemed scarcely germane.

As the baby squealed and squirmed in her lap, she darted looks of pure venom at the poor man, which portended much stronger stuff in store for him once she got him alone. Suddenly there was a blessed silence. The child had stopped momentarily, but in the next instant had cracked its mother across the face with an open palm, then broken into a drooling giggle.

Madam Muk swelled dangerously, then glared at her husband. His name was Nagu but in formal company she called him George. On those rare occasions when she wished to affect a certain tenderness, she called him Babu.

"Babu . . ." The lips snarled into a smile of tortured benevolence. "Come take Baby on your lap. Give Mommy a rest, do." Her English lilted but her eyes scorched him.

"Of course, my precious." Mr. Mukherjee rose and prized the yowling infant from its mother. As he did so, he happened to glance down at the attractive knees of Katrina Van Meegrin.

Mr. Mukherjee admired women in general, and youngish women in particular. He assumed, or took for granted, that this admiration was reciprocated. He was a vain cock of a man with tumbling raven hair and a cold flashing smile you knew he practiced before a mirror. His walk had some of the bravado of a parade strut. He had a paunch belly, flared trousers, and shiny tasseled shoes. His stubby fingers were studded with an array of various rings, and the sugary odor of vanilla followed cloyingly in his wake. He had a number of quirks, by far the most disconcerting of which was a habit of scratching his genitals quite unselfconsciously every several minutes or so.

The change of position had had a felicitous effect on Baby Muk. For several minutes he sat quietly in his father's lap while Mr. Mukherjee made little cooing sounds and beamed proudly down upon him. But in the next moment the yowls resumed at a decibel level heretofore unmatched. The nerves of the occupants of Cabin 5 were sorely stretched.

Kyle Van Meegrin reached down to the paper bag between his feet. It contained the complimentary gift luncheon the Prebaltiskaya had provided every member of the tour. Each bag contained two sandwiches. One consisted of a strong, reeking garlic salami, the other of a gray meat of indeterminate nature—both made on dark, stale bread; each also contained an apple and an orange, a bottle of Vichy, and a bottle of Russian beer.

Van Meegrin asked his wife if she might like a sandwich. She shot him a stricken look, as though she were about to be ill. The heat of the compartment and the noise of Baby Muk had taken their toll.

Van Meegrin patted her arm and winked. He pulled out one of the bottles of beer from the bag and opened it with the brass bottle opener screwed to the cabin wall. Pouring several ounces of it into a glass, he watched with cold clinical detachment a number of particles of foreign matter drifting languidly down through its cloudy, sullen depths. Without drinking any, he put the glass aside, and struck up a conversation with the American girl and her French lover.

Throughout the course of the tour these two had sought to stay aloof from the rest of the group. No one was even certain of their names, although they had heard him call her "Kate," and she call him "Claude." The only additional information they had was that she was a graduate student at Georgetown taking a year in Paris, and that he was studying law at the University of Paris.

Their total absorption in each other was the target of innumerable jokes. In the daytime they'd participated in all of the sightseeing tours, but in the evenings after dinner they never joined the others for the outings to the Kirov or the Circus, or for a rubber of bridge in the cardroom of the hotel. They preferred instead to retire directly to their room.

Europe was flooded that summer with many such couples. They were mostly American girls who had found French or Scandinavian lovers, all terribly earnest and "no-nonsense" in rough clothing with knapsacks crammed full of "serious" books and only the most rudimentary amenities. Clearly educated, conspicuously Spartan, but obviously with plenty of traveler's checks in their pockets, they took great pride in such rough, hearty paraphernalia as blanket rolls, alpenstocks, wool knee socks, and pointedly proletarian laborers' boots, all purchased from the best camping outfitters in London, Rome, and New York. Many of them had walked through the fjords and across the deeply wooded lake country of the Swedish Wärmland.

The young couple in Cabin 5 had reached Leningrad, like Stern, by taking the overnight ferry from Stockholm, sitting up all night in the hard chairs of the *sitzky,* and boarding the Green Train the following morning at Helsinki. They were quiet and unobtrusive. Unfailingly polite but uncompromisingly private. Speaking little and observing much, there was already about them a sense of long-term intimacy, an old-fashioned uxoriousness that Stern found oddly touching.

The Van Meegrins were closest to them in age and no doubt outlook. With Baby Muk now shrieking uncontrollably, Madam and Mr. Mukherjee glowering silently at one another, and all of them confined for the time being to their steamy cabin, it was not at all surprising that both these young couples would turn to each other for solace.

Professor Shapley saw the helicopter first. It was at that moment circling so low over the train that he could feel the concussive thudding of its blade in the pit of his stomach. At one point it canted to its side like a whale breeching, so that he could see the red star and Cyrillic lettering stenciled on the cabin's sliding door. On the engine cowling above the cockpit he could discern clearly the Arabic numerals 1355.

There was little doubt that it was a Russian Air Force helicopter—an MI-26 used for transporting motor-rifle subunits or airborne assault brigades. Why, however, it hovered and circled repeatedly overhead, he could not say.

Grant Shapley was a wry, leathery sort of man who seldom spoke. When he did, it was usually to make some droll, but often keen remark. He was a paleontologist by profession, and the chairman of the Department of Paleontology at the University of Wyoming. Stout, gruff, yet dignified, sort of a latter-day Teddy Roosevelt, he was not unaware of the resemblance and affected battered slouch hats and a shiny malacca cane, possibly to reinforce it.

"Quite a show," he remarked dourly.

Mrs. Shapley nodded to the others in the cabin. "I'm sure we won't be disappointed."

There was a touch of irony in her tone. This was, after all, her fourth trip to the USSR in as many years. Her husband—the Professor, she liked to call him—had a particular interest in the fossil remains prevalent in the rock formations throughout the remote regions of the Kazakh Urals.

Mrs. Shapley, like her husband, was a Westerner, born and bred in the cattle country of Montana. She was a big, rawboned woman, pink and scrubbed with the odor of fresh, starched laundry about her. Though she was close to sixty, she had the skin of a woman half her age. She smiled easily and had about her that rough good humor you imagine typical of the women who crossed the continent in Conestoga wagons.

"They asked to see nothing," little Serja Inusen said, clearly puzzled. She rose and stood just behind Shapley, gazing over his shoulder at all the activity below.

Serja was a young woman of possibly twenty-five or twenty-six, heartbreakingly plain but with the whitish-blond hair and startlingly beautiful skin of Finnish women. She had spent most of her adult life working as a cashier in Stockmann's of Helsinki, and had saved her pennies painstakingly in a jar out of her modest salary in order to make the six-hour train ride to Leningrad. "I had thought it would be much worse."

Wilma Shapley rose and started moving about. "Well, if we're going to be here awhile, I guess we ought to eat. What about a sandwich, Professor?"

Food bags from the hotel were produced and shortly Mrs. Shapley appeared to be presiding over a lively Sunday outing.

The remaining occupant of Cabin 1 was one Junji Asawa, a pallid youth from Sapporo with secretive eyes he kept lowered to his lap all the time. He described himself as a student at the University of Tokyo but he looked considerably younger than his nineteen years. He read books all the time and spoke only when directly addressed.

Mrs. Shapley tugged the tail of her husband's jacket. "Professor, what are they up to now?"

He stood slightly stooped, hands on knees, peering out the grimy window up at the circling helicopter. "Hard to tell, but it sure doesn't look like any custom inspection to me. There must be nearly a full squadron mustering down there."

Cabins 6, 7, and 8 were occupied by a Spanish choral group from Valladolid. They had been touring the USSR on a cultural exchange program. There were seventeen choristers in all—ten females and seven males chaperoned by a peppery group director with a huge nose and saucerlike ears out of which tumbled tufts of steely white hair. The pupil of his right eye was scarred by a milky film of cataract. His style was to order the group about in a hoarse, curt

Castilian to which his charges would respond instantly with the giggling irreverence of children. His name was Señor Madariaga, but behind his back the young people called him "El Cangrejo."

The young Spaniards had eaten almost from the moment they boarded the train that morning in Leningrad, tearing open with gasps of excitement bags crammed full of pretzels, pastries, sweet soda, and incessant cups of coffee made with packets of freeze-dried powder and hot water drawn from the big samovar at the head of the coach.

It was food carried mostly from Spain. Certainly little of it was available in the Soviet Union. The Russian coach attendants were astonished by the sheer abundance of it and grew increasingly disdainful of them as the floor of their compartments gradually filled with peanut shells and candy wrappers.

Almost from the moment the train got under way, they began to sing songs and clap their hands in unison as a form of accompaniment. Some of the songs were lively *jotas* and *zapatongas,* but mostly they were sorrowful tunes full of *mi vida*'s and *mi corazón*'s that bespoke a deep, inconsolable longing for home. Though they sang almost continually, it was not at all unpleasant.

When Colonel Dunskoi and his staff arrived to do the preliminary sight inspection, the Spaniards, indifferent to their vaguely threatening presence, continued to sing songs, munch snacks, and giggle surreptitiously at the soldiers.

Cabin 2 was occupied by what the group had come to call the "Italian Quartet"—actually two young married couples from Milan, the Contis and the Lambrustos. They were close friends in Milan and were taking a vacation together. The object of much speculation among the group, the juiciest of rumors had them down as flagrant mate-swappers copulating their way across the Continent.

Both couples were attractive, friendly, and relentlessly fashionable. Their daily wardrobe was a thing of unceasing wonder. Beside them, everyone felt pathetically shabby. Their leather luggage reeked of money. Maximilliano Conti was a corporate lawyer. Tall, whip-thin, with close-cropped curly blond hair, he had classic Adriatic features that had the look of a profile struck on some antique coin. He wore tinted glasses behind which his eyes roamed indolently about. During the daytime his wardrobe comprised for the most part white duck trousers and stylishly rumpled linen jackets draped swaggeringly across the shoulders like a cape. At evening, he always dressed for dinner.

His wife, Sonia, was pretty and laughed a good deal, even when there was nothing particularly funny to laugh about. "Voluptuous" would best describe her; plump, certainly not fat, unfailingly kindhearted and utterly without guile. But for all of this seeming simplicity, she had very few illusions about marriage and constancy, particularly with regard to Max.

Sandro Lambrusto, by profession an arbitrageur for a leading Italian bank, was a shy young man with a kind of stiff Old World gallantry. By contrast, his wife, Silvana, was vivacious and fun-loving. Thin and willowy, she had the pale, attenuated looks of an extremely successful high-fashion model. Her beauty was of a Roman cast, with bold, strikingly chiseled features, large green eyes set within high cheekbones, and a mat skin of palish ivory.

Without consciously straying, Silvana was something of a flirt. Vivacious and strikingly beautiful she found that men frequently misread her intentions. This trait had become a source of continuing friction between her and her husband.

Sharing the compartment with the quartet was a young man from Ottawa by the name of Keith Wales. Possibly twenty-one or twenty-two, he was attractive in a gangling, callow way. He went about all day morose and sullen in the style of young people emulating movie stars. He affected Western dress—boots, jeans, a good deal of well-scuffed leather.

Young Wales had just been graduated from McGill, still with no clear idea of what he wished to do. His parents had treated him to a trip abroad so he might gain time and perspective, they told themselves. It was certainly easier in any event than having to cope with him at home for the summer.

Six days ago when the group had first gathered on the train platform in Helsinki to claim visas and pick up cabin assignments, Keith had somehow managed to attach himself to the Italians, particularly Silvana, four or five years his senior. Surprisingly, she did not discourage him. Consequently, during the course of the five-day tour, Wales, invariably by her side, had grown increasingly ardent in his admiration, even as Sandro grew quiet and disturbingly withdrawn. Several of the Group were actively promoting the theory that Wales had already seduced her. Wales did little to discourage the idea.

The sixth person in Cabin 2 was Jean Blaylock—a New Yorker, thirtyish, and the graduate of a women's college in Massachusetts. Though she'd been out of school a full ten years, she still affected the dress and mannerisms of an undergraduate.

Jean liked to think of herself as an ideologue, and when she spoke, her talk was liberally sprinkled with such buzzwords as "Marx," "Mills," and "Keynes." She could quote from memory the works of Marcus Garvey and Herbert Marcuse.

She was an unfailing champion of the working class but had only a spotty work record herself. When asked what sort of work she did, she generally described herself as a pamphleteer, a revolutionary in the spirit of, say, Tom Paine. She was a propagandist, she said, whose mission it was to rouse the slumbering masses to a state of righteous activism. She lived on upper Fifth Avenue in a triplex left to her by her father, who had amassed a fortune in scrap metal, and she saw nothing particularly incongruous in any of that.

As admittedly tiresome as Jean was, she was good-natured and generous, and rarely lacked for friends.

Her presence at that moment in Cabin 2 lent fuel to an already incendiary situation. She had little use for the Italians. She thought of them as nice enough, but essentially irrelevant. The women were intellectually vacant, and the men were the corrupt vestiges of a defunct European aristocracy in its final death throes.

Keith Wales she thought of as barely pubescent—sexually as well as intellectually. But Max Conti, seated across the way from her, swathed in all of that bourgeois designer clothing, with its "repulsive" little emblems of status—polo ponies, crocodiles, and whatnot—she considered beneath contempt.

Jean was bored now, had been so ever since they'd boarded the train that morning. Indeed, she'd been bored by everything she'd seen in Russia, in fact disappointed by the whole Russian experience. Now, the proximity of Russian soldiers, so many, and appearing so suddenly, sparked her interest.

In his inspection of Cabin 2, the sergeant major had ignored the others but had asked pointedly to see her passport. Mildly flustered but attempting to cover the fact, she riffled through her purse, aware that the eyes of everyone were upon her. Finding it at last, she thrust it at him, making a great show of impatience. He glanced at it quickly, then passed it back to the colonel, standing just behind him.

The colonel, holding it below his belt at arm's length, looked back and forth from the photograph to Jean, squinting his hooded eyes as he did so. When he'd finished, he snapped something in Russian at the sergeant major, who took Jean's passport at once and checked its number against a sheet of numbers listed on a thick pad he carried with him. Apparently finding something, he whispered a few words into the colonel's ear. In the next moment, the colonel turned on his heel, and followed by his full retinue, moved up the corridor.

"My passport," Jean called after him, and started up. The coach attendant, waving a wide cautionary palm in her face, blocked the way.

"He has my passport," Jean sputtered, swatting the man's palm aside. "I want my passport."

"Please to sit," the attendant croaked placatingly; however, he himself looked a trifle rattled. "Soon to return," he assured her, then lurched out after the others.

The sudden departure of the Russians left in its wake a portentous silence. The occupants of Cabin 2 looked back and forth at one another, their eyes full of troublesome questions they were unable to articulate.

"Shit." Jean smiled brashly but she was aware that her heart was thumping. "What the hell was that book they were checking in?" she asked.

"It was full of numbers," Keith Wales said. "I saw it."

"Passport numbers, probably," Max muttered. He seemed bored.

"Sure," Sandro said. "They were just cross-referencing. Have you ever been to Russia before?"

"Never." Jean laughed oddly and sank back in her seat. "But why me?"

Their conversation broke off in the din of a whining truck engine and the clank of heavy metal.

Max Conti fingered the window curtains aside and peered out. What he saw was something of a surprise. Three armored troop carriers had come lurching up the track bed. Their engines whining in second gear, they rumbled to a halt in a great swirl of dust, almost directly athwart them. In the next instant soldiers jumped down from the cab of each vehicle, dashed round the back, unbuckled heavy chains, and pulled down the tailgates. Suddenly, for no apparent reason, three squadrons of Russian attack soldiers with automatic rifles streamed out of the rear of the troop carriers and started to encircle the train.

Conti turned and looked back at the others who had been watching the scene over his shoulder. A somewhat troubled quiet had fallen over the compartment.

"Che cosa," Sonia whispered to her husband, then giggled. The look on his face silenced her at once.

Grant Shapely had been viewing the identical scene from the next compartment. He watched it with all of the dispassionate remove one associates with scientific observation. His eyes appeared to be counting, classifying, collating, and filing data away for further reference.

He watched the soldiers fan out east and west along the track bed, then saw them swing round the rear of the train, finally ringing it like a huge lariat. It was done with a smooth, impressive dispatch.

In a rare display of curiosity, Junji Asawa rose and moved closer to the window. "What is it?" he asked with a kind of hushed awe.

"Damned if I know," Professor Shapely said, and made a low, airy whistling sound.

In Cabin 4 Tony Thomas studied the backgammon board. He sucked the cold stem of his cigarette holder, making a great show of indifference to what was going on outside. Peter Stern stood at the window looking out. The helicopter they'd glimpsed before had continued to circle overhead, but now it had dropped low, only one hundred feet or so off the ground, and hovered there above the Green Train.

"They don't do this for everyone, do they?" Stern mused aloud.

Thomas cracked his crooked smile. "We do seem to be getting the royal treatment."

"Looks like some sort of military maneuvers," Paul Blanton remarked.

Thomas patted the back of his head where a cowlick of hair kept springing up. He appeared to be pondering some tactic on the game board. Blanton turned to him. "What do you think?"

Thomas' eyes counted pips, his index finger poised above the counter. He was silent for a time as though he hadn't heard the question. "I'm not at all sure what I think," he spoke at last, and moved his counter three pips.

Actually he had a very good idea what he thought. Under normal circumstances he wouldn't have been caught dead on this train. There was no first class and it had a rotten bar. But these were scarcely normal circumstances. That very morning he'd received a confidential pouch from home office, London. A tip—it was no more than that, his editor was careful to emphasize, but a very solid one, considering the source from within the Kremlin itself.

Two days earlier, it seemed, a Soviet submarine had been nabbed red-handed on a spying mission in the waters just off the big Norwegian naval base at Hammerfest on the Barents Sea. It was there that some of NATO's biggest and most secret radar operations were conducted.

The submarine had been impounded at a shipyard in nearby Sorgy and the whole crew taken into custody at the naval base. The thrust of the tip strongly implied that the Soviets were now casting about for some pretext to make a retaliatory strike, and if the tip was at all authentic, they had chosen to make it the Green Train. That's how Thomas found himself aboard the train at that moment, instead of enjoying the amenities of the Dollar Bar at the Prebaltis-kaya.

It had passed through his mind that he might have some obligation to inform the others of the situation insofar as it might impinge on their immediate plans. But then he thought better of it. For one thing, they could all do quite nicely without the panic that must inevitably follow on the heels of such a disclosure. For another, it could place him in a very awkward light if it were to appear that he'd had foreknowledge of such a Soviet plan in the making and failed to advise his fifty fellow passengers to immediately make alternate arrangements for reaching the West. For another, though he didn't care to admit it, he had no intention of jeopardizing a once-in-a-lifetime opportunity such as this.

For a journalist, detention on a train at the Russo-Finnish border was not without its benefits, particularly a journalist nearing sixty, who was rather tired, and whose reputation, rumor had it all along Fleet Street, was in serious decline. Something unusual was about to happen on this train. Something big. He could feel that in his reporter's bones. This was no mere defection. These were not silly little war games. They'd been taken hostage here, although, as of yet, no one was carrying on as if that were the case. The climate aboard the train was still resolutely civil.

But Thomas had been around the Soviets long enough to be able to distinguish between their bluster and the real thing. The soldiers and the armored vehicles did not intrigue him half so much as the presence of that very cool full colonel on the train. The Russians did not normally trot out officers of that lofty rank for border checks. That fellow meant business.

This was big. Very big indeed. If he knew their game, and after a dozen years of unblinking observation, he was sure he did, this train full of foreign nationals, mostly Westerners, would be taken hostage at the border and held there until the release of the submarine and its crew had been effected. They, in short, were about to become a bargaining chip in an international auction.

Shortly, every major capital in the Free World would know of the train's plight. The Soviet Ministry of Information, he was certain, would quickly seal off the immediate area from the prying eyes of all Western media—TV, radio, newspapers, magazines, the works. And there he was right smack in the center of it. Sitting atop a monopoly all his own. What a stroke of fantastic good fortune. Had he tried to plan it that way himself, it would never have worked out so well.

In Cabin 3 Señor Gonzaga had fallen asleep. The heat slowly building up in the compartment had finally overcome him. His chin had fallen to his chest and he sat slumped and dozing, snoring volubly in his seat. A small bead of perspiration emerging from the gray entanglement of a sideburn crept slowly down the furrow of his cheek.

Señora Gonzaga, who seemed almost always embarrassed or apologetic about her husband, watched him anxiously. She had found all of the papers that he had unthinkingly mislaid. For her that was not the problem. He had always been a bit careless. In former years it'd had a kind of eccentric charm. But now, on this trip in particular, his forgetfulness had taken on new and alarming proportions.

The Russian colonel who'd departed the cabin several minutes before had rattled her further. She could not say why. He'd been perfectly polite, even solicitous. But now the shouts of the sergeant major outside, the barking of the dogs, the awful hullabaloo of engines, and the grind of heavy machinery in motion truly terrified her. She did not fear for herself or her husband. But she was an old-fashioned woman, and, seeing soldiers, she feared for Isabel and Consuelo, her two unmarried thirtyish daughters. She herself had been a young girl in Barcelona during the Civil War and had been hidden in the cellars of farmhouses in the countryside to keep her safe, not only from the Loyalists, but from the Falangists as well. She had read too about the Japanese in Nanking and the Russians in Berlin at the end of the war, and in her simple heart she feared the worst.

Along with the Gonzagas in Cabin 3 were Mr. and Mrs. Ralph Keck of Ames, Iowa. The Kecks were one of those problematic couples one is bound to encounter on such tours. On the bus, or during the various daytime excursions, no one sought their company. In the hotel dining room at night no one ever sat at their table, but instead sought out other, more congenial company. After dinner, when people went up to the Dollar Bar or to the cardroom of the hotel for a rubber of bridge before bed, the Kecks were never included. There was nothing cruel or consciously exclusionary about this. It was segregation at the subliminal level, as if people had sensed something unpleasant and, without even thinking, gave it a wide berth.

Mrs. Keck was a retired biology teacher, full of pithy sayings and simpleminded homilies. Prayer and parsimony were high on her list of virtues. Undoubtedly a kind woman, she was remorselessly boring and all about her person was the pervasive scent of camphor. While she had been retired nearly ten years, she liked to boast that many of her old students still came to see her.

Mr. Keck was also retired. He had amassed a modest fortune from a chain of shoe stores he had started with a hole-in-the-wall operation in Ames and built into a Midwestern institution. Given any encouragement at all, he'd recite you chapter and verse on the history of Keck Shoes. He'd pioneered the first foam-rubber arch, and the use of the moulage in the preparation of prescription shoes. He had worked hard all of his life and thought of himself as a living paradigm of the American Dream. Hard work, self-reliance, and good horse sense had been the making of him and he recommended the same formula to all others who wanted to "get on." He was a deacon of the Episcopal Church and rarely missed a chance to inform you of the fact. As a result he was ever vigilant for opportunities to do "good works."

For all his seventy years or so, Mr. Keck was seemingly hale and hearty, although the flush that rose from out his collar, suffusing his cheeks, seemed unhealthily high. He had rheumy eyes, with a spray of capillaries that raked the side of his nose. His hair was lank and white as lamb's wool, plastered down, with streaks of pink scalp threading through between. He never appeared in anything other than a suit and a tie, and for a man who had devoted a lifetime to the "romance of shoes," he himself wore only black oxfords of the most unrelentingly plain design.

His manner was deferential, and with strangers he was capable of the most embarrassing self-effacement, full of groveling apologies about his unworldliness and lack of culture. Whenever he offered some remark or observation, he would glance at Mrs. Keck to see if he had earned her approbation.

They had been everywhere since Ralph's retirement, Mrs. Keck liked to say, but not to Russia. They had heard much about the Russians—she spoke with a glow of nationalistic pride in her eyes—and now they had come to have a look for themselves.

Up in Cabin 9 sat the Finnish tour guide, Jatta Palmunan, along with the Kariolainens, a family of native Californians of Finnish descent. There were four of them: the father, in his early sixties, Mrs. Kariolainen, nearly a full twenty years his junior—they had married late. The daughter, Corrie, was a seventeen-year-old high-school senior, a wonderful mixture of the glorious fairness one associates with Finnish women and the fully bloomed, sun-burnished, outdoorsy beauty of California youth. The son, Christopher, whom they called Buddy, was twelve, short, slight, endearingly clumsy, with a quick smile.

The Kariolainens were a hearty, jovial group. Health radiated from them like a warm sun. In their presence the troubled were calmed, the mean grew kind, and the sad merry. They had no conscious sense of their ministry. That was undoubtedly the reason for their success. People of all manner and stripe gravitated toward them.

Mr. Kariolainen owned and operated a prosperous fruit farm north of San Francisco around Shasta. Nearly seventy years ago his parents, migrating from Finland to America, bought the farm for virtually pennies. Today the land alone, nearly a thousand acres, was worth a fortune, and Mr. Kariolainen's cherries and apricots were the most highly prized in the state. On paper they were undoubtedly millionaires, but they certainly didn't carry on that way.

This was their first trip abroad and, of course, Mr. Kariolainen insisted upon taking his family to Finland, where he still had relatives. "It took me sixty-three years to get to Finland," he confided to Peter Stern late one night in the Dollar Bar after several Heinekens. "I intend to return."

The tour guide, Jatta, had chosen to share the compartment with them, first out of simple nationalistic affinity, but then out of pure affection.

Jatta was probably in her early thirties. She was slight, fair, attractive in a flinty way, with wide-set eyes that could be either disapproving or flirtatious. She was athletic—all sinew and tendon. She was married to a Finnish policeman in Helsinki and had two children. But when she was in Leningrad conducting a tour, which was twice a month, she spent all of her evenings and free time with a Russian naval attaché approximately her own age.

She rose now, straightened the blouse of her jogging suit, and ducked her head out into the corridor. Jatta had been taking tour groups into Leningrad on the Green Train for nearly a dozen years. In her time she'd seen travelers detained at the border; she'd seen film, currency, cameras, and other items confiscated without explanation. On several occasions she had even been stuck overnight in Vyborg, unable to leave until one of her group who, for inexplicable reasons, had been detained, was finally given clearance.

She knew the border guards to be suspicious, unpredictable, impenetrably stupid, and when they chose to be, uncannily shrewd. There was very little you could conceal from them. They could be dazzlingly efficient or infuriatingly slow, which was more often the case. They knew the coaches of the Green Train like the backs of their hands, and could scour every nook and cranny of all six cars, plus dispatch the normal customs-passport drill in little over an hour.

Capable of the most arbitrary behavior, and consummate bureaucrats, they knew how to trump up all kinds of pretexts in order to inconvenience the most inoffensive of travelers. They knew how to ensnare one in regulation and formalities, ultimately entombing their victim in a swamp of paperwork. Everything depended upon the mood of the moment, which, without exception, depended on how the USSR stood just then in relation to the rest of the world.

In twelve years, Jatta thought she had seen most everything on the Helsinki-Leningrad run. But what she saw now—the armored personnel carriers, the motor-rifle units moving in on them, the transport helicopter, which was just then hovering inches above the tall grass in the nearby field, the wind from its rotary blades leaning the grass over on its side, the brisk, ordered movement of soldiers encircling the train—this she had never seen before.

Jatta's practiced eyes continued to observe the scene. Despite the unperturbed expression on her face, she felt a fist closing over her heart. "Wait here for me." She glanced over her shoulder at those in the cabin. "I'll see what I can find out." In the next moment she'd ducked out of the compartment and disappeared up the corridor.

Twenty minutes later she was back, but visibly shaken. "I don't know." She shrugged. "They say there's a defector." She knew a number of the border guards, spoke fluent Russian, and that's what they'd told her.

Mrs. Kariolainen looked surprised. "In our group?"

"Could be anyone. There are five more coaches back there, full of other people."

"So what do they do now?" Mr. Kariolainen asked.

Jatta sighed and pulled the window curtain back. "Tear the train apart, probably."

PART II

COLONEL DIMITRI DUNSKOI stood in the tall grass along the track bed not twenty paces from the Green Train. He had found himself a cool spot beneath one of the towering beech trees that had no doubt been a seedling there at the time of Peter the Great.

He was warm and the thick serge twill of his uniform didn't help matters any. Still, he wore his hat and his high boots and his tunic buttoned to the collar, making absolutely no concessions to the heat. The tall purple phlox contrasted sharply against his khaki jodhpurs.

He was a man of probably fifty years, the colonel, thirty of which had been spent in the military. He lived in a dacha outside of Leningrad with his wife and two daughters, both of whom were attending the University of Leningrad, one studying microbiology and the other medicine. The military had been good to him. He had served with distinction and there were rumors afoot that he was about to be elevated to the rank of a major general of the Soviet Army.

Standing by himself off to the side observing the maneuvers of four motor-rifle squadrons, and the various movements of the armored vehicles encircling the train, he felt a glow of satisfaction. It was that feeling of serenity that comes from being completely synchronized with oneself. He never felt this inner harmony anywhere but in the field with the men; not at home, not with his wife or children in the bosom of his family, not with friends sitting and having a drink in a local bar. He was a soldier to his fingertips—a descendant of the legendary fourteenth-century Muscovite and national hero Dimitri Dunskoi, for whom he was named, who'd delivered a crippling blow against Tamerlane, thus liberating Russia from the Mongol yoke. Like his distinguished ancestor, Colonel Dunskoi was only at peace in the field, in the rough masculine company of other soldiers. He enjoyed wearing uniforms; he enjoyed regulation and system, the transmission of orders, and the swift execution of commands.

A short time before, he had issued several commands and they had by now all been executed with impressive dispatch. He too had recently responded to a command from very high up—a command to put in motion the steps necessary to detain the Green Train on the Finnish border. This order had originated not in Leningrad from base headquarters, where it might reasonably have been expected to come from, but, somewhat more disquietingly, from STAVKA—Supreme Military Headquarters, Novgorsk, a far higher authority.

When the order had come early that morning, it had both startled and perplexed him and he telexed back at once for confirmation. Once having received that, however, he never hesitated one moment to carry out the command.

From where he stood in the close, heavy air beneath the trees, his narrow Tartar eyes scanned the length of the train. Stalled there on the tracks, it had the look of some beast of burden worn out by heat and exertion pausing to cool itself in the grass. Butterflies fluttered before the toylike electric engine. The colonel watched them lighting on the iron bumpers and wafting gaily in and out amid the big drive wheels. Two Finnish trainmen had climbed down from the cab of the engine and stood alongside the track bed talking quietly with their hands on their hips.

Colonel Dunskoi had carried out his orders to perfection. But he faced a problem. What to do now? He had a train on his hands that he had been told to detain until further notice. The train was packed with passengers, almost six cars full. Most were Russian nationals, who presented no problem. But here, too, were a number of foreign nationals, civilians traveling back and forth between the USSR and the West on business, plus a tour group of some fifty people. This became somewhat more problematic. Such encounters were fraught with not only tremendous potential for danger but also a risk of embarrassment to the government. How many first-rate officers had he himself known whose careers had gone down the drain as a result of finding themselves inadvertently drawn into one of these episodes?

It was a situation to be avoided. Handled clumsily, it could cost one a great deal. On the other hand, were it a question of the territorial integrity or the national security of the Soviet Union and its people, nothing in his thinking could take higher priority.

The colonel's immediate problem was not so much the detention of foreign nationals. Any number of pretexts could be quickly trumped up in order to keep them around for as long as necessary. His real problem was the difficulty of keeping such a large number of people confined in one place without the physical amenities to do so for any extended length of time. Although experience told him that this action could not possibly involve anything more than a few hours before its satisfactory resolution, he was at a loss to explain the presence of the four squadrons of shock troops plus the helicopters coming out from the air base outside of Leningrad. Why he himself had been ordered to put in a special appearance there, no one had, as of yet, bothered to inform him.

It was now going on toward three o'clock in the afternoon. The train had been stalled on the border since approximately 1:15. The people on board had been confined to their compartments all during that period. The temperature inside the cabins had risen to 88 degrees Fahrenheit, with most of the compartment windows unable to be opened. They had not much food left in the dining car, and the water, while adequate in terms of supply, was tepid and by Western standards barely potable.

Many people aboard the train were carrying bottles of soda water, juice, and beer, but shortly these personal supplies would be depleted and people would then have no alternative for refreshment other than the train's water, which, even the Russians would concede, made people, particularly Westerners, violently ill.

The colonel had already made one single concession to physical comfort. He had reopened the toilets. Not all of them by any means, but every other toilet, meaning that two full carloads of passengers were expected to make do with one toilet.

The problem would shortly become one of sanitation. The condition of the toilets had already deteriorated during the first hours of detention on the border. Because of the order to close half of the toilets, those that remained open for use were in barely tolerable condition, the floors festooned with discarded toilet tissue, and the toilets themselves flushing poorly, barely emptied of their contents. Since, too, the train was stationary, and the waste emptied directly onto the track, the condition of the track bed directly beneath the train would soon become horrific.

For Colonel Dunskoi the problem was not an easy one. It involved carrying out the orders of Supreme Headquarters while not exposing foreign nationals to conditions that were either unsafe or inhumane. What bothered him most was that he had not the slightest idea what had motivated this extraordinary action or how long it was likely to last.

The mood on the train was one of barely contained exasperation. The heat and confinement had become almost intolerable. Nearly three hours had gone by and the border guard had made virtually no move toward implementing the formal customs check. Passports and visas had not been inspected, nor had customs declarations been reviewed. The currency accountings had not been collected, nor had the luggage and compartments yet been subjected to physical search.

All this had to be done before the train could be given clearance. Under ideal circumstances this could take up to an hour. The sun was now just beginning to slant westward. The clock was moving on. Many people aboard the train were booked on flights scheduled to depart Finland in several hours. Others had booked hotel reservations in Helsinki or cabins on the overnight ferry to Stockholm. Friends and relations were waiting at train stations, at air terminals, or in the sanctified quiet of living rooms, suspecting nothing and looking forward to reunions with loved ones.

"The Indian government shall hear of this." Madam Muk's shrill voice jolted Stern out of the drowsy languor of a daydream. The shrieks of Baby Muk resumed, piercing the hot, stale air like an auger.

"Please to resume seat. Hope to depart soon as pozzible." The tired, placative voice of the coach attendant drifted down the length of the corridor. His patience sounded sorely strained.

"She's at it again," Nell Blanton remarked.

Tony Thomas looked up. "What is it this time?"

"She wants them to take her off the train." Frau Kunkel made an unpleasant sound with her tongue. "Says she must get to a hospital at once. Her blood pressure is rising."

"She'll give us all strokes if she goes on like this."

"At least she makes them as uncomfortable as she makes us," Frau Kunkel reflected with satisfaction, then winced as one of Baby Muk's shrieks rent the air.

"You suppose they'd let me make a phone call?" Stern asked. "I'm booked on a flight to New York this evening."

"I doubt it," Thomas replied.

"Doubt what? That they'd let me call or that I'll make the flight?"

"Both, actually." Thomas made a queer face and peered down at the backgammon board. "Anyone for backgammon or whist?"

Nell Blanton sighed and leaned her head back against the headrest of the banquette. She had opened the top two buttons of her blouse just above the point where the plump, freckled flesh of her breasts began to rise. She dabbed at her throat with a small lace handkerchief balled in her fist. "Feels just like Lexington in July." She spoke dreamily with her eyes closed. "If I sit here quietly I can almost smell the wisteria and the scuppernong. When we get to the hotel tonight, first thing I want is a shower and a cold beer."

Peter Stern fretted silently. He wondered about his daughter and what she would think when he didn't get off the Finnair Stratoliner at Kennedy tomorrow. She would wait around there at the gate for a while, thinking that there had been some mistake or delay and that he would appear momentarily.

When he didn't and it had become clear to her that he was not aboard, she would go to the Finnair desk and have the purser check the passenger manifest for the flight. Learning that her father had never boarded the plane, she would then either cable or call his hotel in Helsinki. They would of course tell her that he had never returned from Leningrad to pick up his luggage at the hotel, where he had stored it temporarily, rather than have to carry all of his possessions with him into the USSR for the five-day tour.

She'd be puzzled then, but not necessarily alarmed. Undoubtedly there was a perfectly plausible explanation—they were delayed or they'd decided to stay a day or two more. No doubt he'd cabled but it had not yet caught up with her. She'd wait a day or two, and if he had not yet returned by then, she'd contact the American embassy in Helsinki, the U.S. consul in Leningrad, and the State Department. That's what she would do. By that time she would be worried, but she was a professional.

"Where do you think you're going?" Frau Kunkel snapped at Karl Heinz.

The boy stood there awkwardly and somewhat embarrassed. "To the lav."

"You just went twenty minutes ago," Frau Kunkel snapped.

The boy was mortified. He swallowed volubly. "Yes, but I couldn't get in. There was too long a line."

Frau Kunkel's impatience appeared to rise. "Well then, go if you must." She dismissed him with a wave of her hand. "But don't be long. And for God's sake, if you hear them start the inspection, come right back."

The passengers of Cabin 4 sat in troubled silence, the hot, close air was roiled with unspoken questions and the edginess of half-imagined fears.

"You'd think they'd tell us something," Paul Blanton said.

"Not necessarily," Thomas remarked.

"You will admit this is all a bit irregular?"

"Rather." The Englishman shot him one of those infuriatingly self-satisfied smiles.

Stern shifted in his seat. "Jatta says they think it might be a defector."

"She doesn't know any more than we do," Frau Kunkel muttered.

Stern folded his arms and concentrated on being calm. "Well, I wish to hell someone around here knew something."

"I want my passport back and I want it now."

Jean Blaylock stood in the doorway of Cabin 2 denouncing the coach attendant. He was a gray, weary man with a rather crumpled face. She stood several inches taller than he and shouted over his head as if she were trying to wake a sleeping world. Thin half-moons of perspiration showed above her armpits and a jagged line of sweat beneath her blouse ran the length of her spine like a gash of lightning. She spoke fast and loud, her hands fanning the air. She had the look of an indignant wasp about to sting. "You have no right—"

"Please to return to cabin."

"Tell me why my passport has been confiscated."

"Please to rezume sit." The attendant repeated the words wearily. "Must comply with wishes of commander."

"Where's my passport?"

The attendant never batted an eye. "Please to return . . ."

Max Conti tried to pull her back into the compartment, but she flung his hand off. "Don't 'please' me, my friend. I'm not going back into that steambath until I get my passport."

By that time the row in the corridor had people up and sticking their heads out from compartment doors.

"I'm not budging until I get my passport."

Sensing trouble, the attendant turned and started to walk away. Jean started to follow, then saw the two riflemen at the end of the corridor moving toward her. She turned and, for some incomprehensible reason, started to run in the opposite direction. One of them shouted something in Russian and took off after her.

They caught up with her at the door just as she was clattering down the iron steps to the track bed. One of them hauled her back up, squirming and wriggling like a hooked fish, and began to shout at her. He grabbed her under the arm and tried to drag her back into the car. She began to scream and then kicked him.

By that time people were pouring out into the corridor to see what was happening. The other rifleman started shouting at them, presumably ordering them back to their cabins. When they didn't move, no doubt because they didn't understand him, he thrust his rifle out at port arms and tried to physically herd them back down the aisles.

The soldier trying to drag Jean back onto the train was not having an easy time of it. Nor, for that matter, was Jean, but the soldier appeared to be getting the worst of it. The more physical he became with her, the louder she screamed, and the more alarmed the other passengers grew.

The corridor was now choked with milling, highly agitated people. Jatta, the tour guide, had managed to muscle her way forward to the scene and was now standing out in the vestibule shouting at the soldier in Russian.

At that point the soldier sensed the situation getting out of hand. He paused a moment, an expression of bewilderment on his face.

"Asshole," Jean hissed, and spat at him.

The soldier slapped her across the face with such force that she appeared to spin fully ninety degrees.

The incident occurred directly outside Cabin 4 in full view of all its occupants.

The soldier was about to strike her again. Stern, never a bold man, for some inexplicable reason, even to himself, waded out into the corridor, grabbed the soldier as his arm went up, and stayed it. "There's no need for that." His voice was strangely gentle. "No need for—"

He never completed the sentence. At that moment, the other rifleman, the one herding people back into their cabins with the barrel of his rifle, placed a palm flat against Stern's chest and heaved. To Stern it was as if someone had jumped on his chest. He felt the air rush from his lungs and for a moment he experienced an odd, almost pleasurable sense of weightlessness. He reeled back into the compartment, slamming hard against the far wall, slumping to the floor amid a shower of glasses and assorted fruits that had been standing on the cabin table. His vision dimmed and he thought he would throw up.

People watched the scene transfixed in horror. The other soldier had now seized Jean by the hair and was dragging her bodily up the corridor. But in the next moment someone had grabbed the rifleman by the collar from behind and yanked him backward. The soldier made a gagging sound, bellowed like a stricken bull, and wheeled about in white fury on his attacker. His arm shot up like a shuttle, then paused, trembling as though it were held by some invisible hand. Then the arm came down gentle as a leaf falling to earth as the soldier stood there baffled, looking into the infuriated features of Colonel Dunskoi.

The colonel glared at him a moment, then with the back of his hand cracked him hard across the face. He barked some orders in Russian, and the soldier, dazed and sheepish, executed an about-face and stumbled quickly out, Dunskoi directly behind him, pummeling the fellow as he scurried down the aisle trying to get out of the way of the colonel's fists.

Shortly after, Dunskoi returned, moving slowly up the crowded corridor, where people hovered, still visibly shaken and muttering to each other.

Not a tall man, the colonel appeared to loom large above the crowd. His presence there was salutary. People were calmed. He had gained their trust. Had he taken the other tack, supported his own man, the situation might well have deteriorated quickly.

Followed by contingents of his own staff, he went immediately to where Jean Blaylock sat huddled on the floor of the car, looking oddly small and childlike. Her cheek was flared and swollen where she'd been struck. She was close to tears. One could sense the enormous effort of will she was making to stave them off. The colonel stooped and attempted to help her to her feet. She flung his hands off and rose unsteadily under her own power.

"I am so sorry," he spoke to her in Russian. "So very sorry."

She couldn't understand a word of it and instead glared at him. "Where the hell is my passport?"

"Are you hurt?" the colonel went on solicitously. "Is there anything I can do? I must apologize for my—"

"Fuck off."

Dunskoi frowned. If he couldn't understand the words, he appeared to understand quite well the tone of them. He tilted his head sideward and murmured something to the captain at his side. The young man whispered something back to him in his ear.

In the next moment the colonel snapped his shoulders back, bowed his head in that courtly fashion of his, turned sharply, and moved up the aisle to the next cabin. It was number four, where Stern, who by then had been helped back into his seat by Thomas and young Karl Heinz, was still badly winded and trying hard to regain his breath.

The colonel paused in the cabin doorway as if he were waiting to be invited in. No invitation proffered, he entered of his own accord and moved directly to Stern. He leaned over and took Stern's hand, shaking it with curious warmth. He proceeded to speak in Russian while the captain beside him did a word-for-word translation in perfect English.

"The colonel extends you his best wishes and offers his sincere regrets for any injury or hurt you may have sustained as a result of the unpardonable rudeness of the soldier.

"The colonel wishes you to know that such behavior on the part of individuals serving in the armed forces of the USSR is extremely uncommon, and further, he wishes you to know that the soldier responsible for such reprehensible behavior shall not go unpunished."

The captain droned on, reeling the words off mechanically like something he'd recited on numerous occasions. But on the face of it, that was unlikely. The apology had to be extemporaneous, and for that Stern felt gratitude.

"The colonel wishes to know," continued the captain, "if you would perhaps like to have a physician examine you."

Stern waved the offer aside with a limp twirl of his wrist. "Thank you. I'm quite all right."

Nell Blanton crouched above him. "Perhaps you should."

"Wouldn't be a bad idea," Thomas added. He turned and spoke in Russian to the colonel. Suddenly they were both conversing in lowered voices.

Stern attempted to interrupt. "Tony, I really don't think—"

"He says there's a military doctor back in Vyborg—about forty kilometers from here. He would be happy to send you over with a driver."

"I don't need a doctor." An edge of impatience crept into Stern's voice.

"Are you sure?"

"Absolutely certain."

The colonel waited, looking down upon him sympathetically.

Thomas spoke a few words more to him in Russian. The colonel smiled, tipped his hand to the braided visor of his cap, then turning sharply, stepped out of the compartment, and disappeared down the aisle, followed by his staff.

Thomas beamed round at his fellow passengers.

"What were you talking to him about?" Paul Blanton asked.

"We talked about Stern and the doctor at Vyborg, of course, and then I asked him when he thought we'd get out of here."

Peter Stern, appearing very tired, suddenly looked up. "What did he say?"

"Said he didn't have the slightest idea but he hoped shortly." He made an amused face. "I asked him if there was anything wrong, and he said no."

Grant Shapley sat in his dampish clothing, shirt sleeves rolled above the elbows. His large fist curled round the brass duck-head handle of the cane leaning against his leg.

Everyone in the compartment had been terribly unnerved by the Blaylock incident, particularly poor little Serja Inusen. She'd started to tremble.

Fiddling with the head of his cane, Shapley grew increasingly aware of the tremor in his leg. It had actually started earlier that morning, at breakfast in the hotel, distant at first, and sporadic, then gradually over the course of the morning increasing in duration and intensity. The doctor had told him it would be like this, each spasm occurring within shorter and shorter periods of time. Then finally that numbness, as if all the limb itself were gone and there was nothing between his torso and the floor but air.

Sitting there slowly twirling the cane, pretending to be interested in what the others around him were saying, he timed the spasms with his wristwatch. They'd been coming roughly every sixteen minutes. The last one had persisted for just under two minutes. The one before that had lasted fifty-eight seconds. He continued to time them, vaguely aware that Mrs. Shapley's shrewd eyes were on him, watchful and aware, yet she said nothing, respecting his wish for privacy.

The Professor found that he could precipitate a spasm by raising his heel off the ground while pressing the toe of his foot down hard and holding the position. Shortly after, a ripple of involuntary muscle activity, like the tentative first tremor along a fault, would streak up the length of the leg from calf to thigh.

"I've never seen anything like that before," Serja murmured in hushed awe.

"Like what?" Shapley glanced up, eager to take his mind off the tremors. He was afraid people might notice the wavelike motion of it going on beneath his trousers.

"That business with the soldier and Miss Blaylock. I'm sick to my heart."

"She was a damned fool, carrying on like that," Shapley grumbled. "They're soldiers. They don't know how to react in any other way."

Wilma Shapley bristled. "He had no business hitting her. We're not at war, you know. What's going on here anyway?"

Serja stared gloomily out the dirty yellow panes of the window at the soldiers and the trucks below. "How much longer will they keep us, do you think?"

Wilma Shapley laughed. "You never know with these people." Seeing the fright in Serja's face, she regretted it the moment she'd said it. "I don't think much longer, do you, Professor?"

She looked keenly at her husband, then instantly caught the barely perceptible flutter of his trouser. "It shouldn't ought to be too much longer, do you think, Grant?"

He cast a grumpy look her way. He knew she was trying to assuage the girl. "We're as much a bother to them as they are to us."

During all that time young Junji Asawa did not speak once. He sat in a kind of trance. Occasionally he would gaze out the window, taking a sullen interest in the action of the soliders. But mostly he kept his eyes riveted to the floor, studying his fellow passengers from beneath his shifting brows, contemplating, so it seemed, some large, as of yet inchoate vision.

Leg tremors notwithstanding, Grant Shapley found that vague furtive expression on young Asawa's face strangely disquieting.

Señor Madariaga was due in Madrid that evening. He had left Valladolid two months before with seventeen youngsters from the Choral Society of the local secondary school.

They had traveled all throughout the Soviet Union, from Estonia to Georgia, to Latvia and the Ukraine. They had crisscrossed the boundless immensity of that vast land in trains, buses, and planes, bringing the fiery songs of their sunny homeland to villages high in the Urals and buried deep within the gray, loamy steppes of Central Asia, from Samarkand and Tbilisi to Kiev and

Murmansk. They had sung in Moscow and topped off, the highlight of their trip, by singing in the choir of St. Isaac's Cathedral in Leningrad.

Señor Madariaga was now tired and he wished to go home. A teacher of music at the local secondary school in Valladolid, he worked with young people all year. In the summers, in order to generate some additional income for his large family of eight, he conducted a number of guided musical tours for his more gifted students. He had a genuine fondness for young people, particularly talented ones—singers and instrumentalists. But eleven months a year of teaching and then escorting youngsters about the Continent could be taxing.

His students were still young enough to be frisky and often foolish. They could be boisterous in public and indiscreet among themselves. The young girls were already nubile. Most of the boys were bumbling and callow, but a few among them were somewhat more precocious than their fellows, and could not be trusted alone with the young girls.

One had to be vigilant, and that was exhausting. Two or three there, he knew, had already been guileful enough to slip past his defenses late at night and find their way into each other's hotel rooms. They had devised a system of electric-light signals and wall-tapping to get around him. Well, what of it? All he could hope was that they had been sensible enough to take precautions. But he could not fret too long about that. He was a teacher, not a duenna.

Besides, now there was far more to worry about. He looked up, aware that the youngsters sitting nearby were looking at him.

"Why do they do that?" one of the girls, Celine, wide-eyed, asked.

"Do what?" Señor Madariaga feigned disinterest.

"Surround the train with the soldiers like that."

"Sh, sh." Madariaga pressed a finger to her lips, hushing her. "Quiet, for God's sake. Obviously they're repairing something. That's why the delay." Señor Madariaga didn't believe a word of that. He had an idea that the armed troops encircling the train just then were involved in something far more portentous than repair. But what exactly, he could not say.

His mind raced ahead. They were scheduled to fly an Iberian airliner from Helsinki to Madrid at eight o'clock that evening. It was now well past four P.M. Even if the train were given clearance that moment, they were still nearly three hours' traveling time from Helsinki. If their plane was to leave at eight o'clock, there was no way in the world they could make it from the train station out to the airport in time.

Would they be able to reschedule their flight for tomorrow, that is, if they were lucky enough to get back to Helsinki by tomorrow? And was there a flight out tomorrow? If not, where would they stay until the next available flight, and did he have funds enough to cover the additional cost of bed and board for seventeen youngsters and himself until such time as they could get a flight out? This was certainly not allotted for in his budget.

These were questions he had scarcely addressed. He was a thorough man,

Madariaga, a thoughtful, well-organized fellow. He thought he had planned for everything, even unforeseen contingencies. But who could have predicted this? Had anyone called him aside just then and asked him earnestly what he thought of their chances of getting out of this thing soon, he was just the sort of gloomy fatalist who would have had to say he wasn't all that hopeful.

Ralph Keck had been watching the soldiers too. There was no choice. They were directly beneath his line of gaze. He'd been rolling wads of paper into little balls. He rolled them slowly between his fingers with an air of dreamy abstraction as if he were several million miles away. But he was not. He was right there like the others, keenly aware of everything that was going on about him.

Mrs. Keck was conversing with Señora Gonzaga. Because of the noise going on outside the coach, she had cupped a hand over her mouth and appeared to be shouting into Señora Gonzaga's ear. Courteous, genteel, the soul of refinement, the señora winced at the braying in her ear, but tried hard to be attentive.

Mr. Keck observed his wife. He wore a kindly smile about his lips, but inwardly he was seething. The object of his anger at that moment was ironically not his captors, but rather his wife, sitting there chatting amiably with the Spanish lady, while he was convinced that their lives and all of their worldly possessions were now in the gravest jeopardy.

In some exasperating, perverse way, she appeared to be savoring the experience. Calm and self-possessed, she felt none of the threat that he did. Clearly she was already projecting several months forward to autumn, back home in Ames, musicales and meetings with her literary circle at the library, where she would recount in vivid detail to a group of rapt, obsequious ladies what it was like to be a captive of the Russians. Perhaps she would even write an article, a first-person account for the Ames *Daily Eagle,* of what it was like to be detained by Communists.

He watched her head tilt backward as she laughed at something the Spanish lady had said. He could hear her laughter above the racket going on around him. Light, tinkling, carefree, it was like something overheard at a garden party in the dusk of late summer. It made him furious. Had it been up to him, they would never have been in this predicament. Hadn't he tried to warn her? Told her what these people were? What sort of godless acts they were capable of? Barbaric, unconscionable brutes. The Mongol hordes. Why, they were almost as bad as the Japanese. Pillage and rape were their specialties.

And now, here they were, their captives. Completely at their mercy. They could do what they wished with them. Take their money. Sodomize the women. Banish them all to the gulag, where a person could vanish forever into that vast unending Russian waste. Who knew what horrors awaited them? And it was all Myra's fault.

* * *

The Gonzaga girls were not speaking to each other. But that was nothing remarkable. They seldom spoke to each other. As a study in personality, they were night and day.

Consuelo at thirty-one was the elder but looked younger than her twenty-seven-year-old sister, Isabel. Consuelo was "the good child." Sweet, docile, infinitely malleable, the one who went to Mass each Sunday morning and prayed for the strength to please her parents. She had no more pressing thoughts in her head than a new dress or the private lives of cinema celebrities as reported in the Spanish-language edition of *People* magazine.

By contrast, Isabel was stormy, sullen, perversely contrary. She would not attend church, she was not interested in clothing or cinema stars. Slightly masculine in appearance, but by no means unattractive, she carried within herself a burden of resentment, not against her sister, whom she thought of as irrelevant, but against her four brothers, all of whom had been given the university education she had so badly wanted. Adding insult to injury, these brothers had then been appointed to positions of responsibility in the family's highly lucrative sherry business—positions she was far more capable of filling. None of her brothers, she knew, could hold a candle to her in capability or intelligence.

If one had questioned Isabel's parents about this, they would have readily agreed. But such was the tradition within aristocratic Castilian families regarding the rearing of female offspring. Young women of a certain station in Spanish life were to be raised in a highly insular environment. It was a foregone conclusion that they would do nothing other than marry and bear children.

Consuelo never questioned the system. On the contrary, she subscribed happily and wholeheartedly to it. Isabel, however, from as early as the age of seven or eight, had waged open war against it. This would take the form of fierce battles with her brothers—kicking, scratching, spitting at them, and challenging their daily tyrannizing, their natural assumption that in the order of things, they came before her.

Quite understandably, Isabel had grown into something of a rebel. She thought of her sister, Consuelo, as "the cow." Consuelo pitied Isabel, thought of her as the family's cross, its private grief and shame.

Isabel had friendships that went far beyond the Gonzagas' rigid standards of suitability—actors, artists, intellectuals, bar flies, and habitués of cafés who sat around all afternoon over a glass of sangria or a *fino,* talking poetry and promoting theories of a dangerous and decidedly unsavory stripe.

Consuelo had no friends at all. She never went out without a chaperon, and once outside her home, found the world alien and terrifying. Needless to say, they had little in common, the Gonzaga girls, other than identical lineage and the fact that they both happened to share living space under the same roof. Consuelo had never once questioned her own wishes with regard to whether or not she wanted to spend the summer traveling with her parents. Isabel loathed the idea, fought it from the moment it was proposed, and only relented in the end after a special appeal on the part of her mother, whom she knew could not manage "El Conde" herself. And "La Vaca," of course, could not be counted upon for too much.

Isabel loved her mother dearly. She was the only thing that still kept her at home. For her father she had very little patience. She saw him as the typical Spanish grandee, inept and autocratic, with delusional pretensions of being a poet-artiste who believed that on the basis of a few pitiful scribblings in a handful of esoteric journals he had become a figure to reckon with among the literary cognoscenti of Latin America. She thought him a pathetic fool who had done nothing for his wife and children other than reduce them all—particularly his daughters—to dependent chattel, with himself as their feudal master.

Unlike the rest of her family, Isabel was not aloof. When it came to meeting people, she did not stand on ceremony. If someone interested her, piqued her curiosity, she approached him directly with a mixture of pugnacity and fun that was wonderfully disarming. As a result, she had made a number of friends during the course of the trip. In Leningrad she had grown particularly fond of the young Van Meegrins and they of her. She also liked the American college girl and her *"caballero"* from the Sorbonne.

During the course of daily outings these five had always made up a particularly lively party. Isabel liked Peter Stern, too. They shared an interest in mystery fiction and a mutual love of music. She did not like any of the "Italian Quartet." She thought of them as "slight" and vaguely degenerate. She could have lived with the degeneracy, she thought, but not the slightness. She had an active dislike for Jean Blaylock, whom she had pegged as a "poseur" with trendy political ideas, who was really little more than a sexual adventurer.

Then there was Tony Thomas, whom she'd met in the Dollar Bar of the Prebaltiskaya and later spent a night with in his room. She could not say she liked him—the fashionable cynicism, the raffish gloom, the insufferable British upper-class affectations—but she was attracted to him and did not particularly like herself for the reasons she was attracted.

Across the way from her, her father had nodded off. A copy of García Lorca's *Llanto por Ignacio Sánchez Mejías* had slipped onto his lap, a longish, waxen hand scored with the thick blue venation of age resting limply on the page he had been reading.

"A las cinco de la tarde . . ." Periodically he murmured words beneath his breath, his head nodding, half-drowsing on his chest.

"Un niño trajo la blanca sábana . . ."

Rumpled white hair, disheveled suit, collar open, sticking out above his lapels, and the funny little velvet carpet slippers on his feet, he appeared small and doll-like, and very old.

Looking at him, Isabel felt a pang of pity tighten round her throat, then quickly scorned it, glancing instead at the hideous Mrs. Keck braying into her mother's ear. Closing her eyes, she leaned her head back against the banquette and tried to find peace in the suffocating airlessness of the cabin. Time and again the image of Thomas and the night before at the Dollar Bar came back to her; how he had plied her with vodka, and how she had all too willingly permitted herself to be had—first with alcohol, then with his impressive knowledge of Russian history, and finally, in his room, with his hands and lips, fully confident he had mastered her completely. Well, he had, and how she despised herself for that.

But she had nothing to complain of. He hadn't done anything she hadn't wanted him to, and would no doubt have felt worse had he not bothered to make the effort. Somehow she had expected *more* of herself, and when the moment for that "more" came, she found she wasn't quite up to the mark.

That morning at breakfast at the hotel she would not meet his eye, or even rise to his breezy good-morning. To her, the breeziness reeked of self-satisfaction. It was like a crack across the face. She would never speak to him again.

In the first hour of their detention, people had merely fidgeted, waiting for the border guards and the customs inspectors to board the train and begin their long, tedious activities. In the second and third hours, while still nothing had taken place in the way of a check, there was a great deal of scornful joking turning to dismay. By five-thirty in the afternoon, after the Blaylock-Stern incident, with the sun starting to slip behind the tips of the trees and still nothing happening, the mood had become one of quiet, watchful fear.

In defiance of the order to remain in their seats, people had left their compartments and were wandering freely about the corridors, where at least the windows had been opened and the air was somewhat fresher. The coach attendants appeared to have forgotten, or possibly even overlooked, the order. Perhaps by that time they had recognized that the order was unreasonable in the light of the situation, and unenforceable in the absence of strong, distasteful measures.

By then most people were milling about, everyone with his own explanation for the delay. Several passengers had tried to step down off the train to stretch their legs, but were sharply ordered back up by soldiers moving toward them, brandishing rifles.

Mr. Kariolainen offered a cigarette to Paul Blanton. "What's all this business about a defector?"

"We heard that too," said Kyle Van Meegrin.

Blanton shook his head. "They haven't said anything definite."

Mercifully, Baby Muk had fallen into a deep snoring sleep on his mother's breast. Mr. Mukherjee had seized the opportunity to flee outside to the corridor and mingle freely there among his fellow passengers. Unlike the others, he did not seem the least perturbed, but took the whole unpleasant matter as a kind of adventure. His quick, darting eyes had fastened on Consuelo Gonzaga, standing by herself at one of the open windows. Arms draped outside the train, she was gulping air deeply, as if she feared she was about to faint. She had removed her outer jacket, and her blouse now clung dampishly to her back and stretched across her full breasts.

A small, rather insolent smile flickered at Mr. Mukherjee's lips. He scratched his scrotum through his trouser pocket, then slowly approached.

"How are you enjoying all this excitement, Miss Gonzaga?" His eyes ranged freely over her blouse.

She looked at him, offended, yet oddly flattered by the flash of his eyes. "I'm very warm. Very uncomfortable."

Mr. Mukherjee grew solicitous. He took her arm. "Perhaps we could walk up the corridor and find a cooler spot."

Jean Blaylock had become the hero of the moment. Surrounded by a group of people, she was regaling them with a blow-by-blow description of her encounter with the Russian soldier.

"I'll get my passport back," she boasted. "Don't worry about that. These bastards haven't seen the last of me."

Tony Thomas, wandering past just then, overheard her. "How'd you enjoy your little tiff with Big Brother?"

"No damned different than Big Brother in New York. Or London, for that matter. Military's all the same. They're all fascists."

Thomas made a clucking sound with his tongue. "Goodness, Jean, I thought you'd be more sympathetic to that sort of thing."

"What sort of thing?"

"Regulation. Authority."

She caught the mocking note in his voice. "I have no problem with authority."

"Of course not." He grew more spiteful. "You just don't particularly care for it when it's directed toward you."

Jean rose quickly to the bait. "I won't truckle to police brutality, if that's what you mean. Not in a socialist, and not in a goddamned so-called democratic setting. If one of these monkeys comes at me again, I'll kick his balls."

Thomas roared merrily and swung off down the corridor, making his way through the throngs of milling passengers. He smiled and nodded at people, but he was more than a little vexed.

Moving down the aisle, looking raffish and quite pleased with himself, he caught a glimpse of Isabel standing by an open window, chatting with the Van Meegrins.

"Hello." He sidled up to her, pointing out the window at the field of purple phlox that had rolled down out of the forest. "Pretty, isn't it?"

She turned from the Van Meegrins and looked directly at him. It was a slow, protracted gaze, utterly neutral, conveying the mild bewilderment of an individual momentarily unable to place the face of someone who'd just approached.

Thomas stood there, his smile fading into puzzlement, until at last his usually easy composure faltered, and, clearing his throat, he excused himself and backed away.

The relief he'd found in flight was short-lived. Halfway down the aisle he found himself confronting the looming shape of Señor Gonzaga. Thomas was a good-sized man—six-two, at least—but even he felt short beside the stooping, blighted elegance of the Spaniard.

"She cut you, didn't she?" he said, watching his daughter turn back into their cabin. There was a note of glee in his voice.

"I rather think she did."

"As a child she would cry easily," Gonzaga went on, speaking in the direction of her vanished figure. "All manner of things upset her—the mouse seized by the cat, some foolish fairy tale that did not end to her liking."

"She doesn't care for sad endings?"

"Sometimes even when they were happy, she would cry." Gonzaga laughed and turned to him. "*La tristesse.* One of those determined to be sad. What is it the poet says, 'Half in love with easeful sorrows—' "

"Death."

The old man's brow arched. "I beg your pardon?"

"Death—the line goes 'half in love with easeful death.' "

Gonzaga pondered that a moment, then shrugged. "Well, whatever." He waved a languid arm at the scene of soldiers mustering below on the track bed and suddenly stiffened. "I hate soldiers," he said, as if in response to someone else's remark.

The abrupt shift in mood startled Thomas. The old man took his arm as though for support and proceeded to steer him down the corridor. "When you live in the part of the world I do, you learn to be wary of the military." Gonzaga spoke while his eyes shifted from right to left, seeking open paths through which they might move. "Soldiers in Russia are no different from soldiers in Argentina. The moment you give them a gun, they rush to enact stupid laws they can enforce with them. Show me a general of the army—I've known many, incidentally—and I'll show you the criminal element of society. The scum of the earth dressed up like cinema ushers and elevated to heroic stature."

Thomas, with his facile journalist's eye trained to lump people into easy, workable categories, had long before cast Gonzaga in the role of an effete Spanish nobleman, a poet manqué who scratched doggerel and clever epigrams into a spiral-ring notebook, publishing them at his own expense under some such title as "Thoughts" or "Musings" or "Eternal Verities." Now the sudden burst of indignation took him by surprise.

"Let's be certain then not to give them any cause to use those guns." Thomas addressed him in the softly placatory manner of the sane patronizing the mad.

Gonzaga's brow flickered upward. "Are you always that accommodating to your tormentors?"

Thomas started to reply but the old man went on. "Do you always drop your pants like that and stick your arse out for them to bugger?"

Suddenly there was a loud bang and the train lurched. A commotion broke out at the front of the coach, and in the next instant people were streaming forward in that direction, buffeting past Thomas and the old man still standing there confronting each other. Seizing the opportunity to flee, Thomas started forward with the others, only to hear Gonzaga shouting after him.

"Mr. Thomas."

He turned. The old man stood nearly ten feet away, oblivious of the people shuttling past him toward the front of the car.

"I think you will find, Mr. Thomas," he spoke slowly and a little breathlessly, "that my daughter hates injustice at both the state as well as the personal level. Fascism is not only a disease of governments. Be advised."

There was a sudden jolt and Thomas toppled forward into a mass of flailing arms and legs. All about him people were shouting and screaming. Someone, he thought, had gone down. It was a woman. He had a momentary glimpse of her on her knees, her stocking torn, several people struggling to raise her.

There were shouts and cries. Figures groping for balance.

"What happened?"

"She okay?"

"Someone went down over here too."

They had Wilma Shapley back up on her feet, dusting her off. Several soldiers had boarded the train and along with the coach attendants were making their way forward.

Thomas caught sight of Peter Stern beside him. "What's going on?"

"I don't have the slightest—"

"Someone said they were uncoupling this car from the rest of the train."

Paul Blanton came panting up. "Did you happen to see Nell?"

"She was just back there with the Contis a minute ago," Stern said.

Without a word, Blanton turned and bustled off in that direction. Frau Kunkel came up. She clung to Karl Heinz's sleeve. "I heard someone in the next car say they're sending back to Leningrad for another train."

"What on earth for?" Thomas asked, but already the dim outline of a scenario was beginning to unfold in his mind.

"Please to take seats," the coach attendant barked. "Please to resume cabins, please." He went wading into the crowd just behind the soldiers trying to disperse the knot of frightened passengers at the head of the car, physically herding them back with their rifle stocks and the weight of their own bodies.

"Seats please. Taking seats please."

"I don't budge," Ted Kariolainen fumed, "until we're told exactly what's going on here."

Accompanied by several of his staff, Colonel Dunskoi stepped suddenly from the vestibule through a glass door into the car. Those people standing forward fell back before his bulky, thrusting presence. The captain beside him proceeded to address the group in perfect, uninflected English.

"We regret the jolting you just experienced. As you are by now aware, we are detaching this car from the main body of the train. In several minutes"— he glanced at his watch—"six minutes, to be exact, a new engine will be along from Vyborg to take the other coaches back to Leningrad. All Soviet nationals will be transferred with their luggage onto that train. Those not holding Soviet passports shall remain on board this train until further notice. The Soviet government deeply regrets any inconvenience this delay may cause you. During your stay here on the border you will be guests of the Soviet government. All toilets are now open and have been fully serviced. Supplies of fresh water are being piped into the train's holding tanks, and the samovars, of course, are always open for those of you who wish tea.

"The dining car will be open after six P.M. and hot meals will be served there up until nine P.M. Sleeping arrangements will be provided shortly thereafter."

"Sleeping arrangements?" several voices exclaimed at once. A short muffled groan went up from the group.

"My God," Grant Shapley said. "Can you beat this?"

Paul Blanton's bland, unremarkable features had turned a vivid purple. "You can't just detain people like this. What's going on here? At least tell us the problem."

Jatta, the Finnish tour guide, speaking in rapid-fire Russian, proceeded to pepper Dunskoi with questions.

If the colonel had any inkling of the depth of general outrage, he showed no sign of it. His calm was glacial. He stared round from one member of the group to the next, more like a spectator who had inadvertently stumbled onto the scene, rather than its prime mover, which is what he was.

PART III

GOOD EVENING. This is Dan Rather for CBS News in New York. A bizarre mystery unfolds tonight. A passenger train loaded with hundreds of holiday travelers has literally disappeared. The train, which departed Leningrad's Finland Station at eleven o'clock this morning was due to arrive at Central Helsinki Railway Station at five P.M., Finnish time. Now seven hours overdue, Finnish authorities say they have no idea of the whereabouts of the train.

The first Finnish town outside the Soviet border is Vainikkala, where the train was scheduled to undergo Finnish customs and passport control at one-forty-five P.M. Spokesmen for Finnish National Railways maintain the train never reached there, leading authorities to conclude that the train is still somewhere inside Russia. Soviet authorities deny any knowledge of the whereabouts of the train but do confirm that the train, known as "The Green Train," did depart Leningrad on schedule this morning.

It is not known at this time if any Americans are aboard.

. . . an act of international gangsterism. Norway, a client state of the U.S., continues to maintain illegal custody of a Soviet submarine and its entire crew, this despite repeated warnings by the Soviet government. The submarine, which inadvertently strayed into Norwegian waters one week ago, incurred damages when it foundered on a rock and had to be towed into the Hammerfest naval base on the Barents Sea.

Norwegian authorities have refused to permit the submarine and its crew to leave, insisting that a team of NATO ordnance experts be permitted to inspect the submarine's log as well as highly secret surveillance equipment aboard.

The Soviet government emphatically denies permission for any such inspection and warns both Norwegian and NATO officials that it will take whatever steps necessary to reclaim its property and secure the freedom of all Soviet naval personnel.

This has been *Bremya, The USSR Tonight.*

The BBC has learned this evening from highly placed sources inside the Kremlin that the train known as "The Green Train," which disappeared earlier today on its normal run between Leningrad and Helsinki, has been towed, along with its passengers, to a remote spur of the FIN-

SOV rail line. The spur, which Finnish authorities say has been retired for years, is located just west of Vyborg, deep within the forest. The Russians presumably chose the spot for its seclusion and inaccessibility to high-altitude aerial surveillance.

Kremlin officials vehemently deny any link between the detention of the train and the recent impoundment of a Soviet submarine and its crew alleged to have been on a spying mission deep within Norwegian waters.

Libya's Colonel Qaddafi arrived in Tunis today to meet with oil ministers and Arab leaders for . . .

At eight P.M. they put the lights on in the dining car, although there was little need for them. The long white nights of Russian summer provided reasonable daylight till well past ten P.M., with only a gradual diminution of light continuing until well past midnight. At that moment the sky was a milky gray, and though the baking sun had long since gone, the heat, steadily building in the train throughout the day, continued to radiate from the floors and seats and ceilings of the coaches.

They had opened the windows in the dining car but there was no breeze to speak of. The cool piny air from the forest crept listlessly in over the dusty sills, nudging the stale, dampish air of daytime before it.

Along with the slight relief of ventilation, however, came one significant disadvantage. They had to eat supper amid the swarms of mosquitoes, moths, and other crepuscular creatures that had flowed in through the windows the moment the lights had been turned on.

Supper that evening was a gloomy affair. Starting shortly after seven, they'd been divided into two separate shifts, the first at 7:15, the second at nine o'clock. The food had been prepared in the military commissary at the Vyborg border station, and trucked into the spur. Since there was no dining-car personnel, the meal was served by Russian soldiers, mostly corporals and junior sergeants of the Military Railway Transport Units. For the most part, stocky, boyish-looking youths in brown tunics, they went solemnly about the business of ladling food out of tall aluminum vats and carting dirty dishes off. They were generally polite and correct, in several instances appealing.

The food was adequate if not appetizing. Plates of dark, slightly stale bread were set out on tables along with half-filled pitchers of a thick, tepid juice—plum or pear nectar so syrupy sweet and viscous that it clung to the palate and tended to heighten rather than slake thirst. A bottle of sweetish red Bulgarian wine, not unlike port, was also placed at each table. Those who asked for vodka could have a half-liter, but the heat of the day had left most of the travelers far too depleted for strong spirits.

Supper was eaten in virtual silence. The easy chumminess, the friendly banter and playful jesting that had characterized their relationships throughout the tour were gone. The air was now thick with gloom. People sat in silent little knots of agitation, worry clearly stamped upon their faces.

Rumors of a possible spy or defector among them had raged like wildfire throughout the train, and while publicly everyone dismissed that as nonsense, privately each of them had begun to reassess his fellow passengers in a new, if not disagreeable light. The source of the rumor was uncertain but its mere presence had created an air of hostility and suspicion between people where none had existed before. At that point, still no one appeared to have heard anything of the Soviet submarine detained in Hammerfest.

Later that evening, on the way back to their compartments from the dining car, several of them attempted to step down off the train to stretch their legs and breathe the night air. Once again, they were quickly ordered back up into the coach by the guards stationed at each exit. It was at that time, too, that they discovered that the motor-rifle units that had made themselves so conspicuous several hours before on the border were now bivouacked in the concealment of the forest. From the windows of the train they could see a tight cordon of small fires glowing at regular intervals in the woods surrounding them.

People had no choice, therefore, but to settle into their cabins and try to make the best of things. At the same time, a sleeping coach, rushed up from Leningrad and coupled to the day coach, was being readied for the night. A few halfhearted whist games had sputtered to life and shortly the backgammon and Parcheesi boards were brought out. Up forward, in Señor Madariaga's group, someone had taken out a guitar and the group had begun to sing. They sang softly, without much spirit, wistful, plaintive little songs. One barely heard them at even the lowest level of consciousness and yet the sound of their distant murmuring voices filled the car with a sweet, unspeakable sadness.

"Attention. Attention, please," a hoarse voice crackled over the train's scratchy P.A. system. "Attention . . . Attention, please."

People came out of their compartments into the corridor in time to see the shabby little coach attendant shuffle through the glass doors at the head of the car. He stood there a moment, blinking uneasily into the dim light, surveying the sullen crowd beginning to gather in the aisle.

"Attention, please. Please to inform, sleeping accommodations now ready in wagonz-litz directly to rear of dining car. If you will step forward, please. Make single line, please." A clipboard dangled limply from his drooping wrist. "Will now make compartment assignments in sleeping car, please."

It was past midnight and the silver sky of a typical Russian white night had gone a pewtery gray. Stern lay in his berth, still dressed in his clothes, except that in an effort to stay cool, he had removed his shirt. Earlier he had tried, unsuccessfully, to locate a pair of pajamas in the turmoil of his luggage without having to completely unpack it.

Through the open window of his berth he could hear the hum of crickets and the mad cackle of a night bird in transit through the forest. A light breeze bore on its listless currents the faintly pungent, not unpleasant breath of dying pine fires where the soldiers slept round the train, unseen in the long, slanting shadows of the encroaching forest. From the berth below came the agitated snores of Tony Thomas, panting and winded like a man who had run too long. The whole length of the car, in fact, was a concert of restless nocturnal sounds—coughs and sighs, the creak of mattress springs, people twisting in their narrow berths prior to the oblivion of sleep.

A bit farther down the coach, Isabel Gonzaga sprawled limp in her slip, unable to sleep. A mild sigh of evening air fell lightly across her bare shoulder, brushing her brow like the touch of cool lips. Like Stern, she too listened for something at the open window—some sound, distant and evanescent, borne on the night breezes, retreating deep into the furthest recesses of the forest.

She could hear the drowsy mumbling of her father nearby, and just below, the deep, untroubled snores of Consuelo like those of some well-contented kitchen dog after a fulsome meal. She did not worry about them, and certainly she did not worry about herself. From earliest childhood she had grown into maturity convinced that the matter of her wishes or personal well-being counted for naught. She had often tried to recall some reason or incident to explain why over the years she'd come to feel this way. Certainly no one had ever said as much to her directly.

She worried about her mother, however—that timid, infinitely gentle creature whose soul had been nurtured in another and more gracious time. At sixty-five she still maintained the happy, trustful outlook of a child who would welcome strangers and share her toys and candy with them all. She had only the most kindly thoughts about her fellowman.

Beneath the blanket, Grant Shapley's leg had started to twitch. He thought that if he could sleep, the spasms and tremblings would ease. But he could not sleep. Aside from the stuffiness of the berth, his mind was in a state of strange excitement. It was not the inconvenience of detainment that had so unnerved him. He was certain that was temporary and would soon end. Unlike his fellow passengers, he had none of that xenophobic distrust of Russians that so afflicts the Western traveler in the USSR, and which on a deeper level is fear.

Shapley had no fear of the Soviets to speak of. He had been traveling to the USSR on various scientific expeditions for the past twenty years and had long since ceased to think of that vast land as either alien or mysterious. He was apolitical, and in that sense, he was entirely at home in the Soviet Union. His friendships there, and they were considerable, comprised chiefly scientists; men, for the most part, devoted to the same passions and disciplines as he, all bonded by a single-minded need to compile and share information. For these men, national identity and political dialogue had a way of fading into the background in the face of scientific inquiry.

Shapley was something of a hero among his peers. He was a near-legendary figure, a pioneer in the area of glacial paleontology. His writings were considered seminal in any history of the earth. Known to a small but international network of scientists, he was the subject of innumerable articles and monographs. Because of his identification and classification of it, a special period of the Cenozoic had been named for him. His books had been translated into dozens of languages.

It was certainly not Russia or an arbitrary, seemingly irrational bureaucracy that had so unnerved Shapley that night. It was his own mortality as reflected in the periodic spasms and twitchings of his leg. When the cause of these tremors had first been diagnosed, he made it a point to read everything available on the subject. He was therefore hardly unaware of what course these twitching episodes would take as the disease ran its course in him.

It was not swift death. Had it been that, he would have been greatly relieved. As a trained paleontologist whose time references ranged over billions of years, he was at ease with the notion of eons. His scientist's certainty in oblivion after death was for him a profoundly comforting thought.

Lying sleepless in his berth that night, it was something else that nagged at him. When his condition had been finally diagnosed at the University of Wyoming's School of Medicine, and later confirmed at Scripps, he had made his wife promise that when death finally did come, she would have his remains cremated and the ashes scattered to the winds that soughed across the tall rolling sea of prairie grass surrounding his mountain cabin in the Grand Tetons. Several thousand miles away, sequestered in a dense, strangely primeval grove of Russian forest, he was overtaken by a premonition that he would not be fortunate enough to die at home.

Jean Blaylock punched her pillow fretfully. She had removed her blouse and slacks and lay atop the coarse sheets in bra and panties, trying hard to sleep. But the whispers and occasional giggles from beyond the dusty curtain where the Italian Quartet were berthed had kept her up. At one point she heard Silvana laugh, followed by someone hushing her. She wondered if it was Sandro or Keith. It really didn't matter much. She despised them all.

She managed for a time to ignore the lewd little sounds and at last dropped off to sleep. When she woke sometime later, the whispers and laughter had ceased, and she was shivering.

She needed to go to the bathroom but the thought of climbing down out of the berth and making her way up to the end of the car was not appealing. Actually, the deathly silence frightened her. She kept seeing, too, the face of the soldier as he was striking her. It was not an unpleasant face—boyish, pink, unshaven. In another time, another place, it might even have been attractive. That was its peculiar obscenity. That blush of innocence even as his hand rose and struck her repeatedly, his wild arm scything the air. Once again she saw the awful fright in his eyes, and then the Russian colonel, his slow hooded gaze squinting at her passport, devouring with his moving lips the data entered there, the frown of suspicion beginning to lower on his brow, the captain behind him, stooping slightly to whisper in his ear, and finally the sight of the small white card passed back to the disembodied hand of some unseen person just behind them. Then the passport retreating beyond the reach of her outstretched hand. How isolated and vulnerable she suddenly felt without it. Such were the images and feelings that fled like startled birds across her mind.

The more she thought of it, the more furious she grew. She lay there spread-eagle in the clammy chill of predawn, composing a series of vituperative articles in her mind, "special" to *The Nation,* or possibly a longish essay for *Harper's* or *The New Republic.* It would be extremely well-balanced. She would not come out recanting, or chronicling her apostasy from strict socialist ideology. Far too many of her colleagues and old classmates had already gone that route, bailed out of the cause, careful to make cushy deals with large banks and corporations before doing so. Then there were the others, who wrote books and articles about it. How despicable that lot. All eager to expunge their guilt, to confess the errors of their pasts for public consumption and big bucks. How to grovel and thereby achieve wealth and celebrity. How the public loves a good "whipped-dog" story. The young and arrogant, tamed.

Well, she had no intention of recanting a word. She would not debase herself. She had gone and seen some socialism at the source. What did it matter that it was only for five days? She'd seen the system, noting many of its limitations. She still believed that it was the only hope for mankind. Of course, there was all the bureaucratic idiocy, the rigidity of marionette officiaries, the disagreeable predisposition to seek out victims in order to make an example—she could cite reams about that now. And then, of course, the donkey indolence of the work force, the mindless, knee-jerk obedience of the masses, and the almost paranoid suspicion among the police.

All that notwithstanding, her admiration for the system had scarcely faltered. The system was still evolving and therefor still idealistic enough to correct itself; unlike the West, which had given up all pretense of correcting inequities and had simply sunk into self-indulgence and despair.

Somewhere deep within the forest the night bird cackled. Jean burrowed down into the scratchy, suffocating wool blanket the porter had provided. Even though the night was warm, she had started to shiver.

In the adjoining berth Serja Inusen lay huddled in her bedding. Her eyes were open and she stared straight ahead. In her twistings and turnings, the sheet had wound about her like a shroud, and lying there flat on her back, hands clasped above her flat breasts, she looked more than ever like the handiwork of some notably unskilled mortician.

It would be early in the morning in Helsinki. Her mother would still be sitting up in the little flat on Munkholmen near the waterfront. The poor woman would be frightened now, but still uncertain, and too timid to call the police or the train station for information.

Serja berated herself for having taken the trip, for having been so thought-less and selfish as to leave her mother alone for several days, even though the old woman had urged her daughter to go. What she had done was unforgiv-able. She deserved to be punished. Now the Russians would come and make her open her bags, and they would find there among her pitiful belongings highly incriminating evidence. The towels, the ashtray, and the stationery, all of which she had stolen from her room at the Prebaltiskaya. She had heard that the Russians did not suffer thieves kindly. People were sent off for years, vanished without a trace into the frozen vastness of Siberia, all for the most inoffensive infringements of the law.

She would be found out tomorrow, no doubt of that, and whisked off the train into some plain, black official car. Where would they take her? What would they do to her? What would her mother do? It was not the punishment she dreaded so. She knew she deserved that. It was rather the humiliation of being exposed as a common thief before all these "fine" people that so abso-lutely sickened her.

She heard the toilet flush down the corridor. She put her knuckle in her mouth and bit down hard in order to stifle her sobbing.

> . . . and so, noble father . . . I beg you to believe that what I have done, I have not done impulsively. I recognize how much you have wished . . . counted upon . . . how great your effort in my behalf . . .

Words formed soundlessly on young Junji Asawa's lips even as he scrawled letters hectically onto his pad.

> I have tried . . . I have tried . . . to be the son you have wished for . . .

He wrote, sprawled in his berth, using the scant glow from a pencil flash-light for illumination.

> I have tried . . . I have tried . . . I have tried . . .

The words gushed from him, streaming from the tip of his pencil like a current of electrical force, palpable and living, something he could scarcely hold.

It frightened him. He was never able to speak such words to his father. Such candor would have been unthinkable. Only through the medium of pencil and paper was he suddenly liberated.

> . . . My last two years at the university . . . I think you know . . . have been a nightmare. The decision to leave was entirely my own, and for that I assume complete responsibility. I thought about it long before I acted, knowing full well your feeling on the subject.

Why I ever believed I had any aptitude for technology is a mystery to me. I sit in my classes at the university, overcome by an apathy, an indifference to my surroundings that sometimes frightens me. Worse is the contempt I feel for my teachers and fellow students, all sitting around me, rapt, obedient, unthinking. Drones, all waiting to be programmed to fulfill some dismal drudgery assigned them by society.

As he wrote, he glanced furtively out the window, as if he feared being observed. Beyond the darkness of the grimy pane he could see the waning fires that inscribed the small tight circle round the train where the motor-rifle troops had been deployed. He found their proximity strangely exciting, and as he hastened to complete his letter, he experienced a surge of elation. There was a sense of cutting free. A grand finality. An end to one thing and the beginning of something new.

All the while it had been his plan to go back to Tokyo, strike some sort of decent arrangement with his father, and go his own way. Now that he had written the letter, however, thereby committing his action to paper, he felt that the words had imparted a certain irreversibility to his decision and that he was now free enough within himself to never return.

It was to Paris he would go instead; there where a number of friends, similarly disenchanted with university and homeland, had preceded him. These friends had all been politically active at the university. He greatly admired them. When the time of protests came against the government, against the police, against Japanese involvement with Western military ambitions in the Far East, these people were invariably at the forefront of resistance.

They were not popular with the other students, who could not wait to sell their souls to the government and the new corporate Goliaths of Nippon. These people were outsiders whose views were known to be inimical to the accepted national goals and aspirations. It was known that they met regularly, that their meetings were clandestine and against the rules of the university. They took place off the campus at night and generally in some seedy, disreputable district of the city, along the waterfront.

To be a member of the group was like taking sacred vows. There was something hieratic about it. It involved a lengthy period of study and self-denial, culminating in a critical and often physically abusive examination at the hands of one's peers. Then, too, a huge catechism had to be submitted to memory. This was not a catechism comprising simple moral precepts, but rather an ongoing economic dialectic that urged widespread redistribution of the earth's wealth, and propounded a new world economic order. This was destined to come about, if not through peaceful means, then through violent ones. But it would come about. Of this he was convinced.

My dear father-san. What I have learned in the last two years would horrify you ... I am no longer the same son you sent off to university. You would be surprised at what I have become.

When he'd finished the letter, he folded it neatly and tucked it away in the pages of a collection of Mishima stories he had been reading on the trip.

Next he rummaged through a small JAL traveling bag into which had been crammed a tangle of unlaundered socks and underwear. With its contents spilling out onto the narrow berth, he at last found what he had been seeking. It was a small sixteen-ounce unlabeled canister. With one of the brass kopeks he still carried in his pockets, he prized the lid up, dipped a tentative finger into the red, jellylike contents, then cautiously sniffed it.

For a while he appeared to reflect on something. Then, replacing the lid, he inserted the edge of the kopeck into the screwhead of one of the green metal panels that covered the bulkhead above his berth. He repeated the operation several times until at last he was able to remove the panel, exposing just beneath it an opening out of which a tangle of tubing and electrical wire spilled, smelling faintly of warm rubber. There was something feral about him as he worked swiftly and noiselessly, inserting the canister into a recess behind the tubing, then finally replacing the panel and screwing it shut.

Kyle and Katrina Van Meegrin slept in each other's arms. Just above them Kate Dubbin and Claude Desfargue lay awake whispering through the night.

Nearby, Mr. Mukherjee snored fitfully, images of lust blazing through his fevered sleep.

Baby Victor had fallen into the blissful sleep of infancy. He lay cradled at his mother's breast. Gone was the petulant grimace of his daytime face. Its expression had softened into a dreamy smile. Madam Muk had swaddled him into a coarse little gown of nankeen out of which wafted the sweetish smell of patchouli. Sleep and silence had made him rather appealing.

Quiet and darkness had finally overtaken the Green Train. It sat now on the weedy tracks, surrounded by the forest, like a beast kneeling in its lair, spent from the day's exertions, its steel flanks cooling in the nighttime air.

Through the broken canopy of trees overhead, stars wheeled and a pale disk of moon rode across the ghostly heavens. The coughs and sighs and creaking mattresses, the full range of presleep noises, had at last subsided for the night.

Outside, posted at each exit, guards stood in the large quavering shadows cast by the coach lanterns. Beyond them, encamped round the perimeter, the motor-rifle troops sprawled fitfully in their bedrolls, inching closer to the dying fires in their sleep.

Several miles away at the small military installation on the border, Colonel Dunskoi pored over a sheaf of recent dispatches from central headquarters. Putting aside his glasses, he rubbed his bleared eyes and dictated several messages to a radio operator who simultaneously encoded and transmitted them back to STAVKA. They involved detailed and itemized descriptions of the colonel's present troop strength; food stores on hand, along with an assessment of hospital and medical supplies. He asked that a military physician be attached full-time to his unit for the duration of the present emergency.

He turned back to the sheaf of decoded dispatches from STAVKA. Lips moving slowly, his restless eyes swarming over the narrow yellow page, once again he read the message from headquarters:

It is a matter of utmost importance that a sense of uncertainty be created regarding the fate of these passengers. To all appearances everything must seem to be cloaked in greatest secrecy. We shall of course endeavor to open a few tantalizing chinks to the outside. Just enough to heighten anxiety. This, plus the vivid imagination of the Western media with their insatiable appetite for sensation, shall do our work for us. . . .

PART IV

GOOD EVENING. NBC News, New York. Tom Brokaw reporting. The Russians are citing mechanical difficulties as the cause for the now nearly nineteen-hour delay of a train and its passengers on the Russo-Finnish border.

Spokesmen for the State Department in Washington admit that they are mystified as to ...

... while Norwegian officials continue to insist that despite the recent detention of a train and its fifty-one passengers, they will go ahead with their plans to inspect the Soviet submarine that recently went aground in the Barents Sea at a point directly off Hammerfest, where the Norwegian Navy operates its highly secret radar installation.

This has been David Craig for the Australian Broadcasting Corporation, Sydney. Thank you and good evening.

Señor Madariaga had been asleep on his back in an upper berth when the noise came. It appeared to be coming from somewhere only inches from his face. Cracking an eye, he squinted into a shaft of mote-filled sunlight streaming through the coach window.

He thought he had only imagined the noise until it came again—a thump, solid, emphatic, with the hollow, concussive bang of an empty steel drum being struck. It appeared to come from the ceiling, or more accurately, from the roof of the coach, then radiate downward through the narrow space between the roof and the shell of the car. It was as if someone were standing above him on the roof directly overhead.

Lying there, Madariaga watched the ceiling of the cabin, his eyes following the muffled footsteps, the path of which appeared to transect his body and recede into the distance. This was followed periodically by another of those sharp, resonant thumps made by a club or a metal rod.

Now fully awake, he was suddenly aware of voices outside the train. Propping himself on an elbow, he looked down from his window. At first there was only the forest, still cool and shadowy from the evening. He stared up at the great canopy of foliage overhead through which a morning sun filtered a shaft of pale green light. There was something of the primeval about it—the huge, gnarled old trees, the dewy glade, the dappled sunlight, the pure unsullied look of prehistory.

But then came the soldiers. Out of the corner of his eye he saw them. First one, then a second and a third, moving through the tall grass along the track bed, their gruff voices preceding them.

There was another thump from overhead, followed by more footsteps. This time they appeared to be retracing their path, coming back the way they had just gone. This was quickly followed by a loud, ratcheting sound coming from beneath the coach. Madariaga looked down. Once again he saw the three soldiers directly below him. They were handling an immense wooden dowel which they swept like a wand along the undercarriage of the wagon-lits, striking the flanges and banging the rods and wheels.

"Maestro. Maestro."

Madariaga turned and gazed down at the dark, sleepy frown of Fantine, the little fourteen-year-old oboist from Valladolid. He had poked his face through the partially open doorway so that his disembodied head stared up at the teacher.

"Do you hear it, maestro?"

Madariaga pressed a finger to the boy's lips, then in a whisper quickly added, "Someone's on the roof, I think."

"Also under the train. I saw."

Madariaga nodded impatiently, then threw his spindly legs over the side of the berth and clattered down the ladder. "Wake the others. Go."

"There's no need. We're all up. We've been up for hours."

The thumping and clatter went on throughout breakfast in the dining car, where they ate rolls and coffee, and the only sound was the anxious little tinkle of teaspoons swirling through steaming cups. Unspeaking, as remote as robots, the soldiers moved up and down the aisle with pannikins of butter and jam, baskets full of stalish rolls dropped unceremoniously onto the plate with large tongs that had the look of dental forceps. Then, of course, there was the inevitable plum nectar, so warm and sweet it hurt one's teeth to drink it.

Jatta suddenly appeared. She swung energetically up and down the car, clapping her hands like a camp counselor. "We must all leave the train now. Finish your breakfasts. Go at once to your compartments. Leave all of your luggage there on the seat, open."

Frau Kunkel's eyes widened. "I am not leaving my things open, unguarded . . ."

"Open." Jatta repeated the word, this time louder and directly at Frau Kunkel. There was an edge to her voice that made it clear this was not the moment for insubordination. "Also, please leave all cameras, film, writing equipment, stationery, pens, pencils, out on your bunks. We will wait outside, along the tracks," the tour guide hurried on. "You are free to walk, but stay well within the perimeter established by the soldiers. Take with you your passports, visas, and currency statements. I repeat: passports . . . visa . . . currency statements. Keep them with you at all times. Do you hear me, Señor

Gonzaga?" She looked pointedly at the startled Spaniard. "These will be checked after the train has been thoroughly searched. Are there any questions?"

"Can you tell us what is going on here?" Isabel asked.

"No, I cannot. Regretfully, I don't have the slightest idea what is going on here."

"How long should all this take?" Paul Blanton asked.

"I am told it should take between two and three hours."

"Then we shall be permitted to go?" asked Señor Madariaga.

"That is my understanding." Jatta looked quickly around to see if there were further questions. The look in her eyes tended to discourage that. "All right. Finish your breakfasts. Go back to the cabins and open your luggage. Leave nothing locked. And—oh yes, use the lavatories now, if you have to. They will be locked and off limits for the duration of the car search and customs check. Do you hear me, Señor Gonzaga?"

For all their odd and various shapes, incongruous dress, all of them scattered, and rambling through the weedy, dusty field, they had the look of a flock of foraging birds. But no ordinary flock. Much more a sort of aviary full of exotic ornithology.

Señor Gonzaga in his rumpled white suit, gliding stately through the hip-high weeds, looked more grallatorial than ever—a stork or an egret promenading a marsh. Señora Gonzaga rambled after him with that short, chesty look of the Arctic puffin.

Tony Thomas, vain and extravagantly plumed, was the perfect cockatoo, while Stern had the look of a distracted pheasant. Frau Kunkel, plodding up to her hips in grass, was fretful and drab as a cowbird. Standing aloof and resentful off to the side, the Mukherjees were a pair of swarthy vultures with their chick. Shy and elusive as the whippoorwill, Junji Asawa crept along the outer rim of the circle, a spectral figure fading against the backdrop of forest, a presence more sensed than seen.

Closer in toward mid-circle, the Italian Quartet laughed and rattled Italian to each other at breakneck speed. They were dressed to the nines, the ladies in great white wide-brimmed straw boaters, the men in light linen jackets, lime trousers, and espadrilles. They could have been a cageful of parakeets.

Jatta, all rapid, darting hops and skips, kept circling her flock like a mother hen. Her usually crisp white jogging suit looked gray and tired, as if she had slept in it. Beside the locomotive, chatting with the Finnish engineers, Grant Shapley stood squat and graceless, like one of those large flightless birds, the cassowary or the auk, earthbound, cheated of the gift of flight, but toughly defiant for all that.

Walking arm in arm with her husband, Nell Blanton was a creature of bright plumage and lilting song, the cardinal perhaps, while Ralph Keck in one of his unvarying dark suits was as sepulchral as a crow. Señor Madariaga with his little troop of choristers was the tough, proud gander out for a stroll with his goslings.

So it was they all rambled fretfully through the grass, traversing the weedy, spongy area along the track, moving back and forth, inhaling and puffing deeply the way people do after a large holiday breakfast.

Their course took them down the full length of the train, over the tracks, and around up the other side, where they would then turn and retrace their steps. Occasionally they would pause to exchange a word or two with fellow passengers, trying hard to ignore the presence of the soldiers, now everywhere in evidence—on the roof of the train, then banging and poking with long wooden probes beneath it. They could be seen inside the coach, too, through the windows, stooped over opened luggage, pulling up seats, checking air vents, and strung out along the whole perimeter where the wide shaggy field met the encircling forest.

Colonel Dunskoi was there too. He stood outside the train in the shade of nearby trees with three of his staff. They hovered obsequiously on either side of him, occasionally venturing a thought. He appeared to listen, but those hooded, imperturbable Tartar eyes, fixed unrelentingly on the train, were evidence of the unbreakable concentration of the mind behind them.

By nine A.M. the day seemed fine. Not yet too hot, although it promised to become so. Young Buddy Kariolainen had dug up a Frisbee. The bright red disk floated on the still air in sharp relief against the azure sky. The wild phlox sprouting in the field, still glistening with dew, seemed even a more vivid, intense purple than the day before. But in the heat of the advancing day, that purple would gradually fade to a dullish gray.

The temperatures round the train were still comfortable from the night. By eleven A.M., however, the hammer of the sun would start to beat mercilessly down upon it, turning the inside of the Green Train into a furnace.

Stern had been looking for a cooler spot. On the northern side of the train, the shadier side, he'd found himself completely alone, peering into a dappled glade surrounded by towering beech and silver aspen. There appeared to be no one else about. He stood in the cool dank shadows beside the engine sniffing the piny, resinous air, watching the trembling of the leaves at the tip of the aspens. There was no breeze and yet they fluttered as if some passing phantom had whispered on them. For a moment everything grew perfectly still except those leaves. Stern was afraid to move lest he shatter the strange perfection of the moment.

As he turned his head, something flashed in his eye. It had come from somewhere in the slanting shadows of the glade. He moved and once again the light flashed, white and brilliant. He took several steps toward it, finally discovering the source.

Not far off, he glimpsed the broken outline of a pond. As he approached, its shape came gradually into sharper focus. It was a fairly decent-sized pond, its surface spangled with sunlight.

It was achingly beautiful. But the thing that moved him, perhaps even more deeply than the scene itself, was the old rubber tire that someone had hung on a long rope from a branch above the water. It was the sort of thing Stern had known in his boyhood Missouri, swimming in cow ponds and lakes among the rough farm youth with whom he'd grown up. He had thought of that as peculiarly American, pure Huckleberry Finn. And now to find it here in the heart of Mother Russia was not only startling but also oddly reassuring.

Meaning to get closer, he took several steps in the direction of the pond. Then, out of the corner of his eye, something distracted him. First perceived as only a slight movement, then suddenly materializing out of the brush, standing silent and motionless, rifles at the port, confronting him were two guards. They stood about thirty feet off, with the frozen immobility of hunters coming suddenly upon their quarry. As wildly improbable as it seemed, Stern was convinced they were waiting for him to make a dash for freedom through the forest. It dawned on him with an almost queasy certainty that he was but a hair's breadth from being shot. It would have been laughable had it not been so frightening. He had not thought of himself as a prisoner until that moment, when it became terrifyingly apparent that he was.

Trying to appear casual, he smiled at them and waved. They stared back at him stonily, never once taking their eyes from him. When he finally turned, he did so quite slowly, retracing his steps with almost breathless fright, all the while feeling their eyes transfixed on his back.

His encounter with the soldier on the train the day before, rough as it was, had, in truth, scarcely affected him. It had been unpleasant, to be sure, but he'd soon forgotten it. This most recent episode, however, was truly chilling.

At the end of the train he stepped over the weedy track and started up the other side, coming out all at once upon his fellow passengers, scattered across the open field.

At the outer rim of the circle where the field met the wood, the motor-rifle troops stood posted at regular intervals, patrolling the wide circle, some of them with large shepherd dogs in tow.

Ten feet or so away, Serja Inusen stood. She was alone, staring up at the coach, her eyes riveted on the window just above her.

She jumped when he approached.

"I'm sorry. I didn't mean to startle you."

She didn't answer, but when he followed her wide gaping eyes, he could see what had so preoccupied her. Behind the dusty glass of one of the coach windows, a military policeman moved, head bowed, shoulders stooped behind the open lid of a suitcase. His actions were clearly visible to them in the slanting light of morning. A second figure, vague and shadowy, moved in the background.

Stern glanced at the Finnish girl. She looked pale and curiously small. "Your compartment?"

She didn't speak, only nodded mutely. She could not avert her eyes from the window.

"I'm sure it's nothing to worry about," Stern went on with bogus cheer. He thought she was about to cry.

More soldiers had climbed onto the roof of the coach directly above them. Still others continued to move up and down the track bed. In the brief time he had been off on the other side of the train, more armored personnel carriers had come rumbling into the area, disgorging detachments of fresh troops and taking back those that had been on duty throughout the night. Departing, they would lurch back out of the field, leaving great clouds of dust billowing in their wake.

Not too far from where Stern stood, he recognized the Russian colonel who'd been so solicitous the day before. He was still standing with his staff, not speaking, merely observing the activity. His features were impassive. At one point he stared directly at Stern, but not so much as a flicker of recognition registered in those heavy-lidded eyes.

Not far from where the colonel and his staff stood, Junji Asawa prowled the area in restless, angry circles. Watching him for any length of time, one might have thought he was drifting dangerously close to the colonel's party, as if trying to overhear their conversation. But his total lack of any Russian made that unlikely.

Asawa was keenly aware that dozens of border police were now inside the train, going through luggage, dismantling seats to peer beneath them, and poking up into ventilator shafts with long metal probes. There were dogs, too, he knew, with sharp powers of scent, trained to sniff out contraband drugs and other chemical compounds. He wondered if they had yet reached his berth and how thorough their search of it would be.

He was not at all concerned about what they might find there. In the event of such a contingency, he knew precisely what he would do. "You would not know your son, honored father, if you could see him now." The words banged about in his fevered head. It was wonderfully satisfying to think of his father reading them.

Asawa turned and drifted slowly back up past the colonel and his staff. Out of the corner of his eye he caught a movement and felt a shiver of delight. He was certain they had noticed him.

The time was fast approaching eleven o'clock. They had been in the field for the better part of two hours and still the search went on. The temperature now hovered somewhere in the upper seventies, with the pale hazy sky giving every indication of its going even higher.

At one point the helicopter they'd seen at the border station the day before came in low over the field and hovered above the train, its blades battering the air and raising blasts of hot dust billowing up about them. They could see the pilot beside his open door, looking down at them. Then it flew on.

People had grown increasingly restless and irritable. Added to that was the keen sense of physical discomfort—the heat, the flies, the lack of proper sanitary facilities in the field. Several times Señor Gonzaga had to be led off under guard into the woods so that he could relieve himself. People had begun to feel a sense of mounting distrust, not only of the Russians but also of each other.

"What's going on here?" Ralph Keck shouted up to the colonel when he reappeared at the coach door. "We have a right to know."

Blanton pushed his way forward. "When do you intend to release us?"

"We have planes and boats to catch. Business appointments," Ted Kariolainen tried to explain.

Frau Kunkel glared. "This is inhuman."

The colonel looked out on the crowd—not at them, but over their heads, as if something in the woods beyond had caught his attention. His indifference to their concerns was chilling.

Jean Blaylock thrust her way up front to a point where she stood directly beneath him. Like a small bantam cock, she stood glaring defiantly up at him. "You have seized my passport and visa. You have offered no explanation. You are in violation of international law, and goddammit, when I get out of here, I will take this to the World Court, to the . . ."

As she spoke, she started up after him. Two soldiers with rifles at the port stepped in front of the colonel. It was at that point that Thomas yanked her back into the safety of the crowd.

"Didn't you learn anything yesterday?" Jatta glared at her.

She made another lunge at the colonel, but this time Stern interceded. "Jean, don't. We're not combatants here. We're not at war."

She glared furiously round at the others, then back at him. "You could've fooled me." She stood there trembling with rage, but for the moment, at least, it seemed she would not force another confrontation.

"It's about time you leveled with us, Colonel." The voice came from the very back of the crowd, quiet, reasoned, but with a ring of authority that even Dunskoi deigned to recognize. It was Shapley, looming large and square, in his shirtsleeves and slouch hat, his jacket dropped over his arm. "You owe us some kind of explanation. Obviously we're not buying the one about defectors."

The captain at Dunskoi's elbow whispered something into his ear. They stood there conferring in whispers for a moment. Then Dunskoi took a step backward and the captain came forward. He nodded, then looked out over the crowd directly at Shapley.

"The colonel is very sorry for this delay, Professor Shapley." The direct reference to Shapley by name surprised even the Professor. "Unfortunately, he feels he can give no fuller explanation of it for the moment."

"Thanks a lot," Jean murmured, her voice carrying forward.

The captain ignored the interruption. "In any event, please be assured," he went on, a tired, oddly likable smile upon his face, "we shall do everything in our power to make you as comfortable as possible during your stay here. On the other hand, it is only fair to advise you that while you are with us, you are expected to comply fully with the customs officials and the border police. Infringement of rules or defiance of authority will be vigorously prosecuted by the Soviet government."

In the next moment, amid an undercurrent of mutters, Dunskoi stepped down off the coach stair. A space opened in the crowd through which he and his staff passed quickly.

The sun was full up now. Waves of heat had started to radiate out of the field. Standing there watching the staff car lurch off in a cloud of yellow dust, the members of Intour Group 409 gathered uncertainly beside the train, as if awaiting some instruction. With the departure of the colonel, the tension of moments before receded, leaving in its wake an air of almost palpable gloom.

Some of the train seats had been disassembled and were now lying outside beside the track. People lingered amid the litter strewn about the weedy, fly-blown field. Many of them, still attired in gay holiday clothes, appeared more lost and out of place than ever. If they had not been frightened before, most of them were thoroughly frightened now. In the next moment, these troubled thoughts were interrupted by the loud gong of a frypan being struck with a ladle to announce that lunch was about to be served.

Stern picked disconsolately at his food. It was cold salmon, so heavily salted that it burned his throat when he tried to swallow it. After a while he gave up trying and attempted to make do with bread and tepid iced tea.

In the dining car the temperature had soared to ninety degrees Fahrenheit—hotter than the outside. There was, of course, no air conditioning, and the coach attendants, for some perverse reason, refused to permit windows to be opened. It nearly sickened one to be in there, much less attempt to eat.

The young soldier-waiters moved about unspeaking with trays and pitchers, up and down the aisles. There was virtually no conversation. The only audible sound was the light chink of cutlery scraping on dishware.

"Anyone sitting here?"

Deeply preoccupied, Stern hadn't heard the question.

"I say. Anyone sitting with you?"

Stern glanced up. "Oh, Tony. Sure. It's empty. Sit down."

Thomas carried a food tray. Bathed in sweat, he had removed his ascot, revealing beneath it a red, wrinkled, surprisingly aged neck. "Bloody steambath in here."

"You'd think they'd open a window."

"Not this lot. They'd sooner die themselves than make anyone too comfortable. It's their way of letting you know they've got you by the short hairs and that things will get a whole lot worse if you don't stay in line." Thomas glanced down into Stern's plate. "Don't like salmon?"

"I thought I did. There's enough salt in this one to choke a horse."

"Poor devils. Still live as if there were no such thing as refrigeration. You'd better eat something. Keep your strength up." Thomas' eyes shifted round the dining car; then, quite suddenly, his voice dropped. "They've found something."

"What?"

"I had it straight from a guard. They found something in one of the loos."

Stern sat in his chair, staring down at his salmon.

Thomas went on in a quiet, conversational tone, eyes lowered to his plate. "Blueprint. Microfilm. Something of the sort. I couldn't get the whole story. It was jammed into the plumbing."

"My God. Do you believe it?"

Thomas sighed wearily. "I'm not sure I know what I believe anymore."

"I mean," Stern went on inquisitively, "they could've planted it themselves, couldn't they?"

"I suppose." Thomas pondered the question. "But what on earth for?"

"As a pretext."

"A pretext for what?"

"How should I know?" Stern snapped. "For something. Possibly for leverage."

Thomas cocked his brow, and then, Stern thought, made the oddest face at him.

Just then, Jatta reappeared, looking worn and frazzled. She was accompanied by a young lieutenant and a sergeant major. In order to get everyone's attention, she tapped a spoon against a water glass.

"Attention, please. May I have your attention, please?'"

Conversation quickly subsided as they turned their heads to where she stood at the front of the car. "I know I told you last night we would be out of here today. I confess I was wrong. It seems we shall be here somewhat longer."

A wave of gasps shuddered through the car. The tour guide appeared very tired as she spoke. Her shoulders slumped and her voice quavered. She had none of her customary zip.

"After you have finished here," she went on with evident distaste, "you must return directly to your compartments and remain there."

"You must be joking," Blanton cried. "It's a sauna back there."

"Can't we at least just stand outside?" Nell Blanton pleaded.

Jatta stared at her dismally. It was as though she held herself personally responsible for everything that was happening to them. Shaking her head, at last she replied, "I'm afraid not. We must all return now to the cabins."

"My father can't be expected to ..." Isabel cried out, then broke off as Gonzaga laid a gently restraining hand on her.

"Don't worry about your father, my child. I'm not going back to any compartment now."

In the course of two days, Señor Gonzaga's immaculate white tropical suit had turned gray with the limp, wilted look of a dying carnation. His body beneath it, however, appeared to stiffen and expand, and on his face at that moment he wore a radiant serenity.

For many of them that day, confinement to the cabins took on the dimensions of genuine punishment. The airlessness, the stupefying heat, the armed soldiers at either end of the car seemingly indifferent to their discomfort, barred them from not only the simple relief of outside air, but of freedom of movement within the coach as well. Returning to their cabins, they discovered that all of their cameras and film, stationery and writing implements had been confiscated.

Announcements crackled over the P.A. system. People were ordered to remain inside their cabins. In those instances when people attempted to resist confinement, they were to be locked in. For people whose notions of confinement were vague at best, the situation was incomprehensible. It had no point of reference to anything they had ever experienced before.

The activities outside the train were no more reassuring. Since the night before, at least three additional units of motor-rifle troops had taken up positions on the fringe of the woods. They did little to conceal their movements; on the contrary, they appeared now to be flaunting them. Additional small bivouac areas had sprung up all around them, and in the field itself a number of what appeared to be contingents of the Soviet Army Artificers had begun to lay a series of drainage ditches and to throw up small jerry-built structures for purposes not readily apparent.

Those inside the train were clearly baffled by what they saw through the windows. But whatever its purpose, none of it was very encouraging. It clearly had more to do with settling in for a long, rather than a brief, stay.

Most of those in Intourist Group 409 tried coping with the adversity with whatever resources they had at hand. Their physical situation was barely tolerable. They sat in sweat-sodden garments gasping for a bit of air to breathe. Some of them had been rendered comatose by the stupefying heat, and as the afternoon wore on and all rules of acceptable attire were gradually abandoned, more and more outer wear was stripped off.

A lunch of salt fish had not helped matters any. One couldn't help feeling there had been an element of perversity in having fed it to people in those high temperatures. Those who had partaken fully of the salmon were now suffering the curses of the damned. They required fresh cold water, but what was available to them was barely potable. Some of them tried to buy Vichy or mineral water from the coach attendants but were sharply rebuffed.

Others tried to play cards and various games. Some, like Stern, attempted to read. But even Inspector Maigret could not ease his discomfort. All the while Stern attempted to follow the good inspector through the winding alleys and byways of the eighteenth arrondissement in search of a maniacal psycho-

path, a mounting sense of unease boiled like an overheated pot not far below
the surface of his seeming calm.

Within each of the nine compartments, going on within each individual,
innumerable such interior conflicts were beginning to unfold. Ralph Keck,
still attired in his dark suit, eyeglasses slightly askew, had been going on at
great length along lines he had started on in the dining car at lunch. "You can
disappear without a trace in this country," he said. "They'll take everything—your money, your jewels, your—"

"Oh, for God's sake, Ralph," Myra Keck snapped. "Shut up."

Keck gaped at her. "Can't you see what they're doing? What their game
is?"

It was at that point that Señor Gonzaga rose to his feet and, somewhat
unsteadily, started to undress.

In Cabin 5, Madam Muk, kohl leaking at the corners of her eyes, sari
blotched with disks of sweat beneath the arms, informed the occupants that a
pair of valuable sapphire earrings was missing from her traveling bag.

The obvious thing would have been to suspect the border police, who'd
been in the cabins all morning inspecting the luggage. If they could confiscate
cameras, why not then earrings? Madam Muk was a bit more complex than
that, however. She had been fuming for hours at the spectacle of her husband's gushing attentions to Trina Van Meegrin. Her jealousy therefore took
the form of direct accusation. Trina was mortified—stung to the point of
speechlessness. She couldn't defend herself. Tears rimmed her eyes. A loud,
bitter altercation ensued, including Kyle Van Meegrin, Kate Dubbin, and
both Madam and Mr. Mukherjee, who was obliged to take his wife's side—all
this, even as the piercing wails of Baby Muk rose like a siren above the din.

In the interval of returning to their cabins after lunch, Nell Blanton had
somehow wound up in Cabin 2 with Sonia Conti. Jean Blaylock, who had left
the dining car with Stern, was now compelled to remain with him in Cabin 4.
Once inside a cabin, any cabin, passengers were prevented from returning to
their own.

It was all perfectly amiable at first, but after a short dose of heat and confinement, the mixture of Jean and Tony Thomas proved to be too combusti-
ble.

"Wonderful, the efficiency of these police states," Thomas remarked offhandedly.

"Britain has more police than the USSR. Everyone there's a bloody cop.
Right from the prime minister on down."

"But they don't carry Kalishnikov rifles."

"No—just those clubs for skull-bashing. Particularly if you're a West Indian in Brixton or a laborer on strike."

"Try striking in Russia or Poland. They'll teach you a thing or two about
skull-bashing."

Jean made a disagreeable sucking sound at him.

Thomas laughed scornfully. "Face it, Jean. You're one of those road-company revolutionaries with a bag full of credit cards for when times get tough. Your ideas are all secondhand and irrelevant."

Stern tried to head them off, but Jean saw the red flag waving and lunged. "Talk about road-company performers—you with that ascot and cigarette holder and that phony upper-class accent. Don't tell me they spoke that way in Chiswick when you were a kid."

She laughed at his astonishment. "Oh yes. I've learned a bit about you. One of your colleagues, part of the press corps at the hotel, gave me an earful one night."

"Oh? What else did you learn?"

Stern and the others watched it all with queasy fascination.

"It's a very slim biography," Jean barged ahead with spiteful zest. "No background to speak of. Just an overambitious working-class kid who taught himself Russian in the British Army and was glib enough to talk his way into Fleet Street. In a year or two he parlayed that into a correspondent's job, getting himself posted to the London *Times*'s Moscow Bureau, became an overnight Kremlinologist, put on great airs, affected ascots, cigarette holders, a huge ennui, and carried on like something out of bad Noël Coward."

There was a moment of silence while they waited for Thomas to reply.

Finally he did. "Am I supposed to be ashamed of all that?"

"Sounds to me like a success story," Stern said heatedly. "I should think you'd be proud of it, Tony."

Jean ignored the remark. "It does seem he goes to great lengths to cover up his prole origins."

"I bet you wish you could boast some good prole origins, Jean," Blanton taunted.

"My prole origins are just as good as his," Jean snapped. They all laughed, except Jean, who failed to see the humor.

Suddenly they heard shouting in the corridor outside, followed by pounding on a door and the thud of running feet.

Karl Heinz was up first, then Stern. They hurled the door back, only to find a number of other doors firing back with sharp reports all down the corridor. Several of the guards bolted past, all streaming toward the point from where the commotion was coming.

The door of Cabin 3 flew open, revealing the large lumpish figure of Myra Keck behind it, her mouth twisted into a hair-raising scream. A brownish blur of motion was visible just behind her as she burst through the doorway and fled down the corridor, making shrill little yipping sounds as she went.

The soldiers who'd rushed there in response to the shouts leapt out of her path. She was a large woman and they quickly recognized the imprudence of trying to stop her. They were about to give chase, but just then Señor Gonzaga appeared, a leprous white apparition framed in the doorway, smiling angelically, and naked as a jay.

Though he was naked, Gonzaga's departure from the cabin was far more decorous than Mrs. Keck's. Looking first right, then left, he raised a leg and stepped into the corridor with an almost regal mien. It had some of the pomp and grandeur of a coronation march. The Russian rifleman standing closest to him stepped aside with an air of surprising deference.

To be perfectly precise, Señor Gonzaga was not entirely naked. He still wore his shoes and socks, and as he swayed majestically down the aisle, Stern caught the expression of one of the border guards just visible beneath the patent-leather visor of his cap. It evinced not the slightest hint of surprise. Quite the contrary, the features were a mask of stony impassivity as they followed Gonzaga's gartered calves and strangely youthful buttocks receding down the passageway.

The last glimpse they had of the old man, he was being whisked off between two strapping, somewhat embarrassed Russian guards and bundled into the rear of a waiting truck. Señora Gonzaga's stricken face appeared at one of the windows. Even from behind the sooty glass it was possible to hear her pathetic, keening wail, an unearthly sound reminiscent of the sunrise cry of muezzins.

Faces now appeared, mute and gaping, at every compartment window. Claude Desfargue had managed somehow to prize his window open, and stood watching the bizarre sight of a naked old man being marched off by a small force of guards.

At the border installation at Vyborg, Colonel Dunskoi sat at his desk working. For the office of a high Soviet officiary, it was unusually Spartan. Part of a shabby, unprepossessing compound of randomly organized barracks, wood structures, and water towers, the office was poorly ventilated—cold in the winter and suffocatingly hot in the summer. It would be safe to say that at that particular moment the colonel was almost as physically uncomfortable as were his captives on the Green Train. But in Dimitri Dunskoi's case, the discomfort was more or less self-inflicted.

Having inspected the train site that morning, and duly noted the overall condition of the passengers, he had cabled general headquarters:

> . . . It shall be difficult to maintain order much longer, not to mention the general health and well-being of passengers aboard the train. From my own personal observations, I have noted several passengers of advanced age, one or two of whom I imagine to be in fragile health.
>
> For that reason, I respectfully suggest that it would be prudent to pull the whole group back to Leningrad without further delay and billet them in more suitable quarters, where detention would be more manageable and considerably more humane.

Dunskoi had sent the cable several hours earlier. Already he had the answer on his desk before him. Reading it made his heart sink.

For reasons that should be obvious, STAVKA does not wish at this time to return Intourist Group 409 to the ease and comforts of civilization. It is better for our purposes to keep the pressure on by extending the period of detention. On the train we can control conditions, making them rather more or less harsh as the situation demands.

The affair is presently receiving major coverage in the world press. Already we have unofficial but "highly concerned" inquiries from the Swedish, French, Finnish, and American legations in Leningrad.

Now that the idea of espionage has been successfully planted among the detainees, you will commence with their interrogation. This in itself should occupy your time for a number of days while international pressure mounts for a settlement.

It is vital that when you finally select your suspect it be a plausible choice—"plausible" meaning "not too obvious" so as to better lend itself to general credibility. Also, by all means, it should be a "sympathetic choice," meaning an individual who is generally liked and whose victimization will arouse anguish among the others.

After reading this directive, Colonel Dunskoi sat for some time staring at the blank unpainted pine wall opposite his desk. Though it was only three o'clock in the afternoon, his office was dark, full of gathering shadows from the drapes drawn against the heat of the day.

Elbows on the desk, chin resting in the palm of his hand, he appeared to be deep in thought. After a time he removed a sheet of plain paper from his drawer, along with the passenger manifest of the Green Train, and proceeded to draw up a list.

Passenger	Citizenship	Determination
Asawa, Junji	Japanese	negative
Blanton, Paul	American	negative
Blanton, Eleanore	American	negative
Blaylock, Jean	American	negative
Conti, Maximilliano	Italian	negative
Conti, Sonia	Italian	negative
Desfargue, Claude	French	negative
Dubbin, Katherine	American	positive
Gonzaga, Enrique	Argentine	negative
Gonzaga, Margarita	Argentine	negative
Gonzaga, Consuelo	Argentine	negative
Gonzaga, Isabel	Argentine	positive
Inusen, Serja	Finnish	negative

Kariolainen, Theodore	American	positive
Kariolainen, Janet	American	negative
Kariolainen, Corine	American	negative
Kariolainen, Christopher	American	negative
Keck, Ralph	American	negative
Keck, Myra	American	negative
Kunkel, Irma	German	negative
Kunkel, Karl Heinz	German	negative
Lambrusto, Alessandro	Italian	negative
Lambrusto, Silvana	Italian	negative
Madariaga, Augusto	Spanish	negative
Mukherjee, Nagu	Indian	negative
Mukherjee, Rashi and child Victor	Indian	negative
Palmunan, Jatta	Finnish	negative
Shapley, Dr. Grant	American	positive
Shapley, Wilma	American	negative
Stern, Peter	American	positive
Thomas, Anthony Beech	British	negative
Van Meegrin, Dr. Kyle	Dutch	positive
Van Meegrin, Katrina	Dutch	negative
Wales, Keith	Canadian	positive

On a separate piece of paper were the seventeen names of the members of the Spanish choral group. With a single stroke the colonel drew through these a long unbroken line.

When he had completed his list he sat for a time in the dark, shadowy quiet of his office, rubbing his burning eyes with the heels of his palms. Most of his staff had gone for the day and, with the exception of an orderly or two and several guards, he was alone. He didn't mind that. He rather enjoyed solitude, the pleasure of inaction.

But shortly that, too, was interrupted by the ringing of the phone. It was his private line. For a moment he was tempted not to answer it. He knew it was his wife, Katerine Ivanovna. Knowing that it annoyed him to be disturbed while on duty, she seldom called him there, except in emergencies. Instantly, therefore, he anticipated some unpleasantness.

For a while they chatted quietly to each other in muted voices, full of warmth and intimacy, dropping here and there bits of small, innocuous information. Once or twice they even laughed. It was her way, he knew. Then casually, almost as an afterthought, she mentioned Masha, their daughter, and the fact that police officials had again been there that afternoon, questioning her, politely to be sure, about their daughter's activities at the university and her friendships with individuals of known or suspected dissident leanings. These activities and friendships, they respectfully wished to advise, were being carefully monitored by the authorities. They very much regretted having to be the bearers of unpleasant tidings, but nevertheless, in view of the colonel's position, they preferred at this time to take no specific action. However . . .

By the time Dunskoi had put the phone down, small white crescents had erupted on his knuckles from the clenching of his fists. His first inclination was to call his daughter in Leningrad and advise her in no uncertain terms that if her activities caused her to fall afoul of the authorities, she could not call upon him to intercede, as he had done several times before, in her behalf. Further, he wished her to know that if his promotion to major general were in any way jeopardized, the responsibility for that would fall squarely at her door.

When at last he reached for the telephone he was smoldering, but when it came to dialing, his fingers trembled. The effrontery, the ingratitude, the thoughtlessness of the child to so embarrass him, to compromise a reputation he had so carefully nurtured over a period of twenty years. Did she not realize? Did she not care?

In the end, unable to complete the call, he slammed the phone back down on the cradle and stalked out.

Throughout dinner that evening a soldier played the accordion—lively Russian folk tunes for the most part. Then he offered to take requests. The service had been somewhat less stiff, and the food itself, roast chicken, markedly improved. They had opened the windows in the dining car and at the conclusion of the meal they passed around with slivovitz and brandy. It was a kind of grudging, albeit tacit, apology for the unpleasantness of the day, and conceivably a way of trying to make amends. Thomas didn't see things in quite the same light. "Beware Russkies bearing gifts," he murmured aside to Stern while tossing off his brandy pony. "Russian generosity is generally the prelude to onslaught."

While they lingered over coffee and liqueurs, Dunskoi suddenly appeared at the front of the car, accompanied by several of his staff. He moved easily down the center aisle, nodding and, through interpreters, stopping occasionally to chat with people.

It was all a bit disarming and for a moment they were reassured. The colonel's amiable presence there was a guarantee that everything would soon be well. Surely they would be leaving tomorrow, first thing in the morning. Jatta herself was beaming. Many of them there even felt a surge of affection for the colonel.

But once having traversed the length of the car, he turned to address them. What they saw then in his face was quite different from the easy cordiality of a moment before. Once he started to speak, by means of the captain's translation, the transition was startling:

"As you no doubt have observed, our people have been busy all day today on this train. Based on information intercepted by the Soviet government over the past several days, the military border police at Vyborg have been advised that documents containing highly secret data were taken from the Polyarny naval station on the Kola peninsula. With additional information, we have reason to believe that an individual or individuals presently aboard this train are in possession of those documents. I can now inform you that this is the reason that you have been detained here over the past forty-eight hours."

He paused a moment and gazed tellingly about the assembled group. "The documents of which I speak have been located in a washroom of the train. They were secreted in a blind drain behind a sink. Knowledge that the drain was out of use, and dry, hence perfect for the concealment of documents, could only have been known to someone fairly intimate with the layout of these coaches.

"Since blueprints designating the plumbing and sanitation lines of these cars are kept in confidential files with the Ministry of Transportation in Leningrad, we are forced to conclude a strong possibility of complicity between the individual who placed the documents in the drain with employees of the rail line or the ministry in Leningrad.

"Earlier I said I regretted this discovery. My life, and indeed yours, would have been a great deal easier had we found nothing. Yes, we are in possession of the stolen documents, but now, so it seems, I am obliged to stay put right here until I can uncover the person or persons responsible for attempting to spirit these documents out of the Soviet Union.

"Most of you, I fully recognize, are entirely innocent of any wrongdoing. You have already been delayed two full days and have had to endure conditions that I recognize as . . ." He stared at the ceiling, searching for the precise words. ". . . shall we say less than ideal."

A snicker rippled through the car, then broke off abruptly as the announcement continued.

"As things stand now, I do not know when you can expect to leave here. To some extent it depends very much upon you. Tomorrow I have instructed my men to proceed with a round of interrogation. This can be unpleasant and, unfortunately, time-consuming."

The colonel waited for the muttering and gasps to die down. "On the other hand, it would be so much easier if the individual or individuals responsible were to come forward—either now, as I stand here addressing you, or if it is more desirable, in the privacy of my office. The door is always open."

The captain gazed round apologetically at the conditions of the dining car. "This car, we are well aware, is warm, and we do not wish to keep you here any longer than is absolutely necessary."

During the course of the captain's translation of his talk, Dunskoi stared straight ahead, his eyes fixed on a distant wall, as though he were scarcely present. His face wore a mask of utter indifference.

The conclusion of the announcement inviting the guilty party to come forward was followed by a portentous quiet. In that silence, Dunskoi had his answer. Stiffening, he threw his head and shoulders back. "So—in that case then, interrogation begins promptly at nine A.M."

The colonel and his staff turned and left abruptly.

By ten P.M. Stern was sprawled across the seat of his cabin, feet up and engrossed in one of his Maigrets. He had a great fondness for the inspector from the Quai des Orfèvres. There was an affinity he felt they both shared. He liked to imagine himself taking a beer or a calvados with Maigret at the Brasserie Dauphin around eleven P.M., just before the inspector would return home to the walk-up apartment on the Boulevard Richard Lenoir, full of its funny old *fin de siècle* furnishings of no great distinction. Hand-me-downs from generations of relatives long dead, beads and brocades, overstuffed velvet chairs with sprung seats and hair-oil stains glistening at the headrests.

It made Stern sad to think of the two of them, Inspector and Madame Maigret, alone there in the apartment with the high ceilings and the occasional blare of a horn sounding up from the street below, as the two of them sat down to a dinner of cassoulet, or possibly the inspector's favorite, a *civet* of rabbit. There would be the quiet clink of silver, the periodic pop of the uncorking wine bottle as Maigret poured. The long, not uncomfortable pauses between talk.

He looked up suddenly at the sound of voices in the corridor outside. It sounded like two, possibly three voices, coming from somewhere at the front of the car. The voices were not loud, but due to some peculiar acoustical property in the construction of the cars, they carried hollowly down the length of the coach. They conveyed no sense of real anger, but in tone they were argumentative.

Stern kept his gaze fixed on his book, pretending to read. But as the voices grew more voluble, more edgy, once again he was forced to look up, surprised to discover that the others in the compartment were listening too.

"That's not what I said."

"Well, then, what exactly did you say?"

"I'm saying, what if they don't?"

"But they have to. They can't just . . ."

"Who's to stop them?"

"World opinion, for one thing."

"You know what you can do with world opinion?"

"There are laws, international treaties . . ."

"Laws and treaties don't amount to a row of beans when it comes to a couple of superpowers throwing their weight around."

Nell Blanton's merry eyes smiled at Stern. "It's Paul and Ted Kariolainen."

"What are they arguing about?"

"When are we going to get out of this. Paul says soon. Ted says not so soon."

Tony Thomas pushed his pips dispiritedly along the backgammon board. "I'm with Kariolainen there."

Stern watched the Shapleys drift past the cabin door. Shortly more voices and footsteps filled the corridor.

Karl Heinz bounded up and stuck his head out the door. He was seventeen and still had that boyish quality of loping. "Looks like some kind of meeting up front," he said, then stepped out into the corridor and ambled off in that direction. He was not particularly interested in what was being said, but he'd seen Corrie Kariolainen up there and he knew that's where he wanted to be.

"Think we ought to go see?" Nell Blanton asked.

Stern sighed, slipped a bookmark into his Maigret, and rose. "Anything's better than sitting around here."

The front of the car was crowded. People milled in the aisle and stood at the open doors of their compartments, following the gist of the talk, occasionally chiming in.

". . . but what choice do we have?" Kyle Van Meegrin struggled to be heard above the crowd.

"None, if you ask me," Kariolainen replied. "You're stuck right here for just as long as they want you."

Silvana Lambrusto threaded her way forward. "But we do have a right to notify our consul of the situation. Our families have to be informed."

"Of course they do." Grant Shapley's quiet drawl was reassuring. "Recourse to a consul or an ambassador in instances of detention is guaranteed by the Hague Convention. It was even expanded several years back during the Helsinki Accords."

Ralph Keck's drooping eyes flared momentarily. "Well then, there you have it."

"Not quite," Shapley cautioned. "Even an ambassador, assuming you'd be permitted to reach one, wouldn't cut much ice with the Russians. Particularly if they've got a bee in their bonnet that someone on board here is attempting to depart the Soviet Union illegally."

There was an explosion of mutters and groans.

"That's ridiculous. It's all made up."

"I agree. But that's the way these people are. They spend a lot of time at suspicion."

"They don't really expect us to believe this spy nonsense, do they?"

"They don't care if you do or you don't," Shapley replied.

"Take nothing for granted," Thomas suddenly spoke out. "Nothing is too outlandish in this part of the world. I agree, the spy story does sound improbable, but something's afoot here. These people are not capricious. They don't initiate actions without some larger purpose. We've been detained here now slightly over two days. Most of us appear to take for granted that whatever the cause of the delay, it will shortly be eliminated. What I am saying is that such an assumption may be unduly optimistic."

Thomas stared at them, as if waiting for someone to dispute him. The implication of his remarks was stupefying. They cast a pall over everyone.

"Please," Jatta cried. "You're alarming people."

"I'm only saying what I believe."

"But are you, really, Signor Thomas," Max Conti called out from the rear. "It sounds to me as if there's something else on your mind."

"I've already said what I think," Thomas replied. "Unfortunately, quite beyond our own personal wishes, we've been drawn into something larger and more complex than we're aware of."

"Okay," Ted Kariolainen conceded the point impatiently. "But what is it?"

There was an odd, somewhat awkward pause before Thomas replied, "I don't know."

"Will you for God's sake, Tony, say what's on your mind," Blanton snapped.

Thomas sighed with an air of great weariness. "Realistically speaking, I suppose I'm saying we could well find ourselves guests of the Soviet Union for a period far longer than any of us might have desired."

"Particularly if one of us here has been so foolish as to—" Keck started to say, but Isabel headed him off.

"Please. Not those stolen secret documents again."

"Why not? Stolen documents are not at all uncommon in this part of the world, Miss Gonzaga," Thomas remarked. "Classified information is traded back and forth here like a commodities market, every day."

Isabel's displeasure with the notion became increasingly visible; the fact that it happened to be Thomas' only aggravated the situation. "If that were the case," she flared, "and mind you, I don't believe for a moment that it is, what exactly are you suggesting we do?"

She'd directed the question at Keck, however, not Thomas. Keck watched her weaving her way slowly toward him. He had a wary, distrustful look about him as though he were watching the approach of a deadly reptile.

His voice quavered as he spoke. "I'm suggesting what has already been suggested to us by the colonel this evening. If there is indeed such an individual among us, whoever she or he may be can spare us all a great deal of discomfort and inconvenience by disclosing their identity right now. One of us here has already had her passport confiscated . . ."

Jean Blaylock purpled. "I was certain you'd be getting to that."

"Well, after all, Jean," Myra Keck reminded her, "they did take your passport."

Stern had been fidgeting restlessly in the rear. "You don't suggest for a moment that because they took her passport, she's some sort of spy?"

"They didn't confiscate anyone else's passport, did they?" Keck replied with an irritating solicitousness, as if it broke his heart to have to bring up the matter.

It was too much for Jean. Her voice choked with indignation as she cried out: "Don't worry that little pea brain of yours about my passport, Mr. Keck. I'll have it back."

Sympathy appeared to be riding overwhelmingly in Jean's favor. Even Keck sensed he had gone too far, and he hastened now to somehow repair the damage.

"I'm not accusing anyone of anything," he said. "All I'm saying is if there's a definite risk here . . ."

"What risk?" Jatta Palmunan's arms flailed the stale air. "Why do you keep talking of risk? Delay, yes. Inconvenience, yes. But risk? I can assure you there is no risk. Both you and Mr. Thomas have no business alarming people . . ."

"I'm alarming no one," Thomas replied. He seemed hurt. "I was asked my opinion and I gave it."

The tour guide disregarded him. "I tell you all once more, we will be out of here soon. Very soon." Her cheeks flamed and her voice rang with conviction. "At this very moment, I'm certain, negotiations are going on . . ."

"I hope you are right, Miss Palmunan." Señor Madariaga shook his head dubiously. "But you have been saying 'very soon' for two days."

There was a moment of silence as they regarded each other across the close, troubled air.

"I must say," Stern finally broke the quiet, "this whole thing about stolen documents does look more and more to me like a pretext for holding us here."

"But why?" Nell Blanton fretted. "For what earthly reason?"

Grant Shapley cleared the gravel from his throat. "Because, as Mr. Thomas said, it obviously serves some other, larger purpose."

Ted Kariolainen turned directly on the Englishman. "Tony, do you know something the rest of us don't?"

Thomas shook his head. "I know no more than anyone else."

"I think we'd all have to agree now," Paul Blanton reasoned, "that our status has advanced beyond that of mere passengers. Or even detainees. We're prisoners now, aren't we?" His eyes swept around from face to face as he said it.

The word infuriated the tour guide. "And I say we are not," she snapped. "All this talk about spies and prisoners serves no good purpose."

"What are we, then?" Keck fired back. "This certainly goes beyond routine detainment. Let's call a spade a spade. We're hostages here. Don't say we're not."

"What troubles me even more than our status"—Ted Kariolainen gazed round at them thoughtfully—"is the state of mind we seem to have reached here. Somebody, I'm not even sure who anymore, drops a word about stolen documents, and suddenly we're all looking for spies and traitors among ourselves."

"Who did start all of this nonsense about stolen papers?" Isabel asked.

"The soviets," Keck said. "They told us right here. Tonight."

"No," Nell said. "We heard it before there was any formal announcement."

"That was yesterday," Blanton fumed. "But that was something about defectors."

"Now look at us." Kariolainen smiled, gazing round at them as if to prove his point. "We know nothing about the legitimacy of any of these charges, and yet we're ready to turn in anyone just so we can all go our separate ways. And that's only after two days of confinement. What's it going to be like if, God forbid, this thing lasts much longer?"

Isabel clapped her hands with great relish. There was a look of delight on her face. "Thank you, Mr. Kariolainen. I thank you for that. Number one, I thank you for not being as gullible as some of the rest of us here. And, number two, thank you for having the character to resist being stampeded into forcing one of our own group into making a foolish sacrifice of himself." She turned a withering look on Keck. "I, for one, would be willing to sit here on this horrid train until hell freezes over before I'd urge anyone, even a spy, and believe me, I loathe spies of any political stripe whatever, to make a martyr of himself just so I could get out of here a bit earlier." Isabel was physically a small person, probably no more than five feet, five or so, but she was capable of rising to a very fine high dudgeon. At that moment, her small, compact being fairly resonated with it. For several moments after she'd ceased to speak, the ring of her voice, never loud, but wonderfully raspy, continued to vibrate through the stuffy corridor like a violin string after it has been plucked.

She continued to stand there, her eyes darting back and forth between Thomas and Mr. Keck. Feeling isolated from the others, Keck appeared suddenly self-conscious and uneasy. He cast about hopefully for support, but appeared to find none. At last his wife came to his side. She took his arm, which at first he made a move to resist, then permitted himself to be led off to their compartment.

In his eyes, he had done his duty to his fellowman. If they failed to appreciate that, it was not his fault. He'd done what he could for them. Now, leave them to heaven.

PART V

K REMLIN SOURCES today disclosed that highly secret documents taken from the Polyarny naval base have now been recovered from a washroom on the Finn-Soviet Express. The individual responsible for this act of espionage, presumably an agent of the CIA, is believed to still be aboard the train. Authorities say it is only a matter of time before the spy is in custody. The train is at present being detained . . . (*Izvestia.*)

. . . that the incident of the Soviet submarine detected in Norwegian coastal waters was not the first such occurrence, but just one in a long series of incursions, particularly several in the vicinity of the Norwegian naval base at Hammerfest. The first such incident was detected in May of 1981, at which time the Norwegian government cautioned the Soviet naval attaché in Oslo . . .

. . . Most of the northern tier of Europe continues to swelter in broiling temperatures of up to forty degrees Centigrade, said to be due in large part to a huge temperature inversion drifting northward across the Strait of Gibraltar from North Africa. . . . This is Per Vokso for *Norge Today.*

"Am I to understand that you accuse me . . ."

"I accuse you of nothing. I merely inform you that you are a suspect."

"That's incredible . . ."

"You surely have had ample opportunity . . ."

"To do what? Steal documents? Ridiculous."

It was shortly past nine A.M. Colonel Dunskoi and Grant Shapley volleyed charges back and forth at one another. The body heat generated between them for the past quarter-hour had been steadily mounting. Not to mention the Professor's astonishment at discovering that the colonel now spoke to him in perfectly serviceable English.

They had come for Shapley promptly at 8:30 A.M. just as he was finishing breakfast in the dining car. They waited for him to finish his egg and tea, then rode him over in a staff car to the border compound at Vyborg, where he was ushered at once into the colonel's office. He found Dunskoi sitting behind a desk riffling through a sheaf of documents.

"Why not? Perfectly plausible. You are no stranger to Soviet Union."

Dunskoi lifted the report at the top of the pile and scanned it through squinting eyes. "You are on intimate terms with many Soviet scientists. You have access to research. People who have access to classified information also have access to you."

"My field is paleontology. I know nothing about naval ordnance. Nor do I care to. The subject, I assure you, would bore me to tears."

"Nevertheless," Dunskoi persisted. "You could sell such information in U.S. for great profit."

"To whom, for God's sake?" Shapley struggled to contain his fury.

"Military-industrial complex. The government. Why not? Why so ridiculous? Is done all the time in United States."

Shapley's jaw dropped. His large eyes blinked with incredulity behind his glasses. "I don't work for the military-industrial complex. Or the government. I'm a teacher."

Colonel Dunskoi smiled his world-weary Slavic smile. "All American scientists work for U.S. government, or military-industrial complex. Especially teacher scientists."

Shapley began to sputter. "My dear colonel, I can't begin to tell you how wildly misinformed you appear to be. The subject in which I happen to have some expertise is a subject, thank God, for which there is no known practical military application. The military-industrial complex, the Pentagon, the Rand Corporation, the Brookings Institution, or whatever the hell have you, would not give me a plugged nickel for the whole damned body of it."

"You are far too excited," Dunskoi said placatingly, and lit a cigarette.

"I resent . . . I deny . . . You have absolutely no right . . ."

While the Professor sputtered, Dunskoi's eyes dropped back down to the file before him, eyes swarming across the page, his lips moved soundlessly reading it.

"If I am to be formally charged—" Shapley resumed his tirade, but the colonel cut him short with a chopping motion of his arm.

"Your last trip to Soviet Union was four years ago?"

Shapley was momentarily baffled. "That's right. Nineteen-eighty-two. I attended a conference."

"Kiev."

"Right." His bafflement deepened. He was embarrassed when the colonel caught him craning his neck to get a glimpse of the report on his desk.

"You enjoy trips to Soviet Union?" Dunskoi inquired.

"Very much. I have been coming, on and off, for twenty years."

"Always scientific matters?"

One does not come for pleasure, Shapley was about to say, but thought better of it. "That's right."

"What are your politics?"

Once again the Professor was thrown off balance. "What on earth does that have to do with anything?"

Dunskoi's eyes twinkled shrewdly. "I am just making conversation. Tell me anyway. In United States, you are Democrat? Republican? Conservative? Liberal?"

"I am not interested in politics or government. Only so far as it impinges on my work. I am a registered Democrat, if that matters at all."

Dunskoi's slow hooded eyes watched him from behind a film of smoke. Shapley continued, unable to stop himself, and aware that his leg had started to twitch beneath his trousers. "But to my mind, all government is a circus populated by creatures with a curious compulsion to perform clever stunts before a camera."

"Such as," Dunskoi's eyes continued to scan the dossier, "detaining a trainload of passengers for several days?"

"Now that you mention it," Shapley snapped back, "yes, particularly when you have to cook up phony pretexts to do so, when all the time you're really after something else."

Dunskoi's brows cocked. "What else? For instance?"

"I haven't the faintest notion. All I know is that this business about stolen documents and spies is ludicrous."

The colonel regarded him gravely through the haze of smoke. Suddenly his head tipped back, his eyes closed and he laughed softly at the ceiling. "It's a pity this world was not designed by professors and intellectuals."

"If it were, you would not see people detained on trains for days and forced to submit to the shabby indignity of this sort of interrogation."

"Doubtless everything would work superbly." The colonel winked spitefully.

"I don't claim anything would work at all, but for one thing we would dispense with secrecy, and knowledge and information would flow freely between people without the encumbrance of dull-witted functionaries. But why are we going on like this?" Shapley pounded the desk with his fist. His leg fluttered in his trousers. "You've brought me here to accuse me of stealing classified documents from the Soviet Union."

Dunskoi raised a cautionary hand. "I have not accused you. Not yet. I have informed you that you are a suspect."

"In that case, show me these alleged documents I am supposed to have secreted in the lavatory."

"I do no such thing," the colonel retorted.

"In that case"—Shapley stiffened—"in the absence of concrete evidence, I shall answer no further questions."

Leaning his stout frame forward, the Professor started to hoist himself on his cane. Once on his feet, he made a quarter-turn. A look of puzzlement leapt in his eyes, along with the odd sensation that there was nothing but air between his torso and the floor. He toppled over with a bang.

"You are a student of political science?"

"That's right. A graduate student."

"At Georgetown University in Washington?"

"That's correct."

"Citizenship, U.S.?"

"Correct."

"You are preparing to enter the foreign service."

"I hope to," Kate Dubbin replied.

Colonel Dunskoi glanced up from the papers on his desk and regarded the pretty young woman seated across from him. "You don't look like a diplomat to me," he growled.

"Oh?" Her brow arched. "What does a diplomat look like?"

Dunskoi ignored the question. "I have daughter your age. She is studying microbiology at Leningrad University."

"Does she look like a microbiologist?" Kate asked, unable to resist the impertinence.

The colonel frowned. "I don't know *what* she looks like. To me, she changes each day. One day she is physician; the next day . . . who knows?" He shrugged.

Kate smiled. Somewhat mystified, she was certain she had not been called there to discuss the colonel's domestic arrangements. "That's typical of the young all over the world."

He looked at her quizzically.

"Changeability," she added.

"In my time, it was unheard of. My father was a soldier. I never considered doing anything else."

"Are you happy?"

"Happy?"

"With your choice."

Another frown furrowed his brow, as if he sensed that the interrogation had veered from the professional. " 'Happy' is perhaps not the word, but I could never have done anything else."

"How do you know, since apparently you never had the opportunity to consider alternatives."

He regarded her through eyes half-closed. She returned his gaze with wise, gentle, possibly amused eyes glowing from a face burnished copper by the summer sun. "You've kept your knowledge of English a great secret," she added.

"May we return to interrogation?" he said, suddenly stern.

"Please do. You were saying that as a student of government . . ."

"I know what I was saying." Dunskoi watched her over the arch he had formed with the tips of his fingers. "It is my duty to inform you that as a person whose background lies in the area of international affairs, you are a prime suspect in the theft of these documents."

"I am a student of government," Kate pointed out with quiet deliberation. "That doesn't mean I am employed by government. I think the connection you're making is a bit simplistic."

Dunskoi's fingertips drummed lightly against each other. Pondering his reply, he appeared to be whistling soundlessly to himself. A phone rang in the outer office, followed by a buzzer sounding at his desk. He snatched the phone up, rattling irritably into it in Russian, then returned it to its cradle. "What is the purpose of your trip to Soviet Union?"

"It was not to study government." She laughed, regretting it the instant she saw his eyes. "It was not even planned. I happened to be traveling for the summer with a young man . . ."

Dunskoi's eyes scanned the passenger manifest. "Monsieur Desfargue?"

"That's right. We were in Helsinki, and we figured we were so close, why not have a look?"

"And did you like what you saw?"

For the first time during the course of the interrogation she appeared uneasy. "Some of it." She spoke tentatively. "Some of it we didn't."

"Such as?" The fingers drummed somewhat faster but the hooded eyes seemed more impassive than ever. "Was it the people? Their shabbiness? Their lack of possessions? The drab uniformity of everything? The absence of pretty things to purchase in the shops? The drunkenness in the streets? The government-controlled press? And . . . oh yes. Of course. The complete absence of genuine human rights?"

His voice had grown increasingly sharp as he enumerated this litany of well-known ills. Perhaps he had sensed that in the almost casual attitude of their preliminary discussions, he had lost some of the momentum and psychological advantage of the professional inquisitor. If that were so, the harsh, clipped manner he now displayed quickly restored the relationship to its proper balance. The young woman was visibly unnerved, but not so much as to be cowed.

"Yes. Those things bothered us. But of course, you've heard all that before."

"Often," he replied curtly.

She felt a rush of heat to her face. "I am sorry if—"

"I must again advise you," he ran over her words. "You are suspect here. Our investigations conclude that you may well be one of those responsible for stealing classified documents."

"But I would like to—"

"The interview is over. You may go."

The drainage ditches and the plain pine wood structures that the artificers and the construction troops had labored over the day before had taken shape overnight in the form of a block of low, flat-roofed sheds meant to serve as a bathhouse with lavatories. Half were intended for male, the other half for female use.

Temporary cisterns had been dug beneath the lavatories; drainage ditches went out from either side of the compound, channeled into leeching fields, and water was pumped up from the pond below.

"Ah—there you are." Tony Thomas whirled into the newly erected facilities. "I looked for you at breakfast."

"I preferred a shave to plum nectar and tepid tea."

"Finish up and come with me."

Stern rinsed his blade beneath the lazy stream of steamy water. "Why?"

"La Gonzaga. She's sick."

Stern was unimpressed. "What is it? The old boy?"

"They won't let her see him. They don't tell her anything. All they say is that he's fine. She's worried sick."

Stern sluiced the remaining lather from his face and dried off noisily with a towel.

"She hasn't eaten since yesterday noon," Thomas rattled on, "and this morning she complained of pains in the chest. Couldn't catch her breath."

Stern buttoned his shirt. "Has anyone sent for a doctor?"

"She wants to see you."

"Me? Why me?"

"She wants you to go see the colonel. Thinks you can do something with him."

"Good God."

"That incident the other day. The soldier knocking you down, and the colonel's kicking the bloke's arse, and apologizing to you profusely. She noted that well, and now she thinks old Dunskoi would be more inclined to be indulgent to you than to any of the others. She thinks he may feel he owes you one." Thomas thrust shaving gear at Stern for packing into his kit. "Come on, Peter. The old girl's really in a bad way."

"What the devil am I supposed to do about it? Tell them to call a doctor. Ask Jatta to go see the colonel."

"She's already been up there twice. She can't budge him. At the very least, they should permit the old girl to see him. I've offered to go myself, but the Gonzagas want you. Yes, it's true. Don't shake your head at me. I've had all this from Isabel. And I'm not trying to ingratiate myself with her. If anything"—he dropped his voice to a whisper—"it's just the opposite. We haven't spoken to each other since Leningrad and I'd prefer to keep things that way. But that's another story. Look—the old lady is really quite ill. Circulatory problems, I gather. Stress tends to aggravate it. Isabel asked me to ask you, because she thinks we're friends."

Stern threw the towel across his shoulder, snatched up his kit, and started out. Thomas fell into step beside him.

Outside, the sun, already well above the treetops, momentarily blinded them. People had already finished their breakfasts and were standing about aimlessly in the track bed beside the dining car. Several additional truckloads of fresh troops had recently arrived and were being deployed round the area. Supplies were being off-loaded from the trucks, while another motor-rifle unit that had been out there several days was being loaded on.

"Just pop in for a minute," Thomas persisted. "It won't take long."

"There's nothing I can do for her, I tell you."

"I quite agree. But as a kindness to an old lady, you can at least make some effort to show concern."

Stern stood there baffled and fuming.

"If anything were to happen to her, Peter, it would be on your head."

"Oh, Christ. Where is she, anyway?"

"There's a good fellow." The hint of a smirk flashed at the corners of the Englishman's mouth. "Come along. I'll take you."

Stern was actually alarmed when he saw the old condesa. She lay stretched out along the banquette, a pillow beneath her head and a blanket covering her. The silk straps of a slip drooping from her fleshy shoulders indicated that she had not yet dressed for the day.

When they entered the compartment, Isabel greeted them with a worried glance. Consuelo was sitting in the corner of the opposite banquette, whimpering into a handkerchief.

"Thank you for coming," Isabel murmured. She stood aside to let them enter.

Stern nodded to Consuelo, whose large, vacant doe eyes were smudged with mascara.

"How are you this morning, señora?" Stern heard in his voice the bogus cheer of the doctor on his daily rounds. "I hear you're a bit under the weather."

Stern's alarm deepened as he spoke. The old lady was parchment pale, and though the cabin was uncomfortably warm, she was shivering beneath the wool blanket. She smiled weakly up at him, then murmured something. He stooped down to hear better.

"*Siento mucho perturbarlo . . .*" The faintly sour air of dentures rose from her bluish lips. Stern looked up at Isabel.

"She is sorry to have disturbed you," Isabel explained.

Stern smiled down at her. "No problem at all, señora. I shall be seeing Colonel Dunskoi today regarding the matter of your husband." Even as the words streamed effortlessly from him, he tried to stop himself. But the pathetic look of gratitude on the old lady's face was too much for him. Once committed, he strode forward grandly like some august personage who could alter destinies by the stroke of a pen.

The old lady kissed his hand as he made ready to go. Even Consuelo broke off momentarily her stifled weeping.

"I've requested that a physician see her," Thomas remarked to Isabel in hushed whispers as they stood at the open door. She ignored him, addressing instead her remarks to Stern.

"My father will be deeply grateful to you."

When the cabin door had closed behind them and they were walking back down the corridor, the enormity of what he had promised suddenly dawned upon Stern. "What the hell am I supposed to do now?"

"I guess you go and see Dunskoi." Thomas shot him his off-kilter smile. "Don't worry—I'll go with you if you'd like."

"We'd better see about setting up an appointment."

"No sweat, old man." The Englishman gloated above his mustache. "I've already made one for two P.M. today."

Keith Wales had always been successful with women. The thought that he might someday be otherwise had never occurred to him. For a relatively young man of twenty-two, he had amassed more than his share of trophies, and in the matter of Silvana Lambrusto he had no reason to assume that the result of his efforts would be any different. The fact that she was married seemed scarcely to have entered into any of his thinking.

Consequently, when Silvana failed to respond to the numerous signals and various body language he beamed her way—devices that had been virtually fail-safe in the past—he was baffled, then later angry, as though she had somehow betrayed him.

In Leningrad he had followed her about everywhere; however, nothing had come of his attentions there. Still, he had reason to believe, or so he imagined, that there was an understanding between them.

Now, out in the big somber birch forests between Finland and Russia, all the while his ardor heightened, so did his frustration. He limped after her like a wounded hare. In her presence he moped and skulked, struck sullen attitudes because he believed that was attractive and she would notice.

She didn't. An alert, vivacious lady, she noticed many things around her, but not Keith. Her almost blithe indifference to his carefully studied moods, always successful with younger, less experienced women, had begun to drive him to desperation. In plain point of fact, in the matter of Keith Wales, Silvana was manifesting signs of boredom, as if all of his "disaffected-youth" poses, so amusing at first, had worn a bit thin and he was now well on his way to becoming a nuisance.

Poor Keith hadn't the perspicacity or, for that matter, the wit to recognize his fall from grace. He thought of it all as female guile designed to arouse him even more, so his antidote for her playing hard to get escalated into recklessness. The idea that they were in a hostage situation, which had the potential for great peril, did not yet appear to have penetrated his thinking. He thought of the situation as a temporary inconvenience, but one that could conceivably work to his advantage. He was, in short, a young man smitten, besotted with a woman, admittedly a very attractive one, ten years his senior, and he was utterly mystified that she had failed to collapse at his feet in gratitude.

Keith and Silvana had been strolling round the far side of the train—the side where the forest came practically up to the coach windows. It was approximately the same spot where, the morning before, Stern had blundered into the path of the two motor-rifle guards.

Sandro and Sonia had been summoned along with some of the others up to Vyborg for interrogation. Silvana was certain that she would be called that afternoon. She had been walking slightly forward of him, keeping up a string of lively chatter to help her subdue her uneasiness at the prospect of an interview with the colonel.

She did not like the colonel, she said. "That one," she called him. He made her uncomfortable with his "slow eyes and low, smoky voice."

As she spoke, Keith responded in monosyllables with an occasional nod for punctuation. His eyes kept scanning the woods, glancing about and over his shoulder to see if they were being observed. Idyllic and lovely as it was, the spot was unusually deserted.

Walking behind her, pretending to follow her talk, he watched the faint sway of her hips beneath her skirt. A thin-strapped sandal tended to heighten the elegance of her ankle, and the pale French pink polish on her toes aroused him strangely.

He touched her shoulder. She turned, unprepared for the force of his body as they joined. His mouth came down hard on hers. It was one of those bruising kisses, not particularly graceful, accompanied by gagging sounds and the assault of hands.

She stood there imprisoned in his arms, writhing and kicking his ankles, trying to prize his hands from her. He made a series of moaning sounds. Her eyes were open all the while it was going on, and she had the sensation of being forced to witness something comical and vaguely embarrassing. Writhing and struggling to evade his hands, she watched with horror, just over his shoulder, the solitary figure of Max Conti round the corner of the train and stroll into her field of vision.

About a hundred feet distant, he had started down toward them, still not having spotted them. Watching him, transfixed with horror, she went limp in Wales's arms. Interpreting that as surrender, he became more aroused. It was then that Max saw them. He stopped dead in his tracks, and she could see quite clearly the expression in his eyes. It was not surprise she saw there, or even embarrassment. It was more like disgust, as though he had just witnessed the lowest form of betrayal.

With the palms of her hands pressed flush against Wales's chest, she thrust hard, prying her mouth loose from his.

"Max," she cried out, but he'd already turned and was striding quickly back in the direction from which he'd come.

"Max. Max." She knew he'd heard, but he wouldn't deign to turn.

Wiping her smeared mouth with the back of her wrist, she gaped at Wales. She spat several times on the ground, as though trying to rid her mouth of some unpleasant taste.

"Pig!" She struck him repeatedly with her tiny fists while he tried to shield his face. "Stupid pig."

He seemed stunned and hurt, and suddenly very young. He tried to say something, but to no avail. She'd already turned and was fleeing down the track in the direction in which Max had disappeared.

Serja Inusen had started to cry. The young Russian lieutenant seated opposite her appeared greatly annoyed. She'd been called up to Vyborg that morning for interrogation and had naturally assumed that they had summoned her in order to formally charge her with theft.

She arrived with a paper bag in which she carried the cake of soap, the towel, and the several sheets of stationery she'd taken from her room at the hotel. She was now prepared to return the articles, apologize, and throw herself on their mercy.

But once the interrogation had begun in the tiny, stuffy barrack office, it became clear that all the lieutenant wished to discuss was her currency statement. They had gone over it three times and still the Finnish girl had been unable to balance the statement. No matter how she computed it, it invariably turned out that she had in her pocket nearly thirty dollars' worth of Finn marks more than her statement claimed she was entitled to.

On entering the USSR, all visitors are required to file a statement declaring the exact amount of money they are bringing in, specifying traveler's checks, types of currency, and exact denominations. At that point the Russian customs official will also insist upon an itemization of all jewelry that is brought in. They will then also check each article against the itemization.

On departure, a traveler is required to cash in all paper rubles at the Douane in Vyborg. Travelers often hold back a few bronze kopecks as souvenirs, but no paper tender is permitted to leave the USSR because the Soviets are deadly fearful of the possibility of their currency being counterfeited.

The customs officials will then add up the remaining cash to see whether a person has exactly as much as he declared on entry, minus what he converted to rubles at official exchange rates, for which bank vouchers must be shown. All this is to discover whether an individual has been trading money illegally on the black market, which is rampant in the streets of Moscow and Leningrad, and is a crime the Soviets treat most severely.

It was this accounting that Serja could not make jibe. Adding up her vouchers and subtracting them from the sum she'd originally declared, taking into account also the remaining rubles she had converted to Finn marks at the little station bank at Vyborg, she could still not justify the fact that she was leaving Russia with thirty-nine more Finn marks than her expenses in the Soviet Union justified.

Each time she went over the statement under the stern, disapproving gaze of the lieutenant, she grew increasingly rattled. He reviewed her vouchers and sales slips for the few paltry items she'd picked up as souvenirs in the state shops and the huge Ptimorska Department Store on the Nevsky Prospect. With each successive review of the declaration, the young lieutenant's voice grew sharper. At last he suggested that she might have converted some of her

Finn marks on the streets for rates higher than those officially quoted. It was at that point that she started to cry.

"You are certain you only exchanged money at your hotel," he persisted.

"Yes—I told you so."

"Then how come it is you have this additional thirty-nine Finn marks in your purse?"

She shook her head back and forth despairingly. "I don't know."

Their talk was in Russian. Like many Finns, Serja was fluent in the language.

"Maybe you have another exchange voucher in your pocket," the lieutenant persisted. "Look."

"I have looked," she snapped at him through welling tears, and was shocked at her own cheekiness. "But I will look again."

She went rummaging in her bag. It was a deep straw bag, choked to the gunnels with a staggering array of seemingly useless odds and ends. There were a number of inside pockets in the bag. She unzipped these and rifled frantically through them. She carried a wallet in the bag; this too was full of individual sections and secret pockets. Ransacking the bag, keenly aware of his growing impatience, she grew panicky at one point, nearly dumping the contents of it on his desk.

"I don't have it," she cried.

He cocked an eye at the paper bag. "What's in there?"

"What's in where?" By this time she was hopelessly rattled.

"The paper bag. There—right next to your hand. The one you brought in."

"Oh," she said somewhat vaguely, as though its presence there were a mystery to her as well.

She lifted the bag and emptied it on his desk. The towel and the soap cake clattered out onto his desk. The stationery fluttered gently downward, landing not far from the other articles. They were all marked clearly with the identifying monogram and letterhead of the Hotel Prebaltiskaya.

The young officer looked at her shrewdly and shook his head. A loud wail issued from somewhere deep inside the girl. It was a pitiful sound, filling the room with an air of inconsolable grieving. In the next moment, her slight, bony little girl's figure was racked with sobs.

"Stop that," the young man fumed. He was embarrassed and actually a bit alarmed. There were people sitting outside the door, more passengers waiting to be interrogated. He feared the impression those piteous sounds might have on them. "For God's sake"—he wrung his hands—"get hold of yourself."

She started to cram all of her belongings back into the straw bag, but only succeeded in spilling more.

"Sit there," the young man snapped. "Sit there. Leave it alone now. I'll take care of it. Just give me your declaration."

She was barely able to hand the paper to him. He snatched it from her, pulled a fresh form from his desk drawer, and while she sat there slumped in her seat, he completed a fresh declaration, using partly her figures and concocting the rest himself.

"Sign this." He thrust the form along with a pen beneath her nose. She started to read it.

"Don't bother reading it. It's fine."

Nodding her head and whimpering softly to herself, she scratched her name along the dotted line. When she'd finished, he snatched the declaration back, stamped it with a large imposing seal, and thrust it back at her.

"Put it in a safe place now, or you'll never get out of here."

She was about to thank him but he pointed to the door. "Go."

Before she could reply, he rose and propelled her gently toward an exit. She moved dumbly, like a robot.

"Next," he bellowed to the sergeant major outside the door.

"Let me see if I understand you correctly."

"By all means."

"You say that because I am a chemist, I am therefore automatically a prime suspect in this . . . this theft of classified documents?"

"Not simply a chemist," Colonel Dunskoi hastened to interject, "but a chemist who happens to be a specialist in the area of synthesizing fuels—nuclear fuels, to be more precise, of the type used in the most up-to-date submarines."

"That's all quite true," Kyle Van Meegrin conceded.

Dunskoi smiled with evident satisfaction. "Of course it's true. I have it here on your visa application, as well as on the dossier that was prepared on you."

"So, yes, it is true. I admit it." Van Meegrin was somewhat chagrined. "But if I'm a spy, why would I tell you all of that on my visa application?"

"Precisely." Dunskoi tossed his head back triumphantly. "That is what is so brilliant. Who would suspect anything so classically obvious?"

"I assure you, it's just a coincidence."

"Coincidence?" Dunskoi's head shot back again. He slapped his knee and laughed that gruff, raspy, rather musical Slavic laughter. "A brilliant coincidence, I would add. Brilliantly conceived. Brilliantly executed. You see, Dr. Van Meegrin . . ."

The colonel breezed along, just as he had been doing for the past several hours, making it all up as he went, impressed by his own rather considerable powers of invention. From time to time he lowered his voice as if to emphasize the gravity of the situation. His manners were exquisitely civil, even sympathetic. It suggested to Van Meegrin a surgeon conveying to his patient the most dire prognosis.

As Dunskoi continued to spin this elaborate web, he was fully aware that everything he was saying to the young Dutchman was in direct contradiction to what he had told Grant Shapley earlier that morning. Similarly, much of what he would say to the others he had yet to interview would directly refute everything he was now telling Van Meegrin.

Certain that, given the chance, all those who'd been interrogated would seize the first opportunity to compare notes, he was determined that they find no pattern of consistency in anything they'd been told. It was, after all, his job to sow confusion, and in several hours, he estimated, as the heat and confinement wore on, their confusion would become exquisite.

"Ask yourself, my dear Doctor," Dunskoi chatted on amiably, "as a hypothetical Western agent with the task of spiriting classified information on synthetic fuels out of the Soviet Union, whom would the Soviet authorities find a more probable courier—an expert in the actual field of synthesizing fuel, or a person with a completely unrelated background?"

"The latter, of course," Van Meegrin replied immediately.

Dunskoi smiled a smile of intense personal satisfaction. "Incidentally. By your own tongue, you convict yourself."

When Van Meegrin left the office twenty minutes later, he was more than just a bit shaken.

"I've never heard anything so ludicrous in my life," said Jean Blaylock. She was seated in the chair recently vacated by Van Meegrin. "By the way, how did you find out I was a member of the American Socialist party?"

"Quite simple. The names of all members are forwarded to us by party headquarters in Washington."

"So that's why you confiscated my passport? Because my name's on your list?"

"Exactly. But your passport was not confiscated. We merely took it to verify that you are the same Blaylock whose name appears on our list. It shall be returned to you at the proper time, assuming . . ."

"That I've been cleared of these wild charges that I've stolen classified documents."

Colonel Dunskoi's head had begun to throb. "I have told you several times." He enunciated each word with great care and an air of utter weariness. "You are not charged with anything. You are, however, a key suspect."

"Bullshit."

The colonel blinked several times as though he were trying to rid his eye of a mote. "What could be more logical, Miss Blaylock? Or more clever? Stop to think. Who would ever think that U.S. Central Intelligence would utilize the services of a known, registered socialist as a courier to smuggle classified material out of the Soviet Union? Who would be less suspect, I ask you?"

Arms folded across her chest, Jean smiled boldly, and stirred in her chair. "Bullshit."

Again came that tiny tic above the colonel's brow. This time his heavy-lidded eyes closed, and he sighed. "This word you are so fond of, Miss Blaylock," he spoke in a tone of weary forbearance. "You must forgive me. My

English is rather limited. I gather this word you enjoy repeating so often is some kind of American gutter term?"

"On the contrary." Jean's smile grew more taunting. "It's used in the very best society."

"Ah—I see. We have no such word in Russian. The closest we come to it, I believe, is *govno.*" He pronounced it with a rich, almost liquid sibilance. "However, only the scum of the earth use it in Soviet society. And among women, it is simply unheard of." His voice, as he spoke, never rose. But there was something decidedly cautionary about it that even Jean did not fail to note.

"I appreciate the fact that you are a liberated Western woman," Dunskoi went on in his quiet, reasonable way. "But for purposes of our discussion here, I suggest you eliminate all such usage in my presence. You see, I am not quite so liberated as you, and if you persist in this manner, I shall be obliged to treat you without the typical respect afforded a lady in the Soviet Union."

Once again Jean stirred in her chair. The facade of amusement so evident in her smile before showed signs of beginning to crumble. "Is this official party policy?" she snapped.

The colonel smiled gallantly. "This is official Colonel Dunskoi policy. The policy of this office."

The polite imperturbability of his manner had begun to take its toll on her. "I am not accustomed to censorship."

"That is evident from your quite adolescent speech."

She ignored the remark. "May I ask what proof you have that I stole these alleged documents?"

"No proof whatever."

"And your suspicions are based solely on the fact that I'm a member of the American Socialist party?"

"You would not be first party member to sell your services to a hostile government for the right price."

"I am no longer a socialist, however. Or for that matter, a communist."

"But you belong to the American Socialist party."

"I joined it in college as a protest."

"Protest of what?"

"Of American policies in Southeast Asia. We all did. It was the thing to do. Since then I have modified my thinking."

Dunskoi drummed his short stubby fingers on the desktop. "How so?"

"I am no longer technically a socialist. I now see myself more as a kind of ideologue for a socialism of the future. A socialism that is still evolving."

"Ideologue?" Dunskoi pretended to be impressed.

Jean bristled. "That amuses you?"

"I am always amused when wealthy people who have never known a minute's privation become defenders of the downtrodden."

"The downtrodden are not sufficiently educated to even know they are downtrodden."

"For a socialist, even an ex-socialist," Dunskoi continued in his gently taunting manner, "you take an extremely elitist position."

Jean's jaunty smile began to wane and her voice was faintly tremulous. "The only real hope for the downtrodden must come from people who have had certain advantages."

"Like yourself?"

She paused, as if unwilling to commit herself. "Very well. If you'd like, then. Like myself."

Dunskoi smiled. He appeared for a moment to be thinking about something else. Then suddenly he was back with her in the room—substantial, imposing, all brisk efficiency. "Forgive me, Miss Blaylock, I don't think you possess the gifts of self-deception necessary to be a truly believable ideologue."

"What do you suppose I am, then," she lashed back. "A double agent? A spy?"

"That is, of course, possible. You are certainly simple enough." He saw her about to retort but barged right on. "I have met dozens of people like yourself, most in the United States, which is a rich country and can afford to encourage a certain amount of eccentricity. To me, I see a wealthy malcontent, a chronic what-do-you-call-it—bickerer. You disapprove of *status quo,* whatever it might be. Like a spoiled child, you despise all authority and cannot tell the difference between authority that is constructive and necessary and that which is merely repressive. You are self-indulgent and rich enough to support your prolonged adolescence. Like most adolescents, you also have atrocious manners in public." He smiled suddenly and disarmingly. "Otherwise, I'm sure you are a very nice person."

She sat there unspeaking for a time, watching him, marshaling her thoughts and gathering strength. She had a sense now of having lost ground and being under a strong obligation to recover it. "I refuse to be reduced to a stereotype by someone like you." She struggled to control her voice. "Just because I am fortunate enough to have a bit of money does not mean that I'm irrelevant, that my thoughts are trivial. To my mind, you're a worse elitist than the most class-conscious, grasping capitalist. You and this fake egalitarianism of yours with all of its special perks for special people. At least in the United States, we are not hypocrites. We are a class society and we don't pretend we are anything else."

Dunskoi sat stolidly in his chair waiting for her to finish. When at last she did, tears had started to well in her eyes. She punched at them with her fists.

"You are prime suspect in crime against Soviet Union. I shall want to question you further."

She'd finished crying and was now smoldering. "When do I get my passport back?"

"At the proper time." Dunskoi turned away coldly, fiddling with papers on his desk. "You may leave now."

"I want my passport back."

"You may leave now." His tone was brusque and clipped.

"Give me my passport." She stood up and shouted.

Dunskoi pressed a buzzer beside his desk. Instantly a strapping guard appeared.

"Show this young woman out." Dunskoi spoke in his curt, authoritative manner, then roared out with unaccustomed rage, "Next."

The Green Train had begun to smell atrociously, particularly the coach where passengers were compelled to spend a large part of their day. Above those areas where people lived cheek by jowl, a haze hung, yellowish in color and almost palpable—a virtual rainbow of smells comprising everything from poor ventilation and human sweat to unwashed laundry, unbathed bodies, moldy upholstery, and toilets overworked and inadequately serviced.

In warm weather it was worse. The walls of the cars sweated, the air inside became leaden and unmoving. A whole nauseous concert of odors combined to produce a stench of unholy, almost epic dimension.

By eleven A.M. the sun was murderously hot. Keenly aware of the bad feelings generated by the confinement of the day before, the Soviets appeared to relent somewhat. Unable to openly proclaim a softening of attitude, for this would be an admission of wrongdoing, they instead simply permitted people to wander on and off the train at will, and stroll freely about the area just so long as they did not venture beyond the perimeters clearly demarked by the motor-rifle troops.

The armed guards and police dogs, while always present, had become somewhat less conspicuous. It was not that there were fewer of them; on the contrary, people had counted three new truckloads that had come in early that morning. But they had been discreetly deployed to areas of the forest in ways less visible, and certainly less inflammatory to the detainees.

A group of passengers sprawling about in the grass had found shade under a border of trees.

"What day is it, anyway?" Grant Shapley asked.

Paul Blanton consulted a small card calendar in his wallet. "Thursday, the eighteenth. I should be in federal court in New York trying an antitrust case."

Shapley checked his wristwatch. "In approximately twenty minutes I'd be starting a seminar for doctoral candidates in paleontological geology."

"I hope they don't wait around too long for you, Professor," Wilma Shapley joked.

"They well might. They're doctoral candidates. I wouldn't give you a plugged nickel for their common sense."

Shapley laughed heartily. He did it so ingenuously and with such evident zest that the others roared with pleasure.

"We were supposed to be in San Francisco two days ago," Janet Kariolainen said. "Our daughter's due to give birth tomorrow." Suddenly and without warning she started to cry. "I don't understand this." She shook her head back and forth, choking back sobs. "I really just don't understand all this."

"This sort of behavior is not acceptable in the Soviet Union."

"But surely you have the occasional lunatic?"

"Of course. But we don't inflict them on the general public the way you do. We keep them off the streets."

"Not some of the streets I've seen."

Colonel Dunskoi's brow arched.

"Sorry." Thomas grinned foolishly. "Merely an aside."

"A what?"

"Nothing. Nothing at all."

Stern watched uneasily as the mood of the meeting continued to deteriorate. "The point of the matter, Colonel," he quietly interjected, "is that we're all quite concerned about Señora Gonzaga. She won't leave her cabin. She's taken no nourishment in nearly two days. She's an elderly woman, not in robust health."

Dunskoi riffled impatiently through papers on his desktop. He was in no mood for conciliation. Still smarting from his encounter with Jean Blaylock shortly before, he'd had a second call from his wife to report that the situation with their daughter had worsened over the past twenty-four hours—not as a result of actions taken by the authorities, but those taken, imprudently, by the girl herself.

"What is wrong with the old woman?"Dunskoi grumbled while making a great show of signing official papers.

"Something with the heart, I gather," Thomas replied. "It would be quite awkward if something were to happen to her while in captivity."

"Captivity?" Dunskoi bristled. "What captivity? There is no captivity here."

"Of course not," Thomas stammered. "I didn't mean to suggest . . ."

"Free to come and go. Talk to friends. What captivity?"

The Englishman flushed, but he had made his point. He had little doubt it had registered with the colonel.

"And awkward for whom?" Dunskoi went on heatedly. "Awkward for her, or awkward for me?" He had caught the implied threat in Thomas' words. "More awkward for her, I think, than for me."

"I didn't mean to suggest any specific unpleasantness," Thomas hastened to explain.

"Unpleasantness." The colonel gazed at him as if he were mad. "What possible unpleasantness?"

"Well . . ." Thomas shifted uneasily in his chair. "Charges. Recriminations. That sort of thing."

"Charges of what? There has been no crime. No improprieties."

"I only meant . . ." Thomas swallowed hard. "It might be awkward . . . difficult to explain if something were to . . ."

"Explain to whom?" Dunskoi's voice rose with growing irritation. "I don't explain to anyone."

By that time Thomas was beet red. "I certainly didn't mean to suggest . . ." He started then, as a bold diplomatic ploy, to speak in Russian. But the colonel quickly put an end to that.

"Please to speak English. There is another party present here."

"Of course," Thomas blustered. "Of course. I'm sorry, Peter."

It was clear now, even to Thomas, that he was in over his head. He scarcely protested when Stern, of his own volition, decided to jump in. "I think what Mr. Thomas is trying to say is that the poor woman is beside herself with worry, and it would be only humane to relieve her anxiety."

Dunskoi sat hunched and silent for what seemed an inordinate length of time. He appeared to weigh Stern's words, playing them out to their logical conclusion in some elaborate scenario formulated in his head. His irritation, his huge distaste for the matter, was evident. At last he sighed and swiveled a quarter-turn in his chair. "I am so weary of this word 'humane.' "

Both Stern and Thomas leaned toward him at once.

"What makes you think you have to tell me what is humane and what is not? I know what is humane as well as you. Why do you people think that only you know what is humane, and that you have some obligation to come here and teach us what it is?"

"I don't think Mr. Stern intended his remarks politically," Thomas strove to clarify the matter.

"I was speaking on the personal level only," Stern piped up. "I was not implying some larger political context."

"I know perfectly well what you were implying." Dunskoi, still facing the bare wall, fumed in his seat. "As a military attaché for three years at the United Nations, I recall seeing people eat garbage out of trashcans in New York City, and sleep in streets during the dead of winter. Yet you feel no inconsistency, no hypocrisy, telling us what is and what is not humane—pfui." He waved a hand as though he were fanning away bad air.

Stern lowered his head and stared hard at the floor. "What you say is perfectly true. There is starvation in America. But that is only a small percentage of the total population."

"If it is only two people"—Dunskoi pounded the desktop—"it is two too many." Pencils rolled about, papers fluttered before his flying fist. He spun sharply back and pointed a finger accusingly at Stern. "In Soviet Union we do not have as much as you. But no one—not one person—sleeps in gutter or eats out of garbage cans. So do not talk to me about *humane*. Clean up your own mess first."

Stern felt a profound sense of helplessness. Expecting at any moment to be invited to leave, he was distantly aware of the clicking of numbers being di-

Stern felt himself flagging. "Not at all."

Dunskoi seemed delighted by the exchange. He plucked up the official form before him and proceeded to read aloud, his eyes arching periodically over the rim of his glasses at Stern. "Peter Stern. Age fifty. Address 258 East Sixty-third Street, New York City. Citizenship, U.S. Parents born Würzburg, Germany. Immigrated to U.S. 1922. Marital status—separated. Two children. You served in U.S. Army during years 1955–1957. You achieved the rank of captain. Served in Germany as an ordnance expert . . ." Dunskoi glanced up at him over the frames of his glasses. "Ordnance expert?"

"That's right."

"Demolitions?"

"Some."

"You worked eighteen years for a large advertising agency in New York. Retired three years ago. Recently divorced from wife, Constance, forty-six years old. . . ."

"Where did you get all that information?" Stern asked.

"You are irritated I have this information." Dunskoi laughed gleefully. "Part of it you were good enough to furnish on your passport and visa applications. The other part . . ." He smiled slyly. "Like you, we have our sources."

"I see," Stern replied curtly.

Noting his displeasure, Dunskoi relented somewhat. "I'm really quite amazed at your naiveté, Mr. Stern. Of course, we check thoroughly the background of every individual who applies for visa to Soviet Union. With the political climate of the world as it is today, we would be fools not to." The colonel grinned at him. "I see you are not entirely happy to learn that you are the object of research." He lingered over that final word tauntingly. "Why did you fail to provide information requested on your application?"

"Information?"

"Pertaining to religious preference." He held the application up, pointing out to Stern the space left blank.

At first puzzled, Stern then flushed. "Well, what if I did?" he blustered. "The question is impertinent, and simply none of your business." Even as it all came out, he was amazed at his brashness.

So too was Dunskoi. His jaw dropped and he peered oddly at Stern. "Your religious preference is of little importance to me. Personally, I wouldn't care if you were a Hottentot. I only noted this because, aside from that single rather unimportant omission, the rest of your dossier is crammed with information voluntarily proffered." Dunskoi cracked a shrewd little grin at him. "Odd, no?"

"I'm not Jewish, if that's what you're suggesting."

The colonel's head tilted sharply sidewards. "I beg your pardon?"

"I said I am not Jewish, despite whatever you might think."

"I'm not aware that I was thinking anything of the sort. But now that you mention it, Stern is certainly a Jewish name."

"Many Germans who are Lutheran have the same name," Stern parried sharply. "I happen to be Lutheran. As a boy I sang in a Lutheran choir in St. Louis."

The colonel was clearly baffled. "Why did you not then say so on your visa?"

"As I said, the question is impertinent and none of your business."

Dunskoi's frown deepened. "Same question appears on U.S. passport application."

"That's right. I didn't answer it there either." Stern was miffed by the colonel's evident disbelief.

Dunskoi probed a bit deeper. "Nothing wrong with being Jewish."

"Nothing at all. However, as I told you, I'm not. I'm Lutheran."

"Can you prove?"

Stern's jaw dropped. "I beg your pardon?"

"Can you prove? Have you papers? Church-membership cards? Affidavits?"

"Certainly not. Why would I carry anything like affidavits and papers around?"

Dunskoi's frown of disbelief melted into that of an impudent smile.

"Ah, yes. I see now. You are suggesting that if you are indeed Jewish, you would therefore be treated somewhat differently than the others on the train?"

"It wouldn't surprise me."

Dunskoi pondered that a moment. "Worse, I take it, than the others?"

"Certainly worse rather than better." Stern watched his smile harden, and his earlier amiability turn. "But I tell you, I am not Jewish."

"So you keep saying," Dunskoi said pointedly. "In Soviet Union we treat Jews no different from anyone else. But I can see from expression on your face, it is hopeless to convince you."

There was a void in which they both groped now for footing.

"You know, Mr. Stern—Dunskoi tilted back in his chair and crossed his legs—"you and I could sit here and talk for hours, speaking to each other, exchanging nothing but the complete unadulterated truth, and neither of us would believe a word each other had said."

Stern pondered that. "It's very sad, isn't it?"

"For us all." Dunskoi nodded.

A long, troubled silence fell over the room. From beyond the draped windows came the voices of soldiers drilling in the courtyard below.

"Assuming you were Jewish," Dunskoi continued.

"But I am not."

"Granted." Dunskoi waved the objection aside. "But assuming you were, I could spend hours here, give you written guarantees that despite your religion, you would be treated no differently from anyone else . . ."

"I would still not believe you."

Dunskoi smiled. His drooping, lidded eyes gave him the baleful look of a bloodhound. "You see how impossible the situation is?"

Stern did not answer. They appeared to have reached an impasse. The colonel stared at the ceiling, scratching his chin whiskers abstractedly.

"It is my duty to inform you, Mr. Stern"—Dunskoi's eyes scanned the ceiling as he spoke—"we have now narrowed our investigation to three or four individuals who we believe have attempted to spirit classified information out of the Soviet Union. Of those three or four, you are at the very top of the list."

It was as if Stern had always known it, had lived it over and over again in the innumerable bad dreams that had marked his latter years; events turning inexorably and capriciously, merely on a whim, against him, and finding himself powerless to make any plausible defense in his own behalf.

"When did you decide I was the prime suspect—when you decided I was Jewish?"

Dunskoi ignored the remark.

"Why me especially?" Stern persisted.

"Because you are so improbable. Such a pleasant, likable chap that it seems preposterous that you could be involved in anything so idiotic as stealing information for an intelligence-gathering agency."

"Then you admit this is all a bit farfetched?"

"Of course—but no one has ever accused espionage of being particularly logical. And than again, who knows? Perhaps we have selected you as our prime suspect because, as you say, your name happens to sound Jewish."

They regarded each other silently. For a moment they were like two men who had been sharing an ice floe in the middle of an Arctic sea. The floe had suddenly cracked and parted, separating them. The cold dark sea had surged in between them, lapping at the edges of the ice, and now they watched as the distance between them continued to widen, and the darkness came on.

Shortly after lunch the temperature round the train soared to the hundred-degree mark. The heat inside the coaches had grown unbearable. So unbearable, in fact, that the Soviets relented and did not order the passengers back into the cabins for the afternoon.

A short time later, to the amazement of everyone, a directive came down from Vyborg inviting passengers to cool off with a swim in the pond not far from the train. In those suffocating temperatures very few people failed to leap at the offer. Accepting it, however, presented something of a problem. Few of them there had bathing suits, and those who were fortunate enough to have one in their luggage were not permitted back on the train to get it. The captain claimed that they were still carrying out a number of "special inspections" within each carriage, and under no circumstances would passengers be permitted back on the train before those inspections were completed.

The alternative to bathing suits was either no bathing suits or underclothes. It simply came down to a question of how hot you were and just how desperately you needed relief.

For the Americans, particularly the more provincial types like the Kecks, the notion of publicly disrobing on the beach was unthinkable. Even more sophisticated types like the Blantons, as much as they craved the relief of cooling waters, found it hard to accommodate themselves. Less conventional types like the Shapleys and Jean Blaylock had no great problem with partial disrobing and rolling up of trousers and such.

For most of the Europeans, of course, the idea of public nudity on a beach raised scarcely an eyebrow. In short order, therefore, a goodly number of Intour Group 409 were frolicking on the beach before each other in various degrees of undress. Seeing their pleasure, a number of those like the Blantons, for instance, who initially held back, finally abandoned all modesty along with their outer dress, and plunged directly into the spirit of the thing with the others.

At a somewhat more distant point on the pond, a number of off-duty Russian soldiers were coping with the heat in precisely the same manner. Just a short time before, these same men, moving smartly about the train with rifles and sidearms, barking orders and climbing all over the coaches, were enough to chill the blood. Divested of weapons and uniforms, however, shorn of all marks of either professional or national identity, attired in bathing suits and in some cases merely underwear, they looked much like any other high-spirited youths—boys in their late teens and early twenties, noisy, raucous, howling and splashing each other, ogling the younger women passengers shamelessly.

Several had climbed the tree with the tire that hung from a branch above the water. Screaming at the top of their lungs, they swung far out over the pond, dropping through space in awkward, tumbling rolls that ended in great pratfall splashes.

A few of the more daring had begun to show off for the delight of the passengers, swinging back and forth in ever-greater arcs above the water. At the highest point of their swings, they would let go and hurtle outward into space in the direction of the passengers, who watched, delighted, the graceful trajectory of the falling bodies slipping below the murky surface of the pond. A moment of anticipation followed until the divers' heads reappeared, to be greeted by a burst of applause. A large aluminum tureen of lemonade had been sent down from the dining car, along with thick slabs of a sweetish heavy cake made of cornmeal. Shortly they were all partaking of it.

Undaunted by distance, Serja Inusen swam far and clear of all the others. Slight and fair, she had the look of a twig floating on the water. Her skin milk white, and with that property of weightlessness and motion, she could move across a body of water yet leave its surface completely unstirred. She skimmed noiselessly along like some wondrous tiny waterfowl, her chin held high above the water, her lower lip curled above the upper, into a funny little grimace, as if by that action she could keep the rest of herself dry.

She had been swimming like that, paddling about for twenty minutes or so, until, suddenly, she realized she was not alone. Out of the corner of her eye she caught a movement. Slight, barely perceptible, on closer inspection it turned out to be a head bobbing on the surface only twenty feet behind her.

A voice called to her softly in Russian. Frightened, she started back toward the shore. Then she saw the face of a man who, swimming swiftly, had neatly placed himself directly between her and the shore.

He swam closer, so much so that she could see that his hair was blond and cut very short, almost to the scalp.

"Hey, *mushka*," he teased her in Russian, his large horsey teeth grinning foolishly. "Hey, princess," he cried as she started to swim away. "Don't go. Wait. I'll teach you to swim." She recognized him at once as the lieutenant who had fixed her currency statement the morning before. He swam near, and dove beneath her, pulling at her toes as he passed by. She squealed and kicked.

"Idiot," she hissed when he resurfaced, snapping the water from his hair. She marveled at her boldness. Had he been in his uniform, as he was earlier that morning, she'd have been terrified. Now, with the two of them out there, swimming about together in the warm, silken liquid of the pond, he made her laugh.

"You can't count, but I can teach you to swim," he taunted.

"I swim better than you," she retorted.

"Come play with me, *mushka*."

"Go play with your own friends."

She turned and started to swim back. He looked surprised and a trifle hurt, and so she did not protest when he swam along beside her.

Several of the Russian soldiers had been watching them from the far shore and now they shrieked and made catcalls at the two swimmers, hooting a mixture of encouragement and ridicule at their comrade. The two of them glided along, unspeaking, through the inverted images of treetops reflected from the shore, the young man paddling in wide, drifting circles round her, the sleek shorn dome of his head looking like that of a wet otter.

For an instant it appeared they were utterly alone, motionless as frieze figures graven on some antique entablature. Fifty feet or so from the shore the shouts and laughter of bathers wafted out to them across the water. In the next moment he swam directly at her, brushing her lightly on the cheek with his lips as he did so. It was such a shy, clumsy, boyish thing, she laughed.

"Good-bye, *mushka*." He smiled and turned abruptly, swimming back to the other side, where his mates stood and cheered.

When Serja climbed back up on the shore, her fellow passengers applauded her while she blushed and pretended to be furious. It had more the look just then of a day's outing in the country, amid a group of earthy peasants, rather than a pleasant break in the grim daily routine of political hostages.

Of all the fifty-odd passengers of Intour Group 409, only the Kecks had declined the invitation to swim at the pond. They sat, instead, by themselves in a shaded grove out of sight of the others, but not out of earshot.

Mr. Keck had begun the day in his invariable dark suit, appropriately shirted and cravated. But at last even he relented (with the approval of Mrs. Keck) and removed his jacket and tie. He spread the jacket out in the tall grass so that they both might sit on it. She in turn removed her shoes and stretched her toes in her stocking feet.

They sat quietly, not speaking, back to back, stiff and awkward, not at all bewildered at finding themselves alone. Hadn't it always been that way? Alone. It was a melancholy picture, her staring upward into the branches of the trees, Mr. Keck staring down at his hands clasped uselessly in his lap, the two of them so quiet, so profoundly alone, even as the sultry air in the grove all about them rang with the playful cries of swimmers in the pond nearby.

Madam Mukherjee would not remove her sari under any circumstances. Hoisting Baby Muk on her shoulder, she waded boldly into the pond with it on. Thirty or so feet out, she was standing hip-high in the water, swirling the squealing child through the water while the vivid scarlet madras of the sari billowed upward all about her, coiling and uncoiling itself like some huge undersea anemone. It was a pretty picture—the mother and child, for a brief moment no longer combatants, laughing, playing, taking pleasure in each other.

Mr. Mukherjee, however, had few qualms about stripping down. Quite the contrary, in fact, he appeared to leap at the opportunity. Not in the least self-conscious, he stood on the beach in a pair of electric-blue bikini shorts bearing on them the logo of some notable French designer. As an undergarment, it seemed unduly tight and skimpy—designed more for self-display than comfort. Strolling about the narrow strip of beach, stopping here and there to chat with fellow passengers, eyes flashing beneath his brows at the lovely milk-white calves of Katrina Van Meegrin, and at the Italian ladies, who had pinned their slips up to serve as bathing suits, he appeared to suck his stomach in and preen himself.

Grant Shapley had rolled his trousers above his knees, and in his slouch hat and cane, waded knee-high through the water. From time to time he'd pause to stoop down and peer intently at an object he'd spied under the surface. Occasionally he'd kneel and scoop up some specimen of marine life.

Sitting in no more than a foot or so of water near the shore, Wilma Shapley sat chatting with Nell Blanton. Their talk was lively, mostly of home and what they would do once they reached there. Mrs. Shapley was full of plans for that autumn. They would build a stone wall for their garden. At Christmas they'd be visiting children and grandchildren back East. All the while she spoke, her eyes never left the Professor. She watched the slow, ponderous motion of his hulking frame as he waded near the shoreline, his bulging pale white calves looking ludicrous beneath the rolled-up cuffs of his trousers. He stopped to chat with a handful of the Spanish youths darting and splashing all about him. He appeared to be showing them some small living specimen he carried in the palm of his hand. She noted how easily and naturally he fell into the role of teacher the moment there were young minds to reach out to.

Once he appeared to stumble. Still smiling, all the while attentive to Nell Blanton, Mrs. Shapley half-rose, only to drop back once she saw him recover his balance. Nell scarcely noticed, but continued talking, reciting at great length and detail an old family recipe for Maryland crab cakes.

Thus the afternoon wore on. Several of the soldiers ventured over on the pretext of wanting some lemonade, but more probably just to have a closer look at the alien creatures. One of them was the young lieutenant who'd been swimming with Serja.

Despite the barrier of language, they appeared to get on famously. Shapley had reasonably good Russian and, of course, there were the tour guides. Shortly, they were all chatting together, drinking lemonade, exchanging cigarettes, standing about in their underclothes and in various makeshift costumes. (No one had a real bathing suit.) There were occasional flashes of breasts and a bit of pubic hair more or less visible beneath sodden clinging undergarments. But it didn't seem to affect anyone greatly. They were not at all unlike prepubescent children having a bath together, laughing and chatting with the occasional furtive glance at one another's scarcely visible private parts.

"And then what did he say?"

"He asked me about school. What I was studying."

"School?"

"Yes."

"Then he just told you you were a suspect?"

"Yes."

"Just like that?"

"Yes."

"*Incredible.*" Desfargue struck his forehead with the flat of his palm. He and Kate Dubbin had wandered off from the others. They'd found themselves a small copse of birch trees behind a hill, where they'd stripped off their clothes and made love.

They lay together in the tall fronds, still partially coiled in one another, stretching their limbs languorously with that wonderful postcoital sensation of completion.

Desfargue's head popped up again. "But didn't that seem odd to you? Strange?"

"What? . . . My being a suspect?"

"Yes. Of course. Aren't you disturbed?"

"Not as much as you, apparently." She laughed and cuffed his cheek.

He shook his head bewilderedly. He was a dark, lanky young man with a substantial Gallic nose and the sort of features generally characterized as intelligent rather than handsome. He was just completing his law studies at the University of Paris, and like many young men right out of school, he tended to take himself quite seriously. He came from a family of prosperous upper-middle-class merchants and so, of course, thought of himself as a socialist.

"An officer of the KGB accuses you of an act of espionage against the Soviet Union," he went on, growing increasingly vexed, "and you are not disturbed?"

When she looked at him her eyes were amused and terribly wise. "Well, what would you suggest I do, have a nervous breakdown?"

"Oh *merde,*" he sputtered. "Little idiot. Don't you see the implications of it? Why aren't you disturbed?"

"Because, if you must know, I didn't take him very seriously."

His eyes widened. "You didn't?"

"No. And I'll tell you something else. Something odd. Even as he was making those accusations to me, I had the distinct impression that he didn't want me to take him too seriously, either. He was really quite"—she sought for something precise but settled instead for simplicity—"nice. That's all I can say. He was very nice."

Desfargue stared at her mutely. "Sometimes, Kate, you astound me. All that intelligence alongside all of that naiveté. But, of course, that is so typically American."

"Ah," she sighed wearily, and rolled over onto her back. "Here we go again with my poor benighted fellow countrymen."

"It's true, darling. I must say it. In the area of international diplomacy, Americans are simply the most gauche, most simpleminded." He caught the boredom on her face. "Well, it's true. Ask anyone."

"Who, for instance? Another Frenchman? Oh, Claude." She turned suddenly, her arms outspread as if in despair. "Look, darling. I want you to know something because I think it's important for the both of us. I love France. I love Paris and Provence. I love Monet and Satie. I love goat cheese and Beaujolais. I even love you sometimes, although you do try my patience. You had an Indochina long before we had a Vietnam and you didn't exactly win any awards for enlightened humanitarian behavior in Algeria any more than we will in El Salvador. So why, my darling, go on patronizing America? Calling us warmongers and missile rattlers and whatnot. When the Warsaw Pact armies come sweeping across eastern Europe and into Paris, you'll scream bloody hell for us to come bail you out." She broke off. "I'm sorry. That was unkind of me. But you are always prodding me about how awful my homeland is. You are wonderful at pointing your fingers at everyone and telling them what their moral responsibilities are. But then you go and sell breeder reactors to Madame Gandhi and the Iraquis and Exocet missiles to the Argies. What makes you think you're any better than the rest of us? I know there's plenty wrong with America, but then why does everyone want to go there? And why is everyone trying to get the hell out of the USSR? Why are we all locked up here behind this barbed wire? Why can't I cross the border into Finland, the way I cross all other borders? Think about that, darling." She pushed her fingers through his hair. "Think hard about it and someday when this is all behind us, we'll talk about it again. I am fond of you, Claude, even if you are stuffy and overbearing and awfully self-satisfied. I can't help being very fond of you. I even think I love you a little. But if you continue to berate America and talk about us in Europe as though we were the Visigoths, I will start to find that very tiresome." Her voice as she spoke was calm and measured. She was indignant, but there was nothing shrill or unpleasant about it. "However," her voice softened, "whatever happens between us, I will always love France. France is a state of mind so beautiful that I won't permit anyone, not even you, to spoil it for me."

She took his face between her palms. When he started to protest, she silenced him by pressing her lips to his. "Now," she went on in a husky whisper, "if we can just stop being so uppity French and just concentrate on being lovers, which we do superbly, I'm sure everything will be just fine."

Señor Gonzaga showed up at the pond about three in the afternoon, gliding along on Tony Thomas' arm. A radiant smile glowing on his lips, he appeared almost majestic, despite the outlandish costume of drab, outsized odds and ends that the Russians had clearly thrown together in order to cover his nakedness. The effect of this costume in some lesser mortal would have been ludicrous. But Gonzaga, with his great gangling height, striding along, nodding and waving at people as he arrived, had the air of some banished king returning to his homeland after years of exile. His combination of pluck and affection for everyone he saw was oddly touching. But permitting himself to be led all about there by Thomas like some newly won trophy had created the decided impression that it was the journalist who'd somehow miraculously pulled strings to secure his release.

Stern arrived shortly after with Señora Gonzaga, Isabel, and Consuelo. Their reunion had taken place minutes before aboard the train amid tears and kisses and stern warnings about such pranks in the future.

People surged about the old man, pumping his hand, slapping his back. There were dozen of questions, all of which Gonzaga answered thoroughly. Where had they taken them? It turns out, to a little hotel in Vyborg, "nothing too 'luxe,' mind you, but perfectly adequate." They gave him supper. He had a bath in a real tub, watched television (none of it comprehensible to him), and had a good night's sleep. "I was simply not going to spend a day locked up in one of those sweltering little cells on that train." Yes, he would take his clothing off again and walk naked to make a point. If he believed in it, why not? His eyes twinkled slyly, leaving everyone there with the distinct impression that the gentle activism of this old Spaniard had been more shrewd than mad, eminently more sensible than the torture they had so meekly endured.

It was, after all, the kind of activism everyone could condone. It hurt no one. It put no one at risk, except possibly Gonzaga himself, and it had accomplished what its author had set out to do.

"I am delighted you're back"—Jatta patted his shoulder—"but don't you dare try anything like that again."

"Don't worry," Señora Gonzaga assured the guide, "I shall keep him under lock and key."

Isabel shook her head in dismay. "Another jailer, Madrecita? How quickly we forget."

There was laughter. The mood was high and Gonzaga's return had clearly relieved the air of a tension that had hovered about them since he was carried off. The manner in which he'd been marched out the day before had cast a pall. His reappearance now, none the worse for wear (possibly even a bit better), was the cause of renewed hope.

Thomas basked in the glory of Gonzaga's release. Taking all the credit for it himself, he glowed in the approbation of his fellow passengers. Perhaps he had already drafted in his head the way in which he would depict the incident in the series of articles he planned to write once he got back to London. He was canny enough to see that there was a syndication deal in this, if not actually a full-length book with a whopping advance.

Stern, who might justifiably have been the recipient of a good part of that acclaim, seemed strangely indifferent to all the fuss. He was content to sit alone on the beach, perched on a rock, staring out at the water. Preoccupied with his own gloomy thoughts, he appeared to have been completely forgotten by the others now flocking round Thomas and the old man.

To Stern's way of thinking, he hadn't interceded with Colonel Dunskoi on the old man's behalf. And if anyone had asked him for an account of that interview with the colonel, he would probably have given all the credit to Thomas. The episode for him was now history. What was not forgotten was his interview with Dunskoi just after, particularly the latter part of it, after Thomas had left. It had been chilling. When at last he walked out of the colonel's office, escorted by a beefy sergeant major to a staff car waiting outside for him, the full weight of what had just occurred, with all of its awful implications, finally hit him. Going down the concrete walk to the car, his brain swam and he toddled like an old man.

As he settled back in the car, the facade of pluck he wore in Dunskoi's office crumbled as he succumbed to a wave of nauseous panic. The worst of it, of course, was that he had brought the whole thing on himself. That brash, vainglorious gesture of omitting information on his visa application, seeming so highly principled at the time, struck him now as sophomoric and unaccountably stupid. It was he, not Dunskoi, who pressed the subject once it had been brought up. And again, it was he who carried on so defensively as to raise suspicions in the colonel's mind.

Then, finally, that awful business about his being the prime suspect. Even as Dunskoi had said it, Stern was consumed with the terrifying certainty that

he was making it up right there on the spot, and that Stern, with his angry repeated assertions of non-Jewishness, had cooked his own goose. He'd given
Dunskoi the perfect opening, a way of capitalizing so fully on a man's fears
that ultimately he must incriminate himself. He'd served up for the colonel a
full flesh-and-blood American secret agent on a silver platter.

The sound of cries and shouts roused him from these uneasy thoughts.
People were streaming past him, moving in a wave up the beach. Kariolainen
lumbered by.

"What's up?" Stern cried after him.

"The old man," he shouted back over his shoulder, then pointed up ahead.
In a crotch of the tree from which the rubber tire dangled some thirty feet
above the water, Señor Gonzaga stood in his underpants, long sodden boxer
shorts that clung revealingly about his scrawny loins. He'd climbed the
rough-hewn log ladder onto the little platform set in the crotch.

"Good God." Stern rose and followed the others to the place.

"Come down," Jatta screamed up at him through her cupped palms. "Idiot.
Come down at once."

Señora Gonzaga had come limping and panting up. She pointed up at him
waving her hands frantically, and started to wail, "Enrique, Enrique." The
sound of it was pitiable.

The Russian soldiers swimming on the far side had seen him too, and came
running toward them along the shoreline. They perceived the problem at
once—a man well advanced in years, disporting himself in his underwear
thirty feet above the ground, no doubt deranged. If he hit the water wrong, he
could well break his back.

"Come down," Señora Gonzaga shrieked. "Enrique. *Venga. Pronto.*"

Her hands still cupped to her mouth, Isabel shouted, "Papa. You fool.
Come down, at once."

Gonzaga appeared oblivious of the chaos below. His face bore an expression of demented, almost beatific intent. He'd taken hold of the tire, hefted it
in his hands, and tugged hard, as if to get the weight of it and test the play of
the rope.

"For God's sake," Thomas bawled up at him. "Don't try it. You'll kill
yourself."

The soldiers gestured with their hands, shook their heads incredulously,
and jabbered up at Gonzaga in Russian. Señora Gonzaga had crumpled in a
heap, wailing at the base of the tree. Consuelo huddled beside her, eyes rolling and making pathetic little yipping sounds.

"You fool." Isabel stamped her foot, shouting up at him furiously.

Mr. Mukherjee thought it immensely funny. He giggled and clapped as
though he were about to see a circus performer attempt his big number. Sandro Lambrusto sprang toward the ladder and started up.

Stern pulled him back. "Don't, for Christ's sake. He'll jump."

In the next moment, he did. Grasping the tire (not all that firmly, so it appeared from the ground), his legs stretched, his chest appearing to expand, he stepped off the platform, kicking out into space. Transfixed, they watched the rope play out its full length and swing across the surface of the placid, waiting water. It didn't go very far. The object (for that's all it was by then) thrashed and flailed at the end of it like a worm wriggling at the end of a hook. There was an audible snap, at which point the rope, the tire, and the object separated in midair, each flying off in a different direction.

"Aiyeeuh . . ." Gonzaga's hair-raising cry rent the quiet cricket-hum of that summer's afternoon as he glided free and hit the water with a loud, sickening splat.

Unspeaking, they watched breathlessly the waves of choppy, concentric circles radiating outward from the point where he'd gone down. When after several moments he didn't appear, Karl Heinz dove in and started out toward the spot. Keith Wales and Sandro dove in too, along with several of the Russian soldiers.

Señora Gonzaga was beside herself. Down at the water's edge, Isabel stood ankle-deep in her shoes, sinking into the mud.

Karl Heinz had reached the place first and dove. The others circled the spot and were diving all about the point where he'd gone down. But in the next moment old Gonzaga's head bobbed up on the surface, fifty feet or so from where the frantic divers were searching for him.

"Aiyeeuh . . ." Once again that bloodcurdling ridiculous war cry ripped from the old man, triumphant, exuberant, self-proclaiming. He swam in long graceful strokes to the shore and clambered crablike up the bank, green weeds streaming from his head and nose, boxer shorts drooping unheroically below his buttocks.

Back up on the shore again, the crowd surged about him, laughing and pumping his hand. The Russian soldiers stood off to the side and gawked with wonder.

"Bravo. Bravo." Madariaga embraced the old man and murmured words in his ear. Lunatic and suicidal as it was for a man of seventy-six, Gonzaga was flushed with the high of it. It had been for him a gesture, a kind of affirmation, possibly toward his captors an act of defiance that spoke eloquently of a life force in people that didn't necessarily grow old and infirm with their bodies but stood unbending until the end.

"Let me understand you correctly. You say it was you who carried these documents onto the train, then secreted them in the drain of the lavatory?"

"Yes."

"And you say it was another man, a researcher at Polyarny, who passed you the papers at Gatchina?"

"Yes."

"With instructions to carry them to a Major General Breen at NATO headquarters in Brussels?"

"Yes."

"Where you were then to be paid two thousand dollars?"

"Yes."

"And you do not know the name of the man who passed you the documents?"

"It was not told to me."

Junji Asawa spoke listlessly in quiet monotones, his eyes fixed uneasily on the floor. In his chair, seated opposite Colonel Dunskoi, he appeared small and huddled. Strangely doll-like. Barely moving, there was something lifeless and chilling about him.

It had been close to five P.M. when the young Japanese man was admitted to the colonel's office. He'd been summoned at the train site and told to report there at three P.M. He appeared promptly at the designated hour, but Dunskoi, for reasons of his own, chose to keep the youth waiting for close to two hours.

If that was a tactical stroke of the colonel's, part of some carefully orchestrated program of harassment designed to rattle Asawa and make him more accessible to interrogation, the colonel got more than he'd bargained for. The fact that Asawa, when informed he was suspected of high treason against the Soviet Union, immediately, even eagerly, confessed to it, threw Dunskoi completely off balance.

"Tell me, Asawa, why did you allow yourself to become involved in this?"

"I knew the documents were crucial to the Soviet Union and I was determined not to permit them to fall into the wrong hands."

"The wrong hands?"

"The United States."

Asawa had said it unblinkingly and with such striking candor as to earn the colonel's begrudging admiration. There was no doubt, Dunskoi concluded, the youth was utterly mad—confessing to crimes that were wholly fictitious. But to what end?

The colonel stirred in his chair. "Let me understand you again. What you are telling me is that your reason for taking these documents was not to sell them to the Americans, but to foil an American plot against the Soviet Union?"

"Yes." Asawa's wide puppy eyes rose slowly from the floor, imploring the colonel. "I now seek sanctuary in the Soviet Union."

Once again he'd winded the colonel. Dunskoi sat there hunched above his desk, eyeing him warily. "Sanctuary from what?"

"Japanese government agents," he replied unhesitatingly.

"What are they seeking you for?"

"Treason."

"Against whom?"

"Imperial Japanese government. I fled there seven months ago."

"What was the nature of your treason?"

"I prefer not to divulge at this time."

Dunskoi frowned. "You have given this some thought, I trust?"

"Yes."

"And you are certain you wish to take sanctuary in the Soviet Union?"

"Yes."

Dunskoi's tongue glided slowly across his lips. A tremendous weariness had overtaken him. He was suddenly too tired to continue. "Very well," he said, snapping the folder before him shut. "Such requests are processed by the state police and the Ministry of Immigration. I shall secure the appropriate forms, but I must advise you, it is a lengthy process, and if you are wanted for crimes of treason by a foreign government, the chances are slight that your application will be honored. You may go now."

Asawa rose quickly, indeed, almost sprang to his feet. Bowing his head, he mumbled a few words and backed uncertainly out. For several minutes Dunskoi watched the door out of which the youth had passed, his eyes fixed on the spot and slightly frightened, as though he'd seen some ghostly, not especially reassuring portent of things to come.

He would secure all the forms for the young man, as promised, even going so far as to appoint someone to assist the youth in completing them. There was no question, of course, that he would ever permit the forms to reach any of the appropriate agencies. A blunder of judgment of that magnitude could be the end of his professional life.

His exhaustion was awful. The sour, burning chyme of partially digested food made his mouth taste foul. He'd had another, somewhat more alarming call from home that day. He must return to Leningrad immediately to confront the police, who had now charged his daughter formally with acts "inimical" to the Soviet Union and "unacceptable" in a citizen of the USSR.

Outside the low squat barracks building at Vyborg, a car waited to drive Asawa back to the train site. Outwardly he appeared composed; inside a fire had started to smolder and was shortly to rage.

He was certain his request for sanctuary in the USSR would be denied. The colonel had rebuffed him. He could read that in the man's eyes and also from the scornful expression on his face as Asawa had made his proposal. Doubtless the colonel would now turn him over to the Japanese consul in Leningrad, who would then return him to Tokyo to his father, and to those Japanese agents who sought him for treason. But against whom? And for what? What agents? But there were agents, weren't there? His mind swam. Moving along a road winding through a birch forest, he experienced a woozy sense of disorientation. He was no longer in Russia. Not at all. He was in Japan, driving down the great Tokaido Road jut below the shadow of Satta Mountain.

But there was the colonel again. In his mind he kept confusing him with Father-san. Both wore that same genial mask tinged with a trace of mockery.

In the next instant a small reddish canister secreted in the bulkhead above his berth flashed before his eye, then vanished. They had not found it. They had searched the car all morning, and still they had uncovered nothing. He had duped them. He alone, by himself. The fearsome, almost legendary Russian state police.

Ironically, he was disappointed they had not found it. He had worked out in his head an elaborate, quite brilliant explanation for its presence there. Now he grieved the loss of another opportunity to gull his captors. They may have denied him sanctuary, but they would live to regret it.

The driver, glancing up in the rearview mirror, saw reflected there a youthful mien of Oriental caste, so bland and impassive as to be enigmatic. He had no way of knowing that behind that trancelike gaze, within that small wiry frame huddled in a corner of the car, something strange, and as yet unformed, beat wildly.

PART VI

$\blacklozenge \blacklozenge \blacklozenge$ A BC NEWS has just learned from sources in Helsinki the names of Americans still being detained in the Soviet Union on that Finn-Sov day coach known popularly as the Green Train.

They are:

Mr. and Mrs. Paul Blanton, Lexington, Kentucky
Miss Jean Blaylock, New York City
Mr. and Mrs. Theodore Kariolainen, Shasta, California
Miss Corine Kariolainen, Shasta, California
Mr. Christopher Kariolainen, Shasta, California
Mr. and Mrs. Ralph Keck, Ames, Iowa
Mr. Peter Stern, New York City

For more on that story, we go live to the UN, where the General Assembly has been in emergency session since noon. . . .

In response to charges made today in New York by the Soviet ambassador to the United Nations, State Department spokesman Richard Graylin issued the following brief rejoinder:

"The government of the United States categorically denies any conspiracy, covert or otherwise, to steal classified material from the Polyarny naval base at Kola. Further, it views the continuing detainment of the Finn-Sov day coach in the gravest possible light. There can be no excuse for interdicting the freedom of fifty-one innocent people. If allowed to persist, this action can only result in the most dire consequences for U.S.-Soviet relations."

This has been Roger Mudd. Thank you and good night for NBC News.

Good evening. This is the Voice of America beaming its nightly news broadcast to the peoples of Eastern Europe Bloc countries and the USSR.

This evening fifty-one people from various parts of the Free World, passengers on a day coach from Leningrad en route to Helsinki, are completing their third day of enforced detention in the Soviet Union.

The USSR claims to have proof that a passenger aboard the train was attempting to steal naval data of a highly secret nature. But a recently defecting Soviet diplomat, speaking today from Geneva, attributed the detention of the train to a Russian pretext for holding hostages until it can secure the release of its T30 submarine and crew presently being held in Norway on charges of spying.

Western travelers in Moscow and Leningrad have cited instances of antagonism and harassment on the streets as well as at various border checkpoints. Soviet authorities tonight denied a request on the part of the International Red Cross to visit the train, maintaining that all passengers are in good health. . . .

With yet another year of failing crop production in the USSR, Moscow has asked the U.S. for an additional six million metric tons of wheat, which the U.S. State Department has already approved. . . .

"I-23 . . . B-15 . . . G-60 . . . B-12 . . . N-31"
Janet Kariolainen rolled the numbers off her tongue.
"B-9 . . . N-45 . . . O-66 . . . I-29 . . ."
Those playing bingo did so with an air of dejection, like people trapped at a dull party. They'd had their supper early that evening, eating dispiritedly in the bright sunshine of a summer Russian twilight. The lights had been left off in the dining car so they might open the windows, but not so much as a breath of air stirred through the place. Grant Shapley pushed a chip with his stiffened forefinger into the I-17 square. If he heard the numbers, it was only at the subliminal level.

His mind at that moment was several thousand miles away in a marsh with small horses no larger than a collie dog. They stood motionless in a brackish pool, up to their bellies in water. From the point at which they stood, the earth had the look of a flat, arid disk stretching for miles to a distant ridge of low purplish mountains. A number of small creatures—rodents, carnivores, marsupials—lingered by the pool's edge and drank. There were shrewlike animals resembling hedgehogs, and large batlike creatures that darted noiselessly through the stunted trees.

At one corner of the pool a small primate sat gliding its small clawlike hands slowly over the surface of the water as though he were signing his name there in a large, sweeping calligraphy.

It had the look of a painting, this image in Shapley's mind—a primordial scene of tranquillity beneath which lurked a sense of imminent violence. The horses were called *hyracotherium,* considered the "dawn horse" of North America, and the monkeylike creature was called *shoshonius,* possibly the antecedent of the modern-day *tarsus* of Southeast Asia.

It was a landscape nearly forty million years old, the end of the Eocene. The profusion of wildlife inhabiting the area had either journeyed there to die or had been carried there by streams or in the jaws of carnivores, then buried in a succession of marshes.

Shapley knew these to be the archaic mammals that had evolved after the disappearance of the dinosaurs who were themselves now well on their way to becoming extinct. That process would go on for perhaps another several million years, at which time many of the modern groups of animals would emerge and begin a major migration from Europe and Asia to North America.

It was in the shadowless, sultry calm of that scene that Grant Shapley wandered, even as his stiffened forefinger pushed the bingo chips across his card, hearing, but not hearing, the dull recitation of numbers.

In eons, the subtropical forests and swamps of that period would become the deserts of today, and the creatures within it, fossilized in stone and amber. Eggs, skulls, skeletons, jaws, and crushing mandibles that once could rip and tear flesh were now toothless, desiccated things, caught in the grinning leer of death.

Shapley stood on a gentle bluff above the scene where the wind soughed above the desolation. He knew the place well. It was in the area of the Wind River Basin, about fifty miles west of Casper at the base of the Big Horn Mountains, where the last great herds of wild horses still roamed. It was not more than a mile or so from his lodge.

Black, low scudding clouds came rolling down out of the north. There was a distant roll of thunder and the feathery leaves of the big aspen lining the tracks began to quiver with the imminence of rain. Several of the passengers gathered in the vestibule between the coach and sleeping car to smoke cigarettes and have a breath of air by the open door.

"It's as if they've completely forgotten us." Paul Blanton shook his head dispiritedly back and forth.

Thomas struck a match to the tip of his cigarette and said somewhat spitefully: "What did you expect—the President to send in the Fifth Marine Division?"

"Come on, Tony." Stern scowled.

Jean Blaylock muttered something and stared out the open door where the guard had lit his lantern for the night and taken up his position.

"I tried to tell you all before, but you preferred not to listen. The wheels of diplomacy, particularly in this part of the world, grind exceedingly slow. It's best we all know that."

"How much longer do you think this can go on?" Ted Kariolainen asked.

"I'm not a clairvoyant," Thomas replied wearily.

Ralph Keck said suddenly, "Why not hold a prayer meeting?"

Isabel looked up, astonished. "What on earth for?"

Keck shot her an impatient look. "Because we're captives here in a godless land. We need to reaffirm our faith."

"We'd do better forming an action committee," Paul Blanton said, "to deal with these people at some official level and protect our rights."

A murmur of approval rippled through the group.

Myra Keck rose to her husband's support. "What could be more effective than appealing to the Almighty?"

"I suspect he prefers Christians to atheists," Isabel chided.

Keck frowned. "We're all the Lord's children, Miss Gonzaga."

"Possibly you are," Isabel joked. "I fear I can only hope for foster-child status."

There was a burst of laughter.

Keck attempted to disregard it. "These little gatherings would be ecumenical. We're not seeking converts here—only an outlet for our spiritual beliefs."

"Belief—in what, exactly?" Jean Blaylock demanded.

"For heaven's sake, Jean, it's only prayer," Sonia Conti said. "Nothing serious."

"But I don't care to pray."

Janet Kariolainen touched her arm soothingly. "Surely it can do no harm. And it might possibly even help."

"I don't need help, thank you." Isabel's hackles were rising by the minute. "And if the time comes that I do, I reserve the right to call upon someone of my own choosing."

Keck seemed baffled by all the contention he'd aroused. In his mind he was merely trying to help. He had their best interests at heart. It was so obvious. Couldn't they see that? "That's your choice entirely, Miss Gonzaga." He tried to sound unruffled. "You're excused."

"Thank you. That's very Christian of you," Isabel shot back. There were snickers and barely muffled laughter.

Keck strove to restore the gravity of his purpose. "Who else here would care to join our little prayer group?"

As he waited for people to volunteer, his face assumed a stony, fixed look. The silence was embarrassing. It was Janet Kariolainen who came to his rescue. "I'd be happy to," she piped up. "So would Corrie and Buddy. Won't you come, Ted?"

Kariolainen looked around. He appeared to lift his back and shoulders to their full height. "Why not? I'll give it a whirl."

"What about you, Margarita?" Mrs. Keck looked directly at Señora Gonzaga, taking her completely by surprise.

"Yes. Of course," the señora consented, but she appeared none too thrilled at the prospect.

Isabel scowled. "Why, Mother? You know you're doing it just to be polite."

"No, no dear," the señora assured her. "I think I'd actually enjoy it."

Mrs. Keck glowed inwardly, as though she'd just triumphed over the forces of evil. "And what about the señor?" She stared directly at Gonzaga.

The old man wore a bored, slightly impatient look. He stared off in space for a while, pondering the question, then cleared his throat. "Even now as we speak, fully one-half the world is engaged in slaughtering each other over one idiotic religious war or another. All this butchery in the name of piety. Really—it's obscene. I can no longer tell the difference between the devout and the street-corner assassins. In the interests of my own peace of mind I shall forgo prayer."

"I, too," Isabel cried aloud, and took her father's arm.

"I'll go with Mother," Consuelo said.

Gonzaga winked round at the others. "You see, faith has already transformed my little family into a battle zone."

There was a burst of laughter. Keck resented deeply the jocular turn of the meeting. He turned abruptly and gazed about at the others. "Who else here would care to join us?"

Sonia Conti raised her hand. Max Conti was taken completely aback by his wife's action. Silvana, seeing her best friend join the ranks of the prayer group, raised her hand too.

"What about you, Professor?" Myra Keck turned her judgmental gaze on Shapley. He smiled back at her tolerantly. "Thank you. But I think I'll sit this one out."

"We too," the Blantons said.

The Kecks tried to conscript several others for their prayer meeting. But shortly it started to have the look of arm-twisting, at which point resistance hardened.

"Very well, then," Keck said with an unaccustomed graciousness. He stared pointedly at those who'd agreed to join him. "We'll gather in the dining car in twenty minutes. If any of the rest of you should have a change of heart, you're more than welcome."

When the rain came that night, it came hard and fast. It started shortly after they'd turned in for the evening. Bolts of lightning flashed, great claps of thunder banged and rolled about outside. Steady, driving rain hailed on the roof, sending sheets of rain coursing down the dirty windows. With it came a blessed break in the heat. Sprawled in shorts and skivvy in his narrow berth, Stern rummaged through his bags and found an old sweatshirt to pull over his head.

The wind was high as it gnashed round the stalled train, sending sheets of water cascading down the windows and seeping its way beneath the sills into the berth, so that Stern had to wedge a towel into the leaky corner in order to stanch the flow. Lying there listening to the not unpleasant sound of the storm, a multitude of images passed before him ... Constance, his wife, or what was once his wife, on the other side of the world in Santa Barbara. His son and daughter had, undoubtedly, by that time notified her of his situation. She'd probably found it funny, and in a sense it was. On the one hand, the improbability of it—this man with whom she lived for thirty years, ate dinner, and went to bed with each night, suddenly at the center of some grave international crisis. And, of course, knowing him, his fastidiousness, his impatience with the slightest deflection from schedule, with anything unexpected. It was all too funny.

"It is my duty to advise you, Mr. Stern ..." The rich, husky, Slavic intonations of Colonel Dunskoi filled the narrow area of his cabin. "Of those three or four, you are at the very top of the list."

It didn't matter a particle to him that he didn't believe a word of it. It still froze his blood, the mere knowledge that having once expressed it, this man whom he'd never seen before, with whom he'd had no grudge, no cause for conflict, could by the stroke of a pen or the transmission of a phone call, will it to be so. Put forces into effect that would make it so. Manipulate truth so that it worked to his advantage. "You are Jewish, aren't you?" the voice echoed through the cabin.

A gash of lightning threw his berth into momentary garish illumination. When darkness returned, he lay cold and trembling beneath the blankets. A clap of thunder rolled sullenly toward them from the east.

SUPREME COMMAND–NOVOGORSK
Headquarters—Vyborg

Grave displeasure regarding recent reports in Western media depicting conditions at site of detainment as resembling that of "a holiday spa." Swimming parties, songfests, wine served each evening at dinner, soldiers of the Supreme Soviet fraternizing openly with detainees, are only part of the story leaked to Western sources, undoubtedly by members of your own general staff.

The result of this has been to undermine our bargaining position in talks going forward at this time in Helsinki, Oslo, and Washington. As you are undoubtedly aware, in these most delicate negotiations, the general welfare of these people is our principal leverage. If it is felt that these individuals are in no immediate jeopardy, our opponents shall feel under little pressure to resolve the situation quickly. Time plays into their hands, since the longer we detain these passengers, the more surely will the tide of world opinion shift against us in their favor.

It is crucial, therefore, to counteract this impression of a Sunday outing with one of a stern but humane treatment afforded all detainees. For *stern* read *austere,* with particular regard to food rations and living conditions. For *humane* read *no use of physical force;* no laying on of hands except in those problems of extreme intransigence where physical restraint is the only effective response to passenger disobedience. The weapon of psychological intimidation, however, is most heartily recommended.

Dunskoi's eyes scanned slowly through the report. He'd read it twice before, speedily, for bare meaning. Now he was reading more carefully, searching for nuance in what had not been said so much as implied by means of certain phrases, the selection and juxtaposition of certain words, the sequence of events in presentation, piled one atop the other and all orchestrated in such a way as to suggest a situation barely under control. "As you are undoubtedly aware," for instance, reeked of scorn. Worse, even, "members of your own general staff" was wrought of the stuff of courts-martial.

The storm outside his dimly lighted office raged, but it was as nothing compared to the tempests of fright and fury that raged within him. He read on:

Once you have embarked on a course of "depleasurization," our own people will then plant stories in the Western media of "grim conditions aboard the Finn-Sov day coach." They, in turn, shall charge us with inhumane behavior, even atrocities, all of which, of course, we will vehemently deny, thus ensuring that the story will be swallowed whole cloth in the West. This in turn shall bring pressure to bear on all aggrieved parties, particularly those with nationals detained aboard the train, to proceed with all due haste to the bargaining table.

On another, but unrelated note, we deeply regret the news regarding your daughter. Expulsion from university may seem unduly harsh, but undoubtedly you see the necessity of it. The virus of sedition spreads quickly if permitted to go unchecked. Unfortunately, this virus appears to have taken hold among certain of our young people. Perhaps this is due to a new climate of permissiveness within our institutions of higher learning. . . .

Dunskoi seethed. ". . . but undoubtedly you see the necessity . . ." The unctuousness of it, along with the sick delight it took in chastisement. He balled the missive in his fist and flung it hard against the wall. A crack of thunder cut the power and plunged the office into darkness. When the light came up again a moment later, he was on his feet striding heavily up and down the length of his office. He was a man desperately in need of strenuous physical movement in order to dispel the bile boiling over inside him.

"*Govno.*" He muttered the word he'd forbidden Jean Blaylock to use. "*Chort poderee . . .*" He spat more epithets into the stalish air, then kicked the wadded ball of paper he'd flung into the corner.

"Swine," he ranted on. "They'd love to see me go down. I can see them gloating now. Sending their most earnest, heartfelt regrets. 'Dear Dimitri Alexandrovitch, what a pity. How lamentable it had to come to this. . . . My dear fellow. Please know you can always count on us . . .' *Govno. Merde.*" That they should question his loyalty; impugn his competence as an officer . . . After thirty years of service. The effrontery. And to think now that they would punish him for the activities of his own child, as misguided as they were.

A vein, engorged and swollen, throbbed at the back of his neck. The room swam before his eyes. It was nearly one o'clock in the morning, but he could not wait until dawn. He would call now. Confront her with these charges. Have it out with her now. And yes, if it were necessary, if it came to that, disavow her once and for all. She must understand that she could no longer depend on his protection. She was of an age now at which she must assume responsibility for her actions. And he no longer could, or would, be part of that.

Asawa lay in his berth and dreamed of the Golden Pavilion. It shimmered on the surface of a pond, its image inverted amid a still reflection of flocculent white clouds. The clap of thunder that had just boomed overhead shattered the image. It went up in smithereens, a billion shards of timber and terra-cotta tile shooting skyward. It had a rather festive air like fireworks hurtling skyward, blooming at the peak of their trajectory into a gorgeous umbrella of multicolored sparks, then showering slowly downward.

He was filled with a sense of unspeakable elation, not at all unlike the effect of chewing certain herbs he'd experienced with friends at school. There was the elation, of course, but with it came the extra dividend of vastly heightened perceptions—mystical and frightening, a visitation from something otherworldly, and yes, yes . . . the allure of something terribly dangerous.

"My birthplace was a lonely cape that projects into the Sea of Japan, northeast of Maizuru." He could recite the text of it by heart, hearing in his head the limpid, breathless exhaustion of its sound. Within it was contained the ebb and flow of tides, the drowsy murmur of two voices after lovemaking.

Asawa thought about the pavilion and the young acolyte and he was happy, he told himself. The logic of his own actions was as ineluctable as that of the young man's. Cause and effect—so natural, so ordered and precise. The freedom of choice to take action, seemingly so elusive, is always there. All one was required to do was to reach out and take it, like the acolyte at the Golden Pavilion in Kyoto.

A guard carrying a lantern trudged past on the track, so close he could hear the man's heavy grunting breaths. The shadows cast by his lantern swayed dizzily on the ceiling above his berth, and for a moment he watched the undifferentiated shards of light and shadow break up, then reassemble themselves quite unmistakably into the eyes of his father peering down upon him. They were not at all unkind.

But when the light had fled and the crunch of boots had receded into the distance, the eyes were still there, as if embedded in the ceiling. He could reach up and touch them, so close they were. Or was it only the faint guttering glow from one of the fires where the soldiers camped behind a screen of trees? If so, then why did he shiver so in the dark? But, of course, it was cool outside. Even chilly. The temperature had dropped rapidly and the air in the sleeping coach was suddenly chill. The steel of the inner walls and the ornamental brass/chrome appointments of the berth were suddenly cold and clammy to the touch.

"I am happy," Asawa whispered up at the eyes, as if he were trying to placate them. "I wish you could be too."

Then something curious occurred. The eyes were no longer those of his father, but rather the eyes of Colonel Dunskoi, with whom he had spoken that day. As opposed to his father's, these eyes were shrewd and pitiless.

Asawa lay for some time shivering beneath his blanket, strangely comforted by the sound of the rain lashing against the coach, watching the eyes of his father and the Russian colonel alternating back and forth on his ceiling.

"I am happy," he kept saying over and over again to the eyes, so that after a time his voice achieved the drowsy, lulled effect of incantation. "I wish you could be too."

When he could no longer reason with or apologize to the eyes, he grew sleepy and clamped his own eyes shut against them. Then, once again, the Temple of the Golden Pavilion floated upside down on the surface of the pond before him.

Somewhere in the early reaches of the morning, Katrina Van Meegrin's head rose from the pillow as though she'd heard something, and half-expected to hear it again. A golden wave of hair fell across her cheek as her head tilted toward the window in an attitude of listening. Still half-asleep, she was not at all sure that what she'd heard was not part of her waking dream.

It had been, so it seemed to her, a dull thud, a heavy muffled sound as of something dropping near her head. Now, wound in her sheets and looking out of a single cocked eye, she scarcely recalled what, if anything, she'd been listening for.

The sound of Kyle's snoring in the berth below was reassuring. Shortly she fell back on the pillow and was fast asleep.

Not long after, Max Conti, turning on his side, heard the same sound— dull, muffled, heavy, a soft bang near his head. But he'd been up, lying awake, waiting for the dawn, and so there was no confusion in his mind as to the source of the sound. It had been the sound of his window being closed from the outside.

Before retiring for the night, he'd opened it about six inches for air. As a safety measure these windows were designed to open not much beyond that.

He'd watched it all as it was happening, and could hear the person, presumably one of the guards, standing out on the track in the rain, grunt as he reached up and hauled it down. That was followed by a short hissing sound, and then the heavy crunch of boots fading into the distance.

He didn't think much of it at the time, except that possibly the guards had decided to close any open windows of the sleeping coach in order to keep the berths and their occupants dry. He recalled thinking that was quite decent of them, and fell back off to sleep.

Claude Desfargue stirred, then turned in his narrow berth. Wound in his sheets, he'd been dreaming that he had died. Something had brushed past his head only inches away, but on the other side of the wall fronting the corridor.

He heard the scrape of slippered feet scurry down the corridor, followed by the giggle of adolescents. He muttered something, then sat up and shook his head, cautious not to bang it against the sagging mattress above, inscribing the curve of Kate Dubbin's sleeping figure.

Still adjusting to the light of the morning, out of the corner of an eye Desfargue grew vaguely aware of movement outside the cabin window. When he turned in response to it, he saw nothing save for the white curdling vapors of fog licking at the panes. So thick it was, it appeared to have palpable weight. It coiled and leaned against the coach like some orphaned creature wanting to come inside. The visibility beyond the window was virtually zero.

The noise of slippered feet came rushing back up the corridor. He slid the cabin door open several inches, only to be greeted by a burst of laughter and the gust of wind left in the wake of several youths scurrying past. Following them came the robed, distraught figure of Madariaga in hot pursuit.

"Hey, it's five o'clock in the morning, for Christ's sake."

The worn, harried face of Señor Madariaga peered in at him as though he were a total stranger. He appeared out of breath and happy for an opportunity to pause. "We're locked in here," he said, a look of incredulity upon his face.

"Locked in?"

"The scum have sealed us in here like sardines and gone off."

"Are you sure?"

The youngsters had run ahead into the day coach, leaving the two of them there staring at each other.

Kate Dubbin's drowsy head appeared from above. "What's up?"

Desfargue waved impatiently at her. "Go back to bed."

Her head descended somewhat further. "What the hell's going on?"

He snapped his head in the direction of Madariaga. "He says we're locked in and the Bolshies are gone."

A cabin door across the aisle slid back, revealing a wispy wraithlike spirit in white pajamas. It was Serja. "What is it?"

Several of the Spanish youths came skidding back through the car. Madariaga flung a hand out and collared one neatly, then proceeded to denounce him in a hoarse, peppery Spanish while the others roared gleefully from a safe corner at the end of the coach.

By that time six or seven additional heads poked out through partially opened cabin doors up and down the length of the car. There was a crossfire of indignant voices followed by a quick barrage of questions and answers. Just then, Tony Thomas sauntered in. He was attired in a silk robe. Along with his lighted cigarette holder, he carried a mug of coffee and a hard roll. "Breakfast's on," he sang out melodically.

Stern tossed his legs over the side of the berth and let them dangle. "Tony, Madariaga here says we've been locked in."

"That's right."

"And that the Russians are gone. Pulled out."

"That's right." Thomas nodded and took a large bite of roll. "I heard the trucks pull out in the middle of the night."

"I did too," Trina Van Meegrin cried from the far end of the car. "At least I think I did."

"Someone came by my cabin and closed the window during the night," Max Conti said.

"Mine also," Stern agreed.

Thomas munched his roll thoughtfully. He appeared to be enjoying the moment. His eyes twinkled merrily. "Try opening yours, Peter."

Stern moved back into the berth, positioning himself on his knees before the window for maximum purchase. Grunting and straining, he tried several times to lift the window. What had worked before with relative ease was now unbudgeable.

"No go, ay?" Thomas smiled sadly. "They've been sealed with a spray of some sort. Probably epoxy."

"That must have been the hissing sound I heard," Stern reflected aloud. "And the doors? Locked too?"

"All of them at the exits. But we have free access from one car to the next."

Ralph Keck, robed and slightly rumpled, shuffled out into the corridor. His eyes blazed with triumph. "Didn't I say so? They've left us here. Just abandoned us."

"No such luck," Thomas reassured him. "I'll lay odds there are dozens of Russian sharpshooters still out there observing your every movement from the concealment of the woods."

"But why?" Nell Blanton's voice had the sound of a plaint. "What's the purpose?"

"Psychological, no doubt," Thomas remarked. "Leave us alone to contemplate the error of our ways."

"Errors?" Jean fumed. "What errors?"

Isabel Gonzaga had been scowling at them from the far end of the car. "What Mr. Thomas means is that we have not complied with their wish that we make a sacrifice of one of our number."

"I'd say that's a fairly reasonable assumption, Miss Gonzaga." Thomas beamed a wicked grin at her.

"Well, by God," Keck thundered. "If that's all they want, we'll find out soon enough who the guilty party is among us."

"And if we don't have a guilty party?" Ted Kariolainen asked ironically.

"We can always appoint one," Grant Shapley grunted. "I'd vote for Keck here. As spies go, he's pretty likely."

"You may think this is a joke, Professor," Keck fumed. "There are those of us who still hope to get out of this thing alive."

"And don't care what they do in order to accomplish that." Isabel approached them down the center aisle. "If someone here has stolen confidential documents, I urge, I entreat you not to reveal the fact. It's no one's god-damned business but your own."

"There is no earthly reason why the safety of all the rest of us should be jeopardized," Keck flung at her.

Jatta Palmunan, appearing suddenly from the dining car, pushed herself between them. "I must ask you, Mr. Keck, not to keep alarming people with your talk. Yes, we do appear to be locked in here. Don't ask me why. Yes, the Russians *do* seem to have disappeared completely. Once again, don't ask me why. On the other hand, the dining car is supplied with several days' provisions. There is plenty of water in the holding tanks. The toilets are all service-able. That certainly doesn't make it appear that it is their intention to endanger our lives."

"Then kindly tell us exactly what is their intention," Kyle Van Meegrin asked.

The young Finnish woman was about to reply, then thought better of it. Instead she stared hard at the floor and shook her head slowly back and forth.

A gloom, thick and palpable as the fog outside, hovered above the occupants of the dining car as they had their breakfast that morning. Mrs. Shapley, Kate Dubbin, and Frau Kunkel functioned as a kind of short-order kitchen staff. They made toast and coffee in prodigious quantities. A large crate of eggs stamped "Produce of Fiume" was found in one of the large cold lockers, but oddly, for a dining car there were only two fry pans. There were also several crates of oranges, and the inevitable fruit nectar, so sweet and thick and warm it made you queasy to drink it.

Breakfast preparations proceeded smoothly, but once the food arrived at the tables, people ate little and there was virtually no talk. Shortly after, they proceeded to range freely up and down the train, exploring it in earnest.

"Appears to be some sort of VIP lounge," Thomas proclaimed, leaning into the compartment from the corridor outside. He stood aside to let the others peer in. Previously the place had been kept locked and off-limits to the passengers.

By the modest standards of the Green Train, the accommodations in the spacious private compartment behind the dining car were sumptuous. It was equivalent to three standard compartments in the day coach. It contained its own toilet, small kitchenette and refrigerator, as well as a fully stocked bar. By day it served as a sitting room with an attractive settee and upholstered chairs; this, as opposed to the hard wooden benches of the second-class day coach. By night it converted neatly to a bedroom with four wide bunks that pulled out from the wall.

"We've struck the mother lode." Thomas knelt before the small portable bar, extracting bottles of vodka, Scotch whiskey, and champagne. In the refrigerator they found tins of Iranian caviar and smoked salmon. Over his shoulder, he passed the supplies back to the eager hands of those waiting just behind him.

"That and a bit more," Stern said, but he was not looking at the food. An edge of something in his voice made the others turn, then follow the line of his gaze to one of the cabin windows above the bunk, where a thin, diaphanous curtain drifted slowly back and forth before an open window.

A bright grin flashed on Blanton's face but before he could say much, the big paddlelike hand of Tony Thomas fell across his mouth. Pressing a silencing finger to his own lips, Thomas pointed with his head in the direction of the ventilator mesh above the kitchenette, then to the P.A. speaker mounted above one of the bunks.

Stern crossed to the window. It stood open slightly more than a foot, but try as he might, it resisted being opened any farther. While several of the others feigned loud casual conversation, Kariolainen on one side and Stern on the other struggled to raise it higher. But it would not budge.

Once out in the corridor again, they whispered excitedly to one another.

"It's only about fifteen inches," Thomas spoke rapidly, "but someone could squeeze through."

"Someone very thin." Kariolainen looked doubtful.

"And someone very smart," Thomas said. "Smart enough to grasp the significance."

"Of what?" Blanton frowned. "What is the significance? What exactly does this person do once he gets out? Assuming he gets past the guards and over the border—what then?"

"The first thing"—Kariolainen grew excited—"is he notifies the authorities and our families of our situation. He pinpoints our exact whereabouts and informs the Free World of exactly what's going on here."

"Puts additional pressure on them," Thomas added.

Revelation came grudgingly to Blanton. "What's the nearest Finnish town?"

"Vainikkala," Thomas said. "Right over the border."

"How far?" Stern asked.

Thomas shrugged. "Ten kilometers. Maybe six, seven miles straight due west, through the woods." He pointed the direction with his finger. "A young chap could cover it in a few hours."

Blanton shook his head skeptically. "What makes you think he'd get through? You said it yourself, Tony. They're probably out there, even if you don't see them."

"True," Thomas agreed. "But on the other hand, they can't see you either."

They turned to the window, where the fog coiled and uncoiled like a serpent against the pane.

Thomas winked at them over his shoulder. "At least for the moment, they can't."

* * *

The voices of the Spanish choristers swelled to the rhythms of a Catalan folksong. They had been gathered and assembled in a corner of the dining car directly beneath another mesh-covered ventilator. Señor Madariaga conducted, one eye on his singers, the other on the group of individuals talking heatedly at one of the tables.

Outside, the rain had resumed and the fog had thickened. Mugs of tea and bouillon passed back and forth out of the galley to the passengers assembled there. Word of the open window had quickly gotten round. Curiosity and hope had drawn them in droves to the dining car.

The thrust of activity was centered round the table where Blanton, Kariolainen, Stern, Thomas, and a half-dozen others had gathered. Whenever their voices grew loud, Señor Madariaga's singers poured on additional decibels to drown them out in the more than likely event of listening devices concealed behind the ventilator mesh.

Paul Blanton had grown increasingly distressed with the course of developments. "I think you have to warn people."

"Of what? Getting caught?" Thomas waved the thought aside disdainfully. "The worst they'd do would be to bring the person right back to the train."

"What about getting lost?" Isabel asked. "Those woods out there are big and deep."

"Not a chance," Thomas said. "It's a straight line due west."

"That's if you can hold a straight line through the woods in this fog."

"Even if you can't," Kariolainen said, "you can just follow the train tracks."

Thomas shook his head. "Not all that easy. The area near the rail line is swarming with Russkies. You have to stay in the cover of the trees but keep the tracks on your right."

Up until then, Jatta Palmunan had kept her silence. Now suddenly she flung her hands up in despair. "I'm sorry. I cannot permit this. As long as I have the responsibility for bringing you out alive. For whatever the advantages to be derived from this, I find the risks involved unacceptable."

"Then you don't fully understand the advantages," Thomas snapped back. He looked quickly about at the others. "Does anyone else have any problem with this?"

"I do," Blanton fretted, "but I don't know what the alternatives are."

"There aren't any," Stern said.

"Precisely." Thomas glowed with satisfaction. "Unless, Miss Palmunan, you're suggesting we just sit about here indefinitely."

It wasn't until that moment that the young woman understood how limited her authority was. "We must wait. We can't risk lives," she pleaded. It was impassioned and sincere, but fruitless. By that time even she knew the decision had already been made.

A long sigh issued from Blanton's lips. "Okay, that settles it. Who goes?"

Thomas nodded and gazed up the length of the car where the others sipped mugs of coffee and bouillon. "We need someone thin."

"And young," Stern added.

"What about one of the Spanish kids?" Kariolainen stared hard in the direction of the choral group. At that moment their voices soared in a booming rendition of "La Paloma." "Or for that matter, my kid."

"Too young," said Thomas. "We need someone older, but not antiquated."

"I'll go." Van Meegrin pushed forward.

Thomas frowned, pointing to the young Dutchman's paunch.

"You'd never get through the window. What about Mr. Conti?" Thomas suggested. "He's the right age and certainly the right size."

"What about you?" Max threw the question right back at him.

"I'd go in a minute," Thomas said, "but I don't have the stamina for that sort of trek."

"Or the stomach," Isabel remarked cruelly.

The words stung, but Thomas ignored them. "Peter," he went on hurriedly, "I know you and Blanton are both a bit long in the tooth for this sort of thing. Mr. Kariolainen and Mr. Mukherjee—you'll forgive me, gentlemen—are both a bit too broad in the beam. . . ."

"What about me?" Isabel piped up. "Or perhaps Miss Blaylock. We're both the right size and the right age."

Jean Blaylock, who'd been strangely silent during the course of the talk, suddenly sparked to life. "No thanks. I'm afraid I'm not one of your Outward Bound crowd."

Isabel stiffened. "In that case, I'll be happy to go by myself."

There was a long, uneasy silence. Thomas lit one of his Balkan Sobranies, sending a plume of gray smoke spiraling slowly upward. "I think perhaps not."

Isabel flared, "You think, you think." Madariaga's choral voices soared beneath the ventilator. "Why is it you who always seem to be thinking for everyone else?"

Stern tugged her back gently. "Tony's right. I think a man, preferably a young one, stands a better chance of getting through."

Grant Shapley patted his stomach with an air of amused self-deprecation. "I regret this overindulged gut of mine more or less disqualifies me from the running. But if it's of any use to anyone, I think it's well worth a try. If only to remind folks we're still out here."

For a moment they listened to the hail of rain on the rooftop, and the angry sound of trees lashing about on the outside.

"It appears, then"—Thomas' voice grew clipped—"we have no volunteer for flight."

"I'll go." A voice tentative and barely audible sounded from a point somewhere behind the others. Several figures within the outer circle parted and the small, frailish figure of Asawa appeared, moving forward with the stiff, rather

stilted motions of a marionette. He came to an unsteady halt at the table before Thomas. When he addressed him, he did so staring over the
Englishman's head into some dreamy vacancy. "I would consider it an
honor."

Thomas appeared to be at a loss for words. He cleared his throat and cast
his eyes about for help. "That's very good of you, Asawa," he said at last.

What followed was a bleak, awkward silence. Asawa quickly grasped its
significance. Keith Wales lurched into the breach. "I'll go."

It was as though Asawa had never petitioned for the job. He was completely forgotten in the sighs of relief. For Wales, the opportunity held a score
of advantages. For one thing, and perhaps most obviously, freedom. For another, in the last day or so, ever since the unpleasant episode with Silvana,
he'd felt a distinct sense of strain in the company of the Italians. It was as if
they'd all known of it by then and were simmering quietly. The air all about
them was charged with silent accusations and reproachful glances. It had
been entirely his fault, of course, and the awareness of that had only just
begun to dawn upon him. He had not the least wish to be confronted now by
Sandro or Max on that score.

But also, the proposition appealed strongly to his youthful sense of the romantic. Possibly he might even redeem himself. He imagined Silvana frightened and pining away until news of his heroic flight reached her. If he failed,
the worst that might happen would be, as Thomas had said, the Russians
would bring him back to the train. There would even be a bit of cachet, he
imagined, attached to that. On the other hand, if he succeeded, why then the
possibilities were limitless.

"You're sure?" Thomas inquired.

"I'm sure."

"No doubts? No reservations?"

"None whatsoever."

"You don't have to do this," Jatta pleaded. "These people can get quite
nasty. Think it over. No one will think you a coward."

There was a moment when he appeared to seriously weigh the proposition.
Then suddenly they were all about him, clapping him on the back, congratulating him as the voices of the choir soared upward into the vaulted corner of
the car. The acclamation was simply too much for him to resist.

Even as they all surged about Wales, no one saw Asawa turn and slouch
down the aisle toward the exit, head slightly forward of his body, limping
stiffly.

It was no easy matter getting Wales on his way. It had to be done fast.
There was no telling how long the blessing of the fog would last. It would
have been naive to assume that the Russians would have left no one at all to
watch over the train and its controversial cargo.

The main force with all of its support groups had clearly pulled out.

Doubtless there was a skeleton force of some sort still out there somewhere in the forest. The fog would be working against them as much as it would be working for Wales. The point now was to exploit that fog as fully as possible.

Stern gave Wales his raincoat. Ralph Keck produced a pair of rubber boots from his luggage. Just before his departure, a number of them crammed telephone numbers and addresses of families and loved ones into Wales's pockets. While good-byes and last-minute instructions were administered, a number of the group ranged up and down the cars, making loud conversation so as to thwart whatever listening devices had been planted about them.

The worst part of it was getting Wales's head through the opening. Of course they might have tried simply smashing the window. But it was thick and shatterproof. They had no heavy, portable objects with which to attempt this, and even assuming they had, the noise created by such activity would doubtless have brought whatever military personnel was still in the general vicinity running.

For all of Wales's sleekly trim athletic figure, it took a great deal of pushing and grunting to squeeze him through the fifteen inches of available space between the sill and the bottom of the window frame. Finally out, hitting the wet, spongy ground below with a heavy squishing sound, he stood looking up at them, startled by the sight of their anxious faces lining the windows, already a touch of doubt chilling his initial enthusiasm. His nose and forehead were bleeding slightly from where he'd scraped patches of skin from them, squeezing through the narrow space.

A bag of food and a large jug of water followed him out. People waved handkerchiefs and looked teary. Dabbing the bleeding areas about his nose with a Kleenex tissue, he appeared to be scanning the windows, looking for one face in particular. But if he'd made this gesture to impress Silvana, it had earned him naught. She was nowhere to be seen. Nor, for that matter, was Sandro.

Thomas thrust a long, bony finger out the open window. "Just follow the track, but remember, keep well to the cover of the forest."

"What are his chances?" Stern asked, after Wales had loped off into the woods, and the others had dispersed into their compartments.

"No better than one in ten," Thomas murmured with the brusque knowledgeability of the professional specialist. "But even if he's caught they won't harm him. He's a Canadian from whose country they'd like to buy more wheat, and what they definitely don't want are charges of inhuman treatment plastered all over the Western press."

Stern sat mulling that over for a time. He stared out the window into the fog-shrouded forest as though he were still searching for a glimpse of Wales's phantom figure receding into the trees. "What I still don't quite grasp," he spoke aloud as if to himself, "is why they'd suddenly just pull out like this. And why, in God's name, after sealing us up in here, tight as a drum, they'd leave one window open like that."

He turned and looked directly at Thomas, whose eyes were staring back at him oddly. "Oversight, no doubt," he replied curtly. "Where the devil is that Asawa fellow anyway?"

From there things went downhill precipitously. Shortly after Wales's departure, Baby Muk started to whine. It began slowly, gradually gaining in volume and resonance until the air was riven by his shrieks. It went on remorselessly throughout the morning, with the effect of driving people into their cabins, huddling behind closed doors to insulate themselves from the shrill, ceaseless cries.

By midmorning the Monopoly and Scrabble boards were out, and the poker games were in full force. When Baby Muk's wailing commenced, the Van Meegrins, who shared the compartment with the Mukherjees, along with Kate Dubbin and Desfargue, had no choice other than to flee. They made directly for the dining car and sat up all morning playing bridge, while the rain drilled morosely down on the rooftop.

Peter Stern tried to lose himself in one of his Maigrets, while Paul Blanton retreated to his cabin and tried to sleep. Peeved and anxious, Thomas prowled back and forth from one car to the next, puffing endless cigarettes, leaving in his troubled wake the reeking burned-dung stench of black Yanidje.

The morning wore on interminably with no seeming break in the weather. Having started with bridge in the dining car, the Italian Quartet had split up after about an hour. Sonia switched to a poker game at the next table. Sandro, in something of a funk, had drifted off elsewhere. Jean Blaylock had left Cabin 2 a half-hour earlier and not been seen since. Only Max and Silvana remained, both pretending to read and be supremely unaware of one another. The seat 7C, lately occupied by Keith Wales, served to separate them. His luggage, still piled in the rack above the seat, smelling of old canvas, seemed to resonate with a host of charges and unpleasant memories.

Several times Silvana glanced up from her book to find Max's reproachful gaze on her. At such times he didn't look away, but kept staring directly at her, as though awaiting something. She folded her arms and gazed out into the fog-bound trees. "You have a filthy mind, Max," she said at last.

"I wish the filth I saw the other day was merely my imagination."

"It was, but in a million years I could never convince you of that." She continued to speak, staring out the window with sharp antagonism. "I certainly didn't encourage it, if that's what you think. And I will not apologize or attempt to make explanations. Least of all to you."

"Then you admit there was something—"

"I admit no such thing," Silvana snapped, and took up her book again.

Max was silent. "Sandro's my dearest and oldest friend," he resumed after a time.

"And for that reason, I am sure, you can't wait to tell him what you saw." She turned on him with a scornful little laugh. "You're such an awful hypocrite, Max. Poor Sonia could fill volumes about your squalid escapades. Even

I could supply a chapter or two there. Your 'oldest' and 'dearest' friend would be surprised, eh, Max? But, there too, I certainly didn't encourage it."

"You never encourage anything, do you, Silvana?" His tone was taunting. "Yet this sort of thing always seems to happen to you."

"I didn't encourage him." The tawny wave of hair along her cheek swirled with the snap of her head. "If you wish to tell Sandro . . ."

"How you could have led this boy on . . ."

"Oh, Christ." She started to rise but he pushed her back down.

"Now you've got this idiotic, overheated youth stumbling around out there trying to impress you. At best he stands a very good chance of being run down by guard dogs and soldiers . . ."

From where he sat he could see the flush of crimson rise like a welt against her throat.

"I think I must get away from you." She bolted up, then wheeled sharply. "I don't suppose that if I told you what you saw the other day was him forcing himself on me . . ."

Conti appeared to reflect a moment. "That is not the way it looked to me."

There was an air of finality about it. The prosecuting attorney rendering his final summation. It was so full of male self-serving, she wanted to strike him. She was a hair's breadth away from doing so, but instead, she flung her hands up in despair. "Tell Sandro. Do whatever the hell you please."

"Sandro has eyes for himself. He is very clever and he will know what needs to be done." He sighed and resumed his reading.

Mr. Mukherjee had been lurking in the corridor, reluctant to return to his cabin. He'd told Madam Muk that he was stepping out for a few minutes to stretch his legs and would return shortly. In truth, he was as anxious to escape the noise of the child as everyone else in Cabin 5.

Once outside the door, he gulped the stale air of the corridor as if it were fresh and bracing as a sea breeze. The sullen pout always visible in the presence of his wife had quickly transformed itself into a bright flashing smile. He was like a child who'd duped his teachers and gotten out of school for the day.

The corridor of the day coach at that moment was quite empty. Up forward, Jean Blaylock had just exited the loo. Not anxious to return to the confinement of her cabin, she loitered in the vicinity of the samovar, toying with the idea of a cup of tea, not that she particularly wanted tea. What she really hoped for was that someone might approach her so that she could rebuff them.

"Ah, Miss Blaylock." Mr. Mukherjee undulated forward, full of flowery charm. "Our ordeal continues, does it not?"

She muttered something and shot him an irritated glance which he construed to be wholehearted agreement. He was encouraged to continue. But just then one of his child's shrieks splintered the air, followed by a barrage of Hindi epithets from Madam Muk.

"I must apologize for the disturbances of my son. The circumstances, you will admit, are both difficult, not to say unnatural, for so small a child, and . . ."

As he rattled on it struck her that he stood unnecessarily close, brushing up against her from time to time. He spoke directly into her face, his eyes dropping from time to time to her breasts. The cloying scent of chypre wafted all about him.

He was talking of India and his home in Bombay. Had she ever been there? What a pity. Such a beautiful land. She began to simmer when he started to speak of caste and its great virtues. Westerners failed to truly understand its necessity. But, of course, he too was not totally unsympathetic. He allowed as how some might suffer unduly under such a system. If she ever came, what a privilege it would be to show her about, the Government Palace, and the Royal King's Club, where he was a charter member. "Only the best people, you know . . ."

Several times his hands touched her—a sleeve or an elbow, once on the shoulder where it struck her that it lingered a bit too long as he continued to regale her with the sights and pleasures of his homeland. All the while his long, bony fingers exerted a tremulous pressure on her, the intention of which was ambiguous. That unfortunate habit, too, of unconsciously scratching his genitals through his trouser pockets every several minutes was not helping matters.

So dazzled was he by the impression he was convinced he was making, he failed to note her growing displeasure. At one point she frowned directly at his hand, which had come to what appeared final rest on her shoulder. "I do admire you so." He leaned uncommonly close and spoke into her ear.

"Can I get you a cup of tea?" she asked, by way of breaking up the clumsy situation.

He appeared baffled by the question. "No—I think not."

She lifted his hand with a no-nonsensical firmness and dropped it from her shoulder with a flick the way one might perhaps discard something soiled. "In that case, bugger off," she said, and swept down the aisle.

Mr. Mukherjee stood there mystified. He was not quite certain what had happened, but in his mind he had certainly not been rebuffed.

Just a young, inexperienced girl, he thought. Probably flustered by the attentions of an experienced older man. He sighed, his eye drawn to a gathering of people in the dining car. Sweeping a comb several times through his thick raven hair, he proceeded forward.

For a while he watched the card playing and accepted a cup of tea. Consuelo Gonzaga was there, and once again he fell into conversation.

This time he fared better. Quickly sensing she was terrified by their general situation, he played deftly upon that. His way was light and airy. Where the flowery charms and quick intimacies had irritated Jean, they flattered Consuelo and reassured her.

Had she ever been to India? he started again. What a pity. If she ever came to Bombay, she must permit him to take her around. By no means unattractive, Consuelo had a kind of overripe bovine physicality that aroused men. She was dark and short. Her clothes seemed always too tight and, like her mother, she had the sort of timidity and shyness of which people invariably take advantage.

Mr. Mukherjee felt his hunting instincts quicken. Gazing at the card players and the others standing about there amid the din of unceasing chatter, he feigned a headache. "It's very noisy here, isn't it?"

"Yes."

"Very distracting."

She agreed, although she wasn't distracted at all.

"Perhaps," he said, his eyes fastened on the rising swells inside her blouse, "we might find someplace more quiet to talk. What do you say to that?"

She stared down at the floor as though she hadn't heard him. Then at last she spoke. "If you'd like."

He looked around and over his shoulder like a man about to steal something, his eyes searching for a discreet trysting place. Her eyes never rose from the floor as he led her off.

Outside the dining car she caught her breath when he pressed close to her in the vestibule, caressing her with his eyes. Passing others in the corridor of the day coach, they tried to appear casual. Mukherjee's greatest fear was the ever-present possibility of his wife suddenly emerging from the compartment. But as they passed Cabin 5 only a sweet, oddly untoward silence could be heard from behind the door.

At that time of day the sleeping coach was completely deserted. Consuelo and Mr. Mukherjee stood at the head of it, peering into the cool, shadowy vacancies. They had the look of a pair of frightened children about to trespass private property.

The doors of many of the bunks stood open, revealing a general chaos of discarded pajamas, rumpled sheets, and unmade beds.

"Would you walk back to my bunk with me?" He spoke softly with a slight breathlessness. When she looked at him, he smiled down at her strangely. "I'd like to show you a snapshot of my home in Bombay. It's in my bag."

Something resembling prudent judgment registered in her eyes, then vanished in a trice. Sensing little resistance, Mukherjee breathed more quickly.

She permitted him to take her hand and lead her tripping through the car. The Mukherjees slept in Cabin 8 toward the rear of the sleeping coach.

"Just let me see if I can find it." He swung the door of the compartment aside and made a pretense of rummaging through some papers. "Here—here it is," he giggled excitedly. "My house in Bombay." He stepped aside, inviting her to enter. He'd spread some snapshots out over the unmade bunk. She bent to examine them while he stood behind her, admiring the curve of her buttocks.

"You see the one there with the swimming pool." He leaned over her so that the curve of his body conformed with hers. When his hands reached up and cupped her breasts, she said nothing. Emboldened by her silence, he spread his palm across the breadth of her buttocks and pushed gently forward.

By noon people had started to wander up toward the dining car from various parts of the train, drawn there by the warm eggy fragrance of dough rising, as well as the simple need for human contact. Most of them had spent the better part of the morning confined to their cabins.

Several games of bridge and poker were still under way. Fortified with an ice bucket and two liters of Russkaya appropriated from the pillaged lockers of the VIP lounge, Tony Thomas, suffused with spirits, presided over a table of rapt, eager listeners. Stern had heard most of it before in Leningrad—the true-life adventures of Mr. Anthony Beech Thomas, the world-traveled correspondent, Kremlinologist, bon vivant, and raconteur who'd covered History as it was being made, the privileged intimate of kings and heads of state, even movie stars.

Stern wandered forward to the galley and poked his head in. Nell was there by herself, swirling a ladle through a pot of melting chocolate. Drops of sweat beaded her forehead and she muttered oaths beneath her breath.

"Is that lunch?" Stern asked.

"If we're lucky." Hands swaddled in a large towel, she pulled open a pair of oven doors and tugged out a large chocolate torte. "They're not exactly set up here for anything too ambitious."

She set the torte down on a butcher's block to cool.

Stern stood above it, inhaling the warm, doughy fumes. He spied the chocolate simmering in a shallow pan and moved toward it with a spoon. He started to dip in, but Nell swiped the offending hand with an adroit swish of her towel. "I'm afraid you're just going to have to wait."

"For what?"

"For lunch."

"When's that?"

"In about twenty minutes, if everything doesn't fall apart."

Stern smiled. Her hair was in disarray. Her cheeks glowed from the heat of the galley, and she wore a chef's apron wound several times about her girlish middle. "What are we having?"

"Deviled eggs. Russian pumpernickel. Sliced ham. Tomatoes. Sardines. Some other kind of pickled fish. Coffee, tea, and . . ."

"Chocolate cake."

"If you're a good boy." She moved off to one of the larders.

He stared round at the general mayhem of the place. Dishes, bowls, platters, whisks, ladles, a variety of parts from a mixing appliance, were all stacked in the big aluminum sinks. "You do all this yourself?"

"Irma Kunkel was here with me up till about ten minutes ago." She blew a

wisp of hair out of her face as she toiled with the delicate business of extracting the torte from the pan without breaking it. "Señor Madariaga's kids did
the breakfast dishes."

"You don't see this in terms of any long-range career plans?"

"God forbid. I came in here for therapy. I just had to get out of that compartment. Paul still there?"

"I think he's taking a nap."

She laughed mirthlessly. "If that isn't Paul to a tee. The world's going up in
flames but he still must have his nappy." She howled as she set the torte to
cool on a drainboard near the window. She pulled off her apron with a flourish and pushed the hair from her face. "How about a belt of chablis?"

"You're kidding. Where'd you get it?"

"Found it in one of the lockers. Been cooling all morning." She pulled a jug
out of the refrigerator along with a pair of chilled goblets.

"My, my." He was full of admiration. "You've got it all together, don't
you?"

"Not exactly." She handed him a goblet. "But enough. Cheese. Milk. Ce-
real. Even meat, of a sort."

"What sort?"

"Nothing you'd care to eat."

"Tell me."

"Some kind of creature. Badger maybe. Damned if I know." She gulped
the chablis, closed her eyes and let it slide down her throat. "Heaven, isn't it?
French. The real thing." She cocked an eye at him.

"When's the last time you had a woman?"

Stern's brow arched. "I beg your pardon?"

"When's the last time you slept with a woman?"

"None of your business."

Nell shrugged. "Don't get huffy. Just being friendly."

"Too friendly." Stern frowned. "When's the last time you slept with a
man?" He didn't expect a reply.

"The other night in Leningrad."

"Very funny."

"I didn't say it was Paul."

He was momentarily flustered.

"But it was," she quickly added. An awkward silence followed while he
watched her knead more dough and tried to think desperately of something to
say. But finally it was Nell who filled the gap.

"As a matter of fact it wasn't the other night in Leningrad." Her eyes were
fixed intently on the dough as she spoke. "It was some time ago."

Stern watched, mesmerized, her hands slowly, rhythmically, stretching and
pulling the dough.

"And you?" she asked without raising her eyes.

He sighed as though to say: "Oh God, let's not get into all this"—then made a funny, rather futile gesture with his shoulders. "About four weeks ago. Just before I left New York."

"Who with?"

"A widow. Friend of Connie's and mine for years. Her husband died a few months ago."

"And you were both at loose ends?"

"In a manner of speaking." He was suddenly annoyed. "Listen, why are we talking this way?"

"Well, we're both a bit horny." She looked up, smiling with an oddly pointed gaze into his eyes. "This is just a harmless way of getting it off."

Stern, struggling to hold her gaze, felt himself coloring.

"Don't look so worried," she said.

"Who's worried?"

"I'm not promiscuous, if that's what you're thinking. And besides, trains aren't exactly designed for that sort of thing."

"Bad physical setup," he agreed, attempting to match her glibness. "Cabin's too small. Berths too narrow. Walls too thin."

"Particularly if you happen to be a screamer and a shouter."

"Are you?"

"I tend to be quiet and very deliberate." She spoke with deadly solemnity. "But when truly aroused, I bite."

A portentous silence descended on them for a moment, then suddenly they both burst into roaring hoots of laughter.

"Why are we doing this?" he said. "I mean, talking dirty. Like a pair of adolescents."

"It's fun," she said, and gulped her chablis.

It was then he noticed she was flushed a bit too—a warm, roseate glow that crept upward from beneath her open collar and fanned out across her throat. He knew it wasn't just the wine or the heat of the oven.

"Have you ever been promiscuous?" she asked with a sudden and oddly touching naiveté.

"Not in thirty years of marriage," he shot back almost too quickly. "I'm incurably middle-class. Have you?"

"Once . . . at the Palmer House in Chicago."

"Who with?"

She pulled the dough, then stretched it into long, tubular shapes. "A divinity student."

A chuckle rippled at his lips, then died quickly when he realized she was in deadly earnest.

"A divinity student?"

"He was half my age. He picked me up in the lobby. Or I picked him up. I don't recall which."

"Probably the latter," Stern said with amusement.

"Probably," Nell agreed. "Anyway he was looking to fall from grace."

"And you assisted him?"

"Almost. Halfway through, I caught a glimpse of myself in a mirror beside the bed."

He watched her intently. "And?"

"Having a sense of humor is a real detriment to a good sex life. All those flailing arms and legs, those grunts and sighs, the inadvertent flatulence . . . I started to laugh. He was deeply offended. So I got up, put my clothes back on, and left. Leaving his grace still intact."

"But just barely."

She gulped her chablis and laughed. "I don't think his heart was really in divinity. If he's actually a pastor today, I fear for the young women of his congregation."

"It's something you have to be born to, I imagine. Like dentistry," Stern remarked soberly. "No such thing there as an acquired taste."

They laughed again and she poured them more wine.

"Now, tell me," Stern said. "What were you really looking for there?"

"In the lobby at the Palmer House?"

He nodded and watched her eyes narrow above the rim of her glass.

"Revenge," she said as though it were the first time the thought had occurred to her. "I was up there with Paul. Supposedly a little spree for our twentieth anniversary. And he was spending all of his time every day seeing clients."

When she looked back at him again her eyes seemed quite merry but there was something unspeakably sad about her.

"I'm very middle-class too," she said. "Not your basic Emma Bovary. I'm not good at sneaking around. I don't like cocktail lounges, or motels, or hotel lobbies. I'm just a forty-six-year-old lady who's a bit afraid of getting older. I still like to be touched and held by a man. Paul's sexual requirements have become erratic and somewhat undependable."

There was no embarrassment as she spoke. Her voice was a quiet monotone with no trace of emotion. It had about it something of the feel of the confessional.

"Why are you telling me all this?" he asked.

She'd laid the dough in strips into a cake pan and popped it into the oven with a loud clap. For a moment he thought she was angry. But when she turned again, there was that quiet, slightly wicked smile flickering at the corners of her mouth. "We're not always going to be stuck on this train, I hope, and I'm just putting you on notice."

Keith Wales came stumbling to a halt, nearly toppling from the force of his own momentum. He'd been on his feet the better part of five hours with no idea of where he was or how much farther it was to the border. He stood now in a dense pine grove, trying to peer through the fog. More ominous yet, he was no longer certain that he was still traveling due west. Within the course of his flight, he'd been forced on several occasions to take wide swings in order to bypass obstacles—once a lake and once a deep gorge. He'd proceeded on the theory that he must stick to the cover of the woods, yet keep the train tracks on his right. But several times the sound of voices in the forest drove him farther from the tracks, and subsequent efforts to correct his position tended to confuse more than they clarified.

It hadn't sounded difficult several hours back when Thomas had first posed the proposition. But his watch now read 1:14 P.M. He'd been under way since roughly nine A.M. If the Englishman was right and Vainikkala was only ten kilometers from the train, he should have crossed the border an hour ago.

The rain had stopped but water dripped incessantly from the trees. Barging through the undergrowth had sent cascades of chilly water sluicing down on him into his collar, down his back. His clothing and shoes were sodden, and to add to his woes, the temperature in the forest had dropped precipitously. The air was suddenly cold, yet he could feel pockets of perspiration under his clothing.

Standing there in the mist-hung grove, panting like a winded animal, it dawned on him that he might be lost. Still, that seemed improbable. He felt reasonably certain the train tracks were not far off to his right. Had he actually lost his way, and inadvertently gone off on a northeasterly tack, he would by this time have intersected the rail line. And, to his knowledge, he hadn't. Of that he was quite certain.

The other possibility, that he'd gotten turned around in the fog and was now moving southeast, or worse even, straight east on a path back to the train, was too awful to contemplate.

Still, he'd heard of things like that happening. He was not quite ready for panic, but he was increasingly conscious of something starting to stir within him, some rising, tossing, unbridled thing with which he sensed himself beginning to contend.

He started walking again, this time more briskly. It was well past lunch and he was hungry. He took an apple from the bag of food they'd given him, and as he lurched and stumbled forward through the brush, he chewed, not tasting anything and spitting the flesh and pips out as he went.

Branches and bracken lashed at him. His clothes were studded with thistles that pricked at him through his trousers. Worse even, the thick muddy ooze beneath his feet gulped at his rubbers, nearly pulling them off.

He thought of those on the train and envied them. They were still captives, to be sure, but at least they were dry and warm. He thought, too, of Silvana, and wondered if she thought of him. He wished that she could see him just as he was this moment.

He plunged forward, muttering to himself, cursing the wet and cold, the lash of branches at his cheek. He wondered about the size of the forest. How big, how vast was it? He didn't know. He couldn't see more than a foot before him. Could a person simply wander off the face of the earth here into some trackless, uncharted wilderness, never to be heard from again?

It had not occurred to him before because it seemed so improbable, but he might now actually have to face the prospect of a night in the woods. He was hardly prepared for that. He had barely any food, only a jar of fresh water, and no matches. No one had thought of more extensive supplies since the journey was looked upon as brief and not particularly challenging.

Suddenly up ahead loomed a formation of rocks he was certain he'd passed hours ago. Yet logic told him that couldn't be. He'd been moving straight due west. He had veered once or twice, to be sure, but it seemed to him he had always corrected his position. The trees at this point were huge and deep, great stands of tall conifer from which emanated an air of almost human malevolence. They were seductive and had a way of beckoning you, luring you on.

In the next moment, for reasons unknown even to him, he started to run, no longer at all certain in which direction he was going. His feet squished through mud up to his ankles so that he had to pull each one out with great effort.

When he'd started to run he was well past wanting to reach the border station at Vainikkala. At that point he wanted only to reach someplace where there was civilization and people.

Winded, he kept running, terrified to stop and unaware that he was crying. It was then he heard the dogs baying, the loud crack of branches in the undergrowth, and the hoarse barking of the Russian guards pushing toward him.

He listened again, leaning on a tree, his heart banging against his ribs. As the baying and shouts came closer, to his surprise he didn't flee. Instead he turned and ran shouting toward his pursuers.

" 'Why do the nations conspire, and the people plot in vain? The Kings of the earth set themselves and the Rulers take counsel together . . .' "

Ralph Keck's voice droned on through the stale, unventilated air. At the head of the dining car, he stood before his small congregation, his pulpit fashioned from an aluminum sidestand used for stacking dirty dishes. He read from a pocket psalter he carried about with him everywhere, his aged, freckled hands holding open the little book, tremulous on the page.

" 'He who sits in the heavens laughs; the Lord has them in derision. Then he will speak to them his wrath, and terrify them in his fury, saying . . .' "

Sonia Conti's eyes wandered to the window and out to the surrounding forest, where they fastened on a raven perched at the tip of a distant tree. She was thinking of Max and at the same time keenly aware of Silvana beside her following Keck's lips with her eyes and murmuring almost soundlessly the words after him.

The Kariolainens all sat together at a single table. Young Buddy leaned against his father's thigh daydreaming of canoes and mountain streams high up in the Cascades. Señora Gonzaga and Consuelo sat just across from them making a valiant effort to follow the meaning of Keck's reading. Mrs. Keck, seated by herself off to the side, appeared to preside over it all. She had about her the alert, vigilant air of a watchdog.

All of them there, both pastor and parishioners, looked terribly trapped. And there was fear now that the Shoe King of Ames would be unable to resist the temptation of delivering some sort of a sermon at the conclusion.

Not a particularly gifted orator, Keck had a high, thin voice that, when charged with emotion, had the quality of an unoiled hinge. But he genuinely wished to give comfort and courage to his congregation. It was not his fault that he failed to see he was not succeeding. " 'Now, therefore, O Kings, be wise; be warned, O Rulers of the earth. Serve the Lord with fear . . .' " The last word emerged at a near-shriek, as if torn from the air. Startled, Sonia Conti flinched, making an audible gasp just as the raven lifted heavily off from the treetop and flapped westward with an awful squawking.

Knowing she and Ralph were doing the Lord's work, Myra Keck observed the proceedings with a glow of triumph. Whatever trials lay ahead, the Lord's strength, she knew, would be there to sustain them.

It always had in the past, through the tough unsettled early days of their marriage when she had been the principal force and backbone of their little family. It was at a time when Ralph's drinking and aimlessness had become a town scandal, life-threatening not only to him but to his wife and children as well. There'd been a period of almost a year in which a judge had at last reluctantly separated him from his family for fear of the bodily harm he might do them. There was no question of his being able to work.

In the institution, fifty miles outside of Ames, where she visited him without exception three times a week, she would read to him from the Bible—he who'd never touched a Bible in his life—out on the big side porch with the majestic old copper beech trees that enveloped them in cool, healing shadows. She would read mostly from the Psalms or Proverbs, and from Matthew and Mark, reading over and over again those sections describing Christ's ministry in Galilee, his laying on of hands, the healing of lepers and of the halt and lame. She would read to Ralph before and after supper, until at last he'd fall asleep and she would turn out the light, leaving the Bible at his night table open at a page for him to read first thing on waking in the morning. Then she would tiptoe out of the room and drive the fifty miles home to Ames.

Ralph left the institution after eleven months. In that time he had exorcised his demons and learned to pray. When he came home he went to work in a small local shoe store. A year later, he bought the store. Five years later he owned a half-dozen stores around the state and was just breaking ground to build his own factory with which to supply his growing chain.

In all that time he had not once touched alcohol, and having found God, never left him again. Indeed, he had a terror of losing God, and of losing

Myra too. He knew how much he owed her, and for her part, she never let him forget it.

"Don't you see? It's inevitable. Marx predicted it all, over a hundred years ago."

"And it still hasn't happened."

"It will, though. Don't kid yourself."

"When it does, I'll put everything I own to the torch, rather than let the state get its grubby hands on it."

"Anything rather than share with the less fortunate. That's what I call Christian charity."

"Communism has nothing to do with charitability."

"That's where you're wrong. If Christ were alive today, he'd be a loyal card-bearing member of the Communist party."

"Tell that to a Polish priest. If J. Christ were alive today, the Commies would have to crucify him all over again."

It was Isabel and Jean Blaylock having a shouting match. They were in Cabin 3, with Kate Dubbin, Desfargue, and old Gonzaga adding their own fuel to the fire.

"Have you ever lived in an authoritarian state, Jean?" Kate Dubbin asked.

"I've lived in one all of my life. America."

Kate groaned. "Oh, come now. You don't seriously . . ."

"Don't you see?" Desfargue leaned toward her. "What she's talking about is not the fascism of the state, but the fascism of technology. The dehumanization of people into robots. That's Western fascism."

Kate flung her hands up in despair. "What I don't get is, if you're all so damned fired-up about the system, why didn't you come here sooner, stay longer, learn the language—instead of this five-day farmer's tour we've had. A trip down memory lane into jolly old imperial Russia. 'See the home of the czars. Walk in the lush gardens where Peter and Catherine walked. See Leningrad by night from the deck of a boat on the moonlit Neva.' Is that supposed to be Russia—all that hype in the glossy brochure they give you? 'See the great cathedrals—the Kazan and St. Isaac's. See the glories and the untold treasures of the Hermitage. See what the czars and the church gave to Mother Russia. But if you're looking for what's come out of this land since 1918, the so-called miracle of the People's Revolution, you may be disappointed.' "

"I came, like you, to have a look," Jean said. "I'm not so dumb as to believe that what I saw was perfection. But I'm convinced it's still the only hope the world has for equality and justice. A fair break for everyone."

"Then what you're saying," Isabel said, "is that we take the part of the world that is productive and self-sufficient, the part that provides goods and jobs, and dismantle all of that so that everyone can be equally hungry and miserable."

Gonzaga clapped appreciatively. "Bravo, Isabel. I quite agree. Give people a chance to own something. Make them entrepreneurs. Give them a stake in the game and you'll soon see what human ingenuity can do."

Jean Blaylock scowled. "What you'll soon see is a handful of rich guys with billions of poor guys indentured to them."

"Then that is perhaps the natural order of things." He smiled as he watched her lips curl with contempt. "In the end, we are not all the same and cannot be legislated so by the drafting of laws and the waving of wands. All my life I have had servants. On my estates and in my vineyards. They have been with my family for generations. We know each of them as if they were our own flesh and blood. Every family is permitted to keep and sell at market half of everything they produce. Many have prospered. Others, less enterprising, have not fared so well. But all are treated with regard and dignity. If you came to them today with an opportunity to go and grub about on some state-operated commune, with extravagant notions about equalizing opportunity for all, I am certain they would look at you as though you were mad."

"That's because they're stupid and uneducated," Jean flared.

Gonzaga's smile was pitying. "Your great esteem for the working poor, Miss Blaylock, is truly touching. You call America a police state. You amaze me. An intelligent woman, with a keen sense of fairness, you've just had your passport confiscated without the courtesy of so much as an explanation; you're sitting locked up, imprisoned on a train unable to leave a country; your eye is still black from a soldier's fist. I ask you, Miss Blaylock, and you too, Monsieur Desfargue—does not anything of what has happened to us here in the last 5 days give you pause?"

"Do you think we'll die here?"

"What a crazy idea."

"Why would they just go off and leave us like this?"

"Corrie, you're letting your imagination run wild."

"Aren't you frightened?"

"Of course I'm frightened."

"I'm glad you said that. If you'd said no, I'd know you were lying and I would have hated you for that."

Karl Heinz laughed and shook his head in bemusement. "I can't keep up with you, Corrie. You're too complicated for me."

Karl Heinz Kunkel and Corrie Kariolainen sat by themselves in Cabin 9 amid the smearings and crumbs of midafternoon chocolate cake. They had been talking earnestly the way young people are apt to, exchanging secrets, amazed and delighted at how often their inmost thoughts appeared to coincide.

"You need to have a calling," Karl Heinz said with grand solemnity. "All life is meaningless without some sense of struggle."

"Yes, I feel that too," Corrie replied. "To have a calling, a commitment . . . That's what really matters. Most of my friends are only interested in material security. They have no conception of hard work or personal sacrifice."

They grew silent for a time, saddened by the vacancy of everyone's lives except their own.

Corrie was smiling inwardly to herself, with a smile as old as time. "I can't believe you've never been to the States."

He hadn't, he confessed, but he planned to come in the not distant future. He thought he might like to attend university in the States. He looked at her hopefully. Then, by all means, he must come to northern California, she said. Up around Shasta, where she lived, not far from the Oregon border. She'd show him her father's fruit farms with their fabulous apricots and big dark cherries. And she had horses, too. Did he like to ride? He'd been on ponies as a child, but never on a real horse. The sort of horses he'd seen in movies in Würzburg about the Old West. A John Wayne sort of horse. Was the American West really as big as it looked in the movies?

"Bigger," she laughed. "Much bigger. You can't begin to imagine. Wyoming. Utah. The Dakotas." Why didn't he think of coming next summer? She'd take him down to Palo Alto. Show him Stanford and the U. of C., where she hoped to go. They had a great school of veterinary medicine. She loved animals and that's what she wanted to do. More than anything.

The rain had stopped. The fog had begun to lift. The trees beyond the rain-streaked windows looked dark and foreboding. For the moment they seemed terribly alone. Karl Heinz's fingers fiddled with a thread in his shirt. He appeared to be pondering something—struggling for words with which to articulate it. "You know," he said, his eyes scanning the dripping trees beyond the window. "This may sound crazy . . ."

"Yes?"

"But I hope the Russians don't come back, and that we stay here forever just like this." He looked up at her questioningly. "You know what I mean?"

"Yes," she laughed. "I hope so too."

He laughed happily with the sound of a saw rasping like mad in his throat. "Even something as rotten as all this"—his grateful eyes swung round the compartment of the train—"something really fantastic can come out of it."

Asawa lay in his berth all day. He hadn't bothered to dress, but stayed in his pajamas puffing innumerable cigarettes and scribbling into his pad. He slept on and off, fitfully, in a numbed daze. Images of home, the ghosts of a troubled past, fled across the ceiling of his compartment.

He propped himself on an elbow and peered into the small oval wall mirror affixed to the wall above his berth. The face he saw there was no more his own. It was Mizoguchi, the acolyte and hopeless stutterer, the outcast youth with his lank hair and pimply skin, seeking companionship and acceptance among the other acolytes in the temple.

At lunchtime Asawa heard voices in the corridor and footsteps trailing past his door. Through the walls of his berth he heard the frantic chatter of the Spanish youths, and at one point the voices of Jean Blaylock and Miss Gonzaga in a loud altercation.

He was hungry but he would not deign to leave his compartment. He would not join the others in the restaurant car because there he would have to sit at table with them and possibly speak. He hated the obligation of simple conversation because he was certain that he, like Mizoguchi, would stutter. And then too, of course, he knew that they despised and pitied him, had witnessed his humiliation before the Canadian that morning, and were, even at that moment, laughing behind his back.

At a certain point between those long, seemingly interminable hours between noontime and dusk, he'd stood up on his berth and once again unscrewed the panel in the bulkhead near the ceiling. He poked about in there until he heard it click dully against the canister. He swept the pencil back and forth until he'd dislodged the lid and plunged the point into the red, gelid substance. Withdrawing it, he brought the point close to his nose, inhaling the nearly odorless fumes as though they were the musk of some exquisite deadly flower.

It was gray outside when they'd gathered in the dining car for supper. The time was well past eight o'clock and after a search they found the switches that illuminated the car. They came in twos and threes, straggling into the car in desultory fashion, unspeaking, looking anxiously about, as if waiting for a captain or a waiter to seat them.

Van Meegrin, Stern, Jatta, and Isabel threw themselves into the task of providing supper. There were sufficient provisions in the train's larder to whip up a passable stew.

Still full of barely suppressed anxieties, Stern pitched himself into the business of providing a sauce of sorts for the boeuf bourguignon. Into cans of concentrated beef stock he chopped onions, scraped carrots, and hulled peas. They could find no decent Burgundy, but Thomas had discovered the keys to the locker where cases of the Bulgarian wine were stored, and that had to do.

Jatta cut slabs of grayish meat into small bite-size chunks and marinated them in bowls of wine. Working in his shirtsleeves, Van Meegrin stirred the large caldron with a big wooden paddle and served up steaming portions in the coarse crockery they'd found stacked in a dishware cupboard.

There was little conversation. All that was heard throughout dinner was the nervous clink of stainless steel ringing on the crockery. Several times Tony Thomas tried to engage his dinner companions in talk, but the air of dejection was too thick to dispel.

They were nearly finished with dinner and on their dessert when the electrical hum of the train's P.A. system suddenly switched on, followed by a great deal of loud crackling. Startled and still chewing, they all looked up at once, staring as if at the noise itself coming from the loudspeaker. In the next moment a voice was speaking to them.

"Good evening, members of Intour Group 409. This is Colonel Dunskoi. I take the opportunity to address you on this fifth night of your detainment in the Soviet Union. We trust you are as comfortable as possible under the circumstances.

"It is regrettable," Dunskoi went on above the electrical crackle, his voice tired and pitying, ". . . that one of your number took advantage of our temporary absence to attempt to escape. That was most foolish and you will shortly see why. This individual is presently back in custody. He has apologized for his actions and, further, he has now admitted to complicity with the American agents of the Central Intelligence of attempting to spirit classified material out of the Polyarny naval station in Kola."

A gasp of disbelief went up.

"We now have reason to believe this individual was not working alone. He had an accomplice here on this train. As of yet, he has refused to identify anyone. The moment he does so it will become possible to process your immediate release. This can be accomplished within a matter of hours. It is very much, therefore, to your advantage to discover the identity of this person among yourselves and to prevail on him or her to do what is not only wise but honorable. Without this, you may all expect to be detained here indefinitely."

"So," Blanton muttered, "there you have your reason for the sudden mysterious departure."

"And the single open window," Stern added somewhat more ominously. "It was a setup to produce a scapegoat, and we fell right into it. Now they want another."

"Quiet," Thomas hissed. "There's more."

"Because of our continuing concern for your well-being," Dunskoi droned on through the crackling speakers, "doctors will be here in the morning to conduct physical examinations. Please be ready promptly at seven A.M.

There was an audible click and Dunskoi's voice was suddenly gone, along with the hiss and crackle of the speakers.

"I don't want to be examined by their doctors," Nell Blanton said when the speakers had been turned off.

"I think you'll find you don't have much choice in the matter," Thomas said. "When these people get interested in your well-being, they can be pretty forceful about it."

There was a sudden commotion at the head of the car, followed by shouting and a blur of motion. The door of the dining car flew open with a bang and something was shoved in. It was Keith Wales.

You could not tell at once, of course. He was swaddled in white bandages his head wrapped mummylike, so that all one could see was the tip of his nose, still bearing the identifying scrape mark from the morning's tight exit through the window. Several holes had been cut in the bandages to leave room for sight. Within those holes, a pair of terrified eyes rolled wildly about behind the bandages.

"My God." Nell's hand flew to her mouth. "Oh, my God."

"Looks like they drove over him with a backhoe," Kariolainen said.

Stern's heart thumped in his chest. He could not associate the broken moaning thing staring wildly out from the bandages with the healthy, self-confident young man who'd slipped off into the woods that morning.

Wilma Shapley was now crouching above him. "What happened to you, child? Can you talk?"

They surged forward, crowding all around him, trying to hear. What they saw was disquieting. A lump of sodden muddy rags; the body limp and spent, seemingly boneless. One shoe had been torn from his foot, half the bare heel exposed beneath a sock half-off. In addition to the head swaddled in bandages, the left hand was bound in a makeshift tourniquet from which blood oozed.

Trying to reply to Wilma Shapley's question, Wales's mouth twisted crookedly and they could see where a tooth had been knocked out and the jagged stump of another showed beside it. When he tried to speak, he had no control over his lips. He struggled to shape them into words but his voice was no more than a hoarse, dry rattle.

"Give him air." Shapley pushed people back and away. "For God's sake, let him breathe."

Kariolainen herded people off. "Let's get him to his cabin," he snapped at Stern over his shoulder. "Wash him up and get him into bed."

"Careful—there might be broken bones."

He groaned when they hoisted him. Stern, sagging slightly beneath the sinking weight, thought he was going to be sick. Max and Karl Heinz locked hands and made a kind of sling onto which Wales, nearly screaming with pain, was lifted and carried back into the sleeping coach.

After they'd disappeared through the glass doors of the vestibule, the others hovered about, speechless. They were frightened and confused. Silvana appeared to be in a state of shock. Sandro put his arm about her waist and half-carried, half-dragged her back to their compartment.

"They're back." Buddy Kariolainen's boyish shout brought them wheeling about, scurrying to the windows. The boy clung to the glass as if he'd been pinioned there. The others pushed forward and crowded every window.

Peering through the milky dusk, they saw dozens of trucks rolling into the area, troops, hundreds more than were there before, off-loading from the motor transports, streaming through the cat's cradle of searchlight beams swerving all about the area. Then, suddenly, like some nightmarish engine of hell, a huge T54 attack tank came smashing forward through the underbrush, moving up to the train, its 60mm cannon looming before them, the black round hole of the muzzle pointing directly down their throats.

All about them were the barks of dogs, the shouts of guards running, taking up positions round the train and at every exit. The clatter of boots sounded overhead on the rooftops, seeming to stamp about with an almost malicious delight. Then came the heavy thud of feet clambering up the coach steps and rifle troops pouring into the outer vestibule.

PART VII

A CLOAK OF MYSTERY has descended over the Russo-Finnish border tonight. Soviet authorities have taken steps to close down completely all access between the two countries. At three key checkpoints along the five-hundred-mile border, Vyborg, Priozersk, and Vyartsilya, all passenger and commercial traffic has ground to a halt. Air traffic in and out of the Soviet Union still appears, at this time, to be unaffected. It has been recently learned that elements of the Soviet Baltic Fleet, stationed at Severomorsk naval base on the Kola Peninsula, have been put on full alert. Terming the action "unwarranted" and an "act of terrorism," the Finns have formally closed their consulate in Leningrad and called all personnel home.

—John Roland, Channel 5 News

. . . dispatches from the Kremlin tonight report that an agent of the American CIA was seized aboard a Finnish train late today attempting to spirit documents of the highest classification out of the Soviet Union to the West. Traveling with a forged Canadian passport, the individual confessed to accepting two thousand dollars in U.S. currency from a U.S. general in Brussels. Another passenger traveling with an American passport, but suspected of being an Israeli agent, is also under surveillance.

Yet another instance of U.S. bullyboy strong-arm tactics, and a demonstration of its ruthless determination to use its lackey client states to achieve its unholy goal of world domination.

This has been a special report of the People's Revolutionary Alert. Radio Tehran.

A detachment of rifle troops came early to the train that morning. Those people who had not yet finished their breakfasts were told to leave them in place and form two columns outside—men in one, women in the other. From there they were marched in formation with rifle troops on either side of each column to a group of large trailer vans that had been drawn up in the fields overnight.

The size of the force attending them had grown appreciably, as well as the number and variety of equipment supporting them. Innumerable heavy trucks were parked in long rows throughout the area—ambulances, motor troop transports, mobile maintenance trucks, water carriers, in addition to three helicopters circling almost continuously overhead, not to mention the huge, incomprehensible presence of the T54 tank drawn up directly outside the newly erected fence to oversee the activities of fifty-one unarmed men, women, and children.

The surrounding woods, too, teemed with troops patrolling every inch of perimeter, but by far the most disheartening sight of all was the twelve-foot barbed-wire fence thrown up during the night in a narrow, suffocating little noose encircling the train. A guard with a police dog stood at attention in a sentry box beside a tall gate built into the fence overnight.

The doctors there were mostly women. Bulky, square, no-nonsense ladies in white smocks with thickish ankles and orthopedic shoes. For the most part they looked more like locker-room attendants at a health spa than physicians.

The examinations were carried out in the trailer vans, one person at a time. Each van was fitted out with examination tables, radiology units, and a field laboratory in order to do blood and urine analyses on the spot. The examinations took approximately forty minutes each while the others waited queued up in the tall, weedy grass outside the vans.

It was a peculiar examination, by no means unprofessional, but rudimentary and unsophisticated by Western standards. Urine and blood samples were taken, as well as a series of X rays of the heart and lungs. The radiological equipment used for that purpose looked quaintly antique and, to Stern's mind, dangerous.

The lady who examined him was a jolly, florid soul who spoke English, told him his blood pressure was high, and asked him what was worrying him. The fact that she was able to ask it with a straight face was some sort of huge accolade to her professional detachment. There was a great physicality to the examination along with an almost prim decorum. The doctor whacked and thumped him about good-naturedly, but auscultation was conducted with all his clothing on.

Only at the end when she put a rubber surgical glove on did things get a trifle sticky.

Stern looked at her askance. "Is that necessary?"

"Hemorrhoids and prostate. Must be checked."

"I have difficulty with neither."

"Please to let me be the judge."

"I don't see the purpose."

"It gives me no great pleasure either. Please to drop trousers."

"I shit and pee beautifully," Stern snapped.

The doctor was unfazed. She smiled a weary but implacable smile. She was a heavy young women who appeared as though she'd been raised on a diet of potatoes and cream pastries. Her clothing was permeated with the sharply ammoniacal odor of dried perspiration. She had a sweet round face and though she looked middle-aged, she was probably no more than thirty or so.

She dipped her rubbered finger into a jar of petroleum jelly and, sighing, turned back to him. "Please. Like a good fellow now, to bend over."

It was well past the lunch hour and still they were waiting to be examined. Those, like Stern, who were among the first to go through had to wait out in the field outside the vans for the others to be processed. Under the surveillance of two armed guards, they could not wander freely about but were required to squat or kneel or sit in place within two neat columns, so that when the time came for them to leave, they could rise at once into marching formation.

The guards overseeing them were sullen to the point of hostility. When addressing them, for whatever reason, they shouted and sometimes made menacing gestures with their fists or rifles. This marked a dramatic departure from only days before when these same men swam at the pond with them, shared cigarettes, and partook of cake and tea together.

At one point Max Conti came close to physical harm. Standing in line with the others, he lit a cigarette. One of the guards came over and proceeded to denounce him in Russian. The form the denunciation took seemed out of all proportion to the crime. The guard shouted and stamped his feet, flailed his arms about. Max stared back at him quizzically. He had not the faintest notion of what he'd done wrong.

"The cigarette. The cigarette," Grant Shapley explained. "He wants you to put out the cigarette."

Unable to see what his cigarette had to do with such a tirade, Max grew more mystified than ever. He shrugged at Sandro standing beside him. Sandro shrugged back.

The gesture appeared to outrage the guard, who, unfamiliar with Italian body language, thought he was being ridiculed. He started to scream and came at Max, who raised his hand. A mistake surely. The guard unslung his rifle and started to swing the butt. The other guard followed suit. At that point Tony Thomas shouted something at the guard in Russian. Whatever the words, they had the desired effect. Perhaps it was the shock of having an Englishman address them in their native tongue, but the guard's rifle froze in mid-air with the metal butt plate inches from Max's cheek. Had it struck him at the force it had gathered, it would have opened his jaw.

Having determined to make an example, the guard could not now very well just walk away without appearing to have somehow backed down. Instead, he reached up, snatched the cigarette from Max's lips, and flung it aside. He stood there glowering at Max, attired in his smartly rumpled linen jacket and pale lime trousers. The guard appeared to be just waiting for any sign of defiance. When it didn't come, he slung his rifle back on his shoulder, muttered something, and started off. But in the next moment he wheeled about, thrust a finger under Max's nose, and rattled off another burst of machine-gun Russian. With the exception of Thomas, and possibly Shapley, none of the others there knew what the guard had said. Its tone and intent, however, were unmistakable.

Gonzaga happened at that moment to be standing next to Desfargue. All color drained from his face, the younger man turned and gave him a long, uncomprehending look. The old man smiled back at him, nodding his head as if to say: "You see?"

Across the field the women were faring not much better. The guards were no less rough on them for being women, possibly even a bit rougher. While there was no laying on of hands, they were shouted at a good deal more, ordered about, and asked to do a variety of trivial, utterly purposeless things, no doubt part of a conscious policy of intimidation and harassment designed to achieve maximum docility among them.

When it came someone's turn to enter one of the medical vans, the guards fairly shrieked and flailed their arms. This was intended to make each lady bolt up and rush into the van with all possible dispatch. It was ludicrous, and for some of the older women, like Myra Keck or Señora Gonzaga, it was simply impossible. The guards appeared to make no distinction on the basis of age. In cases such as these, the guards would poke the women with their rifle muzzles, not roughly, but insistently, until the curtain at the rear of the van was drawn shut behind them.

Not long after Madam Mukherjee disappeared behind the curtains of a van, a burst of shouting and screams was heard outside. First, they heard a male voice, gruff and authoritarian, then Madam Muk's voice shrieking above it. A stream of Hindi poured from behind the curtain.

Several of the guards bolted forward. The curtains were thrust aside and they barged into the van. Several moments of silence followed. Baby Muk, who'd been left with Nell Blanton for safekeeping, started to cry.

When the silence in the van persisted, Sonia Conti went forward, intending to find out what was happening inside. A guard nearby immediately came forward and with his hand pushed her brusquely off.

Everyone there had seen it, and for them that sudden laying on of hands changed their world completely. Until that moment they had all somehow taken it for granted that there were international laws, vigilant commissions that protected their rights and kept them safe from physical abuse. That comforting thought went by the boards with that brusque shove.

Another outburst exploded from the van. It was clearly Madam Mukherjee. An officer standing nearby heard it and he too hurried up the ramp into the van. The ladies waiting outside pushed slowly forward as if drawn by some invisible tether. Shouting, angry guards herded them back. Baby Muk squirmed in Nell Blanton's arms. As if divining his mother's predicament, he sent up a series of pitiful bleats.

In the next moment Madam Muk appeared. She was being escorted out of the van by the Russian officer. He returned her to her place in line, saluted her, and moved smartly off. The others clustered about her. She was quite ruffled and overcome. As she spoke, the old fire returned to her voice, only to be broken occasionally with a half-sob she'd quickly choke back.

The doctor inside the van was a man, she said, and he'd insulted her with his hands. She would not submit to the sort of procedures the doctor wished to pursue. No doctor in India would dare to take such liberties. She was close to tears as she went on, but suddenly seeing her child in Nell Blanton's arms, she made heroic efforts to recover control. She took the baby from Nell, and laughing and squealing, she hugged him and chucked him under the chin until he cooed and giggled with pleasure.

Suddenly she saw the men across the field queued up before the vans waiting to be examined. "Babu." She waved frantically in that direction, but they were too far off to be certain that Mr. Mukherjee was there, or if he were, that he'd be at all aware of her plight.

"Babu. Babu," she cried out again. This time the guards came over and told her to be quiet. Immediately Baby Muk sent up a piercing yowl.

At that moment, a female attendant signaled from the van for the next person in line to enter. It was Frau Kunkel. She looked around at the others, a little shaken but clearly firm. "If that doctor touches me wrong, I'll break his fingers."

"Numbness?"

"Occasionally."

"In the morning?"

"Mornings mostly. Getting out of bed."

"The leg goes out from beneath you?"

"Sometimes."

The doctor paused and, tilting his head, appeared to step back as if the better to scrutinize his patient. "And the tremors."

"When I'm tired," Shapley replied. "When I've overdone myself. Sometimes, too, after a hot bath."

"The eyes?"

"I can see you straight ahead. A nice young fellow with a pleasant smile."

"And the peripheral vision?"

"Mostly gone. Very little left."

"What my American colleagues call 'tunnel vision.' Classic. And ophthalmoscopy?"

"Positive."

"Spinal fluid? Brainwave tests?"

"Positive. Confirmed."

The young physician folded his arms. His head tilted slightly to the side, he regarded the older man from beneath thick, bushy brows. "How long have you known you have demyelinization disease?"

"Eight months. I think I actually knew I had it nearly two years ago. I simply didn't have the courage to go and have it confirmed."

"So." The young man sighed as if groping for some thought. "You appear remarkably calm about it."

"There's not much reason to get too exercised. It won't change anything."

The doctor laughed oddly and nodded his head. "I'm afraid that's true. Still, you have a right at least to be angry. Most of the myelin sheath is gone from the optic nerve."

"I know. I shall be completely blind soon."

"Probably." The doctor shrugged. "But perhaps not. I've seen remarkable cases of remission."

"Thirty percent, I gather, never recover any function."

"But seventy percent do. The odds are nearly three to one in your favor."

"I guess this is a case of the glass that is either half-empty or half-full."

"And for you, I take it, it has always been . . ."

"The former. Classic pessimist."

They both laughed, having achieved a curious intimacy in moments. Shapley continued. "I take it there's a great deal of multiple sclerosis in the Soviet Union."

"Ah, yes. That's how I became a neurologist. My mother suffered from it. She lived a good long life. She only died last autumn, but for the last ten years she was a vegetable."

Shapley noted the quick, almost funny shift of expression in his face.

"Forgive me, Professor. How clumsy and stupid of me."

"Not at all. Actually it was remarkably apt." Shapley chuckled with a certain self-irony. His ease was so natural that the young man laughed as well.

"What is your name?" Shapley asked.

"Spassky. Ivan Spassky."

"Where did you learn your excellent English?"

The young man's face lit up. "In America. I spent a year there. At Northwestern University."

"Evanston?"

"You know Evanston?"

"Oh, yes. I lectured there one year. I have fond memories of the place. We lived on the lake."

"I lived in Chicago. But I was mostly at the medical school. It was an exchange program. I went specifically to study with Dr. Ruysdale, the top man out there in demyelinization diseases. Outstanding man. You must see him. I shall be happy to write you a letter of introduction."

"I'll make a point of going." Shapley's eyes twinkled mischievously. "If ever I get back to the States."

The doctor's eyes dropped with embarrassment. He looked quickly around, then under his breath said, "Nonsense. It's all such nonsense, this."

There was an awkward silence as both of them sought for other topics to discuss.

"Is it all right on the train?" Spassky inquired. "Do they make you comfortable?"

"As comfortable as you can be, I suppose, after six days in a train, living and sleeping in the same clothes."

"Yes. Of course," the young man said. He was about to say something more but checked himself. "Well, aside from your other problem, your heart is fine. Lungs, blood pressure, everything else tip-top." He used that last expression with an almost childish delight, as though he were showing it off.

"Before you go, let me give you something for those tremors." The doctor bustled to a small metal cabinet and fished out several vials of tablets. Next he scribbled something on a piece of paper. "Try some of these. They're steroids. And the antispasmodics are for the tremors."

Shapley squinted at the label on each vial. "I already have both of these in my bags."

The young doctor seemed bereft. "Ah, but of course. You're light-years ahead of us there."

"But I can certainly use more," Shapley added quickly, more out of a wish not to hurt him than any faith in the recommended therapy.

"And here is Dr. Ruysdale's address and telephone number." He pressed a small piece of paper into Shapley's palm.

Shapley glanced down at the paper, then tucked it into his vest pocket. He took the young man's hand. "You've been very kind. Dr. Spassky—I shall remember the name."

"My pleasure entirely. An opportunity to refresh my English." The young man paused, his smiling eyes trailing away. "I have good memories of your country."

Shapley noted the circumspect lowering of his voice as he said it. "I too have very pleasant ones of yours."

Then as they shook hands, the young man said very earnestly, "Try to understand us. This business with our submarine and our sailors. This thing you have done to us. It's very bad. Very, very bad."

The men and women were marched back to the train in two separate columns. The men arrived first, the women twenty minutes later. This had been carefully timed and the reasons for it became quickly apparent moments after they reached the site. In their absence another sleeping coach had been drawn up to the train and coupled onto the rear. The order of the cars now following the engine was the restaurant car, followed by the original sleeper, next the day coach, followed by the new sleeper.

The men were marched into the area past the sentry box and through the gate of the barbed-wire fence. Within the wired enclosure, a number of signs with arrows had been hastily mounted on rickety wooden tripods. Each was written in several different languages, but their hand-printed messages were identical—Messieurs/Dames, Herren/Damen, Caballeros/Damas, Gentlemen/Ladies—all with bright red assertive arrows pointing each sex in different directions.

Their natural line of movement was, of course, to their old quarters on the day coach. But when the column started veering toward there, the guards shouted and thrust the barrels of their rifles in the direction of the last car.

Kariolainen scowled. "What the hell is this now?"

"Don't you see?" Paul Blanton muttered. "They're going to separate us from the women."

Kariolainen made an odd face.

A detachment of railroad transport troops was hosing down the cars; another was shoveling the human waste that had accumulated on the track bed beneath the lavatories and carting it off in trucks. The train, dusty, gray-green, looked diminutive and surreal within that improbable setting of barbed wire and armed troops swarming over the face of it.

Of the fifteen men that had started out that morning for the hospital vans, only fourteen returned. Ralph Keck had complained of severe chest pains during the physical examination and was rushed from the vans directly to a military hospital in Vyborg. Keith Wales was in no condition to march anywhere. He was permitted instead to remain in his compartment and be examined by a doctor there. Since being brought back to the train, he was kept under twenty-four-hour special guard. No one as yet had been permitted to see him.

"They're not separating me from Janet," Kariolainen said with disquieting grimness.

"Easy, old man," Thomas, standing near him, replied. "Don't try anything foolish."

Kariolainen stared straight ahead, apparently disregarding him. But in the next moment he replied in a quiet, decidedly ominous tone, "What I do won't be foolish."

They tramped up to the rear door of the sleeping coach. Several guards were already there awaiting them. They carried clipboards and assignment sheets and barked out names and new berth assignments. Their manner was curt and openly antagonistic. It had the distinct look of the new policies of a new regime.

"Conti, Maximilliano."

"Kunkel, Karl Heinz."

"Lambrusto, Sandro."

"Desfargue, Claude."

"Gonzaga, Enrique."

"Asawa, Junji."

The names rocketed forth like cannon shot into the bright vivid air. As each man came forward, he was assigned a new berth in the sleeping coach. Those who were slow to respond were shouted at and sent back to the rear of the line to wait to be called again. If it hadn't been so unnerving, Stern thought, it would have been laughable, even banal, this petty tyranny, like the hazing administered by counselors during the first week of a summer camp that prides itself on discipline.

"Thomas, Anthony Beech."

"Kariolainen, Theodore."

"Kariolainen, Christopher."

"Keck, Ralph."

When no one responded for Keck, the sergeant major shrieked the name. Thomas tried to explain that Keck had been taken off to a hospital. The news so infuriated the sergeant major that he had them all line up again and stand outside for another half-hour while he performed another head count.

Outside the enclosure, the women were forced to wait in line until every man had disappeared inside the train. When that had been accomplished, they were then marched, stunned and bedraggled, into the enclosure, where the process began all over again. They were put in the charge of three rather fleshy matrons who wore gray smocks and addressed them in clear, stentorian tones. For most of them, the morning had been terrifying. Learning now that they were to be segregated from the men did not help matters. Madam Muk, still rattled from her encounter in the medical van, was in no mood for fresh surprises. Since the incident she had some desperate, almost anguished need to see her husband, if only for the solace of inflicting on him heaps of abuse for having abandoned her to the indignities of a lecherous physician.

Now told that she would not be able to see him, loud pitiful sobs broke from her lips. The sound of it was so stricken and heartrending that it further unsettled the others and infuriated the guards. They came streaming at her from every direction, confronting her where she stood holding her child in her arms, as though she were defying them, trying to make them feel shame.

The guards stamped their feet, flailed their arms, and berated her at the top of their lungs. It was at that point that Jatta interceded. She flew at the guards and argued hotly, going toe to toe with them. But where restraint had characterized their behavior in the early days of detainment, a unified front of hostility and direct aggression now took its place. Still, there was no physical abuse, but one sensed it hovered in the air all about them and that they now lived on only a razor's edge of civilized behavior.

When Myra Keck was assigned her new berth, a young lieutenant, gallant and sympathetic, called her aside to explain the situation with her husband. It had been presented to her tactfully and in the most reassuring light possible. But even as she was being told, Mrs. Keck crumpled at the young man's feet and had to be helped to her berth by two strapping guards straining visibly beneath her sagging girth.

In the privacy of her cabin, Trina Van Meegrin cried. In her absence their luggage had been moved in from the day coach. Kyle's possessions, she noted, had been subtracted from her own, presumably to be transferred to quarters on the men's sleeping coach.

A sense of desolation overtook her. She kept looking about, half-expecting him to appear. Just out of her teens, she had never been away from home before—never out of Holland, not to mention behind the so-called "Iron Curtain." She wanted to cry out for Kyle to come and get her, to take her home. She needed desperately to be with him, in the safety of his arms. She didn't like these people; certainly not the Soviets, and for that matter, not even her fellow passengers. Oh, some of them were all right, of course, but even before this awful business of the train, she had reached a point where the well-known adage about two much familiarity had more than proved its point. She wanted to go home now to the small cozy flat in Rotterdam, to their tiny bedroom overlooking the canal, where the cat slept on the bed with them as they lay in one another's arms.

Not more then twenty minutes ago she'd been delirious with joy. She couldn't wait to get back to the train to tell Kyle that she was pregnant. The doctor who'd examined her had confirmed her suspicions. She was in the eleventh or twelfth week, the doctor calculated. But sitting here in the musty, airless quiet of her berth, her rifled baggage all around her, she was convinced she would never live to see her unborn child, or, for that matter, her husband again.

Not easily intimidated, Irma Kunkel was a tough, resilient lady. She did not suffer fools graciously, and she had little patience with outdated notions of female squeamishness. The daughter of a Munich butcher, the sights and sounds of the abattoir, from childhood on, had inured her to brutality. Her only vulnerable spot, if it could be said she had one, was Karl Heinz.

The sudden realization that he'd been taken from her triggered a panic. With Karl Heinz's disappearance, some deep-seated, long-repressed terror of her early years, something that had lain dormant for decades, far beneath the surface, had leapt fearfully to light.

The fact that she knew he was no more than fifty yards away with only a length of a day coach between them did little to assuage her fright. She was convinced that he could not function by himself, that in her absence, without her to see to his needs, the boy would disintegrate.

Karl Heinz was seventeen years old, soon to turn eighteen. Shortly he would go off to university. He was already poised for flight. She had never faced that fact before. She had put it conveniently out of mind. The fact that he had been a particularly gifted student, intelligent, innovative, enterprising, highly motivated, and self-sufficient from early teens on had somehow managed to elude her. Even when she looked at him now, she saw not a young man on the brink of maturity but a child of possibly five or six, inept and bumbling, crying and reaching out to her for assistance.

Now something had altered all that. This unorthodox vacation, which she herself had dreamed up (principally because her husband had insisted they not go) and then demanded that Karl Heinz accompany her, had been the instrument for separating her from her child. Only that morning she'd had breakfast with him in the dining car. She was still a mother then, seeing to his toast and that he drank his juice. Now they'd taken her boy from her. Just like that. An act, a decree, the impulse of some august personage, arbitrary and impersonal, had in effect dislodged her from her rightful place in the universe. She was suddenly alone now and trying to cope with a terror she scarcely understood.

With an almost inspired perversity, they'd put Señora Gonzaga in with Myra Keck. No doubt they'd assumed that their nearly identical ages made them compatible. Isabel and Consuelo were separated as well—Isabel with Silvana Lambrusto, and Consuelo, to her mortification, with Madam Muk.

With rubbing alcohol and a whiff or two of spirits of ammonia waved beneath her nose, Myra Keck had revived from the shock of the news of her husband. But she was now only a faint echo of the commanding, self-possessed figure she liked to think she was. She trembled. She whimpered. She sat limp as a rag doll in her seat, staring blankly off into space, or clung pitifully to the little Spanish noblewoman beside her.

For Señora Gonzaga's part, she had troubles of her own. Of her own medical problems, she scarcely thought. As for Isabel and Consuelo, they must do for themselves. But who would take care of "El Conde"? Who would get him up and get him dressed? See to it that he ate and attended to his needs? Certainly not he himself. Someone would have to look after him. But who among the men would give a slightly demented old Spaniard the time of day? The English journalist had helped once before, but she had a nagging distrust of him. All of those courtly flourishes, those kindly attentions, she imagined, he wrote down in a ledger, fully intending to redeem them at some future date, with compound interest.

There was Mr. Blanton, who'd been thoughtful and considerate in the past. But it was the sort of spotty, uneven benevolence that in hard times is quickly scrapped.

There was also the old professor. She knew from Mrs. Shapley that he had grave medical problems. Poor woman. She must be beside herself with worry for him. And, of course, there was Mr. Stern, whom she liked and trusted above all. He had gone out of his way once before to help them. Could she prevail upon him again? In the past several days he'd seemed remote and preoccupied. He'd been so accessible in Leningrad. While there had always been an air of something sad about him, he'd always been chatty and full of amusing anecdotes. But in the last several days or so, something new and wholly untoward appeared in his manner—something that discouraged approach. Still, of all of them, he seemed the only one to whom you could make an appeal based on some principle higher than personal self-interest. Though she didn't like to think it, the fact remained: he was the most usable.

She had no idea if they were to be permitted any contact with the men. No one had bothered to enlighten them on that score. They were separated by the mere length of a coach car, but with armed guards posted at either end of the car they might as well have been at opposite poles of the earth. How to reach him?

Myra Keck had been staring out the window with a dull, slightly vacant expression on her face. She held a handkerchief balled up in her fist with which, from time to time, she dabbed at her mouth.

"Are you all right, my dear?" Señora Gonzaga sat down beside her and took her hand. It was easier to like Myra in grief, she thought, than in all the insufferable vanity of her well-being. "Can I get you something? Would you like a bit of tea? A glass of water?"

Mrs. Keck stared back at her with a dazed, pitiful look. She moved her lips tentatively but no sound emerged. When at last she seemed to recognize Señora Gonzaga, her eyes filled with tears. She put her arms around the older woman's shoulders and wept inconsolably. Frail, tiny in relation to Mrs. Keck, the old lady held and rocked her as though she were a child. It made a curious picture, the two of them, like a pituitary giant being attended to by a small child.

Mrs. Gonzaga thought of her husband, ignored, uncared for, abandoned by the others, and wanted very much to cry herself. "What did you say, my dear?" she asked, trying to decipher the choked, garbled noises that broke from Mrs. Keck.

"Ralph . . . May I see Ralph?"

"Of course you can, my dear. In a day or so, when he's feeling better." She was sure of no such thing. Suddenly her face brightened. "I'll tell you what, though. We can write him a letter now at the hospital. It will cheer him up."

"A letter?" Mrs. Keck grasped eagerly at the straw. "Yes. A letter. Can we?"

"Of course, my dear," Señora Gonzaga replied in the manner of a person trying to pacify a heartbroken child. "Of course we can. I have stationery in my bag."

She went to her bags stacked on the seat and found the small piece of hand luggage in which she kept toiletries, medications, and sundries.

The moment she opened the bag, however, something struck her. It was the disarray—not blatant, but enough to show that in her absence the bag had been searched. Items had been removed and then put back, but not in any recognizable order. There was no attempt to conceal the fact that the bag had been searched. Nothing was missing from it, however, except the stationery and pen and then, of course, she recalled they'd been confiscated days before.

She looked for another bag, which contained most of Enrique's belongings—his medications, toiletries, and underclothes. That was missing completely. She presumed, or at least hoped, they'd been transferred to the new coach where the men were billeted. Her own bags remained on the seat untouched. But now her anxiety for her husband quickened.

When she looked up again she was trembling. She had nothing in her bags she wished to hide, but the thought that some stranger had pored over her things produced the extremely discomforting sense of personal violation.

Suddenly she remembered Myra Keck. Turning back, she saw her sitting there, staring out the window again with that listless, chillingly vacant look about her. The childish eagerness of moments before at the prospect of writing a letter to her husband was gone. She appeared to have completely forgotten it. Fortunate for her, thought Señora Gonzaga, since now there was neither paper nor pen with which to do it.

In the privacy of his berth, Stern too had been going through his luggage. What there was of it was simply a single canvas bag. Like Señora Gonzaga's, it had been searched. Unlike hers, however, not merely searched, but rather ransacked. Nothing had been taken, but there had been no attempt to put things back, to reconstruct the arrangement of things so as to give some semblance of its former order. The disarray, the scattering and mistreatment of his belongings, looked intentional and very intimidating.

Kyle Van Meegrin was in the adjoining berth. Stern rapped on the thin partition dividing them. "Kyle, have your things been searched?"

On his side of the partition, Van Meegrin looked around. His bag sat unremarkably on the seat. "Wait," he called out to Stern, "I'll check." It was an old battered gladstone. He unzipped the top and went through it quickly. "Everything appears to be here," he called out again.

Stern pondered a moment. "They haven't messed things up, have they?"

Van Meegrin looked again. "No—not particularly."

Stern had a queasy feeling. A premonitory chill crept over him, like the small choppy waves at the shoreline that are harbingers of things far bigger to come.

Gonzaga drifted by and poked his head in. He stared down with an amused frown at the various articles strewn about. "Hello. What have we here?"

"They appear to have searched my bag," Stern remarked, mildly distracted.

"The swine. Does not look to me like the typical customs check."

"To me, either. Did they search your bags?"

"I have no doubt. But I can't find my bags. Have you seen them?"

Stern gave him a long, searching look. "Aren't they in your berth?"

The old fellow cracked an odd little smile. "I'm sure they are. But I can't seem to find my berth."

In a burst of truly inspired matching, they'd put Nell in with Sonia Conti and Serja with Jean Blaylock. The latter were just then sitting about morosely, doing their best to ignore each other. Jean sat, knees crossed, at the edge of her berth, glowering and swinging her foot fretfully. "What the hell are we supposed to do here now, will someone please tell me?"

Serja looked extremely uneasy. "Do you suppose we can walk out?"

"Outside the train, you mean? I doubt that."

"No. Just down the corridor." Serja fidgeted. "I have to go to the bathroom."

"Well, for God's sake then, go."

"Do you suppose they'll let me?"

Jean could barely conceal her impatience. "If they don't I guess we're all in big trouble." The moment she'd said it, she regretted her facetiousness. "Look," she said, making a weak feint at civility, "why don't you just ask one those lady sumo wrestlers they have walking around out there?"

It was evident that Serja was not enthusiastic about the prospect. She seemed miserable. "Well . . ." She floundered. "I feel so helpless having to ask permission to go to the bathroom—like a child, or some poor senile creature. Is this their way of humiliating us?"

Jean rose and went to the door. Sliding it open, she looked up and down the corridor. It was virtually deserted except for several of the matrons standing about and smoking at the far end of the coach.

"Toilette," she called out. "Toilette."

One of the ladies came trundling down.

"Toilette," Jean said once again when the woman stood before her.

The matron frowned. She was a gruff, hearty *muszik* type with a red face and immense forearms.

"Toilette. Toilette." Jean pointed her finger at the Finnish girl. "The lady . . . toilette."

"Ah, toilette. The lady." The matron nodded with dullish comprehension. She took Jean's arm in her great paw and started to lead her out. Jean yanked her arm back. "Not me. That lady. Over there. Her." This was followed by more frantic finger pointing. Serja rose and started tentatively toward them. She was mortified.

When she reached them, Jean took the matron's hand and placed it solidly on Serja's. The two of them stood there, awkward, bewildered, looking at Jean.

"Toilette. Toilette." Jean flew at them like an angry wasp, a maniacal grin frozen on her face. Hand in hand they fled down the corridor looking like an old dowager and her attendant.

Jean sat alone in her berth, knees crossed, swinging her foot, its rapid motion a perfect index of her agitation. Never one to be plagued much by uncertainty, a great deal of pluck had gone out of her over the past several days. She felt frightened and betrayed by everything. Betrayed by the Soviets. Betrayed by the Americans. Betrayed by her family and teachers. She'd put in a great deal of time, but at mostly the wrong things. Tony Thomas, that most improbable soothsayer, had been right. All of her ideas were secondhand. She'd not had an original thought in her head for years. She'd traveled down a number of roads, all of them dead ends. Whose fault was it, the system's or hers? The nagging realization that it might have been the latter rankled. She had wanted to serve, to be useful in some larger, more significant context. But as a revolutionary and a reformer, she'd been a dud.

Sitting there by herself, hands clasped in her lap, caught in a wholly uncharacteristic moment of reflection, she looked ironically like a perfectly well-mannered, well-behaved, docile little girl. She sat gnawing at the inside of her lip, ragging it until it was an open sore, making it shriek with exquisite pain. She wished she could cry, but she couldn't.

All the while this painful reassessment was going on, she was aware, but only dimly, of an odd, not immediately identifiable odor. Warm and possibly a bit rubbery it was, and fleeting. It wafted like a puff of bad air through her troubled consciousness, and was quickly gone.

She did not know, nor had she any way of ever learning, that the former occupant of the berth she presently occupied had been Junji Asawa.

No one had seen Keith Wales since the evening before, when he'd been brought back to the train. He'd been taken at once to his berth and placed under twenty-four-hour guard. No one had been able to see or speak with him. At the urging of the others, Tony Thomas and Ted Kariolainen had both tried.

Military physicians had already visited Keith twice that day to dress his wounds. At mealtimes a soldier brought him a tray of "soft food" from the restaurant car.

On one of those occasions, Sandro Lambrusto was passing the berth just as the soldier was entering with the tray. He had a clear view of Keith sitting up, his bandages removed and just being changed by the doctor. His face was purpled and swollen. Sandro stopped. He wanted to look in and say hello, ask how he was. But when he tried, the guard shouted at him and slammed the door shut.

Later, Thomas cornered one of the doctors coming out of Keith's berth. Speaking in his most amiable and disarming Russian, he tried to pump the man for information. The doctor was extremely tight-lipped and volunteered little. They continued to chat. Thomas offered him one of his Balkan Sobranies and soon the fellow was relaxed enough to speak in vague generalities.

Yes, he said, the young fellow had been caught in the woods. Damned fool. He'd got himself royally lost. He was in rough shape when they found him. He'd obviously been running and tripped over something, falling face-first on a rock. Broke his nose. Blackened an eye and knocked out a few teeth. When they'd gotten him back to headquarters, cleaned him up a bit, and treated his injuries, he confessed he'd attempted to steal classified documents. Hid them on the train. Then when the documents were discovered—some in the loo and some in his own luggage . . .

"His luggage?" Thomas' jaw dropped.

"Right. Can you imagine how stupid? That's when the kid got really scared and spilled everything." The doctor laughed heartily. "Now he must sign a confession."

"They say he has an accomplice aboard too," Thomas prodded.

"Right. And believe me, my friend, they won't rest till they find the poor devil." The doctor inhaled deeply on his cigarette and blew a lengthy plume of smoke into the air above them. "So you're from London, you say? I was there once. Lovely city."

They marched the women off in two columns. It was shortly after noon and they thought they were being taken to lunch. This time, however, they were ordered down from the sleeping car and told to assemble in two columns alongside it. They were pointedly instructed not to talk to each other or try to communicate in any way while moving in formation.

All of these movements were carried out by the corps of matrons in their gray smocks, booming commands in loud, harsh voices. If they thought they were being taken to the restaurant car, they were quickly disabused of that notion. They marched instead directly past it and on to the newly erected facilities that served now as the bathhouse.

Once inside, they were told to disrobe and then go two by two into the eight available shower stalls. They were given a total of four minutes to bathe and wash their hair, then told to come out and dry off.

Emerging from the showers, they discovered that their clothing had been collected and in their place they found stiff gray smocks similar to those worn by the matrons. In place of their shoes and stockings, each was given a pair of white cotton anklets and rubber thongs.

Protests, cries of outrage followed. Jatta demanded an explanation and was told by the matrons that the clothing had been taken to be fumigated and laundered. Each article of attire had been tagged and would be returned to the rightful owners within several days' time. This was necessary, they claimed, for purposes of hygiene. When asked why they had to bathe all together at one time, they were promptly informed that now that it had been established that there were spies aboard the train, and that one had already tried to escape, a single bathing period for everyone made far more sense from the point of view of general surveillance.

The women listened with an air of scorn and disbelief. Isabel couldn't resist a remark about the hygiene of the gray smocks. Who'd worn them before, and were they really clean? In all fairness, they appeared to have been boiled in water and smelled sharply of some acrid detergent. They were starched to the point where once on, they felt like quick-drying plaster applied directly to the skin.

Serja was taken from the shower crying and nearly hysterical. "We're never going to get out of this," she cried. "It will go on and on. They'll find one excuse after another to keep us . . ."

The matrons converged on her and quickly hustled her from the stalls. Her wet naked body, suds sliding from her narrow shoulders and small sloping breasts, made her look frail and pathetically childlike. As she kicked and squirmed in the grip of two barrel-chested matrons, her cries echoed horribly through the bare, cavernous sheds. The effect of that noise, those yelps and pitiful bleating cries, was devastating. Several days ago, a number of the others would have rushed to her aid. Now they merely stood mute, leaning against the walls in their shapeless gray smocks, trying to ignore what was happening. Thoroughly cowed.

The route they took back to the train was circuitous. It involved a wide swing round the wire perimeter, approaching the dining car from the opposite direction. The purpose of this elaborate detour was not immediately clear; what was clear, however, was that it was not for purposes of mere exercise. As they moved on, the intent of the detour became more apparent. By that curious maneuver, the guards were preempting any possibility of the men and women seeing each other, of mate seeing mate, parent seeing child, friend seeing friend.

Once the women had all been trooped into the dining car, the men were then ordered out of their coach and assembled in double columns at the rear of the train. From there they were herded to the showers to repeat identically the operation just completed by the women.

If there had been a feeling before that the meals provided in the dining car left something to be desired, what they were served now made those earlier dinners Lucullan by comparison. The menu that afternoon was a tepid, watery broth of indeterminate flavor, followed by a small marinated pilchard so bony and salty as to be inedible. It was served on a bed of brownish lettuce, its head still on its shoulders and its gray, glaucous eye peering warily up at them. Plates of dark dry bread, several days old, were stacked in untidy heaps at the head of each table. No butter was provided to make it any the more palatable. Gone was the Bulgarian wine, and even the treacly, sweet nectar that had seemed in such abundance before was subtracted. In its place was plain water of a color and appearance that set alarm bells ringing, and a pale, flavorless tea that most of them drank under the dubious assumption that it had at least been boiled.

The meal was capped off with hard, unripe little pears, reminiscent of Seckel pears, mealy in texture and neither juicy nor cool enough to refresh.

Here, too, it was evident their captors were sending some sort of message. Loosely translated, it seemed to say: "If you thought things were bad before, you haven't seen anything yet." The message was underscored by the attitude of the young soldiers who served the meal and then carted off the dishes. In the early days of the detention, these young men had been aloof and distrustful of foreigners. But they had never been disrespectful. The attitude now was one of overt hostility, and it was unanimous, to a man, so that one could only conclude that the shift in tone was the product of official policy newly created in fresh orders sent down from headquarters.

What did it all signify? They could only conjecture. It looked very much like the sort of ambiguous application of intimidation that cannot be characterized as brutality but achieves the same results; namely, a softening-up procedure designed to make people malleable and rid them of their more fractious individual quirks.

When they spoke later among themselves about the meaning of this new hardening, they reasoned that it appeared to have a direct linkage with Colonel Dunskoi's speech of the night before, particularly that part dealing with the need to secure a signed confession and charging that Keith Wales had not acted alone but in collusion with an accomplice.

"This can't be true."

"But I can assure you it is."

"I don't believe you. What proof? What basis?"

"I've already told you."

"A space unfilled in a visa application? Ridiculous. Show me these alleged documents."

"At the appropriate time."

"When is that? The appropriate time. Tell me."

"I've already said. At the appropriate time."

Stern cocked his head at him. "Will you, for God's sake, make yourself clear?"

"I think I already have." The Russian captain seemed unperturbed. Stern quickly recognized him as the young translator always seen trailing dutifully about at Dunskoi's heels. "There is now reason to believe that you are an agent of the Yad Vashem."

Stern's jaw dropped. "The Yad what?"

"Vashem—the Yad Vashem."

Stern laughed a short, cheerless laugh. "I don't even know what that is."

The young man made a smug, amused face. "Oh, come, Mr. Stern. Really."

"I tell you, I've never heard the term before."

"Surely you know that the Yad Vashem are the Israeli intelligence forces."

"Oh, I see—it's this Jewish thing again."

"We also know that you are a highly skilled interrogation officer for Yad Vashem. Your specialty is compiling dossiers."

"My God." Stern shook his head in bewilderment. Exhausted, he laughed bleakly to himself. "I tell you, I am not Jewish. I told Colonel Dunskoi the same thing."

The Russian officer gave Stern a fishy look. He was a young man, almost boyish-looking, with a pink, beardless face and the penetrating, humorless eyes of the professional technocrat. His name was Grishkov.

"Where is Colonel Dunskoi? I want to see Colonel Dunskoi."

"Colonel Dunskoi has been recalled to headquarters."

"When will he be back?"

"I have no way of knowing."

"You know perfectly well. You just won't tell me."

"I have no wish to pursue this discussion."

The young man riffled through a stack of papers on his desk, making a great show of ignoring Stern.

Stern's chagrin had transformed itself into amazement. "You summon me here. Now you have no wish to pursue the matter."

"I have already told you." The young man enunciated each word with crisp distaste. "We have reason to believe you are an Israeli operative, an accomplice of the Canadian agent, Wales."

"Wales is barely out of diapers. He couldn't agent his way out of a paper bag." Stern felt his head swim. "I demand to see this stolen classified material."

"You shall see. I promise you. At the appropriate time."

"You keep saying that. When exactly is that?"

"As I have already told you . . ."

"At the appropriate time." Stern completed the sentence for the captain. "I know, I know."

"However," the young man continued, ignoring Stern's outbreak, "if you wish now to make a written confession, I am sure the impasse can then be speedily resolved. On the other hand, even assuming such a resolution comes about and the others are released, you should not plan on leaving the Soviet Union anytime in the near future."

The last sentence had the effect of a kick in the stomach. He experienced a rush of nausea, a momentary darkening of vision.

The evening before, even as Dunskoi's voice had crackled over the loudspeaker while they ate in the dining car as he'd informed them that Keith Wales had been captured, the colonel was at that very moment a hundred miles away in Leningrad. What they'd heard over the loudspeaker was merely a taped announcement made several hours before.

Dunskoi was now home. He was with his wife. He had seen and spoken to his daughter. What had transpired in those brief hours had the effect of having put light-years between himself and the embattled hostages on the stalled train in the big birch forests outside of Vyborg.

Nor had the colonel returned home of his own volition. He'd been ordered there by his superiors. A wire had flashed in over a special line from STAVKA directing him to turn over his command to one of his senior staff. He must put his domestic affairs in order at once so that headquarters could act promptly in the matter of his impending elevation to the rank of major general of the Supreme Soviet Armed Forces. Already his application had been dangerously compromised by his daughter's activities ". . . unbecoming to that of a citizen of the Union of Soviet Socialist Republics." His commanding officer at headquarters had read him a draft of the indictment the Ministry of Justice had planned to issue imminently unless he could effect some satisfactory reconciliation between his daughter and the state.

Once again after repeated warnings, she had been picked up, along with half a dozen other students from the Academy of Science, at the university. Like their youthful activist counterparts in innumerable Western universities, they walked in a large circle, chanting dirgelike anti-Soviet mottos, while hundreds of mute and unprotesting spectators watched. They called for a rejection of classic Marxism as the official ideology of the state. They called upon the Kremlin fathers to relinquish their stranglehold on all of Eastern Europe. They demanded intellectual and cultural freedom, including freedom of religion. They called for the release of Sakharov.

The KGB plainclothesmen moved in quickly and broke them up. They were herded together and whisked off in black Volgas while the onlooking crowds were quickly dispersed. The Volgas had taken them directly to police headquarters, where they were arraigned. All, that is, except Masha Feodorovna, who was taken to a separate room, offered tea and sandwiches, and treated with the utmost courtesy.

This infuriated her. Perhaps it was intended to. She wanted to be treated precisely as her colleagues were. They, she knew, had been penned up in cells, to be detained there until formally charged, families notified, and lawyers arranged for.

This special treatment, she knew all too well, was because of her father, and undoubtedly carried out at his express orders. It was his way of trivializing everything she stood for. Even in something as serious as "crimes against the state," she was to be treated like some errant child who'd misbehaved.

It embittered her more than ever and hardened her heart against him. She would not accept privilege and special treatment because she was his daughter. She deplored the system of perks and special handling for the apparatchiks of which he was an integral part. She demanded instead to be taken from this separate room and placed in the pens with her friends. This was denied her.

Several days later, when Dunskoi finally saw her, she appeared small and frail, strangely older than his memory of her, although that had been as recent as six months before.

It was at their home on Kammeny Ostrov outside Leningrad on the Peterhof Road. It was a small dacha dating from the nineteenth century, only four bedrooms but charming, with gardens leading down to an old iron bridge that spanned a narrow inlet. From the graciously proportioned, high-ceilinged living room, with its long stately windows, you could catch glimpses of the Baltic shimmering through the noble aspen and birch.

It was a state dacha, given to Dunskoi for distinguished service during the Czechoslovakian uprisings of 1968. He had played a key role in putting down that insurrection. With that had come a quality of life that most professional soldiers of Dunskoi's rank could scarcely dream of aspiring to. The beautiful home in the exclusive community, furnished tastefully in the most up-to-date Finnish design—teak furniture, costly hand-woven carpets, the fully equipped kitchen with built-in cabinets, Formica-top counters, customized Poggenpohl cabinets and fixtures, all of it made available to him at mind-boggling discounts, at special duty-free import shops accessible only to the most highly favored, the anointed, the apparatchiks. And all of it so much finer and more elaborate than anything available on the Soviet market to the man on the street.

Then, of course, came the other perks: the Chaika with a private chauffeur, the privilege of a pass to the hard-currency Beryozka shops where Russians with certificate rubles could purchase imported goods, items that are never available on the Soviet market.

In Moscow they could go to the special section 100 of the Gum department store, and there in a discreetly sequestered emporium, entering through a small inconspicuous door only for people bearing a special identification card, purchase Western clothing, rare Russian delicacies such as caviar, smoked salmon, the finest canned sturgeon, export brands of vodka and prized vintages of Georgian and Moldavian wines, plus all the meat, fresh fruit, and vegetables one could ever want.

That's what Masha hated. Worse even, it made her hate her parents, which in turn made her hate herself. She would not eat the special delicacies. She would not bring friends home during vacation because she was embarrassed by the opulence of her home and feared what they would think when contrasting it with their own.

Standing there now in that grand, assertively expensive room, the walls lined with books and paintings, the seashore sunlight pouring through the long, stately windows, confronted by this stranger she knew to be her father, she felt how the richness of everything there served only to embitter her.

It was a lacerating interview lasting for the better part of two hours. Madam Dunskoi hovered outside the tall French doors, listening with her heart aching to the angry shouts pouring muffled through the plaster walls, and feared for her daughter. She herself would never have dreamed of arguing with Dunskoi in that fashion, of trading such inflammatory words back and forth with him.

"And you simply accept all this." Her words flung out at him, taunting, demanding. "Blind, unquestioning obedience. You expect me to follow too, like a robot?"

Unable to listen any longer, Madam Dunskoi fled to the relative security of her kitchen and tried to busy herself. But the sound of it was everywhere, the awful rise and fall of voices, threats, recriminations, unpleasant memories dredged up out of the past, bearing no relation to the present conflict other than the fact they carried the burden of feelings that had rankled for years, and all of this couched in words so bitter that, having once been uttered, could never be forgotten.

Several times she thought of entering the room, of thrusting herself between them and forcing them to stop. But each time her courage failed her.

Dimitri was fighting for his professional life, for everything he'd struggled for these thirty years. Masha was fighting for principles deeply cherished. She had a sense of equity and justice that could not be easily shunted aside with appeals to patriotism and jingoistic slogans. Not even for the further glorification of her father to the heady status of major general. As far as she was concerned, he'd already had too much. His service on behalf of a system that berated the West for its elitism and greedy materialism while congratulating itself for having accomplished an ideal egalitarianism was laughable.

When Masha had gone in to see her father, she was frightened. Her mouth was dry and her legs trembled beneath her. When she walked out nearly two hours later, cheeks glowing, carriage erect, she looked vindicated, if not positively triumphant. Dunskoi, on the other hand, was shaken.

She'd walked from the field of battle in the library directly out the front door, closing it with a finality that sounded like the clap of doom. She had not even stopped to gather her things, or even to say good-bye to her mother. She had said good-bye, however, to her father, leaving no doubt whatsoever in his mind what course she would now take. Nothing had been resolved. He had not succeeded in altering one jot her determination to defy the authority of the state.

After she'd gone, Dunskoi remained in the library. No sound, other than an ominous quiet, could be heard from there. Several times Madam Dunskoi made her way back to the library and hovered outside the door. But she could not bring herself to enter. She could not bear to see his fury, or even worse, his humiliation. When at last he did emerge, three-quarters of an hour later, he was ashen, his brow a fearful thing to see.

His second meeting at STAVKA was even more unnerving than his encounter with his daughter. It took place in a setting of almost eerie calm. Unlike his meeting with Masha, issues were resolved, matter-of-factly and with devastating dispatch.

A document had been prepared and placed before him to read. All that remained was for him to sign.

"... *Because of conduct unbecoming to, and inconsistent with, a citizen of the Union of Soviet Socialist Republics* ..."

"Understand, Dimitri. We have tried every avenue of rapprochement with her. If it were not for your extremely privileged position ..."

"*It is therefore the opinion of this tribunal that Maria Feodorovna Dunskoi* ..."

Dunskoi's eyes raced across the page, the print swimming before his eyes. "What is this? I don't understand. What does this mean? You do not propose to deprive her of citizenship?"

The man seated across from him behind an immense expanse of highly polished walnut was a full marshal of the Army, a large chesty presence with wattles and puffy eyes that bespoke of too much vodka, and a nose that made a whistling sound when he breathed. From his tunic depended an array of medals and decorations six wide and six deep. In addition, there were service chevrons, shoulder boards, epaulets, arm badges, lapel and cuff oak leaves, even a marksman's lanyard. So much, in fact, it smacked of opéra bouffe—the banana-republic general. But all of that military vaudeville was counter-balanced by a manner of such quiet, unswerving purpose as to be chilling.

Worse even, he had been an old classmate of Dunskoi's at the military academy in Moscow. They had been cadets together. But Yevchenko, who had not been a particularly promising student, was now a full marshal of the Supreme Soviet, while he was still a low-level colonel waiting breathlessly for news of his elevation to the rank of major general. Yevchenko had learned early how to cultivate friends in high places. Dunskoi's pride had made him despise all of that.

"That is precisely what it means," Yevchenko said, "unless you can prevail upon her . . ."

"But I've already told you, sir." He could not bring himself to use the name Arkady, although that is precisely how he'd addressed him all throughout their student days.

"Ah then, you see, my dear fellow. There is nothing for it. I can do nothing. The court will strip her of citizenship."

"For what? My God. She's a child. Her ideas are still immature."

"She's twenty-one, and according to her instructors at the university, her ideas have begun to affect all those around her." The pasty immobility of Yevchenko's face looked like hardening plaster. "I'm very sorry, my dear fellow—it's really all quite unfortunate."

"Yes, yes. Of course. I see."

"Were it not for you . . . your favored position and all of that . . . well, it would have been over with months ago. She would have been sent north and that would have been the end of it."

Dunskoi nodded his head stiffly. "Surely that's not an option under consideration here?"

"Certainly not." Marshal Yevchenko banished the notion with an expansive wave of his arm. The panel of medals on his chest clanked as he did so. "But I don't mind telling you, there were those here and at the ministry too . . ." He broke off in mid-sentence, having deftly applied that small dose of shock. "Put it all out of your mind, dear fellow. That will be the fate of her colleagues, however, who are not fortunate enough to have fathers who are national heroes." Did he detect there a note of sarcasm? "In Maria Feodorovna's case," Yevchenko continued, "she may retain her citizenship, but she will be required to leave the country."

"Leave the country?" Dunskoi mumbled uncomprehendingly. "Leave the country?" To his mind it would be better to be put against the wall and shot. "But Arkady . . ."

Even as the name slipped out, he saw the marshal's caterpillar brows rise disapprovingly. "Leave the country? To go where, exactly?"

"Wherever such people go. Paris. London. Geneva. Of course, we will do everything in our power to facilitate the relocation. Deportation papers are already in preparation."

"In preparation?" It was all moving too fast for Dunskoi.

Once under way, Yevchenko's momentum was inexorable. "We will provide transportation and a certain amount of start-up money. But you do see, dear fellow, under the circumstances she cannot be permitted to remain. Defamation of the state is serious business."

Dunskoi's head swam. He wanted to shout: "This is my child. What do you mean she can't remain?" But, like a soldier, he sat stiff and erect, his head bowed and listening to his orders. How had Masha put it? Blind, unquestioning obedience. That was it.

"I'm afraid this all comes at the worst possible time," Yevchenko went on, affecting great sympathy. "The whole question of your promotion and all that . . ."

Dunskoi was crestfallen. "Of course. I understand."

"That is not to say it will not happen. The Motherland is loyal and does not forget her favorite sons. You understand, of course, appearances . . ."

"Yes, yes, appearances. To be sure . . ."

"We've prepared a paper for you."

"A paper?" Dunskoi could barely get the word out. Alarm bells clanged in his head.

"A document." Yevchenko's eyes watched him coldly as he slid the paper slowly across the glossy expanse of walnut desk. "Read it, Dimitri. See what you think."

Dunskoi's mouth was dry as dust and it seemed to him he could smell the stink of fear in his own sour breath. He did not lift the paper, but read it looking down on the desk, so that Yevchenko could not see his hand tremble. He had the distinct impression that his old friend, watching him through a swirl of cigar smoke, was enjoying it all immensely.

> I, Dimitri Dunskoi, Colonel of the Army of the Supreme Soviet, having duly considered the actions of my daughter, Maria Feodorovna, and finding them to be inimical to the interests and welfare of the Soviet peoples, and unbecoming to a citizen of the Union of Soviet Socialist Republics, do disavow and disown . . .

Dunskoi stopped reading there. Not only would they banish her from her homeland, but they would also demand that he disown his child. He looked up quizzically into the placid, doughy features of his old friend. It was not in Dunskoi's nature to beg, but if he were seeking pity in those eyes, he found none there.

"Take it home and go over it again tonight with your wife." Yevchenko spoke with bogus sympathy. "There's no need to do anything immediately.

But if we are to continue to process papers for your promotion, you will have to have the document signed and back to me by the end of the week." Yevchenko rose as if to signal that the meeting had ended.

Dunskoi, however, continued to sit dumbly in his seat, wrapped in some private rumination. "Can she never return?" He spoke at last, looking up at his superior.

"Of course. There is that option. Remember, Dimi, she still retains her citizenship. However, wherever she is . . . Paris, Geneva . . . she will be constantly monitored by our consular people. And if there is evidence of genuine repentance, then of course . . ."

Dunskoi felt a rush of gratitude to his old friend, which only upon later reflection struck him as obscene. He was standing on his feet now, shaking Yevchenko's hand.

The marshal had the gratified, self-pleased look of a man who has dropped a particularly generous tip into the hat of a beggar. Only then, for the first time during the course of their long meeting, did he permit himself the humanity of a slight smile. "By the way, Dimi, how is Madam Dunskoi?"

The gull wheeled, then came in low over the water, streaking toward the shore. Its claws dropped forward, the legs fully extended, the bird skimmed the choppy surface, canted slightly left, and without warning, plowed into a wave. A small shower of spray burst directly over the point where the bird had impacted with the water, then rose again on a steady incline into the air, the small black curve of a fish squirming in its beak.

Dunskoi watched the flight of the gull move like a black dot up the long curve of the beach, until at last it appeared to merge, then vanish, its cries ringing in the milky twilight.

He trod up the beach along the little cove, following the same curve of land the gull had taken, moving directly into the wind. He'd taken his shoes off and carried them tucked beneath his arm, so that when the chilly water splashed across his feet, they sank into the sand above the instep.

A dozen or so small fishing smacks bobbed up and down on the choppy surface. Unpainted and mostly untenanted, they had the diminutive look of toy paper boats adrift on a puddle. Beyond them, further out, could be seen a whole fleet of such boats strung out and stationary along the vast gray curve of the Gulf of Finland.

Dunskoi relished his walks along the water. Taken in solitude, he looked upon them as a curative, a way of finding his way back to himself after the chaos of daily duties. Breezes gusting off the water tousled his hair and buffeted his trousers. The smell of salt air and rotting kelp was oddly satisfying. He gulped it greedily like a man who'd had no sustenance for days.

The sudden cry of a fisherman in a nearby smack roused him. They were hauling nets up, swollen and sagging with pilchard and herring. For some inexplicable reason, he'd interpreted the shouts as cries of distress. Once more he was thinking of Masha and of his wife, to whom he'd not yet told any of the grim details of his meeting with Yevchenko that afternoon.

Only now did the real significance of their meeting fully dawn upon him. How smug and oily, coldly self-important Arkady had been, full of that utterly bogus sense of earnest concern for an old friend, having his best interest at heart and all that.

"You do see, my dear fellow—under the circumstances she cannot possibly be permitted to . . ."

Dunskoi ground his teeth and leaned hard into the wind. It was nearly ten P.M. Katerine would be wondering where he was. He knew that she was already quite uneasy, sensing that something was up. Not far up the beach was a small pub frequented by fishermen who came there after work for a vodka or a kvass, or a game of checkers before bed. The sad, sweet plinking of a mandolin reached him, carried on the wind from beyond the orange glow of the windows, and it was to that bright warm patch of life embedded deep within the seashore grayness that he made his way.

The bar was packed elbow to elbow with loud, boisterous fishermen. In that smoke-filled air Dunskoi drank several vodkas, alternating between his rage against Yevchenko and his pity for Irena. There was still, more than ever, his exasperation with his daughter.

She had not been raised to question the rules of the state. Such a thing would never have occurred to him or her mother. And now, to jeopardize his career in this manner, everything he'd worked for over the years. The thoughtlessness. The ingratitude. It was inexcusable.

What was it the American girl on the train had said to him several days ago? Not the vulgar one with a mouth like a trencherman. It was the pretty one who wanted to be a diplomat. He'd forgotten her name, but they'd been talking, he recalled, about youth, and she used a word—what was it?— "changeability" to describe the young, and then added something about that being the "prerogative" of youth, a privilege taken for granted at twenty, only to be suddenly withdrawn at twenty-one.

Pretty child, she was, for that is all she really was, a child, he thought, like Masha, for all of her glib worldliness and sophistication. As if the notion that traveling about in a foreign country with a young man certified her credentials as a responsible adult.

Did Masha have lovers like this? he wondered. Young men at the university who plotted the seduction of young girls by first overpowering them intellectually. The pose of political dissidence, he thought, could have strong attractions for an impressionable young girl. But he knew that was being unfair to Masha. She was far more discriminating than that.

Still, they were so similar, these young people, Masha and the American girl—what was her name?—bright, inquisitive, compassionate, so full of ideals and principles for which they would fight you to the death. And so very "changeable."

The mandolin behind him plinked some wondrously sorrowful old Russian tune. Mandolins were so ineffably Russian. Childish, naive, sorrowful. Something in his soul loved sad old songs, the lullabies and chants he'd heard as a youth in the Urals. He loved as well these old Russian taverns near the waterfront, permeated with the sour, winy smell of kvass and strong tobacco, the camaraderie of coarse simple workmen who drank too much and started to cry, not out of sorrow but out of sheer joy to be there in the warm orange light amid the mandolins and one's comrades.

It reminded him a bit of that time when they were young and just starting out, Irena and he. He was a young, newly commissioned officer stationed at the Smolny barracks not far from the Sailor's Church. They lived then at the bottom of the Nevsky Prospect where it grows shabbier and more dingy. Their apartment house was in a narrow, muddy street that ended abruptly in a stone wall beyond which lay the sea. You crossed from there a little alleyway and came out at the back of the Nevsky monastery. Passing that, you'd cross a narrow canal and right there was their shabby little flat.

In the winter it was so cold inside that vapors rose out of their mouths as they spoke. They made love in a narrow bed. In the summer the flat became so steamy they could not sleep in it. At low tide the canals stank. Instead of going to bed, they would spend all their nights out-of-doors, strolling up the Prospect, along the archways of the Moika Embankment, sit on the benches along the Neva, eating an ice cream and watching the dim lights of the flyboats gliding upriver. Since they were young and had no money, as a form of entertainment they would sit and stare for hours at the big dark silhouettes of the Rostral Columns, the crouching hump of the Peter-Paul Fortress, and the soaring needle of the Admiralty Tower against the dazzling sunset of the White Nights.

Pushkin, he remembered, had tried to depict such a night. But even he, with all of his genius, could never come close to it. Dumas had said of those lines that they were only the poetry of man, but that the nights of St. Petersburg were the poetry of God himself.

They had little money in those days, but whenever they had a bit extra, they went to the Kirov. They sat high up in the rear and in that way they had seen Ulanova, Dudinskaya, Konstantin Sergeyev.

Masha's birth followed a tough perilous pregnancy, touch and go, with Katerine sick and depressed every day. Several times they nearly lost the child. At last the doctor wanted to terminate the pregnancy. Dunskoi was willing. He could not bear to see Irena suffer anymore. But sick as she was, she would not hear of it. She had already lost several fetuses and she had a deep, intuitive feeling that this might be her last chance.

The child came on her birthday. It was a girl, scrawny, wrinkled, but squawking healthily. When they looked at her together for the first time, they roared with laughter, but for them she was enchantment. She was the making of their lives. From the moment of her appearance, Dunskoi's fortunes flowered, and from that point on he could never quite separate in his mind the condition of her well-being from that of his own.

That evening, lying beside Irena, the two of them awake, listening to each other's breathing, he went over and over again in his mind the details of his meeting with Yevchenko. Had he heard it all correctly, and had he come away with an accurate reading of the real intent of the message? Was there something he hadn't heard, some crucial escape clause?

Later that evening, having bolstered himself with the consolation of vodka, he recounted the day's events to her. Even as he tried to explain it all, he could hear in his own voice the muddle he was making of it each time he repeated it with confusing variations. There were still too many loose ends, questions yet to be asked. Finally he showed her the document, stamped with the embossed seal of the Ministry of Justice and bristling with its own sense of importance.

They read it together several times and when he tried to explain that he must either sign it or put aside forever any hope of further advancement, his voice cracked.

"Then of course you must sign it," she said unhesitatingly. The response astonished him. He'd been expecting everything but that. Tears, threats, hysteria, defiance, all would have been justified because in his heart he knew she was in great pain.

"Of course?" He repeated her words with an odd, quizzical smile, as though he'd glimpsed in the individual with whom he'd lived for nearly thirty years something he'd never seen there before. "Why 'of course,' Katerine?"

"Because it is you who count now. She has made her choice. Now she must make her own way."

He stared at her speechlessly, admiration and dismay mingling in his gaze. "You mean that?"

"But of course. Absolutely. You've done everything you can for her. What more can you do?"

"There must be more. There has to be more . . . something else . . ."

"You've gone beyond, far beyond what any normal parent could be expected to do."

"You make it sound as if I should expect gratitude from her."

"Not gratitude, Dimi. Loyalty. Surely she owes you some small measure of that."

"She owes me nothing." He shook his head back and forth, waving the idea aside with a violent flick of his hand, as though something repugnant were stuck to it. "Nothing. I want nothing from her." He trudged up and down the length of the room while she followed him with her eyes.

She was a small, pretty woman in her mid-forties, but her once girlish figure had given way to flesh. Her skin was still quite beautiful, however, and her green, slightly protuberant eyes gave her the look of a Byzantine Madonna.

"It is you who count now, Dimi. You've worked too hard to have it all taken away like this. For something for which you are not even responsible. It's not fair. And if she can't see that herself . . ."

He turned and gazed at her. In the next moment he was laughing. "Really, you amaze me. I'm speechless. I come here expecting . . ."

"I know what you expected. That is because you think I have always placed her before you. Correct?"

The thought stunned him, not because of its improbability but because of its accuracy. However, he'd never consciously known it himself, until just that moment when she'd so aptly phrased it.

"Yes," his voice assented with an exhausted croak, "but I'd never blame you for that. She's your blood . . ."

"Yours too," she fairly shouted. "Blood . . . Good blood works two ways. You've done your share, Dimi. And now you're going to get your reward. You deserve it. You're not responsible for her actions. They know that. We must forget about Masha now. It is as if she is no more."

"No more. No more." As he lay there in bed, the words clanged like a dirge over and over in his head.

"You understand," he'd said to her, his voice pleading, when he'd turned off the night lamp, "what you're saying? What it means? Not to see her? Paris . . . London . . . Geneva . . . they're very far. Expensive. Not easy to get papers."

"I understand," she said with an odd finality, then turned her face to the wall. That was the first time that evening she showed any sign of acknowledging her loss. Later, he knew that she was crying, not by any sounds, which she'd effectively smothered in her pillow, but by the motion of the bed responding to the racking inward sobs of her body.

He took her in his arms and they lay there together, unspeaking, enfolded in each other's grief throughout the long watches of the night. Images of Masha flashed back and forth in his head, in no special order, like a slide show. A portfolio of snapshots of a small blond child with pretty hair and startled eyes, an expression that had remained unchanged from childhood to young womanhood.

Toward dawn, with the first thin gash of light in the eastern sky, Irena at last dropped off. He was still awake, however, alert and as agitated as ever. A million thoughts, like sparks flying upward, raged through his head. In his mind's eye he played out a dozen or so "what-if" scenarios to their logical conclusions, none of them particularly consoling. When he'd exhausted himself along those lines, and all the anguish of his guilt about her had spent itself, his mind turned to the trainload of hapless passengers pinned down in the heavy birch forests surrounding Vyborg.

The news that evening on the television had been dire, full of the diplomatic morass into which the situation had been inexorably sinking with each day it dragged on. The level of harangue had escalated on both sides, and what had before been couched in carefully crafted ambiguities had moved now into the area of rather more concrete actions. Both Tass and *Izvestia* had reported that elements of the U.S. Sixth Fleet had steamed out of ports on the Mediterranean and the Adriatic, ostensibly to stage war games in and around the Baltic Sea. Watching the news that evening, Dunskoi had grown increasingly uneasy. He was infuriated with the Norwegians and Americans. They played, he thought, a very cynical game with the lives of innocent people. Lying there, he could imagine the faces of many of the hostages as they appeared that moment. Unable to attach names to any particular face, he knew he liked the old American professor. And the young Dutch couple were pleasant enough. Then, too, there was the American who spied on fellow citizens and compiled dossiers on them for big-business interests.

A decent enough chap, he thought, and he was even able to recall the fellow's name. A Jewish name it was, Stern. He had been foolish enough to try to conceal the fact. Leaving his religious affiliation blank like that was really quite stupid. It had actually called attention to the fact.

A foolish mistake, that. Hardly the kind of mistake one might expect of a professional operative. Certainly not the sort of bungling you'd associate with an outfit like the Yad Vashem. It did really strain all credulity, but if that's what STAVKA wanted to serve up for public consumption, then who was he to quarrel? It was out of his hands now. He had too many other things to worry about. He would have to call Grishkov the first thing in the morning. He wanted reports on the medical status of all detainees, particularly the old fellow who'd suffered a heart attack during the physical examinations.

Then there was that crazy Spanish count. He hadn't seen the last of that one. His wife, he recalled, had heart problems too. It would be quite sticky if something untoward were to happen to her, or to any of these people while under his jurisdiction.

Once more an image of Masha flashed through his mind, followed instantly by one of that man Stern, the one they'd singled out to make a point. He knew that once they'd singled out an individual to make some kind of point, it was very hard, once the machinery was set in motion, to reverse it. It was rather disconcerting for him to realize that he now identified Stern's plight with that of his own child.

Intellectually he had no trouble understanding the nature of Masha's plight. But down deep in his heart he could not yet accept the idea that they could actually take his only child from him. Send her away so far that the chance of his ever seeing her again was remote. The state, he knew only too well, was capable of acting coldly, absolutely unemotionally in matters of national security, of which, of course, treasonable actions stood at the very top of the list.

But surely they were not that heartless. There could be exceptions. He was a hero, held in special esteem by the state. Surely they would make some exception. At least in his case. There were still avenues to explore, appeals to be made in courts that could be fair and impartial. He would not stop until he'd exhausted all such avenues of appeal.

In the end it would be seen that he, Dunskoi, was a loyal soldier and a dutiful citizen, and while it would never occur to him to defy the orders of his superiors and the wishes of the Supreme Soviet, he was not quite ready to sacrifice his only child on the altar of personal ambition.

No one had slept well in the Green Train. For one thing, they had lit the area with floodlights that glared all night long through the windows of the sleeping coaches. This was necessary, they were told that evening at dinner by Captain Grishkov, in order to discourage any repetition of the foolishness perpetrated by the young Canadian. Then, too, there was the constant noise of soldiers and heavy equipment moving about outside the train all through the night. It was as if some conscious, albeit unspoken, decision had been made to break them further by depriving them of the healing gift of sleep.

Jean Blaylock watched, sleepless and wary, from the windows of her darkened compartment, the changing of the guards, stationed at measured intervals all around the high fence. Their comings and goings were easily observed. She watched too the sentry shifting restlessly on his feet high up in the watchtower above the compound. Directly opposite her window and just outside the fence, she had the disquieting view of the T54 armor-plated tank with the huge black bore of its 60mm cannon pointed directly at her.

She had never seen anything quite like it before. Ugly, unimaginably big, when it moved or spun its turret and cupola searchlights, it made a clanking sound and tore the earth about it, like some infuriated creature about to charge.

She longed for sleep but that was virtually impossible. Even if the lights had gone off and all the noise outside had stopped, the heat and airlessness of the compartment were unbearable. Ever since Wales's attempted escape, all the windows throughout the train had remained sealed.

Worse even than the heat and noise was the unpleasant smell that seemed to permeate the immediate area. She had smelled it faintly that afternoon when she'd first entered the compartment. But now with the doors shut for the evening, and in the oppressive warmth of a sealed unmoving train, the odor had become more pronounced. It smelled to her strongly of rubber—the sort of thing you associate with overheated electrical wiring.

"What the devil are you doing up at this hour?"

"I might well ask you the same question."

"Those bloody lights going all night long. Who could sleep? Care for a schnapps?"

Standing near Tony Thomas in the dark, Stern took a warm fruity blast of breath across his cheek. They were in the small unlit vestibule of the sleeping coach. Periodically, as the tower searchlight swept down the length of the train, Stern had momentary glimpses of Thomas' face, stark and strangely transfigured in that lurid light. Then, after, when the light had passed, he could see him only in shadowy silhouette. He appeared to be leaning, rather than standing, against the coach wall, none too firm on his feet.

"Have a belt." Thomas shook the bottle at Stern as though it were a rattle.

Slightly miffed, Stern considered a moment, then took it from the Englishman. "Why not?"

He grasped the bottle round the neck and tilted it to his lips. The darkness had affected his spatial sense and part of the warm syrupy liquid splashed on his chin and ran down the collar of his shirt.

"Good stuff," he sputtered.

"VSOP. Nothing but the best for you, my friend. You had a nasty day, I heard."

"Nothing special." Stern laid on the breeziness. "Just charged with being an Israeli agent and named as a co-conspirator of Wales's."

Thomas took a long pull of the bottle and started to laugh. "So I've heard."

"Funny, eh?"

"Forgive my laughing, old chap."

"Go ahead," Stern said morosely. "You can afford to. They're not hauling you off to some gulag."

Thomas nearly bent over with laughter. "Oh, listen," he said, half-choking, tears running down his face. "If that's what you're worried about, forget it. All just piss and wind. Amateur theatrics. Their way of getting everyone to squirm."

Stern watched with misgivings the tall, wavering silhouette tilt the bottle back and drink deeply. "I'm not sure that as a technique it hasn't succeeded."

About ten feet away through a glass partition he could see the head and shoulders of a guard posted at the coach entrance, his rifle barrel glinting in the door light. "You'd think we were a pack of terrorists in here," he murmured ruefully.

"We are. They've already got themselves a CIA agent and an Israeli operative." Thomas belched sourly and laughed. "No telling what they'll look for next."

Stern peered gloomily into the dark. "Mind if I have another?"

"Help yourself." Thomas thrust the bottle toward him. "Nothing's going to happen to you, you know."

"I wish I were so sanguine."

"When they've all had enough fun, someone in Washington or Moscow will make a phone call and we'll be out of here a few minutes later."

"Is that the way it works?"

"Essentially. Like a pissing match between small boys. As soon as they've determined who can piss furthest, the match is over and everyone goes home."

"How's Wales?" Stern sought to change the subject.

"No one knows. They keep him under twenty-four-hour guard. The doctor comes twice a day, and then a couple of security officers go in and out. Nasty-looking customers."

"They won't give him much peace till he signs those papers."

Thomas drank again. The beam of a floodlight swept across the vestibule and for a moment illuminated his ragged features. His arm flew up to shield his eyes. "Bastards. I gather they want you to sign a paper too," he said when the beam had moved off like a trailing finger down the length of cars.

"To the effect that I'm a co-conspirator. In the employ of the Israeli government. They think I'm Jewish."

Stern watched his head turn, and looked at the dark spots where he knew his eyes to be, staring hard at him. "Aren't you?"

"No, I'm Lutheran, as a matter of fact."

"Lutheran?" Thomas made a harsh, cheerless sound. "With a name like Stern I could have sworn you were a son of one of the twelve tribes."

"A fairly common misconception. Actually, Stern's as frequent among German Lutherans as it is among German Jews. I was pretty supid not reporting my religious affiliation on my visa application."

"You omitted that?"

"Dumb, eh?"

"That's putting it in the kindest possible light."

"I was being principled, you see," Stern went on, growing angrier as he spoke. "I felt it was an invasion of my privacy."

"Privacy? What the devil's that?"

"I used to think I knew. So much for principle," Stern brooded.

Thomas pushed the bottle at him across the dark. "Have another."

"No, thanks." Stern deflected the bottle. "I've heard of people . . . people in similar situations . . . being detained for years."

Thomas sighed. "Rarely. But from time to time, something as lunatic as that does happen. A couple of years ago, two American diplomats were held under house arrest in Leningrad. Still there, far as I know. No explanations. Then an Englishman . . . physicist chap. Defected a few years back. Took up Russian citizenship. Went to work for the Institute of Applied Sciences until they accused him of being a double agent. The British embassy completely disavowed any connection with him at all. They're still negotiating to try to get him out." He looked up at Stern. "That must be at least five years ago."

"Where is he?"

"No one's quite certain." There was an uncomfortable pause. "I'm sorry, Peter. I didn't mean . . ."

"That's okay. I mean, we've all heard things like that. But who the hell would think . . ."

"Precisely." Thomas' ravaged features glowed with the sudden illumination of his match applied to the tip of a cigarette. "Who'd've thought when I first heard about this in Leningrad, it would drag on for six, seven days. I imagined it was only a matter of . . ."

There was a pause, rather long and uncomfortable. Stern watched the slumping silhouette shift position. "What did you say?"

"What?"

"You said something just before—something about having heard this in Leningrad."

"Well, I didn't. I mean, I didn't actually hear anything."

Stern felt a surge of heat leap to his face. "Then what exactly did you hear?"

"Nothing."

"Just a moment ago you said you'd heard about this in Leningrad. Before we left. Don't tell me I imagined that."

"Rumors," the Englishman protested. "I'd heard some rumors. I had an inkling. No more than a newsman's sense . . . "

"That this train was going to be detained?" Stern persisted. "Torn apart from stem to stern? Held up for God knows how long?"

"No. Of course not. Only that they were looking for some kind of leverage to get back their submarine."

"What submarine?"

"It seems the Norwegians grabbed a Russky submarine in the Barents Sea. Took the captain and the whole crew into custody. Accused them of spying."

"When?"

"A few days ago. Just before we left Leningrad."

"And this train was going to be their leverage?"

"Not necessarily."

"Then what exactly was it going to be?"

"Nothing. One of a dozen possibilities they were considering . . . I really don't know. Look, why the devil are you grilling me like this?"

Stern felt his gorge rise. "Where did you hear this?"

"From friends. Sources. Contacts pretty high up."

"You had hints then? Leaks?"

"In a manner of speaking."

"You might have warned us. Suggested we try some alternate route. A train to Moscow or a flight home instead."

"I told you," Thomas said, his manner growing more trapped and evasive. "I knew nothing for sure. A few leaks from sources. Nothing to it, I thought. But it's my job to follow up on things like that."

"Your job?" Stern gasped. "To let innocent people walk into a mess like this, when it was in your power . . . We've got a boy beaten half to death, an old man in the hospital with what looks like a heart attack, people scared half out of their wits—me, probably, more than anyone. And you tell me this is your job? This, I take it, is what people in your line of work call a scoop."

"You've got it all wrong, Peter." Thomas lurched toward him in the dark. "You make it sound as though I had this rigged. As if I were in some sort of collusion with them. I had nothing to do with any decisions to detain this train. Yes—I had heard rumors . . . "

"More than rumors," Stern fumed. "What you had were leads. Strong leads from *'contacts highly placed.'* Your words, Tony."

"Look, don't try to hang this thing on me. I just had leads, I told you. Nothing certain." Thomas started to move past him back into the coach. Stern blocked his path.

"You just had leads—privileged information, but at no time did it occur to you that you might have a responsibility to share that information with the rest of us."

"Why? What would that have accomplished? Panic. A rush by everyone to exchange train tickets for plane reservations? Is that what you'd have wanted?" His warm, fruity breath hung heavily in the air between them. "That would have tipped off the Russkies that we were onto . . . "

His words broke off in mid-sentence as he realized he'd condemned himself.

"Tipped off the Russkies." Stern repeated the words bitterly. "So they might have then canceled your big show, and with that you could have kissed your story good-bye."

Stern had been blocking his way, preventing him from going back into the sleeping car. Now he shoved hard at the weaving shadow leaning against him. Even before the figure slammed against the opposite wall, slumping to the floor, Stern had turned and stalked off.

Not far away in the sleeping coach, Asawa lay restless and awake in his compartment. He, too, watched the soldiers, the sentry in the box overhead, and the changing of the guards. Farther up the track he could see the T54 tank and, periodically, the crew climbing out of the turret, walking about, smoking and stretching their legs. From time to time the head of an officer would appear out of a hatch in the cupola. He would gaze round at the men nearby, exchanging remarks with them, and occasionally he would laugh.

It angered Asawa, their arrogance and self-importance. Their air of invincibility. How did they come by that, he wondered. They were just a crew of men, ordinary mortals like himself. Thrust into uniforms amid the context of awesome weaponry, and suddenly they were swaggering about, stamping their boots, flexing their muscles. Full of bravado and looking eagerly for ways to assert themselves.

But if he despised them, he was honest enough to acknowledge that he envied them as well—to the point of sickness. Uniforms and rigorous training, the sense of shared values, the mystique of men living together, bonded by unspoken codes, they had a camaraderie he craved. And yet he had always spurned the idea of close friendship. He could not be close with anyone for too long without a sense of suffocating entrapment overtaking him.

Lying on his back, he stared upward at the ceiling of the berth and wondered about the compartment he formerly occupied in the first sleeping coach. He had no way of knowing who now occupied that compartment, or any way of contacting that individual. He was not particularly worried about anyone finding the canister secreted behind the bulkhead. They'd already searched the compartment once and not detected it. Why should they now search it again?

Nor was he particularly concerned that the contents of the canister might explode spontaneously. Of course it was an explosive. That's why he'd had it. But it would only explode if someone like himself, familiar with its use, activated it. So there was little worry on that score, also.

But there was one thing that did worry him. The contents of the canister were flammable, and over that fact he had no control whatsoever.

PART VIII

GOOD MORNING. This is Bob Moon. AP News. Sources report today that a task force of American ships including the carriers *Hornet* and *Kitty Hawk*, the battleships *Arizona* and *New Jersey*, along with scores of cruisers, minesweepers, and attack transports, quietly slipped their ports on the North Sea last evening and are now en route to a staging area somewhere in the vicinity of the Baltic, where they will rendezvous with contingents of the British and French fleets.

Spokesmen at the State Department today were careful to characterize the sudden move as no more than "routine naval maneuvers," asserting that the timing of these maneuvers with the present crisis on the Russo-Finnish border was entirely coincidental.

... along with contingents of the Soviet Northern Fleet are converging on the Kola Peninsula this evening. From the port of Murmansk, from headquarters of the Baltic Fleet at Severomorsk, and from the large submarine base at Polyarny, Soviet naval might is on the move, this in response to reports that elements of the U.S. Third and Sixth fleets have streamed out of ports on the North Atlantic and the Mediterranean to group with contingents of the NATO fleet for war games in the Baltic.

This afternoon, the Ministry of Defense and the Admiralty in Leningrad characterized the move as extremely provocative and stressed that the Soviet Navy would take whatever steps appropriate to protect the sovereignty of Soviet shipping in the area. It was learned, too, that STAVKA has put on special alert elements of the Red Army's Eighth Division, now moving toward the Finnish border.

Good evening. This is Novosti signing off.

It had started in the dining car with Ted Kariolainen. When his breakfast was served, he merely lifted his fork and spoon and laid them off to one side. There was nothing defiant about it, or particularly heroic, but it was done with a finality that was unmistakable.

In the space of moments, his son, Buddy, sitting beside him, duplicated the movement, as did Karl Heinz, sitting across from them. On the other side of the aisle, Señor Madariaga, breaking a roll with his hands, suddenly paused as though he'd just recalled some vital bit of information. His back stiffened and in the next moment he returned the roll to his plate. Several of his young charges seated round him broke off their chatter and, as if by signal, stopped eating.

It went on like that, from table to table, down the length of the car. There was no hint of premeditation about it. It took everyone by surprise. It had been spontaneous and completely unanimous. It was as though they'd all been eager to make some kind of protest. All that was required was for someone to make the apposite gesture. Nothing that smacked of defiance or insurrection, but simply the laying aside of fork and spoon and sitting silent and unmoving before trays of uneaten food.

If the Russian soldiers waiting on them noted it, they showed no signs of being impressed. They continued to move up and down the aisle, passing around pots of coffee and trays of food that remained, without exception, untouched.

At most, minute quantities of liquid, juice or water, were taken by those with sufficient foresight to see that the morning ahead might be long and hot. Afterward, they were marched into the narrow wire enclosure surrounding the train. They were then separated into three groups and each assigned to a drill instructor, with the intention of having them exercised.

The makeup of these groups was determined on the basis of age. The youngest group comprised Karl Heinz, Van Meegrin, Desfargue, the Italians, young Buddy Kariolainen, and the full contingent of Madariaga's male singers. The intermediate group included people of the Stern, Blanton, and Thomas vintage, and then the several older gentlemen like Shapley, Madariaga, and Señor Gonzaga made up the third group.

Presumably, the purpose of segregation by age was to tailor the rigorousness of activity to the physical capacity of each group.

One of the drill sergeants spoke English of a rudimentary sort. A big, stolid fellow built along the lines of a telegraph pole, he planted himself squarely before them and proceeded to bellow forth instructions for a set of calisthenics while demonstrating each at the same time.

The two other drill instructors watched impassively until he'd completed his demonstration. Each then assumed a position before his designated group. Gonzaga and old Shapley were not expected to do anything too strenuous, but the two other groups were confronted with a fairly rigorous drill.

Once more the insurgency began with Kariolainen. When the drill sergeant proceeded to count aloud in his booming voice, the others immediately started the exercise. Kariolainen, however, stood still. The effect of that was to bring those who'd started to a sputtering halt.

It took a moment or two for the drill sergeant to grasp that he was counting to himself. When at last he did, he broke off with a frown. His perception of events was not that he was being defied, but that his instructions had been misunderstood. He went through the catechism again, glowering up and down the line. Then, with a great leap into the air, clapping his hands overhead, he resumed his loud, hectoring count. No one moved.

There was a long, awkward silence. The other two instructors exchanged troubled glances with their leader. Baffled, they awaited some sign of appropriate counteraction.

The drill sergeant was a man unaccustomed to intransigence. Puzzled and infuriated, his authority openly challenged with two of his subordinates looking on, he was astute enough to see that the tall blond man in the intermediate group was at the heart of the problem. Face flushed with anger, he made a fast rush at Kariolainen, shouting at the top of his lungs. His English, none too good under the best of circumstances, became virtually incomprehensible. He flung his arms about and kept shouting at him. Out of that screaming tirade, two words sounding vaguely like "step out" began to emerge.

He shouted those words over and over again, but Kariolainen never budged. The drill instructor put his face up close to Kariolainen and started to sputter. By no means a small man himself, he had not quite realized Kariolainen's size until standing directly before him, his head tilted back in order to bellow up at him.

Aside from mere height—nearly six feet, five inches—Kariolainen was a large man in many ways. Barrel-chested, thick-armed, hands the size of squash paddles, all of it fashioned out of the tough, sinewy hide that comes only from years of hard physical labor, he was a sobering presence to even the most combative-minded.

"Step out. Step out." The drill master shrieked and stamped his feet. "Step out. Step out. Step out."

Kariolainen never blinked. "I want to see my wife," he said quietly.

"Step out. Step out of line."

"I want to see my wife," he repeated with that same ominous quiet.

The drill master failed to take heed. Uppermost in his mind at that moment was the fact that his authority had been challenged. He saw this as personal injury, a direct affront he was now under obligation to redress.

Making a sudden lunge at Kariolainen, he attempted to physically drag him out of line. That was a miscalculation. Stern, standing directly beside Kariolainen, had perhaps the clearest impression of the event—the ranting, enraged sergeant, eyes rolling in his head, tugging fecklessly at the big man. He gave the impression of someone trying to yank a huge oak out of the ground. Out of the corner of his eye Stern watched Kariolainen's arm rise slowly with a strange hypnotic grace, then start its descent. Stern never saw the actual impact. It was over too fast. What he did see was the stunned, even hurt expression of the drill master's face, looking up entreatingly at the American. His wobbling legs suggested rubber bands strummed. As he struggled to regain control of them, his ankle went out from beneath him, causing him to twirl in a quarter-circle, then crumple at Kariolainen's feet.

In the next moment whistles were blowing, horns sounded, and guards with rifles streamed into the compound from every direction.

The hunger strike continued into lunch, even though Kariolainen was not there. Perhaps the fact that he wasn't had established it even more firmly as a fact of life. Moments after the drill sergeant went down, a half-dozen or so guards swarmed over the big man and hustled him, unresisting, out of the area. From there he was whisked off in a staff car.

By then it was too late. The virus of rebellion had begun to spread. Even though Kariolainen was gone, his example persisted. He'd shown a way for the others. It was not reckless, full of the vain melodrama of extravagant heroics. All it required was the kind of quiet resolve which by that time most of them were more than ready to expend. Those less inclined to defiance followed anyway, ashamed to be seen as shirkers. So it was, the hunger strike became a tug-of-war, a battle of wills between captor and captives. The waiters moved up and down the aisle, rattling trays of food, but none of it was touched. Though they didn't show it, the Russians regarded the action as extremely dangerous. Not only was it defiance of authority which must be quashed immediately, but there was also the ticklish problem of the physical well-being of hostages of the state. In the ceaseless war of East-West propaganda, charges of inhumanity and brutality against the defenseless could be used to devastating advantage. It would do little for Soviet public relations to reduce these people to a state of tatters and ruin. All the world, even the politically uncommitted parts of it, would note that sort of thing and mark it down for future use.

Understandably, young Buddy Kariolainen had taken the incident with his father that morning hardest of all. Twelve-year-olds are not typically accustomed to seeing armed soldiers swarm over the fallen figures of their fathers and watching them being dragged off to a waiting car and kicked and shoved in.

The boy was bereft and people like Shapley and Madariaga moved in quickly to fill the void. Thomas tried to assure young Buddy that the soldiers would not harm his father, that at most he'd be given a stern reprimand and sent back to the train. "I'll wager he'll be here by suppertime." Thomas winked and tousled the youth's hair.

The boy was nevertheless distraught. The doubt in his face wavered at the edge of tears.

Karl Heinz became a sort of self-appointed big brother. He took Buddy under his wing and he and Desfargue and the Italians played backgammon for hours with him in an effort to distract him.

After lunch Stern fell off to sleep in his berth. He dreamed of his apartment, a top-floor walk-through of a three-story townhouse, the big skylight windows facing north on Sixty-third Street. Seven rooms of almost Proustian clutterment, brocade and ormolu, celadon lamps, Chinese ginger jars, japanned screens, a bowl of handmade calla lilies against a smoked-mirror entryway, branches of pussy willow fanned out in tall pewter urns, Aubusson area rugs scattered over marquetry floors, an amber-colored leather chesterfield around which sat burled-wood antique tables and overstuffed chairs covered in pale pink and aubergine. On the walls were a number of large paintings

in the style of Watteau and Fragonard. Books, plants, and recordings everywhere.

It was cluttered and airless, sealed from light and sunshine by brocaded
draperies and pale curtains that softened the harsh skyline of the city. It was
all Connie's design. She adored collecting and displaying. In his next life, he
vowed, he would live in monkish austerity. Bare walls and large windows.
Perfunctory furnishings. Solitude, pale light, and air to breathe.

Even in these fitful dreams he worried about the plants and the cat, Jones,
and whether or not his landlord, always on the premises, was taking care of
them or not.

A Ming vase overflowing with Oriental poppies shattered into thousands of
fragments as his bleary eyes fluttered open on the blurred features of a guard
stooping above him, tugging at his sleeve.

"Please to come with me."

Stern cocked a brow at the man.

"We go now."

"Where?"

"Please to come."

The conversation appeared to bog down between variations of that parry
and thrust.

"We go now. The car waits."

Stern rose stiffly and threw on his old corduroy sport jacket. Shortly he was
walking, guards on either side of him, outside the wire enclosure, where a
black staff car pulled up beside the compound awaited them.

Once in the car, bouncing and lurching over the open field, he again attempted to discover their destination. "Can't you tell me where we're going?"

The guards seated in the back seat with him maintained a stolid silence,
each staring out of his own window as though the man seated between them
had not uttered a word. Several times Stern repeated the question and got no
more response than a quizzical glance of the driver's eye, reflected backward
in the rearview mirror.

They drove for approximately three-quarters of an hour while Stern grew
increasingly uneasy. In his mind flashed a series of images, starting with his
being spirited north to a labor camp from which all traces of his whereabouts
would vanish forever, to another, of his body pulped and bloody, tossed from
a moving vehicle and left to molder at the side of the road.

In another ten minutes they'd rounded a curve. A series of spires and
domes and bleak gray office buildings loomed up ahead. They were moving
smartly down a highway into what he recognized as the center of the Russian
border city of Vyborg. It was here that the train had originally stopped to undergo customs inspection and from here their strange adventure had begun.

The car nosed down a series of wide, treeless boulevards lined with a seemingly endless expanse of gray, drab, prefabricated dwellings all bearing the
cheerless look of barracks hastily erected. The streets had a ghostly vacancy

about them, unrelieved by either pedestrians or auto traffic. There was not even the sign of a stray cat to signal human habitation.

The car took a sharp dip and swept down a steep hill, intersected at the bottom by the railway station and the Douane. Stern immediately recognized the barbed wire and the sentry boxes elevated on tall stilts. Huddled along the tracks and extending into the nearby woods were the clusters of barracks, sheds, and small administrative buildings that comprised the compound, housing the military transportation units and the border police.

Captain Grishkov rose as he entered and gestured to a chair opposite his desk. "You understand why you are here?" he asked, after he'd been seated.

"I have not the slightest idea," Stern replied.

Without deigning to glance up, the young man pushed a rather lengthy document across the desktop to Stern. "You know what that is?"

"It's a document of some sort. It's written in Russian."

"Please to note the signature at the bottom." The eyes, blank and colorless, rose to meet his. "Can you read that?"

Stern's eyes took in the faint, wavering cursive letters. "It says Keith Wales, followed by the date."

"Today's date?"

Stern shrugged. "I have no accurate impression of what the date is today. One tends to lose track of time in places like this."

The captain disregarded the gibe. "You may take my word for it, it is today's date."

"I take your word for it," Stern replied, a look of mild consternation on his face.

"And that is Mr. Wales's signature?"

"If you say so."

The air of strained civility descended like a pall upon them.

"It is Mr. Wales's confession of acts of espionage against the USSR."

"He signed a confession written in Russian?" Stern stared skeptically at the paper. "If I'm not mistaken, his Russian is limited, if not altogether nonexistent."

"The document was read aloud to him," Captain Grishkov retorted. "I shall be happy to read it aloud to you. Particularly those parts which bear directly upon you."

Stern's jaw tightened visibly. "On me?"

"You will note your name appears roughly midway down the page. It is written in English letters for your convenience."

Stern's eyes swarmed across the page until he saw the familiar configuration of his name floating in a sea of Cyrillic.

"I see it."

"Would you like me to translate the lines pertaining to you?" the captain went on with icy cordiality.

"If you'd like."

A corner of the captain's mouth arched upward into an irritating smile. "Since you are so gracious in the matter, I shall be happy to do so." He reached across the desk and took the document back from Stern.

The young man's lips moved soundlessly over the text until he'd reached the lines he sought, the lines in question. " '. . . in which I, Keith Wales, admit freely and under no duress, that I did enter into an agreement with Mr. Peter Stern, in full knowledge of his affiliation as an agent/operative of the government of the state of Israel to spirit documents of a highly classified nature out of the Soviet Union, with the express intention . . .' " He glanced up at Stern. "Shall I continue?"

"There's no need."

The captain put aside the document and leaned back in his chair. "I need not tell you, Mr. Stern, that the Soviet Union looks with grave disfavor on foreign agents operating within its sovereign borders."

"Quite right," Stern snapped. "You need not tell me."

The captain gave him a long sidewards look intended to suggest patience rapidly vanishing. "Ah—I see now. You fail to grasp the gravity of the situation."

"On the contrary. I grasp it only too well."

"Then I commend you. You are remarkably composed for a man who is facing twenty-five years of confinement in a labor camp."

The young man announced this with the sort of pompous solemnity one associates with magistrates and prelates. He was evidently quite comfortable in the role. If his words were intended to terrorize Stern into quick submission, they had precisely the opposite effect. Ironically, the more dire the picture Captain Grishkov painted, the more dissociated Stern grew by the minute.

"What exactly are you asking me to do?" he asked in a way so coolly distant as to momentarily unbalance the young man.

He blustered a moment before recovering his composure. "A document similar to the one prepared for Mr. Wales awaits your signature."

"A document implicating me in this fiction you've cooked up about spies and stolen classified data?"

The captain's eyes narrowed to thin taut slits. "I caution you, Mr. Stern . . . if you are testing the resolve of the High Command of the Supreme Soviet—"

"I'm testing nothing," Stern shot back. "If the Supreme Soviet High Command has time for such nonsense, they must be an extremely frivolous bunch without enough work to do. I'd like to see Colonel Dunskoi."

The moment he'd uttered the name he knew he'd touched a raw nerve.

"Why?"

"I've already had discussions with him on this subject and if there are to be further discussions, I prefer that they be with him."

"There shall be, of course, further discussions, but I regret they cannot be with Colonel Dunskoi. He has been summoned back to headquarters, and his command now falls to me."

Captain Grishkov reported all this with evident relish. He was actually an attractive young man with high Slavic cheekbones and finely wrought features. Once again he slid the document back across the desktop to Stern. "Why don't you simply sign this and make it easy on yourself?"

Stern stared blankly down at the paper as though it weren't there. Outwardly his calm was impressive. He realized he was playing as much of a role as the captain. However, at that moment he felt he was outpointing him considerably. "I have a strong distrust of anything too easy," Stern replied with quiet civility. "However, to avoid future misunderstandings, I must tell you right now, in no uncertain terms, I am signing no documents. You can beat me half to death as you did that poor boy; you can pump me full of drugs or send me off to one of those lovely vacation spots of yours up north, but I sign nothing."

Leaning far back in his chair, smiling oddly to himself, the captain pondered Stern's words. He too was playing his role and, like Stern, he too thought he was winning. "Ah, then," he sighed wearily, "I see it is to be a contest of wills."

"10/24 Plekhanova." Dunskoi hailed the wizened old babushka. She was trundling a fresh-water wagon through the streets.

She cupped her ear and squinted at him.

"10/24 Plekhanova," he cried again.

"A block down. Behind the Mir, just off Dzerzinskogo." Her voice was like a nail dragged across slate.

"*Vidanya.*" He waved her thanks and bustled forward. It was nearly eight P.M. and the streets teemed with children and old people. Students from the university living in the ancient quarter scurried homeward, bags of books slung across their shoulders.

It was that district near the Sadovya, in the vicinity of Mir Square. In prerevolutionary times it was known as the Haymarket, a disreputable slum district of old St. Petersburg comprising doss houses, drinking shops, and the sort of low dives loved and immortalized by Dostoyevsky.

In the thirties, the square was rebuilt and a large portion of it given over to a park where now modern-day Moscow Boulevard begins. Just off that assertively modern thoroughfare, the quaintness of antiquity teeters uneasily between progress and nostalgia. Narrow winding streets meander through a huddle of intersecting byways, lined with rows of crooked little residences three and four stories high, dating back to the eighteenth century. Their steeply sloped jagged roofs had the look of broken teeth against the milky twilight.

Life teemed in those cramped, cobbled byways. Tired housewives stood mute and uncomplaining in long queues, waiting to buy a few beans or tomatoes. The dim lights of little kiosks and fruit bars twinkled orange through the vapory mists curling in off the river. The great glittering lights of the huge

Apraksin Bazaar nearby lit up the sky. The air smelled strongly of fish.

"Kafe Fregat?" he inquired of one of the outdoor sherbet vendors.

"Right under your nose, my friend." The fellow nodded, dropping kopeck change into the hands of a waiting child.

Dunskoi turned a corner where the window of a tobacconist's shop jutted like a ship's prow into the street. At once he saw the sign and the leaded bar windows up ahead.

Kafe Fregat was a small cellar café frequented by students because of the trendy decor and the good traditional Russian cooking at inexpensive prices. The champagne and vodka were also cheap and very good. You had to descend a flight of stairs to enter. It was a smoky place with low ceiling beams that represented a hazard even to those of average height. Students sat around small tables drinking beer, tugging at pipes, making the sort of terribly earnest "serious" talk that students so delight in. A few chess games were under way in the back. The air buzzed with the traffic of waiters rattling trays of food about the room.

The place was crowded and at first he did not see her. Standing at the entrance, he scanned the room, certain she had not come. Then he saw her. She was sitting toward the rear amid a group of young people—students, no doubt, like herself, from the university. When his eyes caught hers, she looked away and he realized she'd seen him first, but was determined, for the time being at least, not to acknowledge his presence.

The maître d' showed him to a small booth, quite apart from where she sat. He ordered a Russkaya and a coffee, then lit a cigarette and waited.

It took some time. In refusing to acknowledge his presence at once, he realized that she was making a point. He was not altogether certain that it was an augury of good. When the waiter brought him the second Russkaya, she came.

He rose formally as she slipped into the booth beside him. "Would you like something?" he asked. "Coffee? Brandy?"

"Just a coffee, perhaps."

She lit a cigarette and looked off at a group of young people clattering down the stairs through the front door.

"Friends?"

"Not really. They're from the university. I see them about."

Sitting there, small, pretty, intensely serious, puffing nervously at her cigarette, he could not associate her with the child he remembered in Plisetskaya Square who dressed dolls and threw quoits. "This seems a very nice sort of place," he said by way of small talk.

"A hangout."

"Students?"

"Mostly. Some neighborhood people too. How are you?"

He laughed. "You mean since two nights ago?"

"If you're here to pursue that conversation . . ."

He laid his large hand firmly over hers and looked quickly around. "The two men," Dunskoi muttered, without looking in that direction. He'd seen them the moment he came in.

"Which two men?"

"Seated behind me over my shoulder."

She glanced that way quickly. "Police—your sense of smell is as keen as mine."

He didn't say he'd had about thirty years up on her sharpening that particular sense. He went on casually. "Those people you were seated with. They are your friends?"

"Not my co-conspirators, if that's what you're worried about," she replied acidly. "But they are friends. Good friends. They risk their necks just being seen with me."

"You theatricalize this so."

"You suggest that what is happening to me is some sort of theater?"

Something in her eyes beyond mere indignation cautioned him to drop the matter. "We can go somewhere else, if you'd like."

Her eyes smiled with defiance. "Since I've left the university, I don't bother to hide from the police anymore."

"Would you like to return to the university?"

"Not under the conditions it would entail."

At a loss for words, he gazed around. "We used to go to an old *kafe* near here when you were young."

"Ogonyok."

"Of course. Ogonyok. On the Nevsky."

"It's still there. Part of the Metropol."

"That's right. They had a children's café where you once got sick all over me on pastry and ice cream." He laughed, but it sounded forced.

She frowned and looked away. "Father, why do you bother? It's useless."

He reached across the table, took her chin between his fingers, and slowly turned her face back toward him. "It's not useless. And don't look away from me."

"It is."

"I think it is useless for you to make a sacrifice of yourself."

"I don't see it as a sacrifice. It's a principle—a very important ..." She threw her head back, tossing the hair out of her face.

"Why don't you tie your hair back with a ribbon or a barrette or something?"

"I always lose them. Anyway, they don't work. Nothing works."

He took her hand and squeezed hard until she'd recovered her voice.

"I can't explain it," she went on.

"What can you do for this principle of yours shut away in a labor camp, or banished to some decadent Western capital?"

"God forbid I am sent to the West and God help you if you intercede in any way with your big-shot cronies to bring that about. I intend to go where my friends are going. I wish to take the same medicine. No favors, please."

"To some camp in Siberia where you'll rot in the summer with the flies and mosquitoes, and freeze in the winter? How heroic."

"No worse than here." She gazed back at the two plainclothes security police watching them across the room. "Just another prison."

Once again his resolution faltered, and he lost his thread of thought. He'd come armed with forceful arguments all carefully organized in his head. Now, both arguments and organization had gone up in smoke. Even a last desperate appeal to her that she compromise and save herself had flown. He was about to offer her money, then realized that the only thing that could buy would be her undying scorn. Every tactic, in fact, seemed vain and hollow in the face of this quiet, rather ominous calm.

His sense of helplessness angered him. If he were home, or in his office, he'd have brought his fist down on the table. In the Kafe Fregat, only his eyes flared. "Your mother says I should disavow you. They've told me I must make a public disavowal of your activities. I must sign a paper."

"Or else?"

"Or else my career in the Army is over."

"Have they actually said that?"

"In not so many words. But they don't have to. I know."

"Ah." She leaned back, inhaling deeply her cigarette. "Then mother is right. You must sign."

"Don't tell me what I must do," he snapped. "I know very well what I must do."

"I, too, Father."

"You don't know." His voice rose. People seated nearby glanced at them. His voice dropped to an infuriated whisper. "You're still a child. Despite what you think. And you don't know what you're saying. You don't know these people. You don't know what they're capable of." He spoke with his fist clenched and his eyes lowered to the table.

This time it was her hand that covered his. "The mere fact that you sit here frightened by those men watching us, pleading with me to lie, tells me all I need to know. They want me to make some sort of recantation and promise to be a good girl, think no more unpleasant thoughts about the system, detach my brain and go to work, shut up for the rest of my life in some dreary laboratory of the Academy, carrying out research to achieve ends I find despicable."

"It's not for me." He spoke, trying to match her calm. "Don't think it's for me. I'm not asking you for this to ensure my advancement. What do I care for advancement if my child is not here to enjoy it with me? What do you think I work for? If they take my child from me, they take my life. I want my child. I don't want her taken from me."

It occurred to him that he was pleading, and he couldn't bear that. When he looked up again, she was smiling at him and he knew he had lost.

"What can you say of a system that forces you to choose between your life and that of your own child?"

"You think it's any better in the West?" he threw out at her bitterly.

"The West is just as crazy as here. They want economic domination of the world; we, ideological domination. To what end, either? Can you tell me? We merely worship different gods. Both will eventually collide."

Dunskoi signaled the waiter and took out his wallet. He proceeded to peel off a number of bills. "You want me to be ashamed of being a Russian? Well, I'm not. I am proud of my history. I love my homeland. Your forefathers drove Tamerlane and the Third Reich out of Russia, and we too will crush all invaders. I love what my country stands for. I acknowledge faults within the system. In any system there are inequities. Never look for perfect justice or fairness. In any system designed by men, look first for self-interest. But we don't give up because of that. We don't simply opt out because we can't have things our way. I am proud of the role I played in Hungary and Czechoslovakia, the recent trouble in Poland . . ."

"Why do you think you had to go to Poland and those other places? Because those people love you? Can't bear not to have you there?"

Dunskoi's cheeks reddened. When he spoke again, his voice was husky and tired. "If I were asked to go to any of those places again, I would go gladly. I'm a Russian and a soldier. That's my duty."

When he rose and started out, she called after him. "Sign that paper, Father. And forget me."

Glaring back at her, it suddenly occurred to him how closely she resembled the woman he'd courted and married nearly thirty years before. As he stormed out, something in his throat gagged.

Buddy Kariolainen had been watching for the return of his father. He'd been expecting it at any moment. Mr. Thomas and the old professor had pretty much assured him he'd be back by dinnertime. Nothing to fear. The Russians wouldn't dare harm him. Too much bad publicity. They only wished to put a bit of fright in him, then return him to the train.

That evening Buddy sat in the restaurant car along with the others, his father's empty chair beside him. Each time the glass pocket door at the head of the car slid open, the boy looked up expectantly, a smile starting at the edges of his mouth, certain he'd see his father. But his father never came.

The fast that Ted Kariolainen had so quietly launched that morning persisted now with far more stubborn intensity. It was as though the sight of his empty chair and his physical absence tended to make the symbolic presence of the man loom even larger. No one there would soon forget the sight of him, tall and unresisting, shoved and manhandled into a waiting staff car.

For all his youth, Buddy had a keen awareness of the connection between his missing father and these men sitting stolidly before trays of uneaten food. He understood what it signified and it made him proud. But, on the other hand, he was frightened. Moreover, not having eaten all day, he was famished as only twelve-year-old boys can be. The food on his plate, a boiled potato with a sprig of drooping parsley and a reeking sausage of some indeterminate forcemeat, while not particularly appetizing, would have suited him just fine. He hungered for the little paper cup of raspberry gelatin in the upper corner of his tray, but the sense of honor and pride in his father made even so minor a concession unthinkable.

Besides, what would the others have thought? They were just as hungry as he. But that evening, not one of them, to a man, had lifted so much as a morsel of food to his lips, all the while the Russian soldiers moved up and down the aisles removing plates of uneaten food, glancing questioningly at one another.

Later, tucked away in his berth, he was unable to sleep. Images of his father's arrest, the sight of the black doors of the staff car slamming behind him, flashed on and off in his head like the hot pulse one feels at the center of an infection. It kept him awake, though he was deadly tired, and made him want to cry. Only twelve, he already had a good deal of the realist and something of the fatalist about him. He'd never known separation from his parents before. There was, of course, camp, but that was voluntary, and besides, all of his buddies were there. This was something else. It was forced and that's what made it so scary. Outwardly, however, he kept up a good front, a grand show of pluck.

Long after the lights were out that evening, he could hear the sound of Asawa whispering to himself. It had the sound of mice scurrying across the floor.

As he lay in the narrow upper berth, pangs of hunger squeezed his innards and gave him cramps. He'd worn his underclothes to bed—a T-shirt and Jockey shorts. He had no pajamas. Like everyone else, his laundry had been taken off several days before and had still not been returned. The underclothes he wore now, his last pair, were fairly gamy by then, and lying there, he could smell himself.

The whispering sounds from Asawa's berth had subsided into a silence so abrupt it called attention to itself. In their wake came a whole medley of crepuscular sounds seeping in through the sealed windows from the outside. For several brief moments it distracted him from the task of coping with the tangle of emotions and fears that racketed wildly about inside him.

"Are you awake?" Asawa called up to him from below.

"Yes." There was a silence as Buddy waited.

"Are you okay?"

"What?"

"Okay. Okay." Asawa grew a bit frantic. "You okay?"

"Oh, yeah. Sure." Buddy laughed halfheartedly. "I'm fine."

There was another pause and a new silence gathered all about them.

"Your father . . ."

"Yes?"

"Your father . . ." Asawa tried again and came to a stuttering halt.

"Yes. My father . . . what about my father?" Buddy's heart beat wildly, certain that Asawa was going to impart to him news that his father was now back, safe and on the train.

"He is evil man." Asawa spoke in a strangled voice.

"What?"

"He is evil man."

Buddy sat up in the dark and gaped off in the direction from which Asawa's voice came. He'd heard the words, but as of yet, he hadn't truly grasped them.

"My father?"

"Yes. Evil. Bad. Bad. What he did this morning. Refuse to obey order. Expose all to danger. Very serious. Very bad. Anarchy. He betray us."

Petrified, Buddy listened to the words, recited chantlike and at a shrieking whisper. The sounds came hissing and sputtering upward. "Now we have trouble. Very bad. Very bad."

The mattress squealed, as though Asawa had suddenly lain back. The words and the harsh dry whisper broke off, and silence flooded the darkness.

The boy cowered there for some time sitting up beneath his blanket, immobile, darkness thick as black cotton batting pressed against his face, certain that Asawa, crouched beneath him, lay alert and listening to his every movement. He sat there paralyzed with fright, too terrified to move.

It must have been an hour that Buddy sat there in the suffocating dark. As the woods round the train slowly cooled down, the air in the sleeping car grew fresh and chill so that the boy huddled in his shorts and T-shirt, crossing his arms against his chest, embracing himself for warmth.

Outside, he could hear the bark of command for the changing of the guard, then the whine of a truck rumbling out of the compound. Beneath him, rising upward, came the rapid, agitated breathing of Asawa, possibly asleep.

"Evil. Evil . . ." The words banged about in Buddy's head, and when he started to tremble, he was uncertain whether it was a result of the cold or his own rampant fright.

His trembling, plus the chill of the car, made him want to go to the bathroom. He could feel the sharply uncomfortable pressure of fluid in his bladder and the need to relieve it. Yet he was terrified to move lest he wake Asawa and set him off again. His mind whirled frantically, seeking some way to leave the cabin unbeknownst to Asawa.

The top rung of the bunk ladder felt clammy and cold against his bare foot. Even as he'd swung his leg over the side, Asawa's choppy, lurching breaths ceased abruptly. The boy froze in motion, one leg on the berth, the other thrown over the side. For what seemed an interminable length of time he sat poised like a dancer in that awkward position at the top of the ladder, while his heart thumped and he gaped down into the darkness swimming below him.

Suddenly Asawa's snores broke off and the boy was certain he was wide awake, listening to his every move. But then, in the next instant, the breathing resumed, more raspy and agitated than ever, the sort of breathing associated with shallow, troubled sleep.

Something drew the boy on, pushing him beyond the paralyzing inertia of fear. He thought it was the bathroom he wanted to reach, but somewhere dwelling at the farthest reaches of his conscious thought was the knowledge that his mother and sister were a mere thirty yards away, the length of a day coach. But they may as well have been on Mars for all the snares and perils that studded the narrow band of space between them.

The journey down the ladder, five rungs, seemed as perilous as a descent from a mountain peak. For every two steps he'd come down, he'd retreated one back up, certain that Asawa, if not actually awake, was unquestionably just on the brink of waking.

In his childish fright, Buddy was quite beyond the point of grasping the fact that Asawa had made no threatening gesture toward him, nor that it couldn't have made a particle of difference to Asawa whether the boy stayed up in his bunk or not. All he kept hearing were those strangled, crackling whispers: "Evil. Evil."

At last, standing on the floor at the bottom of the ladder, his back turned to Asawa, he half-expected to feel at any moment a hot, heavy hand come down hard on his shoulder.

The next peril on his odyssey was sliding open the compartment door and slipping out into the corridor. He'd grown accustomed to the regular swings of the searchlight swerving across the cabin and he had the keenness of observation to sense that Asawa's greatest restlessness coincided with those silent swerves. The light occurred with the regularity of a pulse, every two minutes or so. Buddy was clever enough to time his exit a minute or so after it had swung past, sufficient time for Asawa to lapse back into fitful sleep.

The door was heavy, but it slid easily, making a low grinding sound as it rolled across its track. When at last it stood open wide enough, Buddy leaned his upper trunk out over the threshold, peering up and down the darkened corridor, slightly out of breath and cranking up courage enough to step out into it.

At either end of the sleeping car, the boy could see the exit lights glowing a strange spectral red. From outside, he heard the sentries laugh and chat under their breaths as they changed guards. He still had no clear fixed idea of where he was going or what he was doing. Was it to the bathroom? He was no longer certain. Yet wherever or whatever it was, he moved toward it with the unerring instinct of a homing pigeon.

The lavatory was at the same end of the car where the sentries had just greeted each other and laughed as they rotated watches. It was to that end he went, the front end, a full car's length closer to his destination than the lavatory at the other end.

The door to the lavatory swung open so easily he nearly fell inward. Stepping in, he locked the door behind him. The air inside was dark and clammy and smelled strongly of urine. Walking barefoot over the dampish tile, he recoiled at the thought of what he might be stepping into.

He lowered his shorts and squatted an inch or so above the seat, the way his mother had taught him when using public lavatories, so as to avoid any possible contact. Listening to the guards chatting outside, no more than the distance of a thin metal partition between them, he wondered what he was going to do next. It appeared he'd reached the end of whatever few alternatives there were. Sentries were posted at either end. He could go neither forward nor backward. Unpleasant a prospect as it was, there seemed nothing left to do but return to the cabin and Asawa.

Still he waited, it seemed for nearly a full hour, perched motionless as if floating above the toilet seat, a wary sparrow on the rim of a birdbath, when it occurred to him the murmur of voices beyond the partition had ceased.

Stepping back outside the door, the last thing he'd expected to see was an empty corridor and the exit, where the guards had stood, now vacant.

It seemed an illusion or possibly a trick. It made him extremely uneasy. When he slid the glass door open and stepped into the vestibule, he fully expected one of the sentries to step forward and challenge him. He even had an excuse prepared for his being there. "I was just looking for an aspirin. I have a sore throat and that's the only thing that helps me."

But no sentry stepped forward, and for a time he stood there in the vestibule by the open door bathed in the eerie red sheen of the exit light.

Possibly they'd taken a break, he thought. Gone off for coffee and a cigarette. But would they have just left their posts like that, unattended? It had to be some sort of trick, like the way they'd simply disappeared the other morning, locking everyone into the train but leaving just one window open, sorely tempting someone to escape.

He started to descend the steps, then ducked back just as the beam of the searchlight swept past the entrance and moved on noiselessly down the length of the train. In the next moment he hopped back down and perched on the penultimate step between the two cars.

He ducked his head out, then pulled it quickly back when he saw the guards at the rear, and up forward at the front of the coach. Up the track toward the middle of the car, he glimpsed the huge silhouette of the T54 tank bathed in the ghostly white illumination of its cupola light.

He searched his mind frantically for a place he might hide. What he wanted more than anything was to break out and find his father. But they were completely closed in, encircled by wire. And the guards posted in the sentry box at the gate seemed far more alert than those at the coach exits.

Buddy shivered in the musty dark of the vestibule, fully expecting the guards to return at any moment. The thought of going back to the cabin flashed through his mind. There, at least, it would be warm. But he thought again of Asawa, and those awful strangled sounds—half-words, half-grunts—and he dismissed the thought from his mind forever.

He started down the coach steps again, his heart thumping madly in his chest. He ducked his head out, and his eyes shot up and down the length of the train. The guards were still there, to the right and left of him. What, after all, did he expect—that they would all just desert their posts and disappear for his convenience?

He scrambled back up into the safety of the car and started back through the glass connecting doors. But this time, it seemed to him, he'd seen something he hadn't noticed before. To his right, in the coupling zone between the two cars, was a ladder clamped to the front of the sleeping coach and leading up to the roof.

No one had noticed his absence until the end of breakfast the following morning. Karl Heinz had been sitting before his tray. He'd taken nothing from it but a sip of tea. It had been twenty-four hours now since he'd taken any solid food. The roll and cheese and the tea steaming on his tray made him almost sick with desire. The thought of how the boy was faring passed through his mind and he looked across the aisle, expecting to see him there. He saw no one at Buddy's place. Beside it was Asawa, smoking a cigarette and staring off into space.

"You haven't seen Buddy?" Karl Heinz asked Shapley, seated beside him.

Shapley looked up slowly from his tray and stared around him. "Doesn't seem to be here. Probably back in his cabin."

Karl Heinz rose, trying not to call attention to himself, and strolled up the aisle, pausing from time to time to exchange a few words with several of the others. "Have you seen Buddy?" he asked Desfargue, then Conti. No one had. Stern recalled seeing him at supper, and Van Meegrin, just before retiring. But he had no recollection of having seen him that morning.

Soon the whole restaurant car was astir with a buzz of excitement. They whispered because the guards, accustomed to doing a head check each morning at breakfast and at night just before bedtime, had not yet discovered the boy's absence.

"He's probably still in bed," Blanton said. "Overslept."

Karl Heinz shook his head. "That doesn't sound like him. He's the first up every morning. He might be sick."

Stern turned to Asawa just behind him. "Have you seen the Kariolainen boy this morning?"

Asawa appeared puzzled. His eyes had a cloudy, distant look.

"Buddy—you know, Buddy. The kid who's in the same cabin as you."

Asawa nodded vigorously. "Yes—same cabin."

"Have you seen him?" Shapley asked with noticeable impatience.

"Yes, I see him."

"Is he back in the cabin?" Karl Heinz asked.

"Yes. In cabin."

The response lacked conviction or even comprehension. A number of meaningful glances passed among the others.

"Perhaps we might stroll down and have a look," Thomas said, watching the sergeant major eyeing them warily at the head of the car.

"Go at once," Gonzaga said, an unaccustomed urgency in his voice.

Karl Heinz rose, pushing his chair back.

"Someone had better go with him," Shapley said.

Desfargue stood up quickly. "I'll go."

Together they sauntered down the aisle toward the sleeping coach with an air of studied nonchalance. At the end of the car, one of the guards stopped them.

"Toilette," Desfargue piped breezily, gesturing in the direction of the lavatory.

The man nodded and let him pass.

Once inside the sleeping coach, they moved quickly, swinging past a succession of open cabin doors revealing a turmoil of unmade beds and open suitcases.

The cabin shared by Buddy Kariolainen and Asawa stood wide open. It was empty. The youth's berth appeared to have been slept in, but it could have been vacant for hours, or possibly only just minutes.

Karl Heinz hovered tentatively in the dank shadows that smelled oppressively of cigarette smoke and old laundry.

The boy's red Frisbee lay at the foot of the bed, uptilted lightly on its rim, and a baseball cap hung on the post of his bunk as if only moments before he'd breezed in from outside and tossed it there. Though it wasn't cold in the cabin, Karl Heinz and Desfargue, gazing at each other, felt a disquieting chill come over them.

"When did you last see him?" Thomas asked Asawa.

"This morning I see him," Asawa stuttered. "In bed. He is in bed."

"He's not in bed." Thomas bristled sharply.

Shapley eyed him. "No one came during the night and took him off?"

"No, no. I there. We talk. All through night. No one come."

Asawa was absolutely certain in his mind he'd spoken to the boy "all through the night." He truly believed he'd seen young Buddy that morning, too. In his mind the events of past mornings had all merged into an undifferentiated present. He could no more separate the details of this morning from those that had occurred any morning before.

The others had no way of knowing that, and while they may have doubted Asawa's claims, there was at least the distinct possibility that they might be true.

After breakfast they were rounded up and herded out to the exercise yard, where, to their surprise, a volleyball net had been strung between the barbed-wire fence on the one side and a stunted birch pole on the other. A fresh white new ball sat on the ground beneath the net.

Blanton groaned. "My God. Are we going to play volleyball?"

"I can use the exercise," Desfargue said.

"You can do mine for me," Van Meegrin sulked. "I loathe leaping about."

Thomas' eyes swept up the court. "This is not just any old volleyball game. Look there."

Stern glanced over his shoulder in the direction Thomas indicated. The sun came from that direction and he had to squint. At the far end of the compound four or five men in headphones were in the process of setting up a camera, complete with booms and sound equipment.

"It seems we're to be in the flicks," Thomas said.

"Christ," Blanton muttered. "Home movies."

Shapley gazed off into the distance. "More like fancy high-tech propaganda so the folks back home can see how well we're all doing."

"Is it to be in color?" Mr. Mukherjee brightened considerably at the prospect.

Max Conti fumed. "I won't be a part of it."

"You don't have much choice, my friend." Thomas grinned. "Here comes J. Arthur Rank now."

A tall, rangy, Aryan-looking gentleman was striding toward them, his scruffy chukka boots raising small puffs of dust as he came. With him was Captain Grishkov, pedaling hard to keep up. They appeared to be in earnest conversation.

When they reached the place where the group clustered, they stopped and chatted a bit longer. Presently the captain broke off his talk with the tall gentleman, turned to the group, and stepped forward.

"Good morning, gentlemen." He spoke with an amiable grin on his face. "I would like to introduce to you Comrade Vilhos. He is a television news director from Prague." Grishkov looked around to see what sort of impression he was making. There was no discernible reaction whatsoever.

"He would like to take pictures of you today," he continued, "so that your families at home can see that you are happy and well provided for. Regrettably, he speaks no language other than Czech. I will therefore serve as his translator. He asks only that each of you conduct yourselves naturally. Do nothing out of the ordinary. We do not wish these films to give a distorted picture of reality. We are interested in portraying only truth. So we have arranged for all of you to play some ball and laugh and joke and have a wonderful time this morning as your pictures are being taken."

Someone behind Stern snickered. Grishkov's patter broke off at once. His eyes darted through the ranks.

In the next forty minutes they played volleyball in fits and starts. Each time they began to play, the director would stop to pose and regroup them. He had some curious idea that the players should be assembled on the court according to height in strict descending order. Conti was ordered out of the game at one point because he glowered too much.

Innumerable poses were staged, often the same pose four or five times. All the while the director instructed them through a megaphone while Captain Grishkov did a simultaneous translation.

The shooting session was tedious and seemed to go on interminably. The moment it was over, however, and even before the camera crew had struck their equipment, the net was taken down, the volleyball carried away, and the men marched back to the sleeping cars.

The Russians only discovered Buddy Kariolainen's disappearance when the men were marched back onto the train. At that point, the morning's head count was taken and it became readily apparent they had one less detainee than they had the night before.

They couldn't quite accept the fact they'd lost someone during the night. So they counted again, and then once again, each time coming up one number shy. With each successive count, Stern could see their agitation mount. At last they had a roll call, whereupon they discovered that it was the boy who was gone.

But at that point they were still unprepared to acknowledge that anyone was missing, that someone had slipped past them. To have done so would have meant admitting that security had been lax, and this would have proved awkward to explain to headquarters.

Also, in the unlikely event that the boy had managed to get out of the compound, he might well be at the border by now. Worse yet, if he'd actually slipped across the border, that could be terribly embarrassing to those charged with the overall responsibility of guarding him. If the boy were to come to any harm in the ten or so kilometers of rough woodland between here and Vainikkala, the damage incurred by the Soviet Union in terms of world opinion would be considerable.

While the Russians were clearly upset by their discovery that morning, they were determined to keep the matter quiet until they could get things sorted out among themselves. At the head of the car, several officers conferred in lowered voices. No question was asked, not a word was mentioned to any of the men regarding the missing boy. However, instead of sending the men back to their compartments in the day coach as they had the day before, they were all ordered back out to the compound to sit or stroll about as they pleased while a new search of the train was begun in earnest.

In the women's sleeping coach, the curtains of all windows had been drawn. This exercise had been carried out by the matrons while the women were off having breakfast. When they returned they found the cabins pitched in gloom and the curtains tightly drawn. They were warned not to open them under any circumstances. The reason for this, they were told, was to keep the cars cool throughout the day. But if that were the real reason, the portentousness of the warning seemed far out of proportion to its stated intent.

What seemed more likely was that, for some inexplicable reason, the Russians wished to prevent the women from seeing the men moving about outside the train. That they were out there, there could be no doubt. They could hear not only the voices of guards barking commands but also occasionally those of their own men replying. They had heard shouts and cries during the volleyball match.

Janet Kariolainen had no idea that her husband was no longer on the train, nor that her son was now missing and the object of a desperate search. Nor could she have had any way of knowing that twelve hours before, she'd become a grandmother and that the infant, a tiny four-and-a-half-pound girl, had been named Janet Marie Kariolainen after her.

The closing of the coach curtains created something of a stir. It served to heighten worries and suspicions. The only plausible explanation for wanting to prevent their seeing the men, they reasoned, was that some of them had either come to harm over the past twenty-four hours or were possibly no longer even present. In that superheated atmosphere, speculation ran rampant.

As of yet, Myra Keck had been given no word as to the condition of her husband since his collapse the day before. All she knew was that he'd been taken off to the hospital with what was presumably a heart attack. She was in a terrible state. Jatta Palmunan had applied directly to Captain Grishkov, seeking permission for the woman to visit her husband in Vyborg. The young captain proved to be singularly intractable, dismissing the tour guide with a wave of his hand and brusque assurances that Ralph Keck was fine.

Señora Gonzaga had great worries too, about the "old *conde*." Who was looking out for him? Seeing that he ate and took his medications and got his rest? Certainly not his captors. She could only hope that Señor Stern, or, possibly, though she doubted it, Señor Thomas, was keeping an eye on him.

Outwardly plucky, Wilma Shapley was sick to her heart with worry over "the Professor." Even Madam Muk's viperish railings about "George" had in his absence transformed themselves into expressions of endearment. Frequently she found herself clinging to the little boy, cooing at him and, in lilting baby singsong, chanting praises to his "Da-Da" and to her "Babu" in the most tender terms.

Later that morning Jatta came through the corridor telling them that they must leave the coach at once. There was an urgency in her voice suggesting that the order was something more than mere routine.

A full squad of motor-rifle troops, thirty men, were waiting just outside the exits to go through the train. Everyone must vacate immediately. They had to search. Why? someone asked. Hadn't they already done that days ago?

Yes, but that was for something else.

Well, what were they searching for now they couldn't just as well have searched for then?

No answers were forthcoming.

Jatta confessed she was at a loss. In a dozen years of conducting tour groups through the Soviet Union, she had never encountered anything to match this group's experience. Still, prudence and simple good sense dictated cooperation. The last thing they needed then was more confrontation. Perhaps, the tour guide said, putting the best possible face on things, this was the long-awaited customs check started seven days before in Vyborg and never completed.

Attired in their gray, shapeless smocks, the women clambered down the coach stairs and out into the dry weedy enclosure. They already had something of the look of inmates at a penal institution.

Down in the compound, the first thing Isabel noticed was the coach where the men were billeted. Except for the sentries posted at either end, it had a strangely vacant air about it. But the windows, all blacked out with drawn curtains, suggested that people were inside there moving about behind them.

Standing not far off, Kate Dubbin observed an unusual degree of activity in the woods just outside the barbed wire. She called Jean Blaylock's attention to the fact. Hundreds of rifle troops moved through the brush, hacking at it feverishly with rifle butts and entrenching tools as if they were threshing wheat. The sky overhead throbbed with the beat of helicopter blades battering the air. Four or five MI-26's flying low circled the area over and over again, occasionally sweeping out over a wider course, then racketing back in to renew their surveillance of the immediate area.

Wilma Shapley watched them disapprovingly. "They're looking for something."

"Or someone," remarked Frau Kunkel.

Nell Blanton appeared dismayed. "You'd have to be Houdini to make it out of this place. Just look at that fence."

Indeed, at that moment the fence seemed higher and more inhospitable than ever. Its dark little knots of pinpoint steel glistened, and its upper margin, canted inward with coils of razor-sharp tin, looked as though it could slice through bone.

Madum Muk wandered round the compound, patting the baby in her arms on the back and gazing wistfully in the direction of the men's coach. The last several days had managed to subdue even the child. He no longer unleashed those ear-splitting wails, but seemed content to find solace with the faintest of whimpers. "Soon Da-Da comes," she whispered in the child's ear. "Soon Da-Da comes."

The Italian women walked up and down the enclosure. They walked un-speaking the entire perimeter of the enclosure, first clockwise, then counter-clockwise, trying very hard not to notice the tank crew on the other side of the fence watching them intently.

Kate Dubbin hovered in the general area of the train. So close was she, in fact, that she could hear periodically the noise of the soldiers moving through the car. It was a terrifying racket, full of banging and thuds and shrieking metal. It sounded as though the train were being disemboweled. She could hear ripping sounds and the loud clang of metal, the shout of men as they swarmed through the cars like hordes of army ants devouring everything in their path.

Standing not far off, Jean Blaylock watched the soldiers moving on and off the train, wondering what they might find in her own cabin. She could think of nothing she had that might be considered even remotely incriminating. But then again, she'd also assumed that her passport was not incriminating.

The two men came for Stern later that morning. He'd been lying in the turmoil of his unmade berth trying to lose himself with Maigret over a calvados at the Brasserie Lipp.

He was not doing too well. His mind wandered. As engaging a companion as Maigret was, he was unable to distract Stern from the nagging worries raised at his interview with Captain Grishkov the day before. Stern swaggered then, surprising even himself by his own cool bluff. Inwardly he was quaking. That written confession with his own name affixed in type at the bottom awaiting his signature, along with those final chilling words, "Do not expect to leave the Soviet Union anytime soon," had gnawed at him all night.

It was odd, even funny, the way the two men appeared. Noiselessly. Stern looked up and there they were—two stolid, squarish-looking men with baggy suits and heavy growths of beard. Unlike the men who'd whisked him into Vyborg the first time, these two wore civilian dress (which seemed more ominous in itself) and had the look of professionals. They were swift and adroit, brusque yet unfailingly polite. From those thick wrists and the bulky frames, he had the distinct impression that they were not to be taken lightly.

Stern inquired where they were going and whether he should take any of his belongings. They answered neither question. They moved him off the train with such smooth dispatch that their departure was scarcely noticed. In a matter of moments he was settling back into the hard rear seat of one of those boxy little Volgas and gliding through the open gates of the fence with the sentry in the box saluting them smartly.

"I thought I made it clear."
"Yes."
"The last time I was here. I told you . . ."
"Yes. That is correct."
"I told you then I had no intention of signing your document."
The captain frowned and pushed some papers around the desk for effect. His eyes studiously avoided Stern's and he seemed even more brusque and self-important than the day before. He continued. "But you have now had time to think things over—to reconsider."

"And I still decline to sign anything."

Captain Grishkov's brow arched. "Anything?"

"Nothing. Not until hell freezes over."

The captain's jaw tautened. "I beg your pardon?"

"An expression. Idiomatic for *never*." Stern could hear his voice rising impatiently. He could see from the captain's quizzical look that the definition had been no more enlightening than the idiom itself. "I simply mean, I will not sign this document. Not now. Not anytime in the future, and categorically and unequivocally, under no circumstances. I am not now, nor have I ever been, a spy. I am not an Israeli agent. I am not Jewish. I am a U.S. citizen. I have not stolen classified data from your naval base. I have no co-conspirators aboard this train. I'm a father and a husband and a taxpaying citizen of the United States."

Stern railed on even as he watched the captain open a gray file folder, pluck something from its contents, and push it toward him. It was a photograph, a three-by-five-inch black-and-white, slightly faded and badly out of focus.

"What's this?" Stern's eyes swarmed over the photo, searching for its significance.

"Perhaps you might tell me," Captain Grishkov replied with an air of deadly cordiality.

Again Stern studied it. What he saw was a group comprising five men. They were sitting around a table full of bottles and glasses on what appeared to be a terrace adjoining some sort of outdoor café. They sat in the shade of a striped awning against a white balustrade behind which could be glimpsed a shimmering expanse of sea. Hebrew letters were scrawled across the fringe of an overhanging awning.

"I don't have the slightest idea what this is." Stern started to hand the photo back.

"Look more closely, please."

He took it back, peering harder for detail, moving it about in the imperfect office light, adjusting the distance between it and his eye for sharper focus. "I'm sorry. I really don't see . . ."

"Note the character. The man in the short-sleeved checkered shirt. Second from left."

Stern looked where he was directed. "It's very fuzzy," he said, but even as he spoke, he had the disconcerting sensation of seeing his own features come slowly into focus.

"Is that me?"

"Quite so." Captain Grishkov permitted himself the faintest glimmer of amusement.

"But I . . ." Stern stammered. "Who are these people? Where are they supposed to be?"

Grishkov leaned back in his chair and clasped his hands across his chest.

"Come, come, Mr. Stern. This ceases to be amusing. You are wasting a good deal of my time and yours with this pose of innocence."

"I've never seen these people before."

"Ah, so." Illumination suddenly suffused the captain's face. "Of course, you had no idea you were being photographed."

A nerve started to throb at Stern's temple. "I really don't know what you're talking about."

"You are seated at a seaside café."

"A seaside café?"

"In Haifa. The time is September 1983."

A burst of mirthless laughter broke from Stern's lips. "Absurd. I've never been to Haifa. I've never been to Israel. Not in 1983. Not ever."

"The men seated with you," Grishkov went on, unperturbed, "are agents of the Yad Vashem."

"You keep saying those words. I keep telling you I don't have the faintest idea what the Yad Vashem is."

"As I am certain I told you yesterday, they are the elite forces of the Israeli intelligence service."

"And as I am certain I told you, I know nothing about Israeli intelligence, or whatever. What is this? What are you trying to pull here? Wait a minute . . ." Something in the photo, something familiar, yet naggingly elusive, had started to take on a more recognizable shape. "Wait just one minute. I see what you've done."

Captain Grishkov started to reach for the photo, but Stern yanked it back away from him.

"That's my passport photo, isn't it? You simply reshot it, then superimposed it onto this completely bogus snapshot." Stern flicked the photograph back at Grishkov with an air of the most scornful delight.

"I must warn you of what you say, Mr. Stern. What you see in that photograph is authentic. It was taken in September of 1983 by Soviet agents." The young man's voice rose and he spoke more rapidly in an attempt to cover the fact that he was nettled. "We have the names of the people seated at the table with you. They are well known to us as Israeli agents. I can assure you, that *is* you in the picture."

"And I tell you that you have lifted that photograph from my passport. Just who do you think is going to be fooled by that?"

The captain grew very still. When at last he spoke, he fixed Stern with a beady gaze. "Did it ever occur to you, Mr. Stern, that I don't have to fool anyone?" It was said with the sort of certitude that sent a shaft of ice through Stern's veins, once the significance of it had sunk in.

"I see," Stern said huskily. He swallowed hard and started to rise. "May I go now?"

"Sit down, please." The young man nodded in the direction of the chair Stern had just vacated. "I have a good deal more to discuss with you."

Once again he opened his folder, and this time withdrew an envelope from the top of the file inside. He pushed it across the surface of the desk toward Stern.

Making no sign of taking it, Stern eyed the small white square of paper warily.

The captain waited, drumming his fingers lightly on the desk. "I think you had better read it."

"I'm sure it will give me no pleasure."

"I shouldn't think so. But it may give you a better idea of the gravity of your situation."

Frowning, Stern moved his head a bit closer to the letter until the words scrawled across the face of it rose up at him from the paper. Mr. Keith Wales was the name of the addressee. It was hand-printed, not written. The address, 14 Foxwell Park Drive, Ottawa, was also handprinted. The postmark near the center at the top, stamped Tel Aviv, was dated September 10, 1983. In the upper-right-hand corner were three Israeli one-pound air-mail stamps depicting a grove of cedar flourishing in the desert.

"Go ahead, why don't you?" Grishkov continued tauntingly. "Read it. Or are you afraid of what you might find there?"

Stern slowly withdrew the single page of stationery folded inside. He edged it out with exquisite hesitation, like a man expecting some sort of joker's prank to spring out at him.

"Dear Keith," it began, this time in a large, flowing cursive scrawl. "Everything is now in place for our little jaunt to Polyarny ..." Stern's eye dropped roughly midway down the page to a small crudely drawn layout of the big submarine base north of Leningrad on the Kola Peninsula. A number of little squares and rectangles with hand-printed labels such as "armory," "docks," "submarine basins," "warehouse," "laboratory I," "laboratory II," studded the page.

Stern's eye dropped down again, this time to the signature at the bottom.

"Do you recognize the handwriting?" Captain Grishkov asked.

"It's mine," Stern replied, his voice so quiet the words were scarcely audible.

"I'm sorry, I didn't hear ..."

"I said it was mine." Stern repeated his words more loudly. "Or rather a clumsy forgery of it."

"You are saying the letter is a forgery?"

"Exactly. Just like the photograph. Obviously copied from samples of my writing taken from my passport and visa. Any handwriting expert would detect it as a fake in a minute."

Grishkov's drumming fingers accelerated on the desktop, his eyes tucked down beneath his beetling brow. Almost as an afterthought he reached behind his chair and pressed what appeared to be a buzzer of some sort. Instantly, as though someone had been waiting there on the other side for just such a cue, the door swung open and two people stepped in. One was a big square-shouldered corporal. He stood just behind a small, dark Slavic type whose eyes were swarming with fear. He stumbled forward into the room, nearly tripping. Possibly he'd been shoved.

The door was closed and there was a loud, rapid exchange of Russian. The man who'd just entered stood in the center of the room, flailing his arms and babbling loudly as Grishkov interrogated him. Several times his voice choked as if he were about to cry. In response to what were obviously questions, he kept glancing at Stern, his eyes swollen with fright. He had the look of a small cornered rodent.

"Do you know this man, Mr. Stern?" Captain Grishkov inquired.

"No."

"You've never seen him before?"

"Never."

"He says he knows you."

"Oh?"

"He is a security guard at the Polyarny naval installation, or rather he was," the captain added hastily. "He says you offered him, but he declined, one thousand dollars in U.S. currency to pass you information regarding new synthetic fuels used in Soviet nuclear-powered submarines."

Stern felt the air rush from his lungs. "He's a liar. I never—"

The fiery little man erupted in a torrent of shouts, all the while waving his finger directly at Stern. Grishkov made a gesture with his head at the big corporal standing off in the corner. In the next moment, the man, still shouting and waving his finger at Stern, was led, or once again shoved, from the room.

There was a long pause while the captain permitted the gathering effect of silence to take its toll on Stern. His fingers lingered about his too-pinkish lips as he appeared to muse. "I'm afraid there is no mistake, Mr. Stern. You have been positively identified."

The captain reached into his lower drawer and fished out a small brown zippered leather bag, such as the kind men use to carry toiletries. The initials on it were in a faded gold and read P.S. Stern immediately recognized it as his own.

"So that's where that went," he said, watching warily as the captain unzipped it, pulling open the top and unceremoniously dumping its contents before him. Two thick packages of U.S. bills in small denominations—fives and tens—dropped out onto the desktop.

"One thousand dollars, Mr. Stern. Count them if you wish. They were found inside your traveling kit."

Stern recalled his ransacked cabin and his luggage looking as though it had been looted.

"Checkmate, as they say, eh, Mr. Stern?" Grishkov radiated goodwill.

Speechless, Stern watched the man, more mesmerized by the audacity of the performance than truly frightened. As of yet, he still barely comprehended, so fast had it all happened.

"Once again, Mr. Stern, I urge you to sign this document." The captain's manner had become almost benevolent as he dangled the paper before him. "I assure you that with what I have here, I am completely within my rights, as specified within the Hague Convention and the Helsinki Accords, to recommend your imprisonment as a spy in the pay of a nation hostile to the Soviet Union."

The captain came to a portentous pause as he watched the effect of his words register like detonations on Stern's face. "Now that your cover is exposed, Mr. Stern, you are harmless to us and, no doubt, useless to your American and Israeli cohorts. In point of fact, you are now useless to everyone. In my capacity here as commanding officer"—Grishkov bristled with self-importance—"I am in a position to recommend that you be sent away for life, or that we extend, in this case, clemency." His voice appeared to caress the word and linger over it.

He waved the confession tauntingly at Stern. "Sign these papers and you may leave here as early as this evening. We will guarantee safe passage to Vainikkala on the Finnish side of the border. However, refuse to sign it, Mr. Stern, and you may count on remaining here with us for the indefinite future."

Something in Stern snapped. "You're doing this because you think I'm Jewish."

Grishkov frowned. Now it was his turn to be mystified. "I can assure you, your being Jewish—"

"I am not Jewish," Stern shouted, then at once lowered his voice. "I am not Jewish."

"You *people* always claim you're being persecuted."

"What *people*?" Stern snapped. "Kindly tell me what *people* you allude to. I'm Christian, just as you no doubt are, or were, and for that matter . . ."

It was then he heard his own voice, not the sharp note of defiance he would have expected, but rather the pathetic wheedling pleas of an individual attempting to ingratiate himself with someone in a position of authority.

The hunger strike had gone on now for the better part of thirty-six hours. During that period, not one of them, to a man, had taken anything but fluids—plain water or, at most, a gulp of juice. For the past four meals, solid foods had gone untouched on their trays.

If the Russians were perturbed by the action, or even mildly concerned, they showed little outward sign of it. But on the evening of the second day of the strike, they at last reacted, and took a different tack. Instead of the bleak, unimaginative rations that had been their lot each day, now, out of large tureens and aluminum caldrons trucked up from the commissary at Vyborg, came a succession of foods designed to break the will of all but the most ascetic of fasters. A planked beef (not the stringy soup meat generally served) and chicken, roasted to a turn, with little roast potatoes, fresh fruits, and vegetables in dazzling variety and profusion.

The dinner had commenced with platters of *zakuska*—Russian hors d'oeuvres—eggplant, fish roe, herring and dumplings, piquant and mouth-watering. To people famished for food, the odors in the place were devastating. The Russians served it without fanfare, unblinkingly, as if it were precisely what they'd been serving night after night. Nothing unusual.

You could see the longing and the faltering resolve in the faces there. Some looked away; some stared straight ahead. Others looked directly at the food with defiance, as if to stare it down. But still, no one ate.

The soldiers passed up and down the aisle, removing one course of untouched food and replacing it with another. Still, no one ate. There was no conversation. It was eerily quiet in the car, each man locked in a struggle with his own conscience and resolve. All one heard was the rattle of trays and the shuffling of the soldier-waiters as they passed in and out of the train's galley.

Young Buddy Kariolainen had been missing since early that morning. There was a distinct but quiet sense of urgency about what had been his fate. Had he escaped, or was he taken off by the Russians during the night, presumably to join his father? If such were the case, that would have been indeed humane—to have recognized the boy's deep anxiety over his father, and by so doing, put an end to it.

On the other hand, if he'd actually escaped, had he made it to the border or had he wandered off into the big trackless forests stretching to the north and south? Asawa had sworn that the boy was in his berth that morning when he'd awakened. But on the face of things, that now seemed improbable, and by now, most people had come to take Asawa's word with a grain of salt.

The Russians had still not acknowledged that anyone was missing, although with their twice-daily head counts, by that time they were surely aware of the fact. Still, for reasons of their own, mostly self-protection with a dash of stiff pride, they preferred to keep silent. Those on board the train had no way of knowing for certain, however, whether they knew or not. As a result, no one spoke out loud about the boy for fear of possibly revealing his absence, thus sending search parties out to retrieve him.

All attempts to learn something of the general disposition of Ralph Keck or Ted Kariolainen had proved fruitless. Nor could they even get word to their wives and loved ones not more than ninety feet distant in the next sleeping coach. For all intents and purposes, they were completely cut off.

As supper concluded that evening, they rose at the command of a sergeant major and filed out. No one knew precisely how it started, but suddenly there was bellowing and an awful row. A circle opened among them, at the center of which Sandro and Mr. Mukherjee appeared to be swirling about at the bottom of a vortex, clawing and tearing at each other.

Plates and silver rained down from the tabletops. Crockery shattered. Whistles blew and soldiers converged on the spot from both ends of the car. Those standing nearest tried to prize the two men apart. Sandro spat and kicked. Mr. Mukherjee howled like some stricken creature.

The soldiers used the butts of rifles to dampen their rage. Finally, back on his feet, still sputtering and kicking in the grasp of a soldier, Sandro looked as though a large cat had clawed his cheek. Mr. Mukherjee's shirt had been ripped down the middle. Blood from a split lip spilled down his shirt front.

"I see what you do," Sandro hissed. "I see. Look in his pockets."

It wasn't necessary to search Mr. Mukherjee. Scattered about on the floor where they'd dropped from his pockets were a few dry crackers and a pear, both badly mashed, where the two men had rolled over them during the ensuing scuffle.

"*Porco*," Sandro bellowed over his shoulder as they shoved him out of the car. "You better stay away from me. I get my hands on you, I eat your eyes out."

STAVKA general headquarters is a large, fortresslike structure situated on nearly one square mile in the outskirts of Novosibirsk. Entirely in keeping with the political tenets of postwar Soviet modernism, stylistically it is a starkly utilitarian structure, trapezoidal in outline and made of concrete block. It is not attractive and it suffers from that most Russian of traits, a strong penchant for monumentalism.

There are no lawns or gardens to soften the harsh outlines of the building. What trees there are, are stunted and scraggly, looking as though they were planted yesterday, and then only as an afterthought. There is no sign out in front of the building, no official plaque to even suggest what goes on inside. The only hint that the Ministry of Defense and the Chiefs of Staff of the Supreme Soviet are headquartered there is a small red-and-white sentry box with a solitary guard stationed in it to the right of the front entrance. All other doorways leading in and out of the building are kept locked night and day.

All activities aboard the Green Train were being closely monitored inside that building. The Soviet High Command was particularly concerned about the progress of the hunger strike. But if a simple hunger strike had caused a certain uneasiness among the General Staff, news that one of the passengers aboard the train was now "possibly" missing produced a crisis situation.

In the midst of the most delicate moments of negotiation with the West, with a sizable number of ships of many nations engaged in naval games of a highly questionable nature in the Baltic, with border closings and large, rather portentous deployments of troops going about on land, the last thing the General Staff wanted at this time was to have to explain the disappearance of one of the hostages. The fact that the missing individual was a child of twelve or thirteen years made such a disclosure not merely sensitive, but acutely embarrassing.

A series of coded messages between Novosibirsk and Vyborg scorched the wires. Threats and recriminations were hurled like thunderbolts at the little customs post near the Finnish border.

"Search Again" was STAVKA's coded reply to a message from Vyborg attesting to the fact that the train and the immediate surroundings had been searched repeatedly for the missing youth. Captain Grishkov had wired back to say they had no idea where the boy had gone or how he'd managed to get free. Security measures over the past year had grown regrettably lax, he managed to point out, thus incriminating his predecessor without actually having to name him.

But Grishkov hastened to assure STAVKA that he would now assume full responsibility for finding the youth and returning him to the train. They had increased surveillance at the border, but as of yet, the boy had not shown up there. It was merely a matter of time.

In the meantime, a number of the General Staff had grown increasingly uneasy with the climate of affairs surrounding the Green Train. In the course of several days it had gone from a neatly contained situation to that of a tinderbox that threatened to ignite in their faces. Notwithstanding the fact that it was a powerful source of leverage in a highly delicate series of negotiations, several of the General Staff were now strongly urging that all detainees aboard the train be withdrawn at once to Leningrad, there to be placed under house arrest in some larger facility, a hotel perhaps, or a hospital. In any event, they suggested something better suited than a day coach for the care and surveillance of a sizable number of political hostages. Among themselves they now freely used that word to refer to the passengers aboard the train.

The hard-liners, however, argued that such a move would be disastrous. Undoubtedly, in the West it would be perceived as a faltering of resolve. Truckling to the pressure of international propaganda, they would lose their most powerful lever—daily accounts, mostly misinformed, screaming in banner headlines from the Western press, along with the hysteria of families and friends uncertain as to the fate of loved ones and imagining the worst.

In the end, the hard-liners prevailed. Accordingly, the decision was made to stay with the Green Train.

On that evening when he'd climbed to the roof of the coach, Buddy Kariolainen had fully intended to join his mother and sister in the sleeping car two cars forward. The day coach, some ninety feet in length, separated the two cars. To reach it, he knew, meant slithering all the way up there on his stomach. With searchlights sweeping over the train every two minutes or so, there was no question of standing up and walking across the roof, or even attempting it on hands and knees. Had he attempted to make a dash for it during the brief period when the searchlights were not sweeping past, the sound of his feet pounding over the rooftop was bound to be detected by the guards below.

Slither he did, still in his T-shirt and shorts, across thirty yards of cruelly abrasive roof still scorched from the day's sun beating down upon it. It scraped his belly and knees as he squirmed and wriggled himself forward.

With lights swinging back and forth overhead and the voices of guards periodically barking around the train, the comforting thought of his mother's arms was a strong goad.

Logic might have told him that sentries were posted all about the entrance to the sleeping car. But logic was not the force driving him just then. It had more to do with fear—fear of the Russians, fear of the strange young Japanese man with whom he shared a compartment, fear mostly for the fate of his missing father.

When he'd successfully traversed the roof of the day coach and was virtually within a few feet of his destination, what a cruel joke to find two guards posted just outside the entryway. He'd fully expected them to be just as derelict as the two sentries supposedly guarding the men's sleeping coach. Sadly, that was not the case.

He waited for them to go, expecting surely any minute they would. However, they failed to oblige him. All the while, the searchlight swept past with terrifying regularity. The last two sweeps, he thought, or possibly imagined, the beams had lingered somewhat longer than usual over his outstretched body. With each successive sweep, he expected the beam to stop dead directly on him, nailing him to the spot, while sirens wailed and dogs howled and guards in heavy boots clambered up the ladder and came stomping over the rooftops toward him.

He had an image of himself being dragged off kicking and screaming into one of those boxy little cars into which his father had disappeared, then driven off to some distant, forlorn place and tossed down a dark fetid hole where rodents would scurry across his bare feet.

He'd waited up there, pinned to the spot for nearly forty minutes, certain that the men were just about to wander off on a break, the way those guarding the men's coach had. The break, at last, did come, but with it came two fresh guards as replacements.

It was foolhardy, he knew, to stay much longer, and yet he hadn't the heart to tear himself away. He was so near his mother and sister, but even nearer the guards. They stood just below him now, unseen beneath a curved overhang at the end of each coach, so close he could hear the murmur of their voices and smell the puff of sulfur wafting upward from the matches igniting their cigarettes.

When at last he turned, it was because the damp night air had chilled him. He was hungry and discouraged, certain that if he remained a moment longer, he'd give himself up to the guards below and plead to be taken back to the warmth and relative security of his compartment.

The only way back was the way he'd come. Over the rooftop. His only recourse now was to try to slip back unnoticed into his compartment. Whatever quirky mannerisms Asawa might have had, they were not nearly so scary as those of the Soviets—the guards and trucks thrashing about all night, the small fires in the woods beyond the wire perimeter marking the sites where soldiers camped, and the big T54 tank, lights glowing on its cupola, looking like some huge awful insect climbing out of the forest.

It took him the better part of a quarter-hour to retrace, on his stomach, the distance he'd covered. But even more cruelly perverse—at last reaching the other end of the day coach, he found the two guards who'd wandered off on a break now returned to their posts.

Again he waited, his knees and elbows so badly abraded that they bled freely over him. He'd started to shiver as the temperature dipped. It seemed there was no going back and no going forward. The searchlights continued to sweep past in their two-minute pulses, and he was pinned down to where he was.

He lay there winded and panting, chattering in his flimsy underclothes spattered with blood. He thought of his father and started to cry—not with his voice, he dared not make a sound, but with his eyes. They filled with tears so that he could barely see. Once or twice he swiped angrily at them with his fists. Then, through the hazy blur of vision he grew gradually aware of something he'd not noticed before. Out of the corner of his eye he saw the lights of the small locomotive glowing warm and orange up ahead. It looked like the toy train they set up every Christmas at home. Home seemed very far away just then.

He lay at the extreme end of the sleeping coach, the guards directly beneath him, and his body pressed so hard and flat against the rooftop, it made his chest ache. To cross from one car to the next he'd have to go back down the ladder of the day coach and up that of the sleeping coach. But with the two guards standing directly beneath him, that was, of course, out of the question.

The other alternative was to stand up and make a running jump. The gap between the two coaches, possibly five feet, was not inconsiderable. With enough running space before him to get sufficient steam up, he felt sure he could handle it. He'd jumped like distances from rock to rock up in the Cascades with Bo. They'd taken some pretty foolish leaps on ledges and clifftops together. He'd never told his father about those.

But to make such a leap meant having to stand up and risk being caught in the lights. It meant having to run at least twenty feet at full speed. Running made noise, as did landing on a hard surface after a long leap. If the guards didn't spot him in the lights, they'd surely hear him sprinting down the roof and landing with a thud on the other side. That, assuming, of course, he landed on his feet, not some other part of him, and didn't break his neck in the bargain.

It was useless to even think about it. But the longer he lay there getting colder and colder, with the light sweeping past overhead, the more plausible the plan became.

If he stood up and made a dash for it, the entire action would have to be consummated in the brief space of time the lights were off him. Two minutes. That was certainly manageable, provided there were no hitches.

The searchlight flashed again, this time seeming to linger on his back with the cruel playfulness of a cat pushing a caught, terrified mouse about with its paw. He felt his courage sputter and had just about made up his mind to surrender to the guards below. Perhaps they would merely return him to his cabin, where Asawa snored away in fitful sleep. It was not so bad. He was cold and hungry by this time, and besides, the alternatives, if there were any, were not particularly attractive.

The lights of the little engine twinkling up ahead beckoned to him. He couldn't say why. There was no reason to suppose that just as here, sentries weren't posted up there. And even if not, what did he expect to find in that gleaming, shimmering, toylike object anyway?

He sighed wistfully, with an air of strangely old-mannish resignation, and started to rise. It was then he heard the helicopter in the air above him. It came straight on, following a path directly toward him, its landing lights and marker beacons blinking red and green in the western sky, its rotary blades battering the air before it.

He had no sensation of thought. There was no moment of conscious decision, of pausing to consider risk. All he knew was that as the great black shape came out of the sky like some huge moth beating its wings across the night, its blades and turbines pounding the air, he was up on his feet and running—first backward to get the space he needed for the leap, then forward for the leap itself.

It was a kind of fool's luck. Without planning, or even daring to hope for it, the timing was exquisite. The path of the helicopter and that of his own, intersected at the moment when the ship was low and directly overhead, the racket of its blades and engine absolutely at their height.

Sprinting right down to the edge of the roof, the distance between the two cars, only moments before looking negotiable, suddenly widened and appeared to him a yawning infinity. He felt himself faltering, but he was now right at the edge and the momentum he'd already built up nullified any possibility of retreat.

In the next moment he was airborne, hair flying, the breeze cool against his cheek, a small wraith in underwear winging through the night. Above him he glimpsed the outline of the pilot in the lighted cockpit. In the pit of his stomach he felt the vibrations of the copter blades as they racketed overhead.

By the time the helicopter had banged past he'd already touched down, making his own stumbling landing just an inch or so from the lip of the overhang on the other side. He fell flat down, pressing his chest to the warm rooftop, just as the beam from the tower searchlight swung past.

For some time he lay like that, face and chest pressed hard against the warm, sandpaper surface of the roof, the taste of metal and asbestos in his mouth. He had no way of knowing if the guards had heard him stumble or land, or even if they'd seen something large and dark hurdle overhead. The noise of the helicopter flying low had been tremendous and its appearance providential.

Whatever they might have seen or heard, he had no intention of waiting around for possible reactions. With the searchlight beam just gliding past, he was up on his feet, streaking across the roof, moving on a direct path to the bright gaudy glow of the little engine twinkling up ahead.

The two Finnish motormen had a rudimentary sitting parlor at the back of the cab: cots, a few chairs, and a little stove, even pictures—Finnish winter scenes—hanging on the walls. It was immaculate and cozy, the sort of thing not at all uncommon in an American caboose.

In accordance with strict Finnish railway policy, two full-time motormen were required to remain in attendance with their engines for the duration of any period in which their equipment was on duty outside the railyards of Helsinki. Accordingly, during the entire period of detention the Finnish motormen remained at their stations in and about the engine's cab, twenty-four hours a day.

The motormen had finished eating hours ago and their pipes had long since burned low when Buddy made his startling and completely uninvited appearance. He'd crossed over the roof of the small tender just behind the engine, shinnied himself down a drainpipe, and whirled like a banshee into the cab.

Having shared the better part of a liter of vodka between them at dinner, the motormen were sprawled on their bunks snoring when the boy, stumbling about in the darkened cab, banged into a scuttle door. It clanged briefly like an alarm. A dim bedside lamp went on and the three of them confronted each other in the uncertain light.

It struck Buddy that they were more frightened than he was. Of course, he had the advantage, coming as he had out of the night entirely unannounced. They'd been asleep with the kind of profound dreamless sleep that only large drafts of vodka can induce. Then suddenly they were awakened with a rude bang to see this small, nearly naked, bleeding specter materialize in the improbable setting of an engine cab.

Buddy blurted something out. He tried to explain. Hearing his own frantic and too rapid babble, and dressed as he was, he had a fairly accurate notion of the kind of impression he was making.

They had no way of understanding his words, but it didn't take much to divine his predicament. They were Finns who, after several bitter wars, bore no great affection for the Russians. Even in his underclothes they knew he was no Russian. He was clearly one of the hostages, and if, as it appeared, he'd somehow escaped, they had no intention of returning him.

Outside they could hear loud voices moving toward them up the track. Guards, no doubt. In a moment or two they'd be there, checking to see if an escaped youth had somehow made his way to the engine. The motormen were out of bed in a flash, half-pushing, half-guiding Buddy to a small metal door at the rear of the cab, possibly two feet in height, that led to a narrow storage area just before the tender, where a variety of tools were kept.

Not a moment too soon, they'd shoved him in and slammed the door behind him. That gesture in itself the boy might well have perceived as threatening. But he, too, had divined something about these two rather wild-looking Finns. He was certain they meant him no harm.

A pair of bulky guards clattered up the ladder into the cab. The motormen were prepared to evade all sorts of questions as to the whereabouts of an escaped prisoner. But as it turned out, they didn't have to. The guards had only come up to inquire why the cab lights had gone on so late in the evening.

One of the motormen explained he'd had to go to the bathroom. One of the guards made a coarse joke and they laughed. The motormen offered the guards some of the vodka still remaining in their bottle. The guards eagerly accepted and, having done so, quickly left.

The two men waited several minutes before they went back to the storage area, this time bringing with them a tray made up of the succulent scraps they had left over from dinner.

"I think you have made the right decision. Painful, yes. But absolutely correct and unflinching in the face of duty."

Colonel Dunskoi watched his old friend with a sense of growing estrangement. The man he'd known for thirty years bore virtually no resemblance whatever to anyone he'd ever known or seen before.

"I admire you, Dimi. Believe me, I do." He waved the sheet of paper before him like a baton, as though he were conducting some exalted symphonic passage. "I know what it must have cost you."

Do you? Dunskoi thought to himself, and lowered his gaze to the floor for fear that some of his true feelings might show in his eyes. So great was his soldier's sense of professionalism that he dreaded anything in himself that might appear to be insubordination. It had not yet occurred to him that he was angry. But if it had, it was, as yet, unfocused anger, directed at no one in particular except possibly himself.

"I can't talk about it," he heard himself mutter, and grew anxious to be gone from there.

Yevchenko was most solicitous. "Of course, my dear fellow. Perfectly understandable. An errant, wayward child. Falling in with the wrong crowd of people. The espousal of dangerous ideas. Most distressing."

Dunskoi nodded distractedly.

Father, why do you bother? It's useless, he heard her murmur at the back of his head where it had begun to ache. The small pretty ovoid face with his own hooded eyes stared back at him.

"I checked with General Staff this morning." Yevchenko rubbed his hands with the bustling air of a man getting down to more serious business. "The papers are proceeding nicely. You should be informed of your promotion no later than . . ."

Sign that paper, Father, and forget me. . . .

"... the first of the month ..."
Mother is right. You must sign it.
Don't tell me what I must do. I know very well what I ...
"... your plans now?"

Dunskoi looked up startled at the man seated across from him, even as the echoes of his own angry voice subsided in his head. "I beg your pardon?"

Marshal Yevchenko looked vaguely annoyed. "I was asking about your immediate plans. What you might like to do now."

"Ah." Dunskoi smiled with false brightness. "Get back to my command as fast as I can. Rejoin my men at Vyborg."

The marshal had been absentmindedly twirling a bronze paperweight in the figure of a whale. His fingers suddenly stopped and a nervous little smile flickered at his lips.

"Yes, I see." He cleared his throat. "That's all well and good, Dimi. Admirable. I can see how, of course, you'd want to. You're such a fine soldier ... But I'm afraid ..."

Dunskoi listened to his old friend, stiffening in his chair while alarm bells started to go off all around him.

"... such an unsettled situation there at present ... hardly be suitable ... view of the unpleasant notoriety attaching to ..."

Dunskoi sat motionless, unspeaking, hearing snatches of words, not stunned so much as baffled. He'd caught the gist of it. He was to go back to Vyborg, but the fact was that he was being relieved of command. Promoted, of course, but relieved nonetheless. He could hang around as sort of a sinecure there on the post. Kicked upstairs where he could get into no trouble. His mind cast desperately about for some suitable response. What he wanted now was eloquence, sharpness of thought, a biting tongue. But he was mute and all he could manage was a dull nod in lieu of any effective rebuttal.

"Quite regrettable, dear fellow," Yevchenko rattled on. "This awful business of the train and hostages and whatnot. Bigger and more complex every day. Not that you couldn't handle it all perfectly well, mind you. But you've just been through a terrible personal ordeal and—"

"What are you trying to say, Arkady?" He heard his voice, faint, snappish, speaking far outside himself. "That because of my daughter's political activities I can no longer be trusted with a command?"

"Not at all, dear fellow." The marshal rose and moved around the desk, coming to a halt directly before him. "Not at all. Why would you think such a thing?"

"It certainly sounds that way to me," Dunskoi persisted softly.

"Be sensible, dear fellow. If that were so ... If you couldn't be trusted, the whole matter of your promotion would be dead in the water. But you see, it isn't. It goes ahead. In several weeks' time you shall be a full major general of the Supreme Soviet. Then is the time to think of a new command."

"I have known generalships in this army that are little more than consolation prizes for failures, for careers ending in disgrace. They're empty. Purposeless. They amount to little more than banishment to the provinces."

"Oh come, Dimi." The marshal laughed gruffly and clapped Dunskoi on the back. "Surely you make too much of this. All we are talking about here is reassignment until the successful resolution of the present crisis . . ."

"Who assumes my command now?"

"Grishkov. He is promoted to colonel. Effective tomorrow at 0900 hours."

Dunskoi took the news stonily and grim-faced. "Yes, I see." His eyes fastened on the puffy, slightly cyanotic lips of his old friend.

"Not your concern any longer, dear fellow. Take my word for it, you're well out of it." Once again he wagged the document with Dunskoi's signature before him. "With this in hand now, everything is put right. Trust me, Dimi."

Dunskoi was on his feet, nodding mutely as Yevchenko threaded an arm through his and half-led, half-dragged him across the room. They stood there with the door ajar, pumping each other's hands. He was faintly aware of people in the outer office watching them. "Yes," he mumbled, too humiliated to meet his friend's eye. "Yes, of course, I do see now. I shall return there for now, but keep well out of the way. If I can be of any help to Grishkov during this period of transition, of course I . . ."

To all outward appearances, to those seated there awaiting an audience with the marshal, the two men pumping each other's hands gave the impression of old friends parting on the best of terms. Even as Dunskoi strode erect and dashing out the front door, he had the sense of all the world crumbling about him. There was no doubt of it now. He was to be promoted to the rank of major general of the Army of the Supreme Soviet in less than two weeks' time. It would mean a quantum leap in terms of salary, perquisites, quality of life available to him. But all he could think of at that moment as he strode out to the waiting staff car was: If they were going to take my command from me anyway, why did I bother signing that paper disavowing Masha? Where are they now going to take my child?

"We're moving."

"What?"

"They say we're going to be moved."

"Who? Who's going to be moved?"

"All of us. Everyone aboard the train. Men and women."

The sound of footsteps could be heard in the corridor, cabin doors sliding back, people surging forward. It was just past ten P.M. and some of them were already in pajamas. They swarmed around Karl Heinz, almost threatening to trample him.

"Where did you hear that?" Paul Blanton demanded.

"From one of the guards."

"Where?" Max Conti demanded. "Where are they moving us?"

"All about." Karl Heinz's eyes blazed. "He said they were splitting us up. Sending us all over the country. To different detention centers."

"Oh my God," Mr. Mukherjee moaned.

"That's bunk," Blanton snapped. "I don't believe a word of it."

A buzz of angry mutters swept down the corridor.

"Quiet," Shapley growled. "Let's hear what the boy has to say." He turned back to Karl Heinz. "Why did this guard decide to tell you all this?"

Karl Heinz seemed embarrassed. "I was trying . . . to find out something."

"Find out what?" Shapley pressed him firmly.

"About the Kariolainens."

"You mean about the boy?"

"Not exactly."

"Ah, you mean about Ted?"

Karl Heinz looked from one face to the next like a cornered animal.

"I think what he's trying to say," Stern said, "is that he was making inquiries about Corrie. Isn't that right, Karl?"

The young man reddened and looked about sheepishly.

Shapley flung his hands up in dismay. "Well, for God's sake. What's all the huffing and puffing about? She's very pretty. So what? So you asked the guard if he could find out about her for you."

"Yes, sir. I gave him money."

Thomas' brow arched. "You gave him money?"

The small knot of spectators pressed in closer.

"Yes, sir."

"And he took it?"

"Yes, sir."

"And what did he tell you?"

"He told me what he'd learned about Corrie, and then he told me about Mr. Wales."

"What did he say?" Max Conti demanded.

"Corrie and her mother are fine . . ." Karl Heinz's voice trailed off.

"And Keith?" Max persisted.

"He's pretty banged up. He's got a broken arm and jaw—a few teeth knocked out."

"Doesn't sound like the sort of injuries you get stumbling on a rock," Paul Blanton said.

Shapley seemed skeptical. "How did you communicate with him?"

"In German. It seems he'd been stationed near Leibnitz. That's where he learned his German. It was very good German, too. I have relatives in Leibnitz, so we started to talk."

"Yes, yes," Thomas went on breathlessly. "And that's when he told you we were going to be split up and scattered all about the country?"

"Yes, sir," Karl Heinz muttered in barely audible tones. He looked as though he himself were personally responsible for the bad news.

Paul Blanton kicked the corridor wall. "Shit."

"Oh, God. Oh, my God." Mr. Mukherjee wrung his hands. His eyes were white with fright.

Van Meegrin shook his head back and forth. "I don't believe it. I just don't believe it."

"Why not?" Shapley asked reasonably. He appeared to be thinking out loud. "It makes perfectly good sense. For security reasons alone. Fifty or so hostages, all sitting around in one spot. That makes for a lot of surveillance. We've had two breakouts already. I can see where it would make very good sense to divide us up into smaller, more manageable units, and just disperse us to different detention centers."

"Oh, my God," Mr. Mukherjee groaned. "Oh, my God."

"And this whole business of the hunger strike," Shapley went on.

"Right." Thomas nodded. "It's easier to suppress that sort of thing in small groups than it is in larger. I agree. From their point of view, splitting us up makes very good sense indeed."

The note of certitude in the Englishman's voice was chilling. Silence descended like a shroud upon them.

"What I'd like to know," Desfargue asked, "is why they keep us here like this? What purpose does it possibly serve to detain innocent people here day after day?"

"They're looking for defectors and spies and God knows what," Blanton fumed.

"Well, now that they have Wales, they've got their spy," Max said. "Why don't they just let us go?"

"Because they're looking for others," Stern said ruefully. "And they've fixed on me."

"You?" Shapley started.

Stern smiled oddly. "I'm afraid there's more to this than meets the eye." He was staring at Thomas.

"More to what? What the devil are you talking about, Peter?" Blanton snapped.

Stern stared pointedly at the Englishman. "Ask Tony. As a journalist he's privy to information we poor mortals only get wind of when it's too late."

Blanton watched the two men glaring at each other. "I wish someone would have the decency to shed some light on all this." He turned back to Stern. "Exactly what the hell was all that supposed to mean?"

Tony Thomas puffed irritably on his cigarette. "Means nothing. It's all a lot of piss and wind. Cut it out, will you, Stern?"

Blanton started to paw his feet like an angry dog.

"If there's something you know, Tony, you'd better tell us."

"I know nothing, I tell you. No more than any of the rest of you. Stern's just blowing off."

Smiling wickedly, Stern watched his uneasiness. In the days following their late-night altercation, Thomas and Stern had given each other a wide berth. Neither had mentioned the incident to the other, nor had Stern passed on to the rest of the passengers what he'd learned from Thomas. It was not out of regard for Thomas that he'd kept his silence, either. He'd seen no purpose in further alarming the others with knowledge that they were being used as pawns in some sort of political auction between superpowers.

"Oh, my God." Mr. Mukherjee fought back his growing panic. "I don't understand all this. I don't want to be separated from my wife, my child. I can't be. I simply can't."

"Nothing like that's going to happen," Shapley blustered, but he too was visibly shaken. "I tell you, we're not alone here. We've not been forgotten. Negotiations are going on this very moment. I guarantee it. Our immediate concern should now be the well-being of Wales and the Kariolainen boy. We still know nothing about Ted, or what sort of shape Ralph Keck is in."

Shapley's talk had the virtue of diverting them from themselves to those whose situation seemed far more dire. But in the process of diverting them, he recalled the parting words of the young Russian physician the day before. "This business with our submarines and sailors. It is very bad." It meant nothing to him then. But now it took on a clear, far more ominous significance. For the moment the others had forgotten about Thomas and Stern's hint of some possible treachery. Shapley was not eager to enlighten them further on the subject.

Hovering at the outer rim of that tiny circle of exposed nerves, Junji Asawa prowled back and forth, puffing his cigarette, moving like some pantherine creature cooped up too long in a cage.

Señora Gonzaga labored over a letter she was helping Mrs. Keck compose. It was directed to Colonel Dunskoi, whom they mistakenly believed was still post commandant. She'd written it on a piece of paper and with a pencil she'd managed to conceal behind a cabin mirror throughout the repeated searches of the train.

" '. . . and so, I most respectfully request,' " Señora Gonzaga read aloud in her thin, quavery Spanish accent, " 'that I be permitted at the earliest possible time to visit . . .' "

Her voice trailed off as she realized that Myra Keck was no longer paying attention to the letter. In point of fact, over the past three days they'd written the letter six times, using the same piece of paper but merely erasing each time. There was virtually no chance that Colonel Dunskoi would ever see it or, for that matter, that anyone functioning as his deputy would either.

Señora Gonzaga had been informed of that fact by a young lieutenant, with great courtesy but in no uncertain terms: written communication of any sort between detainees or between detainees and post personnel, was strictly forbidden. She neglected, however, to pass this information along to Mrs. Keck, not having the heart to do so.

Señora Gonzaga's trembling fingers touched Mrs. Keck's hand. "Myra? Myra, my dear. Do you hear me?"

Mrs. Keck stirred as one rousing from sleep, her hair in disarray and her eyes slightly bewildered.

"Myra? . . . Myra. The letter."

"Letter?" Mrs. Keck repeated the word slowly, as though she were learning how to pronounce it.

"It is finished now."

"Finished now?"

"Yes, my dear. We'll send it to the colonel in the morning."

"That will be nice."

"Yes, dear."

They nodded their heads at each other.

"Would you like a nice glass of milk before bed?" the señora inquired. "I think I could get you one from the porter."

Mrs. Keck nodded with that dazed look in her eye.

"And possibly a cracker too?" The señora became enthusiastic herself at the prospect.

"A cracker too?" Mrs. Keck smiled with a quick, unexpected brightness.

"Good." Señora Gonzaga clasped her hands with delight. "I think I have a little package in my purse."

Isabel pretended to be reading. Actually, she was trying hard to concentrate on the lurid little paperback she'd borrowed from Consuelo out of desperation. This one, like all the rest her sister appeared to favor, was a big, glittery, nine-hundred-page saga about the rich and famous—counts, starlets, and movie moguls, copulating freely, getting richer by the minute, and finally, of course, all getting their comeuppance.

Isabel had read the same page three times now. It dealt with the philandering of Serge, a penniless but "devastatingly attractive" White Russian nobleman with a penchant for large dogs and masochistic ladies. She was quite bored with the nobleman and impatient with the ladies, all of whom, she thought, were dreary beyond description and incomprehensibly stupid to suffer the abuse of Serge. The whole bunch of them, in fact, she felt, richly deserved each other.

Aside from the staggering fatuity of the dialogue, the real cause of her wandering attention was Silvana Lambrusto, seated across from her in the compartment they shared.

Pale, reedy, incontestably beautiful, Silvana might have been one of the heroines in just the sort of book Isabel was then reading—one of those pampered, satiated creatures with names like Danielle or Gabrielle or Francesca, with bored, vacant, beautiful faces—the sort of beauty that sent one desperately casting about for reasons to despise them.

Isabel's initial impressions of this beautiful young woman had been a projection of precisely what she wished her to be—vacant, selfish, narcissistic; no visible interests outside of clothing and self-adornment. In Isabel's scale of values, the very worst that could be said of someone was that she was irrelevant.

She wanted very much to tell herself that Silvana was irrelevant. It would have been so much easier. In that way she could patronize her and so possibly even grow to like her, in that "poor-adorable-little-Silvana" manner of affection, the way one adores a puppy.

But there was nothing puppylike about Silvana. She was neither poor nor little, and Isabel was far too honest a person, ruthlessly honest when it came to self-scrutiny, to clutch at fantasies for long.

Tossed together with the Italian woman by circumstances, forced to share close quarters, Isabel, try as she might, failed to find the vacant mannequin she'd imagined all throughout the trip. Instead, she found a proud, sensitive, and surprisingly shy young woman of uncommon, sometimes startling intelligence.

During the course of the trip through the Soviet Union they had studiously avoided each other, often the first sign of strong mutual attraction. Suddenly thrown together, penned up in the same small area, they were no longer able to avoid one another. What followed was a kind of stiffly elaborate *pas de deux,* a period of parry and thrust in which a single false move might have thrown the whole thing off. It never happened. Instead, as they continued to maneuver warily about each other, they gradually came to recognize within themselves wholly unexpected affinities.

"What's bothering you tonight?" Silvana asked offhandedly.

"Nothing. Why do you ask?"

"You've been reading the same page for the last half-hour."

"How the devil would you know?"

"Because you just lie there on your back and never turn the page."

Isabel scowled. "Well, if you must know, it's a perfectly lousy book."

They laughed like old chums savoring the sort of intimacy born of the fondest of shared memories.

"Why are you looking at me that way?" Silvana's laughter broke off abruptly.

"What way?"

"You have this odd expression on your face."

"I suppose I was thinking how pretty you are," Isabel remarked after a moment of reflection.

"Oh, please, let's not start that." Silvana waved the subject aside with her arms as if it were a puff of bad air. "That's usually the prelude to the conversation that generally concludes with, 'I never realized how intelligent you were, despite the disadvantage of your good looks.' "

"Well, you are intelligent. When we first met, I was rather hoping you'd be much less so."

"So you could dislike me?"

"On the contrary, so I could like you more."

They were laughing again, easy together, close as sisters filling a need in one another. Then too, they were both trying very hard to manage their fears.

Silvana spoke freely of Sandro, confessing in the end to the awful encounter with Keith Wales and Max discovering them. She was almost certain that if Sandro hadn't guessed the situation by now, Max would have told him. She had no idea what effect that might have on their marriage. She had no romantic feelings whatever for Keith and kept referring to him as "the boy."

Isabel spoke of the three or four ill-fated love affairs she'd had over the years. In each case, the man had been outstanding. Far too good. In fact, she confessed that there was something . . . some fatal need in her own peculiar makeup to deliver the coup de grace to any sort of relationship that threatened to become more than mere satisfaction of the flesh.

She spoke of her awful night with Tony Thomas, the need to humiliate herself before a man she considered distinctly second-rate. Afterward, to her dismay, she started to cry.

It was nearly midnight. They finished talking and flicked out the cabin lights. Isabel in the lower berth watched the pale ring of moon shower silvery light across the tips of the tall birch outside the compound. Up above she could hear Silvana's breathing and knew she was still awake.

"Hey, you," she called up to her softly. "You're not sleeping?"

"No."

"I heard something today."

There was a pause. Then the mattress above squealed as Silvana turned and leaned over, looking down at her. "What did you say?"

"Something I heard today."

"Yes?"

"From one of the matrons. She spoke Spanish. It was horrifying, and I don't know yet that I believe it."

She could see Silvana peering down at her through the darkness.

"She said . . . this matron . . . that they were going to split us up. Send us out all over the country. To different camps and detention centers."

"*Santa Maria nobile,*" Silvana whispered under her breath. "Dear God."

"I'm not worried for myself. Or for my mother or sister. But my father will never survive it."

"*Sancta Madonna.*"

"I wasn't going to tell you. I didn't want to alarm anyone."

"But you say you're not sure you believe the woman?"

"I don't know. Something about her. Her Spanish, I think." There was a long pause suggesting puzzlement.

"What about her Spanish?"

"I don't know. It was almost too good. And she just volunteered the information, almost as if she couldn't wait to tell me."

Nell Blanton lay wound in the sheets of her narrow berth, listening to the faint buzz of Frau Kunkel snoring away beneath her. That evening Frau

Kunkel had poured out her heart to Nell. She was sick to death with worry over Karl Heinz. She was certain that without her he would expire, languish like some delicate, unwatered flower.

For the first time, too, she spoke of her husband, how she'd married him but never loved him. The love of her life had been a soldier with whom, as a girl of eighteen, she'd tried to elope. It ended disastrously. Her parents came after them with the police and took her home by force.

Shortly after, she had married Herr Kunkel, a solid burgher of Freiburg, twenty years her senior. She'd had one child with him, Karl Heinz. Herr Kunkel had been extraordinarily kind to her, providing her with more than merely a decent life. In return, she'd become shrewish, cultivated a sharp tongue, and mocked and scorned him.

Nell listened quietly to the cascade of venom and self-hatred that was shortly to follow. By contrast, her marriage to Paul had seemed almost idyllic. Still, many of the details in her own biography had a disturbing similarity to those of Frau Kunkel.

She'd married for very much the same reasons Frau Kunkel had married. At twenty-three, Paul Blanton had already achieved remarkable prominence as a kind of wunderkind within the small world of corporate lawyers. He'd come from one of the first families of the Old Dominion, had been to the best schools, belonged to the best clubs, and was very much on the way up. For the pretty young Lexington debutante, marriage to such a man was perceived by all those who paid serious attention to such things to be a brilliant coup.

Now, nearly thirty years later, two grown married children, grandparents three times over, in all respects still in the prime of her life, Nell felt empty and she was terrified of an even emptier future.

Unlike many of her fellow passengers, she viewed her nearly nine-day detention behind barbed wire with a strange, almost icy detachment. She was not prepared to bet on how soon they might be released. In some curious way, she didn't really care. She missed her grandchildren, but paradoxically, not her own children. She was not the least bit homesick. Of her gracious, antebellum home in a wealthy suburb of Lexington, she thought not at all. By now, with the children all grown and gone, it was just a large, sprawling place full of room after room of heirlooms and period furniture, as cold and vacant as a museum after dark. It was a matter almost of stunning indifference to her whether or not she ever saw it again. There was, after all, very little to look forward to once she returned there. When she thought about it, she was more alarmed about her own personal state of mind than mere detention in a foreign land.

Before she fell asleep that night, she thought of Peter Stern. The fact that she harbored such thoughts about a man she scarcely knew was profoundly distasteful to her. How different he was from Paul, or for that matter from any of the men she had known growing up in Lexington.

He was attractive in a pleasant, sort of offbeat way. Not at all in the mold of the heroic, chivalric, world-beating ideal she'd been brought up to admire.

She thought that by now she'd seen almost everything of what the opposite sex had to offer. Stern was certainly a good, full-bodied example of it, but he seemed nervous and preoccupied—much too self-involved to permit himself a bit of dalliance with a middle-aged married woman. Not that that's what she was thinking of at all. She preferred to think her interest was along the more comfortable lines of companionship. But what was he all about anyway, out there breezing around the continent all by himself, a man at loose ends? Of course, it was the dissolution of his marriage after so many years. But then again, in the brief time that she'd known him, he didn't seem all that broken up about it. What was he after? she thought again. More to the point, what was *she* after? She nearly laughed out loud, imagining the look on Paul's face were he to guess her thoughts just then.

Jean Blaylock woke abruptly from sleep. It was almost as though she'd been summoned. The searchlight outside trailed over the thin coverlet and slipped nervously past.

She was aware of a vague sense of apprehension. Sorrow lingered over her like a vaguely unpleasant aftertaste, and she knew she'd been dreaming. Of what, she couldn't say. She wondered if it had been the dream or the searchlight that had jarred her awake, but so oppressive was the air of sadness about her that she knew it had to have been the dream.

Lying there in the dark, elements of it still clung to her like shreds and tatters of cloth torn from some larger bolt. She had a sudden image of her parents' home in Southampton and of Betty Corcoran, her old, dear, girlhood friend, now dead some dozen years.

The searchlight swept over the coverlet atop her, and the crunch of boots sounded heavily on the track bed below. She felt suddenly very small and alone. In the next moments, however, her melancholy thoughts gave way to a more tangible distraction. It was that odor of burning rubber she'd been smelling the past several days. Tonight it was somewhat more pronounced, and it occurred to her that a small pocket of heat, quite apart from the natural heat built up during the day, was radiating outward from the wall above her head.

Madam Mukherjee lay sleeping, her baby cradled in her arms. The baby's breathing was peaceful and regular; hers tended to be more fitful, with sighs and an occasional incoherent word spilling from her lips.

Across the way Consuelo watched the sleeping silhouette rise and fall with each breath and thought about Mr. Mukherjee. Since that rainy afternoon when she went to "look at photos" in his cabin, she could not stop thinking of him. Lying there, sleepless, all keyed up, she let her mind conjure with a wide range of images of Babu and her in bed.

Consuelo had no great fondness for Madam Muk, and watching her there, asleep and defenseless, the infant cradled in her arms, she took a certain spiteful glee as she gave herself fully to the lustful images rocketing freely through her fevered imagination.

Stern, not far off in the men's coach, dreamed too of a face, old as time, carved out of rock high up on a cliff. Beneath its huge beetled brow, the craterous eyes gazed blank and uncaring across the distant, frozen mountains.

Dawn on the Gulf of Bothnia. A still, gray disk of water, motionless as a lake, stretches into the pearl-gray distance. On its flat, unrippled surface, innumerable blackish dots sit against the encircling horizon.

On closer inspection, the dots take on the sharp conformation of ships. The ensigns they fly are multinational. U.S. carriers, British and French cruisers, German minesweepers, Dutch gunboats, Italian tankers, Russian and Polish heavy cruisers and destroyers—an assortment of vessels representing both Eastern and Western alliances.

None appear to be moving. They sit low on the water like gulls waiting for the morning's hunt to begin. There is a sense of suspended animation, of watching and waiting. They give the impression of having been summoned to some designated point for some undisclosed reason; then, having reached that point in a setting of the most ominous signs, told to drop anchor, wait, and do nothing.

In the center of all that sinister quiet, however, is a small hive of activity. Two large ships standing roughly four hundred feet off each other's bows intently observe one another's movements.

One is the Russian heavy cruiser *Vladivostok,* queen of the Soviet Union's Northern Fleet out of Severomorsk. The other is the U.S. minesweeper *Daytona,* part of the Sixth Fleet's Mediterranean base at Athens. Standing roughly a quarter-mile off, observing just as intently, is the U.S. nuclear carrier *Nimitz.*

The forecastle of the *Vladivostok* has been crumpled. As far back as where its bow numbers begin, a tangle of wreckage, including a forward gun mount and an ASROC launcher, is clearly visible.

On the minesweeper in the area just beneath the bridge and wheelhouse, a huge jagged hole yawns across the starboard hull. The minesweeper, taking water through the hole, perhaps twenty feet wide and nearly as high, appears to list slightly to the side.

Along the taffrails of both ships, sailors are lined up, watching silently as helicopters from the *Nimitz* remove the injured from the *Daytona* and fly them back to the U.S. hospital ship *Calvin,* standing inside the NATO flotilla. There are thirteen injured aboard the *Daytona* and one reported dead.

There is no way of knowing how many injuries the *Vladivostok* has sustained. The captains of both ships have already exchanged abusive messages. The captain of the *Daytona* has charged that the *Vladivostok* failed to heed repeated warnings that it was sailing too close to the minesweeper. Under international regulations, according to the American captain, the *Daytona,* steaming north toward the open sea, claimed the right of way. The *Vladivostok,* he said, had made a number of deceptive and hostile maneuvers throughout the hours directly preceding the collision.

The captain of the *Vladivostok* in his message refuted that claim, maintaining instead that the *Daytona* was not moving north, but on a southwesterly course, and as such was intruding in waters reserved for combined Warsaw Pact naval maneuvers. It charged the minesweeper with spying.

The *Vladivostok* had begun to trail the *Daytona* during the day. It had kept well back of the minesweeper, possibly between a half-mile and three-quarters of a mile distance between itself and the American ship.

In those brief hours of total darkness between one and two in the morning, the prow of the Soviet crusier appeared suddenly off the *Daytona*'s stern, and either deliberately or inadvertently rammed her.

For a variety of reasons, the latter explanation seems more plausible. Since the damage to the *Vladivostok* was not inconsiderable, and could have possibly resulted in its loss, it is extremely unlikely that its captain set out deliberately to risk both his ship and crew for such a questionable prize. After all, if one is bent on such a course, why settle for a minesweeper? Why not go for the really big game, a cruiser, or perhaps even a carrier?

The only satisfactory explanation, therefore, for the *Vladivostok*'s behavior was that its orders were to menace but not actively engage. In the darkness, it had probably misjudged the distance between the ships and come up on the minesweeper too fast and too close to give it sufficient time to turn.

As the first rays of the sun rake the western sky, a flock of arctic gulls wheel round and settle in one definitive motion on the stern of the *Vladivostok.* A faint breeze kicks up out of the west, producing a gentle swell. Bobbing gently on the surface, the gulls watch the helicopters drop down and land on the deck of the *Daytona,* take on the injured, and depart. They watch these maneuvers with the same air of quiet bafflement as do the young sailors lining the rails of the *Daytona* and the *Vladivostok.*

PART IX

THE STATE DEPARTMENT had stern words for Moscow today over an accident at sea involving U.S. and Soviet ships that took the lives of four American seamen in the Baltic. The incident occurred early yesterday during joint naval maneuvers of both NATO and the Warsaw Pact nations.

Sources here deny that the U.S. presence in the Baltic is linked to the now nearly two-week-old hostage situation involving the detention of fifty-one passengers, including thirteen Americans, in a train on the Russo-Finnish border.

Secretary of State George Shultz said late this afternoon that Soviet failure to make any sincere effort toward resolution of the problem was viewed here in the gravest possible light. Cautioning that Americans had grown increasingly impatient with what he termed "Soviet stalling," he said that the U.S. government would take whatever steps it deemed necessary to secure the release of not only the thirteen Americans on board the train, but all the other hostages as well.

He did not specify whether the steps would be in the form of economic reprisals, such as the cancellation of existing trade and agricultural agreements. But without saying so directly, he did not preclude the possibility of direct U.S. military intervention if all else fails.

This is Leslie Stahl, CBS News, at the White House.

At a small secluded villa on Lake Geneva, fleets of official cars have been seen arriving and departing all night. It is thought that the Soviet team negotiating here with representatives of the West for release of the hostages still aboard the so-called Green Train have been summoned back to Moscow.

While unconfirmed reports over the past several days had suggested that most of the obstacles to a resolution of the problem had been ironed out, it would seem now that recent developments in the Baltic involving a collision between U.S. and Soviet ships has caused positions in the hostage stalemate to harden. With the sudden departure of the Soviet negotiating team, all hope for an early release of the fifty-one hostages appears to have gone up in smoke. Fear is now growing for the safety of the hostages as news from the Baltic . . .

—*Züricher Zeitung*

"You have lost the game. There's never going to be a return to your home-lands for any of you. And don't dare to hope there will be."

Those were Captain Grishkov's parting words to the men during breakfast in the dining car that morning. The words came crackling in over a loud-speaker while they listened in stunned silence. Now that the hunger strike had persisted for nearly 48 hours with no visible sign of relenting (other than pos-sibly Mr. Mukherjee's minor theft of fruit), the captain had taken to the air-waves with a vengeance. There were long, rambling diatribes, born, so the captain said, out of his sense of outrage and hurt at the ingratitude of the "in-ternees" for the splendid treatment they were receiving at the hands of the be-nevolent and magnanimous Soviet government.

"Make no mistake," he assured them over the crackling speakers, "it could be far worse." At that point he launched into his frightening "You-have-lost-the-game" speech. "There's never going to be a return to your homelands . . ."

No one knew precisely what the game was to which he was referring, or out of what specific events the speech had grown. From time to time the captain alluded to "recent external events," but at no point did he mention the inci-dent involving the two ships in the Baltic. Leaving them in the dark that way to guess and wonder was perhaps intentional. It had the desired effect of creating confusion and fear.

It was clear the Soviets felt there was potential for a major public-relations disaster in a hunger strike. It tended to enlist the sympathy of the world on the part of the strikers. Second, it simply didn't look good to return people to freedom in significantly worse condition than when first taken into custody.

Señor Gonzaga, a gentleman in his seventies, had existed solely on a diet of water over the past two and a half days. A tall, gaunt, but characteristically hardy individual, the deprivation of food had turned him cadaverous. Over-night, the tip of his nose had seemed to sharpen noticeably and his ears thrusting out above the sideburns had come to dagger points. His eyes ap-peared to have sunk into the skull sockets, causing the flesh around the tem-ples to grow taut and pinched. His skin, remarkably youthful for a man of his years, seemed suddenly wrinkled and sere like late autumn leaves, with an unhealthy yellow pallor.

But if the flesh appeared to be failing, the spirit was feistier than ever. His mind was sharp. He spoke endlessly, and not polemics or tiresome pep talks. Instead, he would regale his fellow detainees with keen, vivid, wildly funny reminiscences of his boyhood in Madrid. There was something about the old man that was invigorating, bracing as ice water. He had all the instincts of the true campaigner. He was not easily intimidated. That same brazen indomita-bility he demonstrated by swinging from a vine fifty feet up over a pond marked his behavior every day of their detention. Clearly he had the spark to rally men. But anyone seeing him from one day to the next would say that physically he was failing.

Shapley was going downhill too, but the signs of it were less apparent. Determined to be a part of the resistance, he'd taken only fluids over the past several days, and those not so much for nutrition as for a means of washing down his various medications. The sudden withdrawal of protein and minerals from his diet tended now to exacerbate the spasms in his legs. As a result he sat more and moved about less. He was afraid to stand up and walk about for fear the leg would give way beneath him and he would fall. Consequently, the lack of all exercise made him feel weak and lethargic.

As the fast wore on, it took its toll. People grew increasingly testy. Naturally, some fared better than others, which, in turn, fed suspicions that there were those among them who were not as self-denying as others. Rumors abounded that some individuals had made private arrangements with porters to bring them food after dark when everyone else had retired for the night.

With exquisite perversity, the guards left trays of food tauntingly about everywhere. One came upon them not only in the dining car but also in more improbable places such as the corridor of the day coach, where platters of cake and cold cuts regularly appeared.

That, of course, sowed more suspicion. The comings and goings of people in the corridors could not be monitored every moment. There was no way of knowing who might slip a slice of cake or meat off one of the trays and devour it secretly while closeted in the lavatory. The resulting suspicion and dissension, of course, were precisely the effect their captors aimed for.

Max Conti and Sandro Lambrusto, the closest of friends for years, had ceased in the past days to speak with one another. They had always sat together during meals and walked together in the compound during the exercise period. Now they openly avoided each other. Desfargue and Van Meegrin came close to a fistfight one afternoon over a sock that each claimed he owned.

Without his daily infusion of vodka, Tony Thomas grew sullen and short-tempered. For a man as socially gregarious as he was, he now preferred to sit by himself and glower. He would say nothing to Stern, who had taken to sitting nearby and watching him with the fixity of a cat intent on a careless mouse. Uncomfortably aware of him, Thomas would try to pretend that Stern was not there, but the effort of ignoring him had proved to be a strain.

He was reluctant to challenge Stern openly, for then the heart of their quarrel would surely become open knowledge, and Thomas was not at all certain how much public scrutiny his unique position on that train might bear. From a purely professional point of view, disclosure of his actions directly prior to departure of the Green Train could well be embarrassing.

For Stern, the fast was no great ordeal. He could have scarcely eaten anyway, so preoccupied was he with charges of conspiracy and threats of trial and imprisonment. The evidence of collusion with Wales seemed flimsy at best. The letters and photographs offered in proof were such blatant forgeries that no one could take their evidential value too seriously. But even so, with each morning, Stern rose fully expecting that day to be his last on the Green Train, so convinced was he that he was bound for the oblivion of some labor camp far in the frozen north.

Arriving on the heels of the hunger strike, possibly as a result of it, came a new dictum from Captain Grishkov—instead of rising at 7:30 A.M., as they had done since the start of their internment, they were now roused each morning at 4:30. While dark shadows were still entwined in the trees, recordings of martial music were blared through the loudspeakers—Red Army Band marches and even John Philip Sousa, whom the Soviets were extremely partial to. Throughout the remainder of the day they were treated to Russian rock music (as a punishment, not a reward), played at decibel levels that were punitive. The music sounded very much like American or British rock, but it became bizarre and other-worldly in the improbable context of Russian lyrics.

At suppertime they played a sort of soothing, vacuous dinner music, lullabies and popular Russian tunes, the equivalent of Mantovani, and finally concluding with a good-night word from Captain Grishkov over the scratchy speakers—a lecture on obedience and cooperation, half-wheedling, half-browbeating, the law of the mushy cudgel.

The third evening of the hunger strike, as they took their places in the dining car for supper, Paul Blanton took up his fork and knife and proceeded to eat. He made no attempt to conceal the fact, nor did he attempt to encourage the others to do the same. He simply appeared to have come to a decision over the past several hours that the fast served no constructive purpose and, for himself at least, he was terminating it.

His action was scarcely noticed at first. The others were too intent on doing precisely what they had been doing during the past eight meals—sitting at their places, hands folded in their laps, staring blankly at their trays of untouched food. It was the sound, at last, the quiet clink of cutlery moving on the steel tray, that brought Shapley's gaze up. Desfargue, nearby, noticed it too. The Frenchman leaned back in his chair, a look of disdain on his features. There was nothing judgmental about Shapley, however. He watched quietly and seemed to understand. He appeared to take no moral position.

Slowly the gazes of others were drawn to the scene. Blanton continued to eat. He exhibited an almost superhuman indifference to the stir he was causing. His manner at that moment was that of a person doing the most natural thing imaginable. When at last he looked up, still chewing thoughtfully, a mischievous little boy's smile flickered about his lips. "I'm no hero, gentlemen," he said pleasantly. Another forkful of food disappeared in his mouth. "Like all of you, I've tried it Ted's way and it's not working. This morning when I got up I felt weak. I can't believe that much will be gained by my getting sick. So, as you can see, I'm eating. I know what you must all think of me, and I'm sorry. But this has been my decision to make, and I've made it."

Silent, unspeaking, they watched him with deadly fascination slice another piece of meat on his tray, then followed the course of his fork as it rose to his mouth.

The young soldier-waiters standing about in the aisles watched him as well. They had no idea what he'd said, but from the reaction of the others they had divined that something significant had just occurred.

"I agree with Mr. Blanton," Tony Thomas said, with visible relief, and picked up his fork. He was followed by Mr. Mukherjee. Max Conti, beside him, extended his palms outward, shrugged his shoulders, and proceeded to eat. It appeared that the resistance was on the verge of collapse.

Then it was Señor Gonzaga's turn to pick up his fork. He tapped his water glass with it several times as though he were calling a meeting to order. "I'm afraid, Mr. Thomas"—he nodded and smiled cordially to the Englishman—"that I cannot agree. You're a far more practical man than I am, however. A few scraps of food, even if they do spell survival, are not sufficient reward for me to trade my freedom."

Gonzaga replaced the fork by his tray and folded his arms, resuming his position of quiet defiance. His words had a signal effect. Several of those who had been teetering at the edge folded their arms in imitation of the old man to show their allegiance with him. Stern was one of those, as were Desfargue and Van Meegrin. Asawa, who'd been following this with his poised, almost feral air of alertness, suddenly folded his arms too. Mr. Mukherjee's jaw slowed from its chewing as if he were reconsidering his position. In the next moment, he swallowed what was left in his mouth and put his fork down. He gazed sheepishly around at the others, then with his hands folded in his lap lowered his eyes to his tray.

Blanton continued to eat. For all intents and purposes, he had stepped out of the skirmish. As he'd said, he'd made his decision. It was not based on lofty moral sophistries or tortured rationales, but on what he felt was right for him. There appeared to be no pangs of conscience about it.

Thomas continued to eat too, but he appeared to be far less easy in his mind. He was more concerned with self-image and how that might be portrayed once the affair was over.

Stern watched the Englishman with an air of immense satisfaction. His eyes twinkled mockingly, but although hunger gnawed savagely at him beneath his belt, wild horses could not have gotten him to swallow a scrap of food with which to assuage it.

As the days of confinement wore on, Myra Keck grew more listless and apathetic. She'd withdrawn within herself and sometimes Señora Gonzaga would have all she could do to rouse the poor woman out of her deepening torpor. At mealtimes she would personally undertake to feed her. Occasionally a physician would come and examine her in her compartment. The physician was brusque and appeared overworked. He would spend ten minutes with her while Jatta attempted to convey to him the nature of her problem. Checking all of her vital signs, he would invariably conclude from them that she was in sound health. He allowed as how she might have been a bit despondent, but "under the circumstances that is perfectly natural."

When he departed, he would leave behind some aspirin and tranquilizers. He had nothing more germane to add.

"Shall I brush your hair, Myra?" Señora Gonzaga inquired softly.

Mrs. Keck slumped against the window of the coach, apparently oblivious to the question.

"Let me brush it out so you will look pretty when we go to visit Mr. Keck at the hospital tomorrow."

Mrs. Keck stirred her immense frame. Her eyelids fluttered. "Yes. That would be nice."

The old *condesa* tottered to her feet. Rummaging through Mrs. Keck's traveling kit, she extracted from it a comb and brush. Slowly and with infinite care she unpinned the wiry pewter-gray hair and proceeded with long, even strokes to comb it out.

"You have such pretty hair, Myra."

Mrs. Keck nodded dreamily. "My mother's hair. I still have a locket of it somewhere in the attic. Now, where did I . . . ?"

"We shall make you beautiful for tomorrow when you see Mr. Keck." The señora warmed to her job. The effort expended seemed cheap enough for such a quiet glow of elation. She sat there docile, full of childlike anticipation for the morning's visit to the hospital, which of course would never come.

The lies Señora Gonzaga told the woman weighed heavily on her conscience. But they were all in a good cause, she told herself, and besides, by the morning Myra Keck would have forgotten everything of what had been promised the day before.

"That goddamned, piss-awful Keck woman." Isabel whirled into the compartment and slammed the door. A stream of Spanish epithets poured from her. "She has my poor mother waiting on her hand and foot."

The tirade broke off in mid-sentence as she gaped at Silvana. "What is it? What's the matter?"

"Nothing."

"Nothing. Why do you say nothing when I see you are crying?"

"I am not crying." Silvana turned her face toward the curtained window. "It is nothing."

Isabel stood there unmoving, riveted to the place she'd stopped when she slammed the door. "My dear." In the next moment she'd crossed the narrow cabin space in a stride and knelt beside the young Italian woman, patting her hand as though she were assuaging a child who'd barked its shin. "Silvana. Tell me. What's happened?"

Silvana opened her fist, where a wad of crumpled paper bloomed slowly like a flower. It was a napkin—the sort of coarse, yellowish thing that was available from the steel dispensers on the tables in the dining car.

There was writing on it—a faint, thin scribble rendered virtually indecipherable from the wrinkling of the paper.

"My darling . . ." it began. Isabel couldn't make out the next few words. What followed was little better, appearing to have been scrawled in haste and not under the most ideal circumstances.

". . . rumor we are moving . . . separated . . . Next day . . . if . . . No regrets . . . Love you always . . . Sand . . ."

Still kneeling beside her, Isabel seemed angry. "Where did you get this?"

"The attendant."

"The attendant?"

"The fat one with the nice smile and rosy cheeks."

"Sandro must have bribed one of the guards to get it to you."

Silvana nodded tearfully. "What do you suppose it means?"

"It means, just as I've said. I'm sure we're moving."

"Yes, but where?"

"Wherever it is they move people like us."

"Like us?" Silvana gaped at her out of wide, teary eyes.

"Hostages. Political prisoners. Detainees. Whatever they call us. They have labor camps. Transit camps. A whole network of these spread across the country."

"But surely they won't . . ."

"Why not? I assure you they've done this sort of thing before."

"Yes, but we're . . ."

"Nothing special." Isabel dashed that hope quite quickly. "If you're thinking that, put it out of your head at once."

Silvana was sitting up now, hands folded in her lap. Her chin dropped to her chest, and she started to cry.

Isabel rose from her kneeling position and sat down beside her. She took her hand and held it tightly. "Cry. It's perfectly all right."

The floodgates opened and for several moments Silvana surrendered entirely to her emotions. They took the form of racking sobs stifled into a crumpled handkerchief. "I've been awful. Poor Sandro. Why does he put up with it?"

"He doesn't strike me as at all unhappy," Isabel offered. "He puts up with you because he clearly adores you."

"I've never been unfaithful," Silvana blubbered between sobs.

"I know. I know that."

"Nine years we've been married. And never. Not once . . ."

"My darling. There's no need to give me assurances."

"There are those who like to say that I have . . . Believe me . . ."

"I do. Now, let's stop all this."

"That bastard Max. And this stupid thing with the Canadian boy . . ."

"Forget it. It's not worthy of discussion."

Silvana fell sobbing against her while Isabel patted her back awkwardly with a sense of growing embarrassment.

"Do you think they'll really separate us? Send us to these awful—what do you call them—gulags?"

"Of course not," Isabel assured her with a great conviction, of which she was by no means certain herself.

"I'm terrified of pain. Will they hurt us?"

"Put it out of your mind. No such thing will happen."

Silvana's tears abated. Slowly she regained control of her voice. "I'm so glad they put me with you, Isabel."

Isabel laughed her shrill, slightly embarrassed laugh. "I am too. Just imagine, they could have put me with my sister."

They roared, smothering the sounds of their mirth, just as they'd smothered those of grief moments before.

"Look," Isabel chattered on, "someday, after all this is over, let's you and I meet in some city. Just the two of us. Someplace gay and resorty. Preferably on the water, and get drunk together."

Delight sparked in Silvana's eyes. "Why not?" she said. "I'd love it. By then, for all I know, I'll be a single woman."

"I doubt that. But if so, all the better. We'll go out and get ourselves a couple of swells."

"And spend all their money."

"By all means." Isabel's head fell back and she laughed at the ceiling. "But one thing, dear . . ." Her hand encircled Silvana's waist and slowly she drew her close. Silvana came, supple, pliant, infinitely yielding.

"As far as what Sandro says"—she indicated the crumpled napkin with her eyes—"this is all simply rumor. You understand?"

Silvana nodded, appearing frightened. "Yes, I see . . ."

"Knowing the state of mind around here, we'll mention nothing of it to the others."

"But . . ."

Before Silvana could protest, Isabel laid a finger firmly against her lips. "Silence," she whispered, then kissed those lips with her own.

"A hundred and three degrees." Squinting toward the light, Wilma Shapley read the figures off the thermometer.

A look of apprehension moved fleetingly across Nell Blanton's eyes.

Madam Mukherjee caught the look and moaned softly. The baby lay quiet, virtually unmoving except for the occasional shudder that radiated through him. He'd been lying that way for several hours, completely uncharacteristic behavior for a characteristically noisy, active child.

"You'd have thought they'd have a doctor here by now," Nell whispered to

Mrs. Shapley, then turned to Madam Mukherjee. "When did you say you called?"

The question flustered her completely.

"When did she call for the doctor?" Mrs. Shapley asked.

"Two hours." Nell checked her watch. "No, three hours ago. Mrs. Palmunan asked the matron and she said she'd call at once.

"Maybe we should try again," Frau Kunkel suggested. "You can't trust these people to get anything right. This baby is on fire."

Once again the long, low moaning sound rose from Madam Muk. "Babu. Babu," she gasped.

"What's that she says?" Mrs. Shapley asked.

"That's her husband," Nell replied.

"I thought he was George."

"Apparently not when she's upset. Then he's Babu or Nagu or something else."

"Nagu. Nagu," Madam Muk chanted softly while watching out of one staring eye the still, limp form of her child.

Mrs. Shapley looked round at the others, then settled her gaze on Madam Mukherjee. "Do we have any baby aspirin?"

The poor woman was in no condition to provide a coherent answer.

"We've been giving two baby aspirin every hour for the past three hours," Nell Blanton said. "It doesn't make a dent. We need something stronger."

"The child doesn't need aspirin," Frau Kunkel snorted. "He needs an antibiotic."

Nell Blanton had begun to display signs of irritability. "Well, if you can tell me where to get some. We can't seem to get anything from the dispensary until a doctor sees the child."

Wilma Shapley folded her arms across her ample bosom. "So we're stuck here."

"Until a doctor comes," Nell replied.

"My child—my baby," Madam Mukherjee entreated them. "He's going into convulsions."

Shivers, like a series of small visible quakes, had begun to ripple with disconcerting regularity up and down the child's tiny frame.

Mrs. Shapley was impatient, but by no means rattled. She'd raised four children of her own, sometimes in conditions less satisfactory than those they faced here. There was not much in the whole repertoire of pediatric disease she had not seen. She turned back to Madam Muk, hovering in a corner, wringing her hands. "Has he had any fluids?"

The Indian woman shook her head, scarcely comprehending.

"She tried to get some juice into him a while ago," Nell explained, "but he can't keep anything down. Just throws it up."

"Is there any more aspirin?" Mrs. Shapley asked.

"We gave him our last about an hour ago."

Mrs. Shapley bent down and placed her lips on the child's fiery forehead, then glanced up over her shoulder at Frau Kunkel. "Would you please ask the matron to step in here a moment?"

Frau Kunkel slipped from the compartment while the others hovered about in the small airless space. Madam Mukherjee wept softly to herself. She seemed utterly spent. The once-pretty sari with its crisp, vivid colors drooped from her, rumpled and sodden with sweat. Kohl leaking at the corners of her eyes streaked her tearful cheeks.

Shortly a clatter of feet sounded in the corridor outside. In the next moment the door swung open and Frau Kunkel was standing there with Jatta and a matron. There was no longer room in the compartment for everyone. Some jockeying followed while those who had been inside stepped out into the corridor to make room for the newcomers.

The matron was a stout young girl with frightened eyes. She glanced down at the baby, and then at Madam Mukherjee in the corner, sensing at once that something was wrong.

Mrs. Shapley started to question Jatta. They spoke in hushed voices. "Is this the one who rang up for the doctor?"

"I think it was another girl," Nell Blanton replied. "The new shift came on after lunch."

"Does she know anything about the call?" Mrs. Shapley asked. "Was there a message left by the first shift?"

Jatta rattled off the question to the matron in Russian, then turned back a moment later. "No message was left."

"So we don't even know if the first shift called for the doctor." Mrs. Shapley smoldered quietly.

Frau Kunkel's eyes glowed with triumph. "You see? Just as I told you."

"This child is burning up." Mrs. Shapley turned with sudden force on the matron. "He has a fever. He's very sick."

Jatta translated the short, declarative sentences as rapidly as Mrs. Shapley fired them at the matron. The Russian girl took them stiffly, eyes closed and chin slightly elevated as though she were being slapped.

"We must have the doctor at once," Wilma Shapley went on relentlessly. "This child is going into convulsions. If something happens, there'll be an inquiry, and you'll have to answer for it."

They watched fright register in the girl's eyes. No sooner had she bolted from the cabin than she was back with her older and more hardened chief—a woman whose face was a mask of gray, doughy skin with large pores. She had the look of someone who'd learned years ago how to say no and fully enjoyed every minute of it.

Mrs. Shapley started again, Jatta doing the simultaneous translation. Madam Muk remained huddled in the corner, whimpering.

"*Nyet . . . Nyet . . . Nyet . . .*" The elderly matron kept shaking her head to coincide with each *nyet*. Several times she started out the door, only to come back in response to some new attack by Mrs. Shapley.

"I have already told you," she said. "The doctor has been summoned several hours ago. He was on call. He's in surgery now. He cannot be disturbed."

"And I have already told you," Mrs. Shapley bore down hard, "this child is going into convulsions."

The matron, easily Mrs. Shapley's equal in both size and tenacity, stood her ground.

"This child . . ." Mrs. Shapley took the woman's arm, walking, but to be more accurate, dragging her to the far side of the cabin out of Madam Mukherjee's earshot. She lowered her voice, but nearly hissed. "This child could die."

"Nyet. Nyet," the matron went on implacably, clearly impressed with her own force of personality. She was a strict, doctrinaire party type, and felt these Westerners had already been too coddled. She would not call the doctor again. The child would be fine. She had seen that sort of thing with infants before, and they were always fine in a few hours.

Could she at least find some antibiotic? Failing that, at least some more aspirin?

"Nyet. Nyet." No medication could be procured without the doctor's prior approval. They would just have to wait. She swept out in a huff, followed by the younger matron as a terrible silence descended on the cabin.

In her youth in Montana in the twenties, Wilma Shapley had seen babies carried off with high-fever convulsions. That was, of course, in the days before antibiotics and other fever-reducing medications. If there were medications available here, it would be a simple matter. But they had nothing, at least until the doctor came, and there was no way of telling when that might be.

Looking at the child now, Mrs. Shapley didn't like its shivering. And particularly disquieting was the slight bluish cast that had begun to darken its normally pink lips. He was burning up with fever, the result, no doubt, of some systemic infection. From the way the child appeared to wince slightly each time it swallowed, there was a strong possibility of strep throat.

The problem was clear-cut. The fever had to be lowered quickly. She knew what sort of interim steps might be taken until the doctor came. That is, if he ever did. The question was, would she assume the responsibility of taking those steps herself? She was suddenly aware of eyes focused on her. In some tacit, almost imperceptible way, the mantle of leadership had in that moment passed to her. The fact was, no one else appeared to want it. Across the way, cowering in a corner, looking utterly lost, Madam Mukherjee gazed at her imploringly.

Kate Dubbin stuck her head into the cabin, startled to see them all huddled there. She quickly grasped the gravity of the situation. "Is there something I can do?" All the while she spoke, her shrewd eyes scanned the child, whose breathing had grown irregular and noisy.

"Do you have any rubbing alcohol?" Wilma Shapley asked.

"No, but let me run down and check with the others."

The child made an odd little gagging sound.

"Don't bother," Mrs. Shapley snapped. "Instead, just bring me some towels soaked in cold water. Quick."

Since his recapture no one had seen Keith Wales. They knew he was still aboard the train because they could see the doctors come and go twice daily to the private compartment in which he'd been confined since his capture. An armed guard stood outside the door twenty-four hours a day.

Going out to the exercise yard that morning, Van Meegrin had passed the compartment just as the door was opening and the doctor was leaving. He had a glimpse of a narrow, somewhat isolated figure sitting in a white smock or nightshirt at the edge of the bed, feet dangling over the side. Something about the attitude of the figure, slumped yet poised as though it were marshaling all of its forces to stand, gave an impression of terrible exhaustion. All about the forehead and front of the face was a kind of cagelike apparatus that had the look of some sort of ghastly medieval torture device.

Later, when Van Meegrin told the others about it, Shapley said they had no doubt wired his jaw. Several of them, including Shapley and Tony Thomas, had made formal requests to see him. But all such requests were summarily denied. Wales was now deemed to be an enemy of the state, they were told, and as such had forfeited all rights of visitation with the others or, for that matter, any form of communication whatsoever.

Stern wanted very much to see Wales. It was vitally important for him to confirm with Wales Captain Grishkov's statement that he had indeed implicated Stern along with himself in a conspiracy against the state.

Stern's request was flatly denied. To his even greater dismay, he discovered that since his last meeting with the captain, he was being watched more closely then ever. Moving about in the compound during the exercise period, rinsing out socks and underwear in the bathhouse, it occurred to him increasingly that wherever he went, whatever he happened to be doing, whenever he looked up, there was invariably a guard standing there watching him intently, with little attempt to conceal the fact.

Stern was among the half-dozen holdouts in the hunger strike. With him were Shapley, Gonzaga, Sandro, Claude Desfargue, and Asawa. The others had gradually and with a certain amount of embarrassment returned to food. Blanton had become their unofficial leader. The rift between eaters and noneaters had grown so wide at one point as to result in an actual but undeclared self-segregation between groups. The noneaters no longer sat with or associated with the eaters. Estrangement between people who were formerly friends became the rule of the day. Feelings of betrayal and embitterment ran high. The word "collaborator" was tossed about freely.

That day at lunch the noneaters sat stolid and unmoving before their food trays while the eaters partook openly. Bad feelings reached an intolerable high. Max Conti accepted a second helping of boiled beef. He happened, at one point, to lean across the table to ask Blanton to pass a salt cellar. Asawa, seated with the noneaters, rose to his feet like some avenging god and with wild eyes flung a salt cellar across the aisle directly at Conti's head. Fortunately, it only struck him on the arm.

Everyone rose at the same moment. There was a convergence of bodies in the aisle. Arms flailed. Several punches were thrown before the guards swarmed into the car and broke them up. Lunch ended abruptly with everyone being ordered out of the car. The crowd was dispersed and people stood about sullenly in the exercise yard until the lunch break was over.

Later they returned to their compartments, where a few dispirited poker games started up. The porters distributed a variety of Russian magazines that no one, with the possible exception of Shapley and Thomas, could read, along with some plain hardcore Soviet progaganda in English prepared by the Ministry of Public Affairs.

Stern made a halfhearted attempt to reread a Maigret he'd read several weeks before. But he could concentrate on nothing. His mind was fixed to the point of obsession on his last encounter with Captain Grishkov. That the Soviets had a Jewish "thing" was quite well-known, and he could not prove he wasn't Jewish. For the first time in his life he experienced a resentment toward Jews, a sense of having been dragged unjustly into their "mess." The possibility that he might actually be removed to Moscow to stand trial on charges of espionage brought him to the brink of panic.

They were bluffing, of course. Such a trial would be a farce, Stern attempted to placate himself. There was no substance to their case, and all the evidence was blatantly factitious.

Just as he began to feel somewhat reassured, he had an image of Grishkov's smug, self-satisfied smile as he said when they were parting, "I don't have to prove anything." Stern's blood turned to ice.

Later that afternoon, he had another jolt. Two plainclothesmen, very much the same sort of squat, square physical types that had driven him to Vyborg before, appeared in his cabin. The overall impression they conveyed was one of barely contained brutality.

One of them spoke reasonably good English. He instructed Stern to open his bags and spread the contents out on the bunk before them.

"What on earth for?" Stern started to protest. His belongings had already been ransacked three or four times. But something in their eyes made him break off quickly. Maigret would not have been intimidated, but Stern was not Maigret. He did as he was told.

It was a single canvas bag. He lifted it down from the luggage rack, unbuckled its two belts, and upended the contents onto his bunk.

The two plainclothesmen stood there just behind him, hands plunged deep in their pockets, watching him spread the contents out on the bunk.

It would be hard to imagine an array of more innocuous rubbish—toiletries, socks, underclothes, several shirts badly rumpled and gray from use, a sweater with a hole at the sleeve, two handkerchiefs, and a pair of cotton khaki slacks.

But there was also a small package of film—Kodak 230. One of the men, the English-speaking fellow, pounced on it, plucking it out of the debris as though he'd found a diamond in some silt.

"What is this?" he demanded.

"Film."

"Film of what?"

"It's film I took in Leningrad. The Hermitage. St. Isaac's. Petrovorets. Things like that. Here, let me . . ." He made a move to retrieve it but the man snatched it back out of reach and jammed it into his pocket.

"Where is the camera?"

"It's been confiscated."

Stern regarded the man grimly. "Will I get my film back?"

"You're not permitted to have film here." The man then grumbled something in Russian to his colleague. In the next moment he was addressing Stern in loud, declamatory tones. "You are to have all belongings packed and ready for transferral by tomorrow morning, 0800 hours."

Stern felt a spasm in his bowels. "Where am I to be transferred to?"

"Please to be ready at the appointed hour." There was no further answer. Both of them turned at once, as in a single motion, and started out.

"When will I get my film back?" Stern called after them. They never bothered to reply.

Junji Asawa lay on his bunk. Propped on an elbow, he watched Van Meegrin and Desfargue play desultory chess on one of those small pocket board games that folds into a neat little leatherette package.

He appeared to be following the play—the maneuver of castle and pawn, bishop in pursuit of king and queen. Whenever a piece was captured, he laughed softly to himself. It didn't seem to matter particularly if it was a black or white piece. He took no sides but appeared to take some secret pleasure from the interplay of both.

He laughed, then appeared to drift off into a languorous half-doze with a smile that lingered on his lips. His mind had wandered to some unreal place with the quaint air of one of those toylike villages enclosed in a glass ball. The scene within this particular glass was a three-tiered Buddhist temple set on the shores of a tiny lake with a range of white-capped mountains dreaming in the distance. Snow drifted slowly downward, whispering on the still surface of the lake and catching in the upturned eaves of the pagoda. It was peaceful there, and cold—the air so clear and brittle you could hear the frozen branches of trees snapping in the forest. The scene darkened to purple violet as the hour moved on toward dusk.

Inside, the priests would be setting the tables for tea. The tiny porcelain cups were set out and the iron kettle was hissing on the charcoal brazier. A fire crackled on the hearth and the cat drowsed on his back in the corner, pedaling his paws fitfully in the air through his cat dreams. Outside, the pale orange light from the temple shimmered like flaming sconces on the half-frozen surface of the dreamy little snow-blown lake.

"We must be ready to move by eight A.M."

"But where?"

"Wherever it is they move people in our category."

"Labor camps? Jails, you mean?"

"No one said anything about jails or camps." Jatta Palmunan was exhausted. "If I knew exactly where we were to be relocated, I assure you I'd be more than happy to tell you. But as it turns out . . ."

Jean Blaylock fumed. "Wherever it is, it's got to be a huge improvement over this."

"I wouldn't be too sure of that," Kate Dubbin said.

"What about the men?" Wilma Shapley inquired.

"Yes, the men are moving too."

"And what am I supposed to do," Madam Mukherjee fretted, "with a sick child, running a high fever?"

"I'm sure they'll make some provision for that," Jatta attempted to placate her.

"They haven't bothered to send a doctor yet," said Nell Blanton. "What makes you so certain they'll make provisions to move the child?"

It was ten P.M. They'd gathered out in the corridor, summoned there by the tour guide, who'd just been informed that relocation was imminent.

"And poor Mrs. Keck. What about her?" Señora Gonzaga struggled to be heard above the general din.

"She's able to walk. She's able to move about, isn't she?" Jatta asked.

"She's on the verge of some kind of breakdown," Isabel shot back. "Any idiot can see that."

There was a general outcry. Fright and anger. Jatta clapped her hands for silence. "Please, please. I'm only conveying to you the orders I've been given."

There was more muttering. More indignation.

"I'm sure they will make provision for people with special problems." Jatta had the look of a beleaguered teacher before an unruly class. "But for the rest of us, we must be ready to move by eight A.M."

"Are we all going to the same place, or are they separating us?" Silvana asked.

"Yes," Jatta replied somewhat vaguely.

"Yes, what?" Kate Dubbin asked. "The same place or separated?"

Jatta looked away, uncertain how best to confront their terrified eyes.

"Well?" Jean Blayblock pressed.

"The impression I got from the captain"—at that point Jatta's voice dropped—"was the latter."

There was a groan of disbelief.

"Yes. Separated. To different places. The captain says it's for our own safety."

"Once they send you to one of these camps," Isabel muttered, "you may as well walk off the ends of the earth. You cease to exist."

"They don't even keep records," Silvana said. "I heard that once you're sent, even they can't find you again."

Consuelo began to weep. Madam Mukherjee unleashed one of her long, keening wails and suddenly the place was in an uproar.

"Please, please." Jatta clapped her hands, appealing to them. "This won't help matters."

"What will?" Janet Kariolainen asked.

No one seemed to know.

In the women's sleeping coach people returned to their cabins, packed their belongings, fretted, fidgeted, wandered back and forth, already looking displaced and en route. The air of uncertainty about the future and the fate of their loved ones created an atmosphere dangerously close to panic.

Wilma Shapley and Nell Blanton alternated between the chore of packing their belongings and tending to Baby Muk. There was no question of Madam Muk handling the situation herself. She was simply beyond the point of responsible action.

They kept changing the towels, soaking them in cool water and rewrapping the child in them every hour or so. They stood by his bunk fanning him with seat cushions until roughly midnight, when the fever broke. With a low, satisfied burble, the child dropped off to sleep, a faint rosy blush beginning to pinken his lips.

Jean Blaylock sprawled on her bunk. She hadn't bothered to change to pajamas. She knew they would wake them early, before light, with Sousa marches, then have them wait about for hours before some clear directive came down.

It was just past midnight, and except for the single red exit light glowing at the end of the corridor, all the other lights had gone out for the evening. A quiet had settled over the car, but it was not a quiet born of peace, but rather one of fear.

From the adjoining cabins came the sound of an occasional cough or the clearing of throats. The searchlight beam from outside cut a wide white swath across her cabin wall and moved on. The crunch of boots sounded on the gravel of the track bed below; a large dog bayed in the nearby forest. Where would she be tomorrow at this time? she wondered. Would her situation be any worse than it was here? Her passport and visa had still not been returned, although, in truth, the others by this time had also had their passports confiscated. Still, she'd been the one they'd singled out from the beginning. What recourse would she have in this new place to which she was being sent? Would it be to someplace where she knew absolutely no one? Even having Trina Van Meegrin beside her would be some sort of comfort.

She thought about her parents and Southampton and experienced a sort of not unpleasant melancholy when at last she fell off to sleep, dreaming of the big old gabled house on the beach. She could hear the roar of breakers pounding up the shore and sniff the clean, bracing stench of salt and drying seaweed at the neap tide.

It had started with a sort of sizzling sound. Dots and dashes tapping out an angry little Morse code. She heard it near her head and in her fitful sleep swiped at it, thinking it was a fly.

It went away for a while, then started again, this time somewhat more insistently. Still, she thought nothing much of it. Not enough in any event to rouse herself and have a look. There was an unpleasant dryness in her throat, and several times she coughed to relieve a tickling there.

It was the tickling that woke her and not the noise, even though the noise was a more persistent nuisance. When her eyes fluttered open she was lying on her stomach, facing away from the wall. Had she been turned toward the wall, she would have seen above her head sparks showering like fireworks, spewing out of the ventilator grate set in the cabin wall above her.

The buzzing that accompanied the sparks persisted, and as consciousness drained back into her, she was aware once more of the smell of burning rubber. The cabin had always smelled of burning rubber, but not quite like this. Tonight the smell had a suffocating pungency to it.

Her eyes had started to tear and a sudden spasm of coughing brought her bolt upright in bed. Out of the corner of her eye she glimpsed the sparks raining down on her berth, strangely gay and festive. Behind those sparks, blue and orange tongues of flame licked at the grating.

In the next moment there was a puff, followed by a blinding glare illuminating the cabin in a stark, lurid light.

It was over in fractions of a second, but it gave the impression of eons. Everything in the cabin—boxes, luggage, medications, cosmetics—all of its chaotic content stood out in bold relief. Jean's mouth opened in the shape of a scream but it was a stillborn scream that died inside her head, for in that moment there followed an explosion. Not truly an explosion, but more a loud gasp, like air swiftly evacuated from a large balloon. Something seared her face and she was aware of being warm all over.

The sparks she'd seen showering from the vent had stopped, and so had the fierce buzzing, but the tongues of flame she'd seen just behind the sparks had begun to extrude themselves like wriggling fingers between the narrow spaces in the grating. It was then she saw that her pillow was on fire. In the next moment the whole wall of the cabin was engulfed in flames.

It wasn't fire that wakened Grant Shapley. It was the shouting and all the movement outside his window. The sharp blasts of a klaxon whooped through the night. Over the ledge of the window frame, and skimming along it, Shapley could see a parade of barrack caps all streaming in one direction. Dogs barked. Guards shouted.

"What the devil is it?" Thomas moaned drowsily from the bunk above.

"Don't know. Something's up out there."

Shapley put his legs down from the berth and felt nothing beneath him but the shock of yawning space. He went down with a sickening thud.

The noise brought Thomas up and almost simultaneously out of the bunk in a single motion. Stepping down, he almost toppled over Shapley's prone form. The stamp of boots came thudding up the corridor and he could hear the loud, urgent rap of knuckles on cabin doors.

"*Von—Natoozshoo—Pozhar—*" a voice barked in gruff Russian. Knuckles rapped loudly on the cabin doors. "Outside. Everybody outside. *Pozhar—Pozhar. Vse-Na-Vyxod.*"

Thomas was stooping above Shapley, struggling to lift him from the floor. The Professor's arms were raised above his head as though he were getting out of a sweater, while Thomas tried lifting him from beneath the armpits. Each time he managed to get him halfway up, the right leg, twitching uncontrollably, went out from under him, and down he'd go again. It was like trying to lift deadweight.

"What's the matter with your leg?" Thomas cried.

"It's a long story," Shapley gasped. "Was he saying something about a fire?"

"Right—we'd better get the hell out of this. Here . . . put your arm round my shoulder."

"You'd better go without me, Tony," Shapley said.

"The hell with that," Thomas fumed. "You're going with me. Lift, for Christ's sake, will you?"

Several cabins down, Stern knew something was wrong but had no idea what. Outside his window he had a perfect view of the traffic streaming up and down the track. For some odd reason, he assumed it had something to do with the engine.

The noise outside his door was frightful. Throwing his trousers and shoes on, he shot his door back and stepped out into the corridor. It was jammed with people being herded toward the exits by the guards. A dense, choking smoke curled above the hectic scene.

Fully one-half of one full side of the women's coach was already engulfed in flames. Isabel and Silvana stood outside their cabin in robes. The matrons and guards were moving up and down the corridor, swinging doors open and shouting at the occupants inside to get out. Above the din inside the car and the frantic bursts of the klaxon outside, they could hear the terrified shrieks of Madam Mukherjee as a pair of motor-rifle guards on either side of her yanked and dragged her toward an exit. Another guard followed with Baby Muk swaddled in a blanket yowling at the top of his lungs.

Two guards came right after, struggling beneath the girth of Myra Keck, still half-asleep and shadowboxing with the smoke before her.

"Let's get out of here," Silvana said, coughing. She grabbed Isabel's arm.

"You go. I must find my mother and sister."

"Your sister's out. I saw them take her with Madam Muk."

"I have to find my mother."

"She's probably out already. Come. Come now . . ." Silvana gaped as flames leapt out of what was once their cabin. "Come. For God's sake, let's go." She started to tow Isabel along behind her.

Their cabin was located roughly a quarter of the way down the length of the car. But with the smoke and heat and people all groping their way up the aisle at once, the red exit light above the door seemed light-years away.

Silvana pushed toward the exit, shouting over her shoulder, coughing furiously, "I wonder if Sonia . . ." She turned to look back at Isabel, but she was no longer there. She'd vanished like a phantom into the swirling brown smoke behind them.

Isabel had slipped cleanly away. In all the smoke and confusion, neither the guards nor the matrons, nor any of the straggling passengers in the rear of the coach, had seen her.

However, Frau Kunkel, plowing her way up the corridor, flailing her arms against the smoke and the impediment of lagging bodies, spotted her at once. "Don't go that way, for heaven's sake," she coughed. "The rear exit is locked."

"My mother. Have you seen my mother?"

If she answered, Isabel hadn't heard it. By that time Frau Kunkel had moved off into the smoke-swirling distances.

Isabel stood now, roughly three-quarters of the way down the length of the car, eyes burning and gasping for air. Under normal circumstances she knew precisely the location of the cabin shared by her mother and Mrs. Keck. But in smoke and whirling darkness, she'd lost her bearings completely. She had no idea where she stood in relation to both exits of the train, and now she'd been informed that the rear exit, as a routine security measure, had been locked for the evening. She knew it couldn't be opened from the inside.

"Mama . . . Mamacita." She started to run randomly from one cabin to the next. "Mama . . . Donde está?"

The heat was rapidly approaching the level of the intolerable. Loud cracking sounds rent the scorched air. She imagined it was rifle shot outside and had no way of knowing it was the sound of windows exploding from the heat.

When she'd gone down almost to the locked end of the car, and found no sign of her mother, she whirled and stared around wildly. The roof over her head had started to buckle and crack. Shortly that too would go up in flames. If she was to get out at all, she knew she must do so now.

"Mama. Mamacita. Por Dios mío. I'm looking for you."

She started back up, stopping to peer into each cabin, using her arms to shield her face from the glare and blinding heat.

"Mierda," she muttered. *"Que estúpido."* How did she know her mother was even still on the train? And what of her father and sister? For all she knew, the guards had already come by and taken them off. *"Mama, Mamacita."* She was shouting and crying and coughing at the same time, flying up the corridor like some demonic, obsessed creature.

It seemed to her she'd hit each of the thirteen compartments. She knew full well that in that light and with that visibility, it would have been entirely possible to have looked into a cabin and failed to see anything, particularly a small, frightened figure cringing there inside.

"Mama," she kept crying out, her hopes rapidly dwindling. Then, roughly halfway back up the corridor, with the klaxon whooping frantically outside, she heard something like a faint, uncomplaining cry. "Isabel? Isabel?" It came like that, in the form of a question.

There seemed no fear to it, no impatience. Just a quiet undemanding acknowledgment of a presence there, as if whoever it was didn't care to make any special fuss about it.

She was sitting, actually sitting up, in one of the cabins, her hands folded in her lap. Fortunately, the cabin she was in was not as far gone in flames as some of the others. She had her purse and a small package beside her, as if she were prepared to go shopping.

Isabel flung herself on her mother's neck. "Mama, for God's sake—what are you doing?"

"I'm waiting for Myra. I'm sure they'll be here for her any moment."

Isabel rolled her eyes skyward and made a strange growling sound in her throat. "For God's sake, forget Mrs. Keck. She's fine. They took her off a couple of minutes ago."

The señora seemed a bit miffed. "Are you sure?"

"Of course I'm sure. *Dios mío*—We've got to get out of here. Can you walk?"

The question further irritated the señora. "Certainly I can walk. What's the matter with you?"

Isabel gently hauled her mother to her feet. "Take my hand, dear. It's a bit hot further up front." Snatching a towel that had been draped over a chair, she wound it round her mother's head. "Cover your face with this. There's a lot of smoke. We'll be fine. Now come."

Oh God. Were they going to die here now, in this fire? The thought crossed Isabel's mind as a distinct possibility. "How dumb. How stupid," she muttered to herself. "Whoever, whatever you are up there—help me to bring us to those stupid little red lights flickering up there by the door."

She felt a docile, trusting, almost childlike hand, cool as marble, slip inside her palm, and they were off, inching and groping their way through the scorched air.

As Stern stepped down off the train, his immediate impression was that of a man arriving late at some gala event. There was something oddly festive about it. He looked around to see if there was anyone he recognized. To his left, one hundred yards or so, the women's coach was completely engulfed in flames. It made a grand bonfire. Sparks crackling and showering upward drenched the sky above in a lurid orange. The compound outside was jammed with hundreds of people—soldiers, guards, detainees, personnel from the train—all swarming about some vague circle, one indistinguishable from the other. A small convoy of trucks streamed in and out of the single exit, blaring horns at each other.

There appeared to be no coordinated effort to stanch the fire. For one thing, there wasn't water enough, or the appropriate pumping apparatus to bring water up in sufficient quantities. If they'd sent for fire-fighting equipment, it was as yet nowhere in evidence. Possibly it had bogged down on the narrow substandard dirt road leading out from the city to the train site.

As of that moment they were carrying buckets of water from the bathhouse to the train. But they had not more than a half-dozen buckets, so the quantity of water and the speed of delivery to the fire site was hopelessly inadequate to the task.

The flames had started to spread from the sleeping car to the day coach. More trucks entered the compound. More soldiers poured out of them. The klaxon continued to whoop. An enterprising young officer had come up with the idea of starting a bucket brigade extending from the pond up to the train. There were more than enough hands about to man the brigade, but unfortunately, nowhere near enough buckets. That didn't appear to stop anyone. At once, fifty or so motor-rifle troops went thrashing off into the woods to establish the line. In the meantime, an urgent call went out for more buckets.

The guards and matrons and porters were making an effort to segregate the passengers from the military personnel. But when the call went out for hands to man the bucket brigade, passengers were conscripted as well. After that, whatever semblance of order had existed before vanished entirely. Orders issued by one set of officers were quickly countermanded by another. The place surrendered to chaos.

Amid the welter of confusion among the hostages, there was a general sense of relief, almost a spiteful joy. There was downright laughter, as if some god were wreaking just vengeance on their captors. The Mukherjees were reunited, all of them in sobbing, laughing embraces. The Van Meegrins clung together like a pair of lost waifs who'd found one another again. Unable to spot

Nell anywhere in the confusion, Paul Blanton went bolting through the compound, wild-eyed, collaring people to ask if they'd seen her. He'd already imagined the very worst when at last he found her with the Shapleys, standing outside the dining car, watching in childlike wonder the soldiers stamping around on the roof, dousing it with buckets of water to keep it cool.

In all of that smoke and heat, Thomas went slouching about in his silk lounging robe, puffing on one of his Balkan Sobranies. Jatta Palmunan rushed up to him, slightly frantic. "Is everyone out? Did you see everyone? Who are we missing? I must do a count."

She kept raking her hands through her hair until he realized that her hair was burning—not actually burning, but smoldering, and not fully aware of the fact, but conscious of discomfort, she was trying to extinguish it. Her brows had been badly singed. "I can't seem to find Miss Gonzaga or her mother." Her voice was almost plaintive.

In the space of a second, Thomas had whipped off his robe and smothered her burning hair in it. Caught unaware, she had not the slightest idea what he was trying to do. She panicked, striking out at him with her fists, and they went staggering about in a curious little apache dance with people scarcely noticing them. Suddenly it dawned on her that he was trying to help, not hurt her. Afterward, when he was certain her hair was no longer burning, they stood there gasping and panting at one another. "Who was it you said you couldn't find?"

"Miss Gonzaga and her mother."

"Isabel?"

"Yes."

"Good God," Thomas groaned, and in the next minute started back toward the train.

There was a loud rending noise, then a crash, followed by the collapse of the outer wall of the women's coach. A sheet of sparks like fiery comets roared upward into the orange sky. Those standing nearby fell backward before the wall of oven heat pressing outward.

The bucket brigade had abandoned all hope of saving the women's coach and had now moved down to the day coach in a frantic effort to prevent that, too, from going up.

Stern found himself pressed up against the wire fence on the outer edge of the storm's eye like a spectator peering in. Oddly, he felt little identification at all with the general spirit of joy and relief. If anything, he felt an alienation from it that bordered on contempt.

He was leaning almost casually against the fence. Its barbs, like a series of small, exquisite prickings, pierced his back. His hands dangled at his sides and he imagined that if anyone in all that welter of confusion were looking at him just then, no doubt he struck a pretty foolish figure, as though he might be stunned or simpleminded, or possibly deranged. Why was he not reacting as the others were? Why was he not part of the communal effort to extinguish the fire that threatened them all? Why was he not demonstrating some sort of human emotion?

Out of the corner of his eye he was aware of a movement nearby. It was sudden and furtive. Startled, he turned and failed to recognize at once the tall stooped figure of Gonzaga only two or three feet beyond him.

His hair was disheveled and he wore his robe. His back to the fire, he gazed at Stern, an ambiguous little smile playing about his lips. Stern took a step toward him, then stopped short, momentarily puzzled. It was the smile, of course, vacant and unfocused, yet oddly suggestive, that brought Stern up sharply. He moved toward him again. In that eerie glow of tower lights and flames, he had the distinct impression that the old man not only didn't recognize him, but hadn't the faintest idea of where he was.

"Señor Gonzaga." Stern inched cautiously forward, as though creeping up on a rare butterfly. "Are you all right?" He had to shout over the roar of the fire and the klaxons.

The old man smiled sweetly by way of reply.

"It's me. Peter Stern." He tugged him gently by the sleeve as if rousing someone who'd been dozing.

The old man nodded. *"Sí, Peter Stern. Por seguro."*

But still he didn't appear to really know him. In the next moment he turned. It was more of a stiff, wobbly spin in which an arm flew up and he was then facing the barbed wire looking outward. He looked at Stern again and smiled that sweetly luminous smile, looking straight ahead through the wire and nodding his head.

Stern's uneasiness increased. "What is it?"

Gonzaga's eyes glinted wickedly. He nodded toward the fence again, that slow, almost ceremonial nod, fraught with some obvious significance that managed to elude Stern entirely.

Stern took his arm with the intention of leading him back toward the compound. But as he started to pull him gently, the old man yanked his arm back.

"Look." Gonzaga pointed with a long, tremulous finger through the fence. Just then a shaft of fire rocketed skyward behind them. It made a great hissing sound. Stern ducked automatically, but the old man never flinched. "Look," he said more urgently, his gray tousled head shaking. "Look."

Stern's eye followed the crooked, trembling finger back to the fence. They were standing no more than twenty feet or so from the front gates. Suddenly Stern saw what had so agitated the old man. Where the trucks had been streaming in and out, the gates hung open, and the little sentry box, always occupied by an armed guard, now stood empty and unattended.

When he turned back to Gonzaga, the old man was smiling and nodding. His eyes seemed to say: "You understand now?"

Stern was not the sort of man to whom thoughts of escape from a penal institution would normally occur. He was simply not cut from that sort of cloth.

Faced with such a romantic alternative, he would instinctively ask a number of practical questions with the express intention of discouraging anything foolish. He had no idea how far it was to the Finnish border, or how, in fact, if presented with the opportunity, one would get there. Once there, one would doubtless encounter barriers and border guards with big, noisy, highly dangerous guns. Then, too, if one were so foolish as to entertain the thought of flight, there was always the image of Keith Wales, his bandaged head and wired jaw, to give one serious pause.

"Come." Gonzaga laughed softly and started to pull Stern toward the open gate.

"Wait a minute." Stern dug his feet into the earth, his eyes swarming up the wooden tower where a guard, distant and impersonal, stood playing the searchlight over the fire. Just across the way, the big T54 tank stood, bathed in the stark white glare of its cupola lights. None of its crew appeared to be anywhere about.

In another moment Stern found himself standing with Gonzaga at the open gate just inside the wire. Gonzaga stood legs wide apart in his robe and slippers, the robe unbelted and open, drifting out behind him. "You see? You see?"

Stern glanced uneasily over his shoulder. But in truth, all he was aware of that moment was the danger of their standing by the open gate with its unguarded sentry box. That alone was sufficient cause to get them shot by some overzealous guard, certain they were about to make a break.

"Go," Gonzaga said.

"You must be mad."

They were standing just beneath the klaxon, and the noise level was intolerable. "Look. Look," Gonzaga shouted. Once again he was pointing with his crooked, trembling finger. Suddenly he seized Stern by the arm and spun him sharply about. "Look."

The rotation had moved him just outside the gate. Momentarily dazed, Stern tried to scramble back in, convinced he was about to be shot on the spot. But Gonzaga blocked the way. Then he saw the boy.

Standing about twenty feet off, he seemed to have materialized out of the forest, a small wavering figure, tentative and spectral. He waited there with an air of expectancy, like a spooked deer, ears pricked forward, ready to bolt.

Something resembling a direct line instantly established itself between Stern and Buddy Kariolainen. It was as though they were tethered together by some invisible cord. The boy, regarding him quizzically, the eyes wide with fear, appeared to beckon him.

Stern took an involuntary step forward, then, losing courage, half-turned and started back. But Gonzaga was just behind him, out the gate, still barring his way.

Another shaft of fire rocketed skyward from the roof of the dining car. There was a deafening roar. Large tanks of propane gas used for the stoves inside the galley had started to explode. The sky above the train went from a deep orange to a pale roseate hue while at the very top of the shaft a huge plume of fiery dendrites streamed down with the dreamy languid grace of sediment falling through water.

There was a burst of shouts and screams. Sirens wailed from trucks, undoubtedly belated fire-fighting equipment, streaming toward the site from the dirt road behind them.

"Go, for God's sake. Go." Gonzaga placed his palms against Stern's chest and shoved. Stern stumbled backward, then had another glimpse of the boy waiting a short way down the road. He swallowed, looked around once more with an air of baleful resignation. Against his own better instincts, his legs started to move away from the compound. At that point, it was all beyond his control. He was moving quickly, a spirited jog, when he became aware of someone moving behind him. Turning, he nearly stumbled as the old man came right up at his heel, nearly colliding with him. "What the hell do you think you're doing?"

Gonzaga winked and flashed his naughty grin. "I'm coming with you."

"My heart was throbbing merrily and my wet hands were trembling. Moreover, my matches were wet . . ."

Asawa sat cross-legged in a lotus position in the dirt near the fence. His head rolled from side to side. He watched the flames consume what remained of the sleeping coach and appeared to be laughing. The words poured effortlessly through his head, falling from his lips beneath his breath, incantatory in effect. By that time the fire fighters had been able to establish a makeshift water-pumping operation up from the pond. Several figures were now staggering about up on the roof of the day coach, playing a weakish stream of water over the car top. Inside the coach, flames licked behind the windows with festive gaiety. The heat on the roof was intense. No sooner had the water sluicing down from the hoses hit it than geysers of smoke corkscrewed violently upward into the air.

The mere recitation of the words now filled Asawa with an intoxicating sense of power. As he recited he rolled his head and rocked back and forth against the wire. Periodically he would laugh. The sound would emerge from somewhere deep within him, a short, violent growl of mirth, ending with a strange abruptness.

He was oblivious of the turmoil going on about him. It was just the fire dancing before his ecstatic gaze that held him transfixed.

He staggered to his feet. The klaxon booming through the forest night roared distantly in his head. Although he was standing almost directly beneath it, with flames roaring and people swarming all about him, he had managed to retire to some interior region of himself, a place of polar tranquillity, icy cold and infinitely silent.

He could not describe the intoxicating sense of power that had come over him. All he knew was that it brought with it the great calm of victory. It was a sense of completion that approached bliss. Within those shafts of smoke it seemed to him he glimpsed the lineaments of his father's face. It made him want to scream with joy. He wished his father could have been there to share his triumph.

Long after they could no longer hear the roaring crackle of the fire, they could still look back and see the great rosy glow of light drenching the sky above the treetops.

They had been under way thirty minutes or so, going straight due west, making good headway through the forest. Stern had opted to stay as close to the train tracks as possible, keeping them as a guide always on his right, while still sticking to the cover of the woods. He knew that as morning came on and the sky grew gradually lighter, they would have to move deeper into the forest. The chance of encountering guards or railway workers, he knew, was far greater in the vicinity of the tracks than farther off in the brush. But for the time being, at least until he was certain of his bearings, they would stick close to the tracks.

They trudged along, barely speaking, Buddy Kariolainen up ahead with Stern and old Gonzaga following along behind. Stern's chief concern now was the old man. He knew the border to be roughly ten kilometers away. He judged they'd already gone about a mile. The old man would have to do five or six more before they'd see the border. The terrain was rough, but thankfully not hilly. So far, Gonzaga had managed to keep up.

It seemed doubtful that he could continue to do so. At every moment, Stern kept expecting to hear behind them the noise of pursuit, trees and branches cracking, the shout of guards, and dogs barking. But there was none of that. In the great encircling dark of night, all they could hear were the crickets, the hoot of owls, and the occasional flap of nightjar wings shuttling through the branches. They plodded on unspeaking, through the dark, each preoccupied with the burden of his own solitary ordeal.

Young Buddy, scouting ten feet up ahead, pushed branches aside, warned them of boulders and other obstacles and when the ground underfoot was uncertain. Ever since they'd started out, he'd been setting the pace. But as the night wore on, the pace had become grueling for Stern, not to mention what it must have been for Gonzaga. Neither of them could be expected to keep up with the boy, and Stern, thinking ahead, was already scheduling a rest period within the next hour. By then it was almost three A.M., and sunrise came early in those latitudes.

Stern still had no idea of where the boy had been for the past several days. The costume he wore provided some information. The rail worker's jacket, the baggy outsize trousers, the big floppy unlaced shoes that kept slipping off his bare feet, suggested that he'd found patrons on the train. During the remainder of the night Stern was to learn bit by bit the story of the Finnish motormen and the boy's two days and nights hidden in an engine tender. He'd been well cared for and was obviously in good health. But harboring him had become a source of contention between the two Finns. They'd started to quarrel. One of them, worried about implicating himself in an escape attempt, was all for turning the boy back over to the Russians. The other, a fearless and peppery man who'd lost cousins and brothers in the last Soviet invasion, would sooner die than return an escapee. Fortunately, the latter was a giant of a man, a persuasive argument in itself, and so, for the time being at least, the boy was safe. Then came the fire. A stroke of fantastic luck. They woke the boy, dressed him in odds and ends, then pushed him out the cab door and pointed him toward the border. By that time even the Finn who'd balked at concealing the boy was assisting in the escape.

When Buddy had finished recounting this story to Stern and the old man, he anxiously asked if they'd heard anything of the whereabouts of his father. Stern said they hadn't. The boy stared hard at the ground for a moment, and then, with no further discussion, the three of them turned grimly back to the trek ahead.

It was Stern's intention to cover as much ground as they could before sunrise. With the first crack of dawn, he was certain search parties and helicopters would be out scouring the woods between the train and the border. If they could make the border before sunrise, the better their chances were of making it across. Failing that, Stern's plan was to lay over in the forest for the day and start out again that evening under cover of dark.

"Are you all right?" Stern inquired of the old man over his shoulder.

"I am well," he replied, but there was a resigned, breathless quality to his voice.

Stern turned. It was a moonless night and there was little light. He could barely make out the features, but he sensed something. Up ahead, the boy, too, had stopped and was watching them.

Gonzaga had started out in the most improbable costume for a night trek through the forest—a pale blue robe thrown over pajamas and a pair of terry-cloth backless slippers that kept flopping off his feet as he tried to plow through the mud and prickly bushes. In that pitchy blackness, a ghostly bluish glow emanated from the robe. From where he stood, Stern could hear the old man's hoarse, rapid breathing. Above the breathing he could hear a faint mysterious clicking sound that he was at a loss to identify. Only later did he realize it was the sound of Gonzaga's dental plate chattering.

"Look, I'm bushed." Stern tried to sound apologetic. "If it's okay with you, I'd just as soon stop here awhile."

Even in that impenetrable dark, Stern could see the tall, lanky figure appear to stiffen. "We don't stop now. They'll be after us soon as it's light."

Stern was well aware of that, but he saw no way of going on with the old man in that condition.

"I'm very sorry, but I don't think you're in any state—"

"Kindly disregard my state. We'll go on now."

Gonzaga started forward with a lurching motion; then, as he came abreast of Stern, he teetered. Stern caught him just as he was going down, taking the full brunt of the old man's weight as it sagged against him.

"We'll go on now," Gonzaga said, pulling back his shoulders, straightening his robe, recovering dignity.

"Look, really . . ." Stern protested.

"I said we will go on." This time the message was brusque to the point of rudeness. There seemed little point in arguing. Gonzaga, Stern knew, would go down in his own time and of his own accord. And perhaps that would be better for everyone.

They started out anew, but at a deliberately slower pace. This time the boy had the perspicacity to see that the effort had already taken its toll not only on the old man but on Stern as well.

Stern reached up to take Gonzaga's arm, but the old man snatched it back, rejecting any offer of assistance. Stern said nothing but merely moved on until once more they had settled back into the grim, relentless drive for the border. There was no talk, just the steady sound of hard, extended effort—panting and sighs—as they started up a long but shallow acclivity.

At one point Stern glimpsed lights far off to the right and heard what he thought to be voices. He imagined they'd strayed too close to the rail line and had possibly stumbled on one of the rail workers' sheds.

They veered sharply left and soon found themselves laboring up another long slope that seemed to rise to the top of the forest. It was slightly past three A.M. when they struggled over the crest of it and broke out into a wide treeless clearing. The air had grown chill. Vapor curled from their lips as they clambered over the top and waded through the tall damp grass.

The sky above them was immense. Big stars hung in the trees between the branches. Smaller ones were strewn across the skies like daisies in a summer field. The air, redolent of clover and hay, was as sweet as anything Stern had ever smelled in a Missouri summer night. It was a curious sight, the three of them standing there, torn, bedraggled, studded with burrs, casting about like lost wanderers trying to regain their bearings.

When they'd crossed the clearing and started to move back into the cover of trees, Stern was suddenly aware that Gonzaga was trailing badly behind. He doubled back to get him.

"Are you okay?"

"Fine," the old man gasped, and rocked slightly on his feet.

"Are you sure?"

"Of course I'm sure." He stumbled forward, kicking a foot out. The torn muddy slipper attached to the end of it arched up and outward in a shadowy curve into the brush ahead.

The old man muttered something and slipped wearily to his knee, slumping there like a floored pugilist waiting for the strength to get back on his feet.

"We're stopping here," Stern said.

"I say no."

"You can't go on. We're tired too."

"Must go on," Gonzaga gasped, and tried to rise.

Stern was adamant. "You're shivering. You're exhausted. We'll all do better with a rest now. Buddy, go see if you can't find Señor Gonzaga's slipper."

The old man sighed and sank back into the tall grass, which seemed to close like water over his head. Stern knelt beside him. In the light of that nearly treeless space Stern could see the mud and coagulated blood caked on his foot and running in streaks above the ankle. "How do you expect to walk barefoot on that?"

Gonzaga sprawled backward on the grass, kicking his legs, exasperated and for the moment defeated. "We don't stop now. They'll be after us."

"They'll be after us whether we stop or not. What's the difference?"

The old man was right, of course, but there was absolutely no way of continuing in his present state. He was utterly exhausted, going on sheer nerves alone.

"It's just another mile or so," Gonzaga pleaded.

Stern said nothing, but according to his own calculations, they'd been under way possibly two and a half hours. If they were lucky, they'd covered three miles. That left another three or four to the border, and who knew what they might encounter there? More guards, more watchtowers. More barbed wire. Surely by this time their absence had been discovered. Still, from all outward signs, it seemed no one was yet tracking them. But that was scarcely a problem for the Russians. All they need do was call ahead to the border with instructions to dispatch an additional company or two of motor-rifle guards to bolster patrols there. Whatever lay ahead for them was not terribly promising. But there was no question now of turning back.

A crunch of twigs and a rustle of bushes brought Stern sharply about. Buddy Kariolainen stepped out of the darkness and started toward them. He was holding up the slipper.

"Good lad," Gonzaga said, snatching it back and jamming it onto his foot, wincing as he did so. Again he tried scrambling back up. This time Stern pushed him down and pinned him there.

"Get off me." Gonzaga thrashed back and forth.

"No."

The boy hovered in the background, watching them silently.

"I'll shout at the top of my lungs."

"Go right ahead," said Stern, never believing for a moment he would. Sure enough, there was a shout, or rather just the beginnings of one. It started loud and clear until Stern clapped a hand over the old man's mouth, cutting it off abruptly in a strangled yawp.

"Are you crazy?"

"We must keep going."

"You'll die. Do you want to die?"

"Not in this godforsaken pisshole of a country. Get off me, you bastard. Get off."

Stern still crouched above him, pinning him to the earth.

"I'll scream. I swear it. You'd better get off me."

Stern knew from the tone of those words that he was beaten. They could not risk another one of those piercing shouts.

Stern sighed and rose to his feet. "Okay, you win."

He and the boy hauled the old man to his feet, dusting him off.

Gonzaga pushed their hands away, lunging ahead so suddenly that the other two had to scramble after him just to keep up. He went two or three steps, made a funny wobbling motion, and went down again on his knee.

"You see?" Stern said. He hauled the old man up by his arm and wound it across his shoulder. "Now, hang on."

This time Gonzaga did not quarrel.

From that point on things grew truly grim. It was not the ten kilometers, surely. Just over six miles is hardly epic distance. It was rather the terrain—the mixture of tall trees and low gorse, the thorns and nettles that lashed out at them when they passed and clawed at their clothing. And then the mud—it sucked them down as they passed over it, so that each step involved kicking out one foot while extracting the other. Then, too, there were the hills, never steep but interminably long, so that marching up each one became its own passion play.

Stern was not an athletic man; not a man in outstanding physical shape. Just a fiftyish sort of man given to good dining and mostly sedentary pleasures, now suddenly saddled with the responsibility of seeing to a man a quarter of a century older and a youth who might be his own grandchild.

Gonzaga was not unaware of the burden he posed. It was not that he'd given up and let himself be carried. Every agonizing step of the way he made his own contribution. He pushed and stumbled; he leaned out in such a way as to relieve some of the weight from Stern's back, and in so doing, took more of it onto his own wobbly legs and bleeding feet.

The boy, on the other hand, was indefatigable. Like the hound straining after the quarry, he was always far ahead of the hunters, visibly impatient with the physical limitations of his elders.

Several times, coming back, he'd find them both leaning against a tree, attached to each other, spent and gasping. He'd squat beside them on his haunches, clownish in his floppy outsize clothes, waiting for them to revive.

Near four A.M., with the first hint of gray marbling the evening sky, it seemed Gonzaga could go no further. He dropped to his knees. "Leave me here. I'll rest a bit, then follow."

But now it was Stern who wouldn't stop. He was beyond caring. Together with the boy, he hauled the old man up and started again.

Stern had lost all sense of time. He no longer had any recollection of how long they'd been going or how many miles they'd covered. There was no certainty they were still heading west. Several times during the course of the night large obstacles—tall rocky outgrowths, and once a fairly good-sized lake, forced them to take wide detours, then attempt to correct their course.

It was only when the sky at their backs started to lighten that Stern knew they were still holding a westerly course. As he moved forward, dragging the weight of old Gonzaga across his back, each step became a painful little odyssey all its own. And still, to his uneasy surprise, there was no sign of pursuit. Each moment he kept expecting to hear the dread sound of barking dogs and shouting guards ringing across the forest behind them. But he heard nothing. The silence was ominous.

With the coming dawn the abundant stars appeared to twinkle more brightly in the pale blue vault of sky. Stern had long passed the point where he was aware of the depth of his own exhaustion. Seeking release from the bone-weary ache of his body, his mind wandered. He was back in New York, in a restaurant. He and Constance were having dinner with friends. It was a Chinese restaurant over on the East Side. One of his favorite haunts. Sampans plying the Yangtze glided across a silvery mural. Pagoda scenes stenciled on blue-white porcelain; sauce-stained lids from aluminum salvers sitting awry like crooked party hats; empty bottles of Tsing-dao; teacups. Chopsticks. Rumpled napery spattered with plum sauce. Half-eaten sherbets melting in tulip cups. Saucers littered with paper fortunes. Gossip and small talk. Quiet laughter. The comfort of old habits, like old friends, grown more dear through constant use.

Why had they quarreled? Where had all that started? Was it in the beginning, or rather imperceptibly at a point somewhere midway, from which time it never truly stopped again? They had stuck together thirty years—an eternity of sorts in the Golden Age of the Ephemeral. Was it after the children had left and Constance, after a lifetime of making a home for others, grasped for some measure of fulfillment in a workaday world?

Surely he could not begrudge her the joy of reengagement she felt. But while she was in the process of starting in anew, he had just begun to detach himself from professional life, and it was there they might have reached the bifurcation in the road.

All this came back to him in the wood and stony silence of a Russian forest, five thousand miles distant from the setting of the actual drama. Over and over again he could play it in his head with startling powers of recall—each argument, the traded insults, once uttered, never retrievable, no matter how trivial the source of the insult.

Gonzaga had fallen asleep on his shoulder but his legs still moved mechanically like those of a somnambulist. He mumbled as if barely conscious and dribbled saliva onto Stern's badly chafed neck. The words sounded Spanish to Stern, and while he couldn't understand them, the single one he seemed to hear repeated with striking frequency was *patria*.

Stern shifted his burden to the other shoulder and, head down, plodded forward. All the while the sky had been lightening behind them. By 4:45 A.M., long ribands of rose and lemon streaked the eastern sky. Ahead of them the forest was still gray and murky. Rags of mist clung to the lower branches of the big pine and birch. The visibility was poor.

The boy kept doubling back, looking at them with an air of exasperation. He wanted to make time. He couldn't understand why these fellows, even granted their advanced years, couldn't do a bit better. By himself, he could have been at the border hours ago.

"Keep going." Stern waved feebly at him. He was so fagged he could barely see the small querulous figure hovering there in the trees. "We're right behind you. Keep going."

It was just as the boy turned again and bolted that he heard it. It came at him over great distances, so faint as to be ambiguous. On his befogged, wandering mind a sort of dull rattling sound had started to register. It seemed to follow them, pausing occasionally for several moments, then resuming again. During the pauses, Stern came to believe that the noise was all his imagination.

Shortly the sounds would resume, and each time they did, they were somewhat louder and came with greater insistence. He had no idea what it was. Although at some deeper, more subliminal level, he knew precisely what it was. The overall effect of that reluctant awareness was to somehow increase his efficiency—make him move faster.

Gonzaga's legs had by then ceased to carry him. They had grown rubbery and no longer made any pretense of functioning. Stern was now carrying, or rather dragging the man, one agonizing foot at a time.

They plugged on in that fashion for the next half-hour or so, all the while that unearthly rattling noise appeared to gain on them. Stern watched the boy for signs that he too heard it. But if he did, he gave no indication. As for the old man, it was doubtful that at that point he heard anything.

At last the sun broke through the dark trailing clouds ahead, sending a shaft of light through the canopy of the forest. There was still a great deal of mist about, curling upward like vapor from the boggy earth. Though an impediment to their progress, it was also a blessing. As long as the mist was there, it provided cover of a sort. But soon the sun would burn it off, and then, Stern knew, the helicopters would fill the sky, flying low, scouring the woods beneath them.

All of Stern's remaining energy was now concentrated on reaching the border. By dint of mental effort, he'd been able to put that fiendish clanking sound behind him. The moment his concentration flagged, however, the noise came flowing back with the annoying persistence of a buzzing fly. By then he had no illusions left as to the source of it.

As an infantry captain in Germany after the war, he'd heard enough such sounds to know a tank when he heard one. Hearing the big American tanks thrashing about in the frozen forests on maneuvers at night could make the blood run cold. It was a fiendish, unearthly sound. On hearing one again in this primeval glade, his visceral reactions were precisely the same. Age had not taught him to fear less. It was an awful sound. In a flash, his mind could see an orange shower of rockets in the sky and hear the growl and pummel of mortars, as if, after three decades, it was all happening again.

In the past ten minutes the noises behind them had grown alarmingly louder. There seemed to be no more pauses. Stern imagined, too, that he could hear the groan and cracking of trees going down and the earth being chewed up. It had the awful sound of something being eaten alive.

What Stern felt at that moment was hard to define. He'd reached a point of exhaustion by then that expressed itself in the form of a curious exhilaration, as if prolonged physical exertion had somehow overoxygenated his brain. He felt strangely giddy. The laughter which had started low began to rise within him to great rollicking hoots. The salt of sweat streaming down his forehead burned his eyes and, plowing forward, he laughed a hearty, therapeutic laugh.

The boy up ahead glanced back at him uneasily. The noise of laughter and the bodily shaking attending it roused Gonzaga. "Are we there?" he mumbled. His head lolled on Stern's shoulder.

"Just a bit farther," Stern gasped, and heaved the old man a bit higher on his shoulder. Just then he saw Buddy waving frantically up ahead, his eyes flashing wildly.

"A fence. A fence," he cried.

Bleary-eyed, Stern looked up and dimly comprehended. "Where?"

"Up ahead. Right through there." Buddy pointed excitedly at a faint light that seemed to glow from behind a tall bush.

Even then, Stern was dubious. He stumbled forward, the old man glued to his back. "Any sign of guards?"

"No one. There's no one."

Stern wavered there, uncertain, disbelieving. "Let's have a look." He set the old man down in a thicket, his back propped against a tree. "Señor Gonzaga ..." He slapped his cheek gently till his eyes fluttered open. "Señor Gonzaga. Do you hear me?"

Gonzaga's jaw hung slack, but his eyes were strangely alert.

"Listen," Stern rushed on breathlessly. "It looks like we may have reached the border. I'm going ahead with the boy to look around. I'm leaving you for a minute, but I'll be right back."

The old man nodded, waving a limp benediction at them. They turned and thrashed off up ahead.

By then the noise of the tank behind them was distinct and unmistakable. Just from the rattle of its treads, Stern could tell it was moving quickly, probably ten miles an hour or better. They, on the other hand, would have been lucky to be making two.

The boy by that time could hear it also, and like young people of that age, he had little talent for self-deception. "Is that the tank, Mr. Stern?"

"I'm afraid it is."

They rounded a curve in what appeared to be a footpath, then pushed through a final fringe of thickets and stepped cautiously out into a clearing. Up ahead Stern could see the morning sky. Framed against it, stretching north and south as far as the eye could see, was a thirteen-foot barbed-wire fence. Like the fence at the train site, at its very top was an additional two-foot apron of coiled tin stripping, honed sharp as razor blades and canted inward.

The boy started for it but Stern yanked him back. They stood there awhile, crouching on the fringe of the thickets, craning their necks left and right. If Stern was expecting a patrol then, he didn't get one. But off to the right, nailed to the fence, he saw a sign. It wasn't all that far off, still the size of the letters made it impossible for him to read.

"Can you read that? Is it in Russian?" he asked the boy.

Buddy rose to a crouching position and squinted at the sign. "Can't tell. Letters are too small."

"Okay," Stern said. "Follow me. Crawl on your belly. Understand?"

The boy nodded, and together, Stern leading, they proceeded to inch their way out into the clearing.

Beyond the fence Stern had a glimpse of meadow and open fields. On the other side of that fence was Finland and freedom. Standing between them, obstructing the way, was that thirteen feet of wire, appearing aggravatingly slight and insubstantial. It gave the impression one might walk right through it, like a cobweb. But the barbs on it were razor-sharp and the steel-drum peelings coiled in loops at the top could cut through flesh like a meat slicer. On the other side of the fence a ditch extended the full length of the wire. The reasons for it were not immediately apparent.

Beyond the wire, Finland stretched lush and verdant, the Free World so tantalizingly close. With ease Stern could toss a rock over the fence—a rock from Russia into freedom. Yet he could imagine no way that he himself could follow that rock.

The distance between the edge of the forest and the fence was a narrow dirt selvage, possibly six, seven feet, no more. Enough for foot patrols certainly, and even for a small truck to travel up and down. Midway across, he could finally read the sign. It was one of those typical border signs in multiple languages: "ACHTUNG. REGARDEZ. ATTENTION. BORDER CROSSING. PASSAGE WITHOUT AUTHORIZATION STRICTLY FORBIDDEN. TRESPASSERS WILL BE PROSECUTED."

Beneath that, in larger letters in the same languages: "CAUTION. HIGH TENSION. 75,000 VOLTS. ALL UNAUTHORIZED PERSONS STRICTLY FORBIDDEN."

The boy crawled back to the fringe of forest. Stern still lay prone, straddling the path with his body, eyes searching the wire for some possible way over, some point of vulnerability that might be penetrated.

When he came back, the boy was waiting for him, crouched in the thickets, his body taut with fright.

"What is it?" Stern asked.

The boy cocked his head rearward. It was the clanking again, this time louder and closer. Stern estimated the tank to be just about within the immediate vicinity. Its engines whined. The cracking of trees in its path made a fearful racket.

Stern started up in a half-crouch. "Come on," he said, thrashing off into the woods in the direction in which Gonzaga lay. When they reached the place, there was no sign of him.

They stood there baffled, beginning to doubt they'd returned to the same spot where they'd left him. Prowling the area in circles, they kicked leaves and branches as if in doing so they might uncover some sign of him. When it seemed they were thoroughly confused, suddenly they heard a hissing sound. They turned in time to see a limp, disembodied wrist rising out of the deep grass and waving faintly at them.

Scrambling to the spot, they found him lying on his stomach, an improbable sight—the old man entombed several feet below ground surface, in a ditch in a silk robe and pajamas, smiling up at them. "You'd better get down here. They're all around us now."

It was a dank, narrow ditch, apparently scooped out of the earth by a backhoe or a bulldozer, then abandoned to the encroaching wilderness, the sort of thing Stern had seen trappers and hunters use in Missouri to stash a kill for a brief time. In his courtly fashion, Gonzaga smiled, rolling over on his side to make room for them, as if welcoming them to his lavish *estancia*. They lost no time in scrambling down the hole, for in the next instant the forest exploded with the noise of crashing trees and the awful tonnage of metal rolling. To Stern, the noise was so big and overwhelming that he thought for a moment that it existed only inside his head. From behind the tangle of brush they watched the big T54 lumber past. Creaking and clanking, it raised a fearful din as it came. Though at least twenty yards distant, they could feel the ground quake beneath them, and at one point the earth on the floor of the depression in which they crouched actually started to crumble and give way from the vibrations.

A lone trooper moved out in front of the tank, a kind of tracker, Stern imagined. Up on the bridge of the tank, the lid of the cupola stood open and Stern had a clear view of the helmeted head of the tank commander poking up from below. He swung past in profile, an erect torso figure scanning the forest through a pair of binoculars and shouting instructions to the tracker up ahead.

The tank was gone in a moment, sliding back into the rising mists like some gray spectral thing that emerges from the deep, permitting a rare glimpse of itself, only to disappear in the next instant. There was something unreal about it, but there was nothing at all unreal about the oily trail of diesel fumes it left behind in its wake.

Unspeaking, they listened to its noise recede, then return, as though it were circling the area, then recede again, off to the left, moving north along the wire.

The excitement appeared to have revived Gonzaga. He seemed amazingly alert. "They're going," he whispered.

Stern peered gloomily after the receding noise. "They'll be back."

Gonzaga cuffed Buddy's cheek with a gentle fist. "Fun, ay, *muchacho?*"

The boy smiled up at him a bit uncertainly.

"We'd better start moving." Stern hoisted his aching body out of the ditch. "They'll be back as soon as they discover the trail's cooled."

"How far to the border?"

"A few hundred feet up that slope."

Gonzaga beamed. "Not bad. Not bad at all." He'd tied a handkerchief round his bleeding foot. A gout of reddish stuff oozed out from beneath it. To Stern it had a fairly ominous look, but the old man appeared unaffected by it. His spirits were high and he seemed ready to go. The mood was infectious, at least for the boy, who also scrambled up out of the ditch.

"Is there any way over?" Gonzaga inquired. "A weak point. A break in the fence?"

"Even if there were, we couldn't go. The whole thing's electrified."

The old man's grin faded.

"Seventy-five thousand volts. We'd be toasted."

Suddenly they heard the whine of the tank's engines behind them.

"They've circled around again. They're coming back."

The boy looked desperately back and forth from Stern to Gonzaga, awaiting some instruction.

"We'd better go," Stern said. The old man was looking at him. He could read his thoughts. "We'll never make it over that fence. The only thing I can suggest is that we keep moving about. Crisscross our own tracks. Confuse them. It takes longer for them to track than for us to move. That's one advantage in our favor." Stern attempted to convey enthusiasm, but his efforts bore little conviction.

Skepticism flooded the boy's eyes, while a great deal of blood seeped through the handkerchief-tourniquet on the old man's foot.

When Stern looked up again, Gonzaga was smiling at him. "You and the boy go. I'll stay here. Perhaps I may be of more use on my back than on my feet." The old man chuckled at some private image conjured up by his own words. The remark was cryptic enough to set off alarm bells in Stern.

By then the tank was chewing up the forest just behind them. They could almost feel the heat of the thing. The foliage around them appeared to yellow and wilt before it. Stern grabbed Gonzaga's hand and squeezed hard. It was an old hand, scrawny as a talon. The bones of it were brittle beneath his grasp.

The old man returned the pressure. "If you see my wife ... my daughters ..."

"We'll be back," Stern said before he could finish. "Don't move from here."

There was a tremor under their feet. A great clatter and banging rumbled at them from their backs.

"Go. Go now." The old man shoved them off with flailing arms. Stern lingered a moment, then turned. The boy was already moving out ahead of him. He took several steps, glancing back for a final glimpse of Gonzaga waving feebly. Then, as if with a sigh, the tousled head slipped beneath the rim of the ditch, the lid of bracken and ferns slid back in place above it, and once more the open hole had become indistinguishable from the forest floor.

Stern and the boy struck out in the direction from which the tank had just come. If it had just covered that area, the chances were it wouldn't immediately be returning there. At least until the present search proved fruitless.

Buddy bounded forward, the tails and lapels of the motorman's jacket flapping wildly behind him. Stern trudged along behind. He could manage no more than a kind of lame trot. The ordeal of having lugged Gonzaga through the night had exacted a heavy toll on his legs and back.

Several times the boy stopped and stared back at him, chafing to go faster but too frightened himself to let Stern completely out of sight.

Stern flung his arms out at him impatiently. "Keep going. Keep going. I'm right behind you."

Shortly they were out of earshot of the tank. Either they'd covered a good bit of ground or the tank had stopped somewhere in the woods and the crew had taken to foot. At least the awful ponderous clanking had stopped and that was a relief.

Their progress slowed in the next several minutes. The terrain grew muddy and hilly. It was covered with a tough, thorny bramble that lashed out at them. The vines were so wiry that it was necessary on occasion to bend down, and with the hand, disentangle the foot.

They were running parallel to the border fence, possibly fifteen or twenty feet just inside the cover of the woods, when the first helicopter came. They could hear it approaching from far off, the dull, concussive throb of its blades thrashing the air above them. It came in low, moving up along the border in the same direction they were heading. To Stern it appeared they'd been spotted by the pilot.

After a while the helicopter circled and racketed back down in the opposite direction. This time they caught a glimpse of its belly through a patch in the forest canopy, gliding low above the treetops. Several times it repeated the maneuver, so that Stern grew increasingly certain it was in constant radio contact with the tank. Badly winded, he signaled the boy back.

"Have to rest a bit. Too risky to go on just now." He flung an exhausted hand at the sky as the helicopter pounded over.

Off to the right stood a dense stand of birch with a thick crown of foliation at the top. It would be difficult to see into it from above, and as for the tank, even if it were to reach there, it would have a hard time trying to maneuver through the grove. Most of the trees were old, first growth—tall and very thick.

"Come on." Stern grabbed the boy's hand. They plunged off together, Stern leading the boy by the hand until the great feathery branches enfolded them.

It was cool inside the grove. The last mists of evening still clung airily to the branches. The floor of the forest there was free of the terrible clinging brambles, and they walked easily now on a mossy, springy floor covered with fragrant pine spills.

At a point Stern estimated to be the center of the grove, they came on a stack of birch, evidently sawn and stored there by loggers. The branches along the trunks had been stripped away, and the trunks themselves studded with a variety of fungal growth, suggesting they'd lain there for a long time or had been stored for firewood.

"Let's stop here." Stern flopped down beside the wood stack. The boy did the same. Stern sprawled spread-eagle on his back. The earth, wet and spongy, seeped into his shirt, cooling his overheated body. "You okay?" he inquired after a moment.

Squatting on his haunches beside him, the boy nodded. But there was a look of troubled doubt in his eyes that belied the nod.

Stern caught the look. "We'll be fine. Don't worry."

Something in his words or manner pressed a button and opened a floodgate in the boy. He turned away so that his tears could not be seen.

Pretending not to notice, Stern let the boy give vent to his feelings. It was over in a matter of moments, and shortly they were both sitting up, peering over the log pile, trying to get their bearings.

"I bet there's something to eat around here," Stern said, gazing about for berry bushes or wild artichokes. As a boy in Missouri, he recalled mushrooming with friends in the woods around his home. "Let's have a look."

Pushing the hair out of his eyes, Buddy bounced up eagerly. Stern struggled to his feet, and with a hand on the boy's shoulder for support, they started moving cautiously round the grove. The search had immediately engaged the boy's imagination. It was a kind of game, like a treasure hunt or hide-and-seek.

For twenty minutes or so they wandered about the grove, finding nothing edible except possibly a rubbery red berry growing on a low bush. There was a waxy sheen to it and the red was of such a vivid hue, it looked lethal.

They passed up the berries but they found a stream with clear running water from which they drank and splashed freely. Except for the birds and the rattle of crickets, the forest had grown ominously quiet. They could no longer hear the tank, and the helicopter had ceased to fly overhead.

Stern had no illusions on that score. Clearly they'd just paused to regroup and rethink their strategy. They were certain to be back, this time, no doubt, with foot soldiers and hunting dogs, far more effective in this type of terrain than heavy machinery.

They returned to the log pile and sat there dejectedly, their backs propped against the wood. Stern searched his head for things to talk about. He knew the boy was thinking of his father and mother and sister. Ironically, Stern was not thinking very much about anything. His survival instincts had dwindled sharply with his energy level, now virtually zero. His concern now was primarily for the boy. The thought of carrying him to safety, restoring him to his family, if indeed anything were left of it, had taken some overriding priority in his mind. It made him feel better since it had the virtue of taking his mind off himself. There was, too, in all of this, some faint echo of his own son and the painful, bewildering, and wonderful years of raising him to maturity.

"Do you think you can hold out for one more day here?" Stern asked suddenly.

A look of alarm crossed the boy's face.

"I mean both of us, of course," Stern hastened to add. "Just until dark."

"Sure."

Stern lay back on the damp earth. "Good. I think I have a plan."

The rest of the day they spent lying about, resting, recouping their strength. Their hunger was great and several times they got up and renewed their search for food. There were grasshoppers in abundance. Stern knew from old Army survival courses that in emergencies, such insects were a perfectly wholesome source of protein. He snatched a grasshopper from a log and held it out to Buddy, its wings fluttering wildly. "If I ate one of these, would you?"

The boy made a queasy face and looked at Stern as if he were joking. When it became apparent he wasn't, he shrugged uneasily. "I don't think so."

They watched the grasshopper beat its wings frantically against Stern's fingers.

"Can't say I blame you." Stern laughed and flicked the creature into a nearby thicket, where it landed on a leaf and leapt away.

They rose shortly and went back down to the stream and bathed their feet and looked for fish they might snatch with their hands out of the shallow streambed. But there were none, and once again they filled their empty stomachs with water.

Several times during the day they heard the rumble of a motorcycle patrol bounce past on the dirt path running beside the border fence. But nothing more—not the tank, or the helicopter, or the dogs. There was only the rattle of cicadas, the occasional quack of wild ducks streaking past overhead, the ceaseless burble of the stream below them, and always, the profound unnerving quiet of the forest.

As dusk began to gather they were startled to hear a funny but unexpected sound.

Stern's head jerked up. "Did you hear that?"

"Sounds like a cow."

"Here? In the middle of the woods?"

The noise came again, this time more distinctly.

"I'm going up to have a look," Stern said.

"Can I come?" Buddy called after him.

Stern could see the boy didn't want to remain there alone. "Sure. But be quiet and keep down."

They emerged from the forest at a point possibly a mile north of where they'd left Gonzaga earlier that morning. In front of them, stretching north and south for as far as the eye could see, was the fence studded with its innumerable tiny barbs. On the fence was the same sign they'd read that morning, its blunt warning emblazoned in four languages across it.

Beyond the fence was a long sloping meadow in which cows grazed. Their bells tinkled as they browsed along the low gorse. Now Stern understood the reason for the ditch on the other side of the fence. It was intended to keep the cows from electrocuting themselves on the fence. On a hill above them, the lights of a red chalet farmhouse flickered through the gathering dusk. It might have been a hillside in Connecticut or southern Vermont, but it was Finland.

They gazed at the scene through the fence until the distant whine of an engine startled them. It was the motor patrol coming back as it did every few hours. They dove back into the cover of the woods and crouched there, waiting breathlessly until a motorcycle with a sidecar attached to it rumbled past. A figure in the sidecar sat stiffly erect, the barrel of an automatic rifle pointing skyward beside him.

They lay there in the thicket for some time after the patrol had passed, knowing that within two hours or so they'd be returning back up the path. It was just past seven P.M. but there was still a great deal of light. Stern knew that there would not be much darkness till well past eleven. "Come with me." He rose up with an urgency that startled the boy.

They moved quickly through the forest back in the direction of the grove. When they reached there, Stern pulled his jacket off and tossed it over the log pile. He grabbed one end of a large birch pole. "Can you get the other end?"

Sensing the move he'd been waiting for, the boy scampered eagerly round the log pile and hoisted the other end.

"Careful," Stern warned. "It's heavy."

The boy hefted it with surprising ease. "What are we doing?"

"Building a ramp."

"Where?"

"Right up the side of that fence."

They staggered out of the grove, the birch pole between them, moving back up to the border. The next hour was spent dragging one birch pole after the next out of the grove up to the place where the edge of the forest and the dirt road met. Each pole they would conceal there in the thickets while they went back for more. It was hard work. Painful and laborious. The trees had once been large and their trunks heavy. The boy never once complained.

By the time they'd hauled a dozen poles up and cached them in the thickets beside the path, they'd worked up a fairly good sweat. The sun had dropped and the dusk was thickening to a velvet gray. Still it was too light for them to risk much more.

"What do we do now?" the boy asked.

"I have to go back and see how Mr. Gonzaga is doing." Stern watched the boy. "You think you can wait here for me?"

Buddy looked at him uneasily.

"I won't be long," Stern added. "You stay here. In this thicket. Right beside these logs. I'll be back in an hour."

It took him the better part of a half-hour to locate the ditch. In that light the terrain was uncertain and everything looked different. But he found it. There was no tank there now, and somewhat more disquieting, no Señor Gonzaga. What he did find at the very bottom of the ditch was a blue terry-cloth slipper, muddied and bloodstained. Nothing more. Nearby, not more than five feet off, he saw deep scars torn in the earth by the tank treads. He could surmise the rest.

When he got back it was nearly full dark. The boy was sitting inside the thicket, just where he'd left him, looking greatly relieved to see him.

"Did you find him?"

"No sign of him, I'm afraid. But there were tank tracks all around the place."

"They probably got him."

"Looks that way." Stern tried not to sound grim. "What have you been doing?"

"Watching the cows. They sure look good. Reminds me of home."

"You have cows, do you?"

"Dad keeps a couple around on the farm. Just for milk and butter."

Stern gazed off distantly. He was thinking about old Gonzaga and his probable fate.

"What do you suppose they're doing at the train now?" the boy asked.

Stern shook his head. He hadn't the slightest idea. He couldn't imagine anything too pleasant.

"Think we can really get over that fence?" Buddy asked.

"We're sure as hell going to try. Better rest now till dark comes."

They'd not slept for twenty-four hours, and as the long dusk finally ended shortly before eleven, the boy dropped off. Stern lay awake, taut, overtired, nerves tingling, his mind drifting back over the long spate of years. He thought of the uncertainty of his prospects for the future in whatever years remained to him, and somewhat to his surprise, he thought, too, of Nell Blanton.

He'd not been unaware of her throughout the course of the trip. Confinement on the train had naturally thrown them closer together. He hadn't been unconscious of her obvious charms, nor of the fact that she seemed in some way to have favored him.

That rainy afternoon in the galley of the dining car when she'd kissed him (not really kissed him—it was the most innocuous sort of peck), he'd been aroused, but full of all kinds of ambivalence. She was, after all, married, and after several months of litigation dissolving his own mess, he was not eager to step back into someone else's. But she was fun, he thought, and quite pretty. It wouldn't be unpleasant.

Just as he was about to drift off, a sound, distant but by that time all too familiar, jarred him back to full consciousness. He struggled up into a sitting position. Full darkness had descended now like a dark cloak about the grove. A whole chorus of twilight sounds—birds, crickets, frogs intoning in a nearby pond—flowed in upon them. But it was the heavy clank and rattle of the T54 tank rumbling back toward them—tireless, persistent, with the dogged malevolence of something almost human—that had him back on his feet and shaking the boy.

Cracking an eye, Buddy looked up at him.

"They're back." He tried to keep his voice calm. "We'd better go now."

The boy scrambled up and in the next moment they were stumbling back up the slope toward the border fence.

The first pole was the most difficult. Stern didn't know what to expect. The poles were long and limber. He wasn't at all sure how much weight they would support. They were awkward to move about, and then, too, the idea of high voltage was terrifying. The wood, he knew, was a nonconductor. But should they stumble or trip, make contact with the fence inadvertently, that could well be fatal.

"Whatever you do," Stern cautioned as they raised the first pole against the fence, "don't get anywhere near the wire."

As they hoisted each pole and jostled it into position, Stern fully expected blue flames and a shower of sparks. They slanted the poles against the fence at an angle shallow enough so that they could be easily ascended. At the most comfortable angle, they found that the tip of each pole just barely cleared the point where the top of the fence ended and the second tier, the apron of tin curlicues, began. If they'd wanted the poles to straddle the fence at that height, the angle would have been far too steep for either of them to negotiate.

"We'll have to take it at the first level." Stern jostled the pole into position. "We can make a dive for it over the coils when we reach the top. Hand me the next. Quick."

By the time they'd set the third pole into position, the noise of the tank shook the forest all about them. Through the dense foliage they could see the eerie glow of its bridge light softly diffused through the trees.

"Next," Stern panted, one eye on the ramp he was erecting, the other on the beam of the tank light swiveling round in quick, angry circles. From where they stood, it appeared to Stern that it had come to a halt nearly abreast of them, one hundred yards off in the woods in the vicinity of the log pile where they'd hidden out for the day. He could hear its big diesel engines idling and see the light swiveling about through the forest. Undoubtedly the tracker had uncovered something in the vicinity of the logs and they were now down there inspecting it.

Stern and the boy had done little to conceal their tracks. Dragging the birch poles up to the fence from the grove had doubtless left a trail a mile wide. It would be only a matter of moments before they'd pick it up.

Stern reached for another pole, the fifth, which he swung up against the fence, rolling it into position against the others, then jamming its end hard into the earth. "Next," he snapped. "Come on. Come on."

The boy dashed back to the thicket and struggled to pull another pole up to the fence. Stern snatched it with an air of demonic frenzy. Just beyond the fence a cow chewing earnestly watched their frantic motions with a mild curiosity.

No sooner than one pole had been shoved and rolled into place than the boy would come thrashing toward Stern, dragging the next. Seven birch poles had now been laid side to side up against the fence in a kind of raftlike arrangement. The width of the ramp was now nearly three feet, still a trifle narrow, not for the boy, but for Stern.

There were three more poles to come. Though he could no longer see the tank through the foliage, Stern was certain it had turned and was now rumbling toward them. The noise of it grew louder.

With the ninth pole in place, the earth all about them started to tremble. Stern could hear the voices of the tracker and the tank commander shouting back and forth to each other in the dark.

There was no time to put the tenth pole in place. The ramp was now nearly four feet wide. Stern grabbed the boy. "Go now. Fast. Just run up and dive over."

The boy froze.

"Now," Stern shouted, and shoved him toward the ramp. "Quick. I'll follow."

Buddy turned and started for the ramp, then hesitated and looked back.

"Go for Christ's sake," Stern hissed. "When you dive at the top, kick your feet clear of the wire."

Eyes wide, looking suddenly very small, the boy turned and bolted up the ramp. At the mid-point, the two centermost logs sagged, and so, it seemed to Stern, began to separate. But in another two steps Buddy was at the top. There was an awful moment in which for a fraction of a millisecond he seemed to pause. Stern's heart stopped as well. The boy stiffened visibly; his back arched, and suddenly he was airborne, rising with the weightless grace of an acrobat. Lofting easily up and over, he landed in a perfect somersault, clearing the ditch on the other side. No part of him had come anywhere near that fearsome second tier of coiled steel at the top.

Stern had little hope that things would go quite so well for him. He had neither the spry legs nor the inherent sense of indestructibility of a twelve-year-old. From behind him came a terrifying grinding and crunching. He could feel the heat of the tank at his back, like the breath of some awful creature running hard. Suddenly the beam of the searchlight fell across his body and stopped, pinning him there in the light. It had the momentary effect of paralyzing him. He heard the voice of the tracker shouting hoarsely, and that of the boy, high and sweet, crying out to him from the other side.

In the next instant, the tank was there, bursting through the fringe of forest, a shower of scruffy birch saplings falling with loud cracking sounds in a neat row before it. They lay down in unison, all at once, as though something large and unseen had leaned against them.

The front of the tank breaching from the trees rose at a steep angle over a mound of earth so that for a moment its treads spun noisily in midair, with a thin, whining sound. Then it was out in the open, on the dirt path, veering ponderously toward him, its noise immense.

"Jump. Jump." He heard the high-pitched shouting of the boy behind him.

The tank had broken into the clear just about seventy-five feet down the path from him. Stern watched the stiff, funny motion of it turning toward him, the beam of its light rotating on the bridge like a toy dragon.

"Jump. Jump," the boy kept shouting. Transfixed by the beam of light falling across his breast, Stern was nailed to the spot. The dirt path was far too narrow to accommodate the tank's full width, so that fully one half of it rode at him elevated at a giddy angle.

He watched the hatch of the bridge start to open and the top of a helmet begin to emerge. The ground beneath him was quaking and the cow in the meadow beside him started to moo.

Stern's journey began with the left foot. It rose, kicked out, hit the ramp, and slipped directly between two parting poles. His foot went through the ramp and slugged hard into the earth below it. He went down on his knee with a sickening crack, scrambling at the same time to extricate his foot, all the while that fearful tonnage came clanking up the path toward him.

He was up in a trice, kicking the poles together, then scurrying on all fours like a frisky monkey up the dangerously shifting birch poles. Even as he went, the poles wobbled underfoot, threatening at any moment to part and drop him to the ground, or worse even, throw him up against the fence.

When he'd reached the apron at the top, he'd already made a conscious decision to quit. The ramp swayed and buckled so he had to go double time to keep his balance. By that time the tank was a mere several feet away, the tracker out front shouting, waving his arms and streaking toward him. The birch poles beneath him rolled and started to pull away from the top of the fence. In that moment he leapt.

It was not so much an act of conscious volition as it was an involuntary spasm—a lunge for something solid. As the poles under him began to drop away, he flung himself, arms outstretched toward some firm anchorage his hands might grasp. The fact that the only such object within reach was an electrified barbed-wire fence seemed beside the point. The ramp was in the process of breaking up beneath him. At that point there was no choice and he took flight.

It was headfirst, like a high dive. He had blessedly no awareness of the leap. He heard the boy shouting somewhere up ahead and felt a sharp tug at his trousers. There was a ripping sound as he barely cleared the apron. His body took an odd turn in midair, and then an additional lunge, as if powered by some internal boost. The earth on the other side was lush and green but it was not soft. There was a bang and he felt a terrible wrenching inside him. His shoulder and right arm bore the full brunt of the impact.

He'd come down backward, facing the fence. Stern had a fleeting impression of the boy running toward him and the cow observing it all with a drowsy, incurious stare.

There was an awful rending sound followed by a shower of blue sparks. Stern could hear gears grinding as he watched transfixed the fence going down before him. He had the peculiar impression of watching something in slow motion—the steel stanchions drawn up out of the earth, the wire snapping in midair with a high ping, and for thirty or forty feet or so, the wire fence lying down like some infinitely weary thing. There was a sizzling sound and more blue sparks, none of which appeared to bother the tank; it was undoubtedly one of those especially equipped with grounding devices enabling it to breach high tension wire.

Where the tank had burst through, a fissure wide as a barge gaped. At the outer edges of the fissure, the tangled broken ends of the wire fence danced crazily in the windless air.

Sprawled on his back, head slightly raised, Stern watched with curious detachment the tank grinding toward him. From its speed and position, and the manner in which it approached, it gave every indication that it meant to crush him. If indeed that was the case, Stern had neither the strength nor the inclination to prevent it. He lay there winded and panting, legs leaden, and with pain of a most exquisite order stabbing up the length of his arm.

On the bridge of the tank in the open turret stood the helmeted commander. He was shouting and waving his arms, seemingly at Stern. Stern could hear the hoarse bark of his voice above the engine's growl even as the tank swayed dizzily toward him.

Then, for no apparent reason, the tank came to a shuddering halt, the engine idling and the heat of its diesel fumes wafting across the narrow space until they were licking warmly at Stern's cheek.

Where the T54 had stopped, clouds of dust rose up all about its flanks so that its outline wavered in and out of focus. A blurry yellow haze drifted toward Stern, raining on him a gritty shower, until his face was grimed with mud and the tears leaked from his burning eyes.

The voice of the helmeted figure on the bridge came at him again. With the engines cut down, Stern could hear him somewhat more clearly. He shouted and flailed his arms, presumably commanding Stern to return to the tank and captivity over the border. If that was the message, Stern had no intention of complying. Frightened and weak as he was, he'd still choose annihilation under the tank treads to lengthy internment in some labor camp while diplomats dickered interminably over his fate in a château in Geneva.

They stood like that, the tank and Stern, stalled at an impasse, neither machine nor man deigning to yield an inch. No more than sixty or so feet separated them. Stern was acutely aware of the boy moving behind him. The word "run" came at him repeatedly over his shoulder as if across great distances. He could neither turn nor respond. He could not bear for even one second to avert his eye from the tank or the helmeted figure on its bridge.

Then something peculiar happened. The tank commander was suddenly still, rather like some mechanical toy that had wound down. In the next moment his arms rose, and with a deliberation that seemed almost choreographed, he undid the chin strap of his helmet, lifted it off, then stood there quietly regarding Stern.

Everything froze into immobility, and an unearthly silence rushed in upon them. Through his bleared eyes Stern squinted at the strange sight. The choking yellow haze still lingered uneasily above them, and through its undulant, gliding motions, the figure on the bridge wavered in and out of register.

At certain moments the dust would thin and seem to drift away, only to return again in even denser concentrations. At those moments the figure would come at Stern in sharper relief and there would be the curious sensation that he was looking at someone he knew. But he didn't know exactly who. In the next instant the figure was swallowed in rags of smoke and dust. Stern was far too overcome with his own perilous situation to pursue the question further.

The boy shouted again. Stern half-rose, an act of the faintest velleity, then fell back facefirst into the cool damp meadow grass. All about him was the sweet, clean smell of clover and cow flop. Somewhere far off in the distance he heard the high whine of a siren and was aware of Buddy's frantic hands trying to drag him out of the path of the tank.

When he looked up, the boy was stooped over on one side of him while a stout avuncular figure in military uniform knelt beside him on the other. They held him under each arm and lifted. He nearly fainted from the pain.

Behind them, the tank idled, straddling the smashed fence—one half of it in Finland, the other half still in the Soviet Union. It appeared to hover indecisively. The helmeted tank commander rose up on the bridge, climbing full out of the turret, shaking his fist at them and shouting.

There was no telling at that moment what they would do or if they really intended to fire. By that time they'd been joined by another motor patrol that had come bouncing up along the fence, moths swirling in its headlights.

"Are you all right?" the man in the uniform asked Stern. He spoke with an accent that could have been French or Belgian, but was more probably Swiss. Then Stern saw the Red Cross armband on his sleeve.

"I think I've broken my arm."

"Can you walk at all?"

"I think so." Stern started to rise. Under his left shoulder, Buddy nearly buckled beneath the weight of him, but squared his feet and stood firm.

"Turn around and start walking toward the jeep on the hill." The man in uniform spoke under his breath with a sense of quiet urgency. "I'm right behind you. Don't say anything. Don't look back."

They started out in single file, the boy first, then Stern, followed by the Red Cross officer. All the while they could hear the angry shouts of the tank commander ordering them back.

"Just keep going." The officer spoke with an air of studied calm. "Don't turn around."

The beam of the tank's searchlight swerved right and left across the path before them, accompanying them up the hill. The tank itself, however, did not venture an inch farther.

Up forward, Stern could see the outline of a jeep. The Red Cross flag flapping gently on its fender shone in the glow from its headlights. From out of those headlights several figures emerged, streaming down the hill toward them. Suddenly the night was full of the white glare of exploding flashbulbs. Stern's head swam from the pain in his shoulder and arm.

Someone was scurrying about them, clicking a camera, shouting instructions that they pose in a certain way. Another man, tall and suave, sidled forward, his hand outstretched. He introduced himself by name, a reporter from *L'Express*, and congratulated them on their safe return to the West. It was at that moment that Stern blacked out.

PART X

ONCE THE JEEP started moving and the chill morning air hit him, Stern revived quickly. On the way, the Red Cross officer, who was a Swiss, explained that some sort of breakthrough settlement had been achieved during the night. The Soviet government had agreed to release all the detainees aboard the train, while the Norwegian government agreed to release the Soviet submarine and its crew.

The settlement had been achieved through intermediaries. Both sides by that time eagerly wanted a resolution, but neither was willing to make the first conciliatory move lest they lose face and thus bargaining power. For purposes of *amour-propre*, therefore, three nations, Italy, Belgium, and Malaysia, as well as the International Red Cross, served as intermediaries. They made the initial overtures and became the conduits for all negotiations, while the two superpowers, sulking off in the corner, eager for some quick, not too unseemly way out, sat back and allowed themselves to be approached.

It was all very funny, had it not been so sad and utterly pointless, the Swiss officer said, laughing heartily. He said they'd learned about the fire on the train early that morning. It had come over on a Reuters report from Bucharest. Were there any casualties? Stern asked. He'd not heard of any, but that was characteristically Russian, to give as little information of a negative sort as possible. He speculated that one of the things that really accelerated the agreement was the fire, and the reluctance of the Soviets to take too much international heat from what had happened aboard the train. It had simply become a hot potato they were eager to drop. What was left of the train was at that moment being driven from Vyborg to Vainikkala.

"Did you happen to see anything of an old man?" Stern asked as they lurched down the road to the little border town. "A Spaniard. Seventyish. In a robe and pajamas."

The Swiss officer shot him a bemused look. "We saw no one of that description."

"He was with us," Stern explained. At that moment they hit a bump. Stern howled and clutched his arm.

"Sorry about that," the officer said.

"I think my arm's broken."

Reaching forward, the officer tapped the driver on the shoulder and instructed him to drive more slowly. He turned back to Stern and the boy. "We'll get that fixed up for you the moment we get into Vainikkala."

They reached the Finnish border town in another twenty minutes. The sun had been up nearly an hour but mist was still rising out of the damp grass surrounding the little train station that served as the border checkpoint.

Though it was only five A.M., the station was already mobbed with reporters, camera crews, and curiosity seekers who'd heard of the settlement during the night and wandered over to see the excitement. Horns blared as cars and vans kept flooding into the area. The train was due to arrive at any moment.

When they drove up, a British *chargé d'affaires* was running up the station platform, weaving in and out of crowds, waving his hand frantically. Red Cross ambulances and personnel choked the little parking lot where they drove in. Off to the side, French volunteer doctors mingled with Finnish Army medical units. There were nuns and clergymen of every stripe and persuasion. UN officials, stout ladies in blue smocks from some local civic organization, dispensing paper cups of coffee and sugar doughnuts. American consular officials from Helsinki had set up a booth. A large American flag fluttered above it and U.S. intelligence officers were placed there to direct operations.

The Finns had thrown up a field hospital very hastily. From the scant, carefully censored reports of the fire, they had no way of knowing what to expect. The waiting room of the station itself had been transformed into a fairly decent-sized communications center. Detachments of Finnish signal corpsmen were installing trunk lines and direct wires to the world's capitals in order to handle the flood of long-distance calls—not only from reporters eager to file front-page stories for the late editions, but to handle the more pressing needs of hostages desperate to reach families and loved ones.

The station platform was jammed with reporters. Several camera crews had gone a few hundred feet up the track, right to the border, in order to get the first shots of the repatriation of the train. The whole thing was now somehow wrested from the anguish of history, turned over to the capable hands of the press impresarios and network czars, there to be transformed somehow into the farce of living-room entertainment. A *son et lumière*, promoted as educational fare, treated with the utmost seriousness and piety, it would eventually emerge as a kind of vaudeville, orchestrated tears and laughter, something to have with your Scotch and chips before sitting down to a good dinner, secure in the knowledge that all was well in your little corner of the universe.

Stern was taken directly over to the field hospital. It was no more than a large square shaped out of white screen panels on rollers set up at the side of the station. Inside, a number of little booths were manned by volunteer physicians, largely French and Finnish, supported by a staff of nurses, a pharmacy, and even a small operating room for emergency surgery, should that be necessary.

A young French doctor examined Stern, told him he had broken his right arm and badly bruised his shoulder. He was going to be fine, the doctor assured him, and put the arm in a temporary cast and sling. He would have to go into a hospital within the next few days to have it set properly.

"Where's the boy?" Stern asked suddenly while all this was going on.

"The boy?"

"The little fellow I came in with."

The doctor brightened. "Oh, that one—he's right over there, waiting for you."

Stern looked up from the table on which he lay and saw Buddy watching him anxiously from a corner. "Stick around. I'll be out of here soon."

Buddy waved back feebly. He looked small and very lost in all of the clamor and confusion.

Stern was able to walk away from the table under his own power. The doctor had given him a small supply of Demerol in case of pain and urged him to have the arm properly attended to the moment he could get into a real hospital.

The Swiss official was waiting outside for him when he came out with Buddy. "Do you want to get into Helsinki now?" He had to shout over the din. "I can arrange a car."

"Thank you. I think we'll wait for the train," Stern said. "We have friends on board."

Outside on the platform, the crowds had grown. The police had cordoned off the station but there was a tremendous amount of traffic and horns blaring on the road outside, wanting to get into the area.

They found a place right near the edge of the platform. Stern kept his good arm firmly round the boy's shoulder so they wouldn't get separated. He could sense the boy was close to tears with exhaustion and worry. "We ought to be seeing your mom and sister any minute," he said with bogus cheer.

The boy glanced up at him, a vague, oddly condemnatory smile on his face. "What about my dad?"

Stern could say nothing. His arm had started to ache and he tried now to keep it out of the way of the jostling crowds. He wanted very much to leave there, but he was determined to stay, at least until he could deliver the boy over to one of his family.

There were three short blasts down the track and a sudden surge of excitement. People pushed forward on the platform. Stern and the boy had to struggle to keep their places as they craned their necks to get a first glimpse of the approaching train.

There was a graded curve several hundred yards up the track from the station, and suddenly the whole length of the train seemed to fill the arc of that curve. First came the little toylike electric engine, limping down the track, sliding toward the station. Though it was now broad daylight, its three headlights were blazing and its horn blasted an unceasing chain of salutes as if to proclaim to all its indestructibility. "I'm here. I'm alive. I'm still with you," it said.

The engine was remarkably untouched by fire. Just behind it came the restaurant car, its windows punched out, shards and spikes of glass depending like broken teeth from its steel frames, but essentially intact.

Farther back, however, the devastation grew worse. The women's sleeping car and, behind it, the day coach, were both completely destroyed. Their metal skins had been thoroughly consumed by flames, and thrusting up beneath them you could see the charred skeletal frames, just the ribs of them intact. The last car, the men's sleeping coach, was missing all of its windows. Its sides were seared and streaked by smoke. The gray-green paint along its sides had bubbled like a fondue from the intense heat it had endured.

They could see all of that in a glance, the whole train teetering precariously on the curving track, threatening, like a very long cigar ash, to disintegrate at the slightest jarring motion.

The innards of the two middle cars had been completely gutted. As the train grew closer, it was possible to see through the exposed framing into the cabins inside. There was something strangely indecent about it, the pajamas, the torched bedding, the contents of burst luggage—hats, gowns, undergarments—strewn in tatters all about, flapping like pennants from the exposed laths and beams that had once been the framework of compartments.

The train came on, rattling slowly toward them. Gouts of vapor wheezed off the engine flanges, spouting through the spokes and interstices of its drive wheels. People pressed closer, awe stamped on their faces, sniffing the stench of burned rubber and carbonized wood, steel twisted by infernal heat into a caricature of its former self.

The engine horn continued to peal as the train came rocking gently up to the platform. There was something majestic in its serene, unhurried grace, in all of the dignity of its splendid wreckage. Gaunt, ghostly faces slid past, looking out from behind the smoked glass, all with that curious air of melancholy that seems to hover about arrivals and departures in busy passenger terminals.

The horn continued to blast even after the train had come to a full stop. You could see one of the motormen inside the cab, tugging the horn-pull with one arm while waving outside the window with the other.

All of the passengers had been moved out of the middle cars and were concentrated in the men's sleeping coach. When the doors opened, several reporters tried to board the train but were quickly repulsed by police and security guards. There was a rush. Consular officials came first, escorted directly up to the doors by armed security guards. Someone's camera was dashed to the ground and a scuffle ensued. There was little civility surrounding the events that followed.

The first to appear at the opening doors were the Russian porters letting down the steps. Nell and Paul Blanton were already standing there waiting to detrain. They'd arrived in torn clothing, Nell, still in her gray matron's smock, looking bewildered, and a bit embarrassed. They were immediately swamped by reporters.

Paul's arm was bandaged. He'd incurred serious burns and was in obvious pain. His remarks to reporters who asked for his "first reactions" were terse, even somewhat rude. He was hurting and in need of medical attention. The bandages he presently wore had been applied by a kindly Soviet matron whose skills along those lines were clearly limited.

Some nameless, but blessedly astute, official quickly discerned their predicament, neatly separated them from the crush, and led them off to the little field hospital around to the side.

Next off were Serja and Jatta. Serja had salvaged from her luggage a little straw boater with a plastic flower and had donned it for the occasion. The tour guide carried a clipboard and looked harried. She tried bravely to impose some semblance of order on the process of transferring passengers from train to platform, but the task was far beyond her meager resources. Even the American and Finnish intelligence pros, moving quickly to seal off and isolate the passengers, were quickly overcome by the sheer numbers of pushing, jostling spectators.

Stern caught a glimpse of Jean Blaylock, looking pale and dismayed at the door. The right side of her face was bandaged. She appeared almost reluctant to leave the safety of the train for the perils awaiting her here. The moment her feet touched the platform, she turned as if to retreat back to the train. A television cameraman shouted at her to wave, but she merely shrugged and moved off aimlessly into the crowd. A Swedish intelligence officer caught up with her and led her to the safety of a temporary holding area set up inside the station.

The Mukherjees and the Shapleys detrained in one group. Mrs. Shapley came first and called at once for medical assistance. Several attendants from the field hospital had been posted nearby with wheelchairs. They had to fight their way through the milling crowds. At last the security police came and physically pushed people out of the way until they'd wedged a ragged aisle through which the chair could pass into the center of the mob.

Shapley was carried down off the train by two of the Russian porters and set gently down in a wheelchair. The porters scurried to get back onto the train, for they were being watched every moment by Russian security police, who remained on board the train. Stern moved quickly to the professor's side. Mrs. Shapley started to cry when she saw Buddy. She knelt and hugged the boy. "Oh, Buddy—your poor mom and sister . . ."

"Did they know he was missing?" Stern asked.

"They found out a few minutes after we were all evacuated from the train. Somebody told us they saw him go off with you, but they know nothing about your being here. They've been worried sick."

Shapley was sitting in his chair grinning widely. He seemed wan and a bit dazed but he was laughing and tousling Buddy's hair. "Your mom was just behind us."

Buddy turned, craning his neck, seeking her out. But in that moment a mob of reporters descended on them and the Finnish paramedics wheeled the professor off, with Mrs. Shapley following close behind.

A cheer went up from a number of the press corps when Tony Thomas stepped down off the train. He waved and then waded into a waiting throng of well-wishers, looking as raffish as he could manage under the circumstances.

The Italian Quartet followed, with Frau Kunkel and Karl Heinz right after. Frau Kunkel spotted Stern and Buddy and pushed her way over through the crowds. For once, she was neither dour nor disapproving. She fluttered all over them. Karl Heinz hoisted the boy in the air. "Where the devil were you?" He started to laugh his nervous, sawing laugh. "Corrie. Corrie," he shouted over a sea of heads at the Kariolainens. They'd detrained at the other end of the car and were now separated from them by a swelling, heaving mob. "See. Look there—your sister and mother." Karl Heinz held the boy up in the air above his head and shouted at the Kariolainens.

"Did everyone get out?" Stern asked Frau Kunkel.

"Everyone." She lowered her voice. "Everyone except the Canadian. They wouldn't release him. They say they're going to try him. Someone said old Gonzaga went with you."

"He did. Right up the the border. But we lost him. He couldn't go any farther. We had to leave him."

"Leave him?" She frowned. "Where?"

"I don't know," Stern murmured, realizing how hollow that sounded.

Suddenly she noticed the sling. "Your arm—"

"Nothing—it's nothing at all."

A look of disapproval crossed Frau Kunkel's face. "You haven't seen the Van Meegrins, by any chance, or the Frenchman and the American girl?"

Stern gazed at her mystified. "Why would I?"

"They saw you and the old man walk out the front gate. Someone said they followed a bit after." Frau Kunkel shrugged. "The gate was unguarded for nearly a full hour until the fire was under control."

"Then they might still be out in the woods," Stern reasoned. "Unless the patrols picked them up."

They grew silent, speculating on the fate of Gonzaga and the two young couples. There was a sudden squeal as Janet Kariolainen swooped down on them and swept Buddy up in her arms. Corrie came right after, fighting through the crowds, holding a small charred suitcase over her head.

"Mr. Stern. Peter ..." Janet Kariolainen tried to embrace him, saw his sling, then instead buried her face in his chest and sobbed. "I don't know what to say ... I just don't know ... "

"We couldn't have done it without him," Stern laughed. "He was our guide. He was the driving force."

"Where's Dad?" Buddy beamed. "Is he here?"

There was an awkward moment as they exchanged uneasy glances. The boy's face dropped.

"We haven't heard anything yet," Corrie said. She was about to go on, but just then Tony Thomas appeared, waving frantically at them. He had a tall, rangy, pink-cheeked woman in tow.

"That's her. That's Mrs. Kariolainen," he explained to the tall woman, nearly shoving them together.

"You're Mrs. Kariolainen?" the woman inquired. "Mrs. Theodore Kariolainen?"

"Yes—I . . ."

"I'm Joan Mosher. U.S. consul's office. Could you come with me, please?"

"My husband . . ."

"Out front." She spoke in that laconic, no-nonsense Down East way. "In a Russian field car. They just brought him over from Vyborg but they won't transfer him unless some member of the family is present."

Janet started after her.

"I'm coming too," Corrie said.

Buddy bolted after them. "Me too."

Karl Heinz watched them go wistfully. Then suddenly he turned to his mother. "I'm going too. Just to say hello."

He dashed off before Frau Kunkel could protest. "Don't go too far," she cried after his retreating figure, then turned back to Stern, looking somehow betrayed.

"She's very pretty," Stern said, by way of sympathy.

"Ach . . ." Frau Kunkel dismissed the idea with a wave of her hand. "You don't suppose I could get a call out to Hamburg? To my husband?"

"I gather they've set up some kind of communications center inside the station. But it's absolutely mobbed."

The din in the station area was deafening, and they had to shout at one another to be heard. Frau Kunkel said something to Stern about telling Karl Heinz where she'd gone, then plunged into the crowd, making her way to the little station house. Stern was left alone.

Nearby the Mukherjees milled about in a little circle with Madariaga and his group. An Italian photographer from *Il Messaggero* was taking their pictures. The young musicians waved and mugged shamelessly. Mukherjee, smiling toothily, posed with his arm about Madam Muk. Baby Muk, of course, had recovered enough of his health to commence yowling.

Nearby, unobserved, Consuelo Gonzaga viewed the scene. She watched Mukherjee perform his antics for the camera. There was a wistful little smile on her face—a smile full of misgivings and pathetic expectations, and already she wore the look of one dispossessed. Consular officials and intelligence personnel tried to get them away from the press, but Nagu was clearly enjoying it far too much.

Farther up the platform, Isabel and Señora Gonzaga stood about at a loss. They had the sad, baffled look of people who'd inadvertently stumbled into someone else's celebration.

Stern moved quickly to their side.

"Have you seen him?" Isabel asked before he could get a word out.

"He was with us," Stern replied.

Señora Gonzaga smiled with a polite effort. "Yes, we know. We were told that. But where is he now?" Her face was gray with worry.

"He couldn't go any farther. He begged us to leave him." Stern attempted to put the best face on things, realizing how bad it must have sounded. "He was in reasonably good shape. I'm sure the Russian patrols picked him up."

"Why, in God's name, did you permit him to go with you?" Isabel fumed.

"You know your father far better than I, Miss Gonzaga," Stern said with an air of helplessness. "He's not an easy man to say no to."

Señora Gonzaga patted his hand. "Of course. Of course." She said it with that sweet, almost fatalistic subservience. "You have been most kind."

"The Russians just released Kariolainen," Stern said. "If the patrols picked Señor Gonzaga up, and I'm almost certain they did, they'll release him too."

"Yes," she murmured without much conviction. Her freckled gnarled old hand covered his. "You must have heard about poor Mr. Keck."

"No, I—"

"He died," Isabel said bluntly. "In the military hospital in Vyborg. They took Mrs. Keck there early this morning to identify him. The Soviet government has offered to fly the remains home."

Stern looked grim. "How long had he been dead?"

"A full week," Señora Gonzaga said tearfully. "And they never thought to notify her—my poor, dear Myra." She started to cry. Suddenly Kate and Desfargue and the Van Meegrins were there, and she was wiping her eyes with a lace handkerchief.

Van Meegrin threw his arms about Stern, overcome with joy. "We followed you out the gates. We were right behind you. Maybe a quarter of a mile. Didn't you know?"

"No, but we knew damned well a tank was following us."

"And we followed the tank," Trina Van Meegrin said.

"It was easy," Van Meegrin went on. "Like following an elephant."

They roared with pleasure and wonder at what they'd survived.

"We came with Claude and Kate," he went on. "We crossed at a big hole in the fence. There was no one there. We walked right through."

"That's where the tank chased us," Stern said. "I was with Buddy Kariolainen."

"Where had he been?" Trina asked.

"Hiding out up in the engine. The Finnish motormen concealed him. I broke an arm going over the fence."

"I just found out I'm going to be a father," Van Meegrin boasted.

Señora Gonzaga caught hold of Trina by the hand. "You must rest now. To have walked all night in the woods . . ."

"I'm fine." Trina laughed and gulped the air. "I'm absolutely wonderful."

"When will the child come?" Isabel asked.

"February," Van Meegrin said.

Señora Gonzaga appeared crestfallen. "My poor husband, Enrique, was born in February. Now it seems we have lost him."

Van Meegrin's jaw dropped. "Lost him? How so? He's just over there in the field hospital."

"The field hospital?" Stern asked.

"Of course. He came with us." Van Meegrin was as bewildered as they were.

"With you?" both the Gonzagas cried at once. "Why didn't you say so?" Isabel snapped.

"I just assumed you knew. We found him wandering in the woods in his pajamas," Trina explained. "We all walked through the fence together. A Red Cross lorry picked us up in a cow pasture and drove us all over here. We took him directly to the hospital."

Van Meegrin looked at them incredulously. "You haven't seen him yet?"

"We didn't even know he was here," Isabel said.

"*Santo Dios.*" Señora Gonzaga clasped her hands. "Where is the old fool? Let me get my hands on him. Isabel, come." The old lady set off at once.

"I'll go with you," Stern said to Isabel.

"Where's Consuelo?" Señora Gonzaga turned around, searching the crowds. "Consuelo. Consuelo. *Donde estás? Venga aquí—inmediatamente.*"

Sure enough, they found him, just as Trina had said. He was sitting at a little table surrounded by three robust, pink-cheeked Finnish nurses. They appeared to be having a marvelous time. Gonzaga was drinking coffee out of a paper cup and regaling them with an account of his escape. Even in his tattered robe and mud-spattered pajamas, he looked quite rakish.

He was just about to bite into a large stollen when they rushed up. His foot had already been swathed in a fresh dressing of impressive size, but nevertheless he rose, a bit unsteadily, in his most courtly fashion. "Margarita."

A tongue-lashing started to spill from the Señora's lips. But she had no heart for it. Instead, she began to weep, alternately kissing him and punching him feebly on the side of the head. Gonzaga, looking tousled and slightly demented, appeared annoyed. He winked at Stern. "When we have a chance, I must tell you about my night in the woods."

"I think I know a bit about it already. We looked for you and couldn't find you. Where did you go?"

The ache in Stern's arm had become intolerable and he asked one of the nurses for a glass of water with which to take one of his Demerol.

By that time the American and Finnish consular officials had managed to round up most of the passengers and segregate them from the press in a holding area in the station until they could be moved to some undisclosed location.

Jatta appeared with a pair of U.S. intelligence officers. They moved toward them in a group.

"We must go now," she said, her cheeks glowing and her white jumpsuit sooty and black with smoke.

"Where are we going?" Isabel asked.

"To a processing center near here," one of the intelligence officers, who introduced himself as Captain Lantz, explained. "It's a kind of passport check and debriefing. We estimate you'll be there one night."

They were led from the hospital back out onto the platform, where the confusion had reached chaotic proportions. Several of the camera crews boarded what was left of the Green Train, swarming through it like locusts, taking thousands of feet of film, clicking shutters, flashing bulbs, and squabbling loudly among themselves over territorial privilege within each car. The air above the platform was now thick with the smoky, putrid smell of burned wood and upholstery.

On the way back to the holding area they passed Madariaga and his group. He'd assembled them in choral formation on the platform, where they'd started to sing national anthems—every one of them they knew—Dutch, French, American, British, German. As they sang, Madariaga paraded up and down their ranks, checking and rechecking to see that all of his charges were accounted for. Some he would kiss and others he would smack lightly on the back of the head when he felt the occasion warranted it.

The holding area was a large penlike arrangement into which a number of cots and chairs had been introduced. It was cordoned off by a thick length of hemp with a half-dozen very large Finnish security police posted at intervals just in case the hemp failed to make a strong-enough impression.

Inside the holding area a number of special phone lines had been set up for the exclusive use of the Green Train passengers. Already there were people queued up in front of each.

Ted Kariolainen stooped over the first one, looking gaunt and a bit overcome, but basically fit. One hand covered his free ear as he tried to speak over the long-distance phone. Janet, Corrie, and Buddy were gathered round him with the receiver passing back and forth between them.

Stern found the Blantons inside. Paul's burns had been dressed in the hospital and both he and Stern laughed when they saw each other in arm slings.

They exchanged accounts of their various adventures throughout the night. Stern recounted the story of their escape and the tank crashing through the fence behind them. All the while Nell looked at him with a soft, enigmatic smile on her lips. He could not read exactly the intent of that smile, but it seemed to say: "All right. Forget about it. Rest now. It's over."

They were taken by bus to a small Finnish inn in the mountains above Vainikkala, a low sprawling red chalet with a number of outbuildings and farm animals roaming freely all about the property.

Several times during the course of their stay at the inn, Consuelo attempted to renew her relationship with Mukherjee. By that time she'd become convinced that something of that order actually existed between them. But even as her eyes sought him across the little lobby or the dining room, his eyes always managed to evade her. Invariably, in the midst of a crowd or while showering sugary attentions on Madam Muk or Baby Victor, Babu was too busy for her.

Ever since their assignation on the train, it had been her persistent fantasy that Mukherjee would approach her, would offer to dissolve his marriage and plead with her to run away with him. He was just looking for some opportunity when they might be alone so that they might plan their future together. But the opportunity never seemed to come, and slowly it dawned upon her that Mukherjee seemed less than eager to bring one about.

That evening Stern spoke to his daughter in New York. She was staying at his apartment, and assured him that the cat and the plants were fine. Her mother had called several times from Santa Barbara. She'd seen his name flashed on a TV screen, along with those of the other hostages during a late-night newscast. Several days earlier she'd seen him on another news show. It was a clip of footage first broadcast in the USSR. He was playing volleyball with a number of other men. "Mother said you didn't look as if you were enjoying it much." She laughed and then started to cry.

That night they ate off crisp white linen and Arabia in the inn's small charming dining room, overlooking the meadows and deep pine forests of Finland. They dined on fresh salmon, ptarmigan, reindeer tongue. There was a good deal of Finnish vodka and cloudberry wine, fresh berries and a huge wheel of Roquefort for dessert.

There was much laughter and high spirits and a few sober moments when they'd all considered where they'd been and how they spent the evening before. When the name of Ralph Keck came up, there were some tears. No one could pretend to have liked him very much, but his death seemed unfair and somehow inappropriate in the midst of all the present jubilation.

"You must have been quite close then," said Stern to those seated at his table. They were recounting their adventures of the night before.

"Not far. A mile or so," Van Meegrin nodded.

Stern seemed puzzled. "Didn't they see you?"

"We're sure they did," Desfargue said.

Stern's puzzlement deepened. "And they didn't try to stop you?"

"On the contrary," Kate Dubbin said. "We had the distinct impression they were escorting us to the border. Making certain we got over."

"I seriously doubt that," Blanton said, dismissing the idea with a wave of the arm.

"I know it sounds crazy," Desfargue said, "but that's the way it looked to us."

"And I'll tell you something crazier," Kate said. She wore on her face the expression of someone about to reveal an extraordinary secret. "The man commanding that tank was none other than our friend Colonel Dunskoi."

There was a moment of stunned disbelief.

"It's true," Kate persisted. "It's as true as I'm standing here. The man up on the bridge of that tank was Dunskoi."

"You really don't believe that," Isabel said.

"He wasn't even at the train, Kate," Nell Blanton chided gently.

"We heard he was transferred back to Leningrad," Van Meegrin said.

Kate persisted stubbornly. "I know that. But I saw him on that tank. I know Dunskoi when I see him. Believe me, I'll never forget that face."

Van Meegrin shook his head skeptically. "I know him too. And I also saw the man up on that turret. He didn't look anything like Dunskoi to me."

"How could you possibly tell," Trina Van Meegrin said. "The helmet covered most of his face."

Kate was undaunted. "I saw him several times from the side and once from the front. There was enough face showing. Believe me, it was Colonel Dunskoi."

They sat there exchanging looks of skepticism. Desfargue at last broke the silence. "If this is so, Kate, why didn't you say anything before?"

"Because I couldn't be certain. Up until now, that is. We got pretty close to the tank this morning. I heard the voice and I saw the face. It's been nagging at me for hours, but now I'm certain."

The more emotional she grew, the more skeptical the glances became.

"I'm certain too, Kate," Stern said suddenly.

All of the chatter ceased at once and they turned to face him.

"I saw him with the helmet off. It was Dunskoi."

They had stopped eating now and sat watching him keenly, full of suspicion and wonder.

"I saw him through a lot of smoke and dust, flat on my back," Stern explained. "I knew I recognized him, but at the time I was just not thinking very clearly."

Buddy Kariolainen, who'd been silent through all of the talk, now suddenly cried out, "It *was* him. I saw him too. I was standing right there. He took his helmet off, just like Mr. Stern says. It was him all right. It was the colonel."

The boy's confirmation came as a thunderbolt. Oddly, it carried more weight than either Kate's or Stern's.

"You don't seriously suggest"—Blanton reverted to his best prosecutorial style—"that this man we've all come to know quite well over the past twelve days—"

"Far better than we'd have cared to," Van Meegrin added.

"—was looking to do you any favors?"

Kate appeared troubled. "I don't know. The fact remains he broke down that fence, then drove off leaving it unguarded. He knew we were trailing only a couple of hundred feet behind."

"He was chasing Stern," Blanton said hotly. "They probably got up so close to the fence they couldn't stop the damned tank. It just barreled through."

"They could've nailed me anytime," Stern reasoned. "I was a sitting duck up on that fence."

"But isn't it strange he should remove his helmet like that?" Nell pondered aloud.

Stern shrugged. "I can't figure that out at all. But I can't figure out lots of things that happened last night." He looked about at them helplessly. "Does anyone know how the fire started? Or where?"

Asawa drank a great deal of vodka that evening. Throughout most of the day, since arriving on the train, he'd been morose and aloof from the others. Now, with the aid of vodka, he talked freely and in a loud voice. He boasted that he'd been a great success, that his ancestors would have been proud of him today, as well as his friends. He went on in a long rambling discourse about how his plan to free them had been a great success. None of it appeared to make much sense, but by that time few people were listening. Halfway through dessert, he fell asleep at the table and had to be taken up to his room.

While they lingered over their coffee and brandies, Señor Madariaga rose unsteadily to his feet. He'd drunk too much wine at dinner and had become somewhat lachrymose.

He gazed around at everyone at the table, particularly his seventeen young charges, and started to speak in a quavery voice hoarse with emotion. "Today I told all my children . . . all my kids"—his arm waved round at them expansively—"that for the rest of our lives, we will always be *one*. Catastrophe and tragedy have bonded us forever. I think that is true now for the rest of us as well." Smiling, he looked round at them with the simple benevolence of the truly humble. "Good grows out of the bad. We'll always be one, my friends. *Siempre seremos uno.*"

"*Hola!*" Gonzaga cried, and clinked his glass with a knife to declare his approval. Stern knew he would talk about this moment, even laugh about it, for years to come. In every human tragedy there was always plenty that could be laughed about afterward. The gift was to have the capacity to be able to recover such moments and cling to them for dear life. He still didn't fully understand what had happened to him, or what he'd been through. What he did understand, however, was that, as of this moment, things would never be the same for him. He had changed irrevocably—whether for better or worse, he could not be certain.

That night Stern slept between starched white sheets with the good smell of laundry soap still about them, and beneath feathery light quilts that felt wonderful in the cool night mountain air. He drifted off to the sou ⸍ ⸍ tinkling cowbells and the soft bleating of goats in the meadow outside h dreamed of a stone face high up in the mountains of some di clime.

Down the road for miles every approach to the inn was cordoned off by security police. They were there to protect the privacy of the newly freed detainees from the packs of reporters camping out all night in the vicinity, still awaiting their chance at the "big story."

In the morning they were taken by bus to the Finnish Army post outside of Helsinki, where they underwent routine processing. This consisted of a perfunctory interview conducted by Finnish intelligence officers, followed by meetings with various consular officials. Passports and visas retrieved from the Soviets during the official transfer at Vainikkala were returned to their owners, along with newly issued air/rail tickets, plus enough per-diem allowance to get each of them home. Their cash and traveler's checks, cameras, film, and airline tickets, confiscated by the Russians during the early days of their detention, were never returned.

Late that afternoon the group was moved under full guard and the strictest security back to the inn, where they exchanged addresses and said their good-byes. The majority of them were staying on for the evening, intending to leave first thing in the morning. The American contingent, minus the Kecks, was to be bused out to Helsinki International Airport that evening. From there they would be flown by U.S. military transport to Frankfurt, where they would be transferred to the U.S. Air Force base outside of Wiesbaden, there to undergo medical clearance and general debriefing.

A small handful of the others—the Van Meegrins, the Kunkels, and the Contis—elected to accept a U.S. invitation to hitch a ride to Frankfurt. The Lambrustos, for reasons of their own, decided to make alternate arrangements for getting back to Milan. Karl Heinz, of course, was delighted at the prospect of a few precious extra hours with Corrie. Already he'd informed a number of the group that on graduation he was planning to attend college in California—Stanford or Berkeley is what he was now aiming for. Frau Kunkel listened silently, a stony expression on her face.

Stern was standing amid a small group of people exchanging addresses. Gonzaga had invited him to go on to Aranjuez with them, to his ancestral home there. He had no plans to go back to Argentina. He'd had it with military governments forever. He would try life among these "so-called new socialists" in Spain. However bad it might be, he said, "it would be nothing compared to the monstrosity from which we've just come."

"If you are ever in Spain, Señor Stern, come to Aranjuez. My home is yours."

"Thanks, but I don't think I'll be back this way for some time."

"Well, when you make up your mind"—the old man winked—"I'll still be there."

Out of the corner of an eye Stern glimpsed Tony Thomas lurking off in a corner. He appeared to be watching him, waiting as if for some opportunity or signal to approach. As Stern turned from Gonzaga, Thomas came slouching toward him, his eyes looking away, not directly at him. "Stern . . . Oh, Stern . . ."

There was an awkward pause as Stern waited for him to speak, but then it was actually Stern who spoke first. "Where've you been? Haven't seen much of you about."

Thomas seemed grateful for the opening. "Very busy. Up to my ears. My paper. Several publishers. They all seem to want me to do a book."

"I'm sure it'll do well. You've got plenty of material." If there was sarcasm in Stern's voice, Thomas appeared anxious to ignore it. "Look, I don't know what to say, exactly . . ."

Stern waited, watching him, as he cast about for words.

"I'm grateful you haven't mentioned this to any of the others."

"I thought about it. It would have served no real purpose. The damage was already done."

"I know what you must think. And I admit there may be something questionable about what I did . . ."

"Or failed to do," Stern added.

"Rather," Thomas conceded. "Or failed to do."

"You did know, then?"

"Up to a point, yes. I knew before we left that something was up. I had no idea where it would lead to or how long it would last. That's why I took the train, of course. Had I warned you all, it would have just been some other group."

"We don't know that at all," Stern said firmly.

"They were looking for some pretext . . . any pretext. And . . . look, it's a big story, Stern. Probably the biggest of my career. Things haven't been great for me over the past few years. This is just what I needed. A shot in the arm. Look—it's my business." His eyes pleaded for understanding.

"One man is dead; the fate of another, beaten half to death, is still uncertain. If you could have prevented that and didn't, then there's something terribly wrong with your business or the way you do it."

Thomas looked away. His mouth moved, yet no words emerged. "Look, Stern—you won't say anything about this, I trust. I mean, about me—to the reporters, or in print or anything?"

Something quite nasty rose to the tip of Stern's tongue, but stuck there when he saw the terrible fear and pleading in Thomas' eyes. "You have nothing to fear," he snapped.

Thomas extended a shaky hand to him. Stern looked at it, then simply turned and walked away.

It was a tearful, slightly embarrassing farewell. The small group piled into a pair of vans along with whatever luggage they'd managed to save, and drove out in a convoy. At the terminal, they didn't go through the main entrance, but instead swung round the back to a darkened, unused runway and transferred directly from the vans onto the big U.S. Air Force transport awaiting them.

* * *

The flight to Frankfurt was a little under two hours. They landed at the international terminal, where more press awaited them. The plane landed on a main runway and taxied up to a gate. Not far from there was a floodlit dais crammed with functionaries.

Intelligence personnel and security forces swarmed aboard the plane at once. They distributed name tags, messages from immediate family, and a general message of welcome to all from the President of the United States, informing them that they'd all been very brave and that the nation was proud of them.

They assumed at that point that they would disembark under the blanket protection of the U.S. military police. That was not the case. Instead, a man in a trench coat boarded, introduced himself as Mr. Bradwell (please call me Buzz), a television news producer from one of the major U.S. networks. He told them in the most earnest and solicitous terms that they would be disembarking not as a group but individually.

The U.S. ambassador to Bonn was waiting outside on the dais, he explained. He would call each of them by name over a microphone. At that point a spot would hit the exit door of the plane and that individual would then step out from behind the door where he or she had been waiting. "Wave and smile. Throw kisses, if you like." Mr. Bradwell warmed to his task. "You will then descend the aluminum stairway to the tarmac and be whirled from there by a security officer to another waiting van. The spotlight will then swing back to the plane, ready to pick up the next individual."

At the same time there was to be a marching band of German youths from a local school who would be playing "Tie a Yellow Ribbon Round the Old Oak Tree."

The producer grinned all the while he was choreographing his shot, convinced they would all be immensely pleased at the prospect of making such a splash on the evening news. He was somewhat baffled at the appalled silence with which his proposal was met.

"This is not Madison Square Garden, is it?" Paul Blanton fumed. "We're not the Boston Celtics, you know."

Mr. Bradwell failed to appreciate the humor. "That's not the same thing at all."

"Precisely," Blanton shot back.

The Blantons, Stern, and Jean Blaylock all refused to be paraded out and would only consent to leave the cabin after the spotlights had been removed. The others agreed to go, but they weren't going to do any waving or kissing or such.

Mr. Bradwell was crestfallen. "America's going to be very disappointed tonight," he said, as though he were addressing a band of traitors.

"America has been disappointed before," Jean Blaylock said caustically. "She'll survive it."

* * *

The next days were a blur of activity. Army doctors. Intelligence debriefers. Laboratory tests. Stern's arm was set finally by a dignified white-haired major who looked more like a professor of English at an Eastern university than an orthopedic surgeon. The arm was put in a cast and he was given a long sheet of instructions for continuing care of the arm and shoulder at home.

The debriefing seemed long, detailed, and needlessly repetitive. Stern sat for several hours with one interrogation officer, and then was referred to two others. They went over precisely the same material he'd covered with the first man: Why had Stern traveled to the Soviet Union?

"Just on impulse. I was so close, I thought: Why not?"

How was he treated by his captors?

"Like a prince," Stern said fliply, and from the stolid expression on the interrogator's face, regretted it the instant the words were out. "There was that incident when I was punched," Stern attempted to recoup something of his reputation as a sober, responsible citizen. He described the events with Jean Blaylock that led up to the episode. "And then, of course," he went on, "they accused me of espionage."

The officer's brow notched upward. "Please continue." He spoke softly.

"Well . . . they insisted I was involved in some sort of conspiracy with this fellow Keith Wales."

"He's the Canadian they're still holding?"

"That's right."

"Can you tell me a bit about it?"

"I've already told the other gentlemen."

The captain's jaw tautened. "I realize that, Mr. Stern, and I'm sorry for the inconvenience, but this is extremely important."

Stern went into the whole thing again, starting with that morning the Russians disappeared from the train and Wales made his abortive attempt at escape.

Next he went into the awkward business of his being mistaken for a Jew. The captain looked up from his note-taking and it was then that Stern noted from the I.D. tag on his shirt that his name was Bloom.

Embarrassed, Stern stammered his way through a description of the episode, all the while the captain, his eyes lowered to his pad, took extensive notes.

"What's being done for Keith Wales?" Stern asked at the conclusion of the interview.

"The Canadian and the U.S. governments are both making very strong representations to the Soviets," Captain Bloom explained. "It won't be easy though. You were very lucky."

When Stern left the man's office an hour and a half later, he was exhausted and felt slightly humiliated.

Twenty minutes later he was back at his room in an officers' quarters on the base, when he was seized with an attack of anxiety. As he reconstructed the interview in his mind, it seemed to him that the captain had known far more about the so-called conspiracy charge by the Soviets than he himself had volunteered.

Of course, Bloom had no doubt spoken to the two other debriefing officers prior to his talk with Stern. In the interim they all might have had time to compare notes. But it seemed to him that Bloom had known things, was privy to certain details that Stern had no recollection of having ever divulged. He'd gone through approximately twelve hours of debriefing that day. He could hardly be certain what he'd said to the other two interrogators, and by that time he scarcely cared.

Arrangements had been made for Stern to fly home the following morning. It couldn't be soon enough for him. He'd be flying out of Frankfurt on a commercial airliner at ten A.M. and arriving at Kennedy Airport at approximately twelve noon, Saturday, where his daughter would be meeting him. Saturday night he'd sleep in his own bed on Sixty-third street. The Kariolainens were booked on the same flight.

Kate Dubbin and Jean Blaylock were both leaving the next day, but on different flights. The Shapleys were flying to Boston to see their children and grandchildren. The Blantons would be staying on several more days for rest and a visit with some old friends in the Rheingau.

They had their farewell dinner together at the Nassauerhof in Wiesbaden, just across from the park and casino. It was a lovely little restaurant adjoining the hotel, called Die Ente.

Throughout dinner, Buddy regaled them with a blow-by-blow description of their night in the forest, his long nocturnal trek with Stern and Señor Gonzaga to the border. They laughed at his description of Stern taking a header over the barbed-wire barricade and coming up face to face with a cow. It was one of the few things they could laugh at that evening.

Stern found himself seated next to Jean Blaylock and just across from the Blantons. Nell had had her hair done and had bought a new dress in one of the smart little shops on the main drag of Wiesbaden. Jean came in a skirt and sweater. She appeared different to him that evening—less combative, softer, and strangely subdued. Throughout dinner they spoke of their plans for the immediate future.

Stern had no plans whatever, he said, unless cultivating the art of doing nothing qualified as a plan.

Kate was flying home to Washington the next morning. Desfargue had already taken a night train back to Paris. They'd decided to give themselves a complete break from each other for a few months. As the plan stood now, they'd meet in New York for Christmas.

When they were having their coffee and *poire*, Jean turned suddenly to Stern, a shy, slightly embarrassed smile on her face. "I suppose I've been a real pain in the ass."

"There were those who were a lot worse."

"Like who?"

"I'll never tell."

"You don't have to." She sipped her brandy. "I think I know."

"Are you glad to be going home?" Stern asked.

"Not particularly. Are you?"

"Yes," he snapped eagerly. "I plan to spend a lot of time with myself."

Nell had been listening, and now she chimed in. "Sounds like you're ready for a monastery, Peter."

"Only if it's one of those places where they make good chardonnay and sing Gregorian chants all day."

He'd said it in his glib, mock-serious way, but apparently she took it to heart. "What makes you dislike people so?"

He started to protest.

"Outwardly, you're so amiable, so accessible," Nell continued, "but that's just a facade, isn't it?"

"I'm not sure I follow."

"I'm sure you do." She shot him a sly grin.

She was right. Of course he did. But he was unwilling to pursue the subject further. All the while, he was aware of Blanton's keen gaze watching them.

"I think I'll see my parents when I get back," Jean said suddenly. She appeared as much startled by the thought as the others.

"When did you decide that?" Kate asked.

"Literally this minute."

"Something I said?" Stern asked.

"No. Something Nell said."

Nell laughed. "I said something that produced a positive result? What was it? Tell me quick, before you forget it."

"That's my secret."

"God," Nell sulked. "Now we're all getting as secretive as Stern."

"I haven't spoken with them in two years," Jean went on. "They live all of two hours from me."

"It sounds long overdue." Janet Kariolainen beamed.

"I hardly know what I'll say to them."

"If I know you, Jean," Nell teased, "you'll think of something."

It was eleven P.M. and Buddy had fallen asleep against his father's shoulder when they broke up for the night.

"If I don't see him in the morning, give Paul my best," Stern said on the way out from the restaurant.

"I will—that is, if I see him." She laughed a bit oddly. "In fact, I haven't seen much of him recently. He's been on the long-distance ever since we got out of Russia. You'll be leaving early?"

"First thing in the morning. They want to get everyone out to the airport before the press gets wind we're leaving. And you?"

"We're staying a few days more. Paul has some clients he wants to see."

The cab they'd sent for rolled up to the porte cochere. A porter snapped the door open for him.

"Can I offer you a ride back to the base?" he asked.

"I have a ride back with the Shapleys."

They'd reached the end of their conversation. Stern cast about for some graceful exit line.

"When we get home, I'm going to ask Paul for a divorce," she said suddenly. He had the impression she hadn't intended to mention it, but at the last minute changed her mind. She laughed. "Don't be alarmed. It has nothing to do with you. It's something that's been simmering for years. This awful business with the train. The way they separated us. Actually, it was a kind of blessing. It's the first time we've been apart for years. Time to think, I mean."

"You haven't told him?"

"He has no idea." She looked down at the waiting cab and porter. "You'd better get going. You've got an early start in the morning."

He reached out to say good-bye and she took his hand firmly.

"Someday when all this is over, perhaps you'll let me buy you dinner," she said.

"Name the time."

"Possibly around Christmas. I plan to be in New York."

"I'd love it," he said. He was not entirely certain of that. He was still too close to the end of one thing to be able to fully contemplate the beginning of another.

She leaned forward and reached up. Her lips brushed his cheek. He was aware of a sudden warmth and the scent of heliotrope rising all about him.

EPILOGUE

WINGING HIS WAY back over the dark watery stretches of the Atlantic. Alone with thoughts. Wives and lovers. Strangers briefly encountered, shortly to be forgotten. The course of human events. So capricious, so elusive, so far beyond the powers of mere humans to arrange. At least he'd endured. He walked out of captivity leading a boy, carrying an old man on his shoulders. It was like some ancient, timeless legend . . . he couldn't recall exactly which.

Nagging thoughts persisted. Dunskoi's actions and behavior on that final night remained as mystifying as ever. The question would never have occurred to him had Kate not brought it up. Then, the moment she'd said it, he knew beyond any shadow of a doubt that it was true. He'd surely recognized the figure standing on the tank's bridge that night partially veiled by a screen of dust and smoke. It was someone he knew. But in all of the tumult and chaos and pain of that moment, he could not put a name to the face.

Doubtless his several encounters with the colonel had been chilling. It was difficult to think of acts of generosity in the same context as someone who'd charged you with "crimes of treason against the state" and threatened to toss you to the tender mercies of Soviet justice.

The annoying question persisted, however. Why had Dunskoi driven a tank through the border fence, demolishing it, then driven off, thereby permitting five additional fugitives he knew to be just behind him to simply walk across the border to freedom?

Was it blind rage that sent him caroming through the fence in hot pursuit of Stern? Surely he could have shot them down at any time as they struggled over the top of that fence. They would have been fish in a barrel. Yet he didn't.

Possibly he knew a settlement was imminent and had been ordered to see that those fleeing the burning train got back into the West unharmed so as to avert any further propaganda damage. Whatever Dunskoi was, he was no blundering hothead. A soldier and a technocrat, a professional to his fingertips, he was far too disciplined and calculating to have acted out of mere blind rage. Blanton had pegged him well. "Ice water in his veins. Nobody's patsy. Out to do no one any favors."

But why did he remove his helmet and stand there staring at Stern? What a strangely vulnerable, ingenuous sort of thing to do in a moment like that. Did he want Stern to recognize him? Was it some gesture he wished to make? If so, it hardly seemed hostile; more like "Farewell and Godspeed," one might have thought, if one didn't know him better. But judging Dunskoi and the forces that compelled him at that moment this was all speculation. Stern would never really know.

The heavy-lidded Tartar eyes floated up before Stern in the darkened cabin where overlunched stuporous passengers watched the spectral figures of a movie drift silently, like aquarium fish, across a dropped white screen. Beyond those cold, uncaring eyes lurked yet another pair, ancient and even more uncaring. Stone eyes, hard as flint and chiseled out of rock born in the furnace of some primal explosion.

They'd crossed the late afternoon of one time zone into the bright morning of another. Below was a gray sea spattered with innumerable islands—the cold, inhospitable desolation of Newfoundland. Up ahead the Maine coast loomed, followed by Boston and the outer Cape, pointed out to them by the pilot. Then the last leg, approaching New York down the long eastern corridor. That sense of anticipation. People up in the aisles. Going to the toilets. Having a wash. Lifting small bags down from overhead compartments.

Below now, the south shore of Long Island. Stern peered down out of the cabin window, following the white lines of breakers rolling shoreward up onto the beachfronts of tiny seaside communities. Places so pretty, so secure in their sense of privilege and immunity. So far from Vyborg.

The plane veered gently left, taking a wide loop out to sea. They were circling now in a holding pattern, in a stack of five other planes, waiting their turn to come in.

There was a high whining sound, followed by a dull thud as the flaps dropped and the landing gear went down. The plane took one of those stomach-raising dips and started down while the stewardess informed them in three languages that they'd started their descent to Kennedy. Temperature and weather conditions were announced. New York time was provided so that everyone might reset his watch. Then the flight attendant was thanking everyone in three languages for flying her airline. "It was a great pleasure to serve you." Next came instructions for all those with connecting flights.

Dropping down toward Kennedy, he could see fishing boats on Jamaica Bay, and then suddenly in the gray-yellow haze Stern watched the glass-steel dolmens of the Manhattan skyline looming up ahead.

Tomorrow would be Sunday. He'd sleep late, he thought. Loll about in bed till ten. Late-morning buns and coffee. The *Times* till twelve. He hoped it would rain so he could stay at home all day. A long, uneventful afternoon. Chopin mazurkas on the phonograph. A bottle of good bordeaux while the late-summer rain splashed incessantly against the panes. A late-afternoon cinema and, possibly, Chinese supper. Dusk at Pearl's. The quiet Sunday of a bachelor. Not an unpleasant prospect.

Suddenly the gates and the crowds. Mostly they were security people and press with special clearance to be there, no doubt tipped off that several of the

Green Train crowd were to be on this flight. There were rumors that more of them were expected in on different flights throughout the day. They streamed right past Stern, necks outstretched, eyes scanning the crowds while he slipped off unobtrusively to the baggage carousel and picked up his luggage.

On his way, he overheard Janet Kariolainen attempting to answer the questions of a half-dozen shouting reporters.

". . . yes . . . yes, our captors were very kind. At no time were we physically abused. We grew very fond of them, and they of us. We went swimming with them once, and they became our friends . . ."

Stern kept right on moving, anxious to avoid the same interrogation.

". . . they fed us and gave us excellent medical care," Janet enthused. "What I learned and what I think all of my family learned from the experience is the need for a greater tolerance and understanding of these people. Really, when you think of it, they're just like us . . ."

Stern glanced back once over his shoulder as if to make certain he'd heard it correctly. Janet continued to talk. Under the prodding of reporters, she'd found her theme, rising by each moment to ever-greater heights of universal love and brotherhood. Kariolainen stood off to the side listening to her, looking incredulous and not a little embarrassed. He was drawn and gaunt from the ordeal of four days' house arrest in Vyborg. Had the reporters asked him for his own reactions to the same experience, they might have heard a vastly different version of the events.

The two FBI men, Gerd and McGrath, identified themselves and pulled him out of line at customs. They kept calling him "sir" and were unfailingly polite as they led him off to a private office while they questioned him, as another man sat in the background quietly looking on.

At first it all seemed perfectly innocuous. They asked for his passport. Routine stuff. Wiesbaden again. Why had he gone to the Soviet Union? How long had he stayed there? Where had he been before? Whom did he see? Then, with the introduction of Keith Wales's name, the interrogation swung into high gear.

The man who'd sat quietly throughout the preliminary questioning rose suddenly and ambled forward. His name, he said, was Inspector Tokentine, of the Royal Canadian Mounted Police (Special Investigative Branch). What was Stern's relationship to Wales, he wished to know.

"None whatever."

"You'd never met him before? In Ottawa? Or possibly Israel?"

Stern's jaw dropped. He thought at first it was a joke. A crude one, but nevertheless . . . Evidently it wasn't. The inspector was dead serious.

"I never met Keith Wales before. I've never been to Ottawa. I've never been to Israel." He found himself responding to questions in the terse guarded style of a defendant. "What's this about anyway? I thought I'd just left all this behind."

"You were unaware of Mr. Wales's espionage activities?"

"Espionage activities?" Stern laughed scornfully. "You've got to be kidding. He was about twenty years old. An overheated juvenile. Not terribly bright. He couldn't espionage his way out of a paper bag."

"The Russian embassy in Ottawa says he was involved in a conspiracy to purchase classified materials."

"They said the same of me," Stern shot back. "Don't tell me you believe that. That was all part of a pretext just to hold us there. They set Wales up for an escape. Not necessarily even Wales. Anyone else who could have fit through that window that morning would have been hung with the same charge. If you were there it might just as easily have been you. It just happened to be Wales. After he fell into the trap, they decided to broaden the scope of their charge to one of full conspiracy. That's when they accused me of espionage. They put together a set of phony snapshots, using my passport photo. Forged letters supposedly in my hand, tying me to some group of Israeli agents in Haifa. Imagine . . ."

Stern's tirade trailed off when he suddenly heard the sound of his own voice, shrill and defensive.

An ominous silence had settled over the room. "And were they right?" Inspector Tokentine inquired in his soft, solicitous voice.

Stern glared back at him, scarcely understanding the question. "Were they right?"

"Are you now, or have you ever been, an agent of the U.S. or the Israeli government?"

Stern shook his head in disbelief. What the situation demanded was a strong, articulate, no-nonsense disclaimer. Hit them with countercharges, the threat of swift, costly retribution in the courts. Governments, at least free ones, always sobered up the moment the word "litigation" raised its ugly head.

But Stern had no such words. His mouth went dry and his brain swam with confusion. "I don't believe this. I don't believe any of this. This is some kind of joke or a nightmare. This really isn't happening."

"I'm terribly sorry, Mr. Stern." The inspector seemed genuinely apologetic. "It's my duty to advise you that the Canadian government has been informed through the Russian embassy in Ottawa that they are holding Keith Wales for acts of treason against the Soviet Union. They maintain that they're in possession of photos and letters that document all of this. Your name figures prominently in their deposition to us as a co-conspirator."

"And their word is better than mine—an American citizen? A veteran? You don't see that they've trumped up the whole thing?"

"They may very well have. The point is that Mr. Wales is still being held there and will have to stand trial. We're trying to secure permission now for his parents to visit him. Had you not been fortunate enough to escape the night of the fire, doubtless you'd still be in the USSR in the same boat with Mr. Wales, facing the same sticky situation."

"Why don't you simply just ask the State Department if I'm an agent, or, as you say, a spy?"

"We already have."

Stern's face brightened. "Well, then, they must have told you."

The inspector sighed wearily. "I'm afraid it's not quite that simple."

Stern frowned. "You're not saying that they've identified me as some sort of agent."

"On the contrary. They absolutely denied knowing anything about you."

"Well, then . . ." Stern breathed a bit easier.

"But of course they would. In highly sensitive cases such as this, the most natural thing for them, for any government, is to put as much distance as possible between themselves and an agent who's blown his cover."

It was all coming too fast for Stern. "But you said they denied . . ."

"Yes, but unfortunately in terms so ambiguous as to raise the most serious doubts about the reasons behind your recent trip to the Soviet Union."

Tiny black motes started to zigzag before Stern's eyes.

"Look," he nearly shouted. "I'm not a spy. I'm an American citizen. I'm a veteran of the U.S. Army. Check the Pentagon. They have my records. Why wouldn't they just come out and say this is all ridiculous?"

A long uneasy silence ensued while the three men continued to study Stern intently.

"You tell us, Mr. Stern." The inspector spoke with the smug self-satisfaction of a prosecutor who has done his job well. "Let me ask you once again. Are you now, or have you ever been, an agent of the U.S. or the Israeli government, or for that matter, any foreign government?"

Stern's look of cornered victim turned slowly to defiance. "You're the inspector. You find out. I don't say another word without a lawyer present. May I go now? My daughter is waiting."

"You're perfectly free to go," one of the FBI men informed him. "As of now, you're not charged with anything. But we must ask you not to leave the general area without notifying us." He produced a card from his billfold and handed it to Stern.

Stern glanced at it, then thrust it into his jacket pocket. "May I have my passport, too, please?"

"We're running a check on it right now. As soon as that's finished, we'll return it by mail. May I help you with your bags?"

He made a motion to help Stern, but Stern waved him off. Snatching the bag out of the man's hand, he stalked out of the office.

His daughter, Laura, was waiting outside. She stood in the midst of a great swirl of activity—passengers, porters, customs and immigration queues. She was looking off in another direction. She had the perplexed and troubled look of a person who suspects she is waiting for someone in the wrong place.

She turned then, staring directly at him for a long moment before recognizing him. Then she was smiling and waving, running toward him.

"I thought I missed you . . . I thought I might have . . ."

"I'm here. I'm fine."

She fell into his arms and kissed him and then she was crying. "Are you sure? Are you sure?" Her eyes swarmed over him.

"I'm fine—just fine."

She studied him more closely. "You look as if you've seen a ghost. What happened to your arm?"

"I'll tell you all about it in the taxi." He laughed oddly. "How's Ed? How are the kids?"

A tall, lanky man with sparse hair, in a rumpled suit, came up to them. "Excuse me. You're Peter Stern, aren't you? I recognize you from all the coverage. My name is Blakely. *Daily News.*" He flashed a card. "Could you spare a few minutes?"

"No," Stern snapped. He grabbed his daughter's arm. "Let's get out of this."

"Dad, is something wrong?"

"I don't know. I'm not sure. Where are you parked?"

"I've got a taxi waiting outside."

They surged out amid crowds of people flowing through a cavernous concourse, half-walking, half-running. Above the din they could hear the crackle of loudspeakers announcing a steady stream of arrivals and departures.

"Just a minute." The reporter jogged along behind them. "Just one question."

They plunged forward, not looking back, fleeing into the swarming onrush of dazzled crowds.

Good evening. This is the six o'clock Channel 2 News. I'm Jim Jensen.

With the successful resolution of the so-called Green Train episode scarcely hours old, the potential for another such incident is at this moment already in the making in the skies over Lebanon, where a United Arab Emirates airliner with 207 people aboard has been commandeered by hijackers and ordered to fly to Algeria. A group calling itself the Argos Section has taken responsibility for the act. Thought to be an extreme faction of Muslim fundamentalists, the Argos Section is . . .